PRAISE FOR AMANDA

'Amanda Prowse is the queen of family drama'

Daily Mail

'A deeply emotional, unputdownable read'

Red

'Heartbreaking and heartwarming in equal measure'

The Lady

'Amanda Prowse is the queen of heartbreak fiction'

The Mail Online

'Captivating, heartbreaking and superbly written'

Closer

'Uplifting and positive but you may still need a box of tissues'

Cosmopolitan

'You'll fall in love with this'

Cosmopolitan

'Powerful and emotional drama that packs a real punch'

Heat

'Warmly accessible but subtle . . . moving and inspiring'

Daily Mail

'Magical'

Now

An Ordinary Life

ALSO BY AMANDA PROWSE

Novels

Novellas

The Game
Something Quite Beautiful
A Christmas Wish
Ten Pound Ticket
Imogen's Baby
Miss Potterton's Birthday Tea
Mr Portobello's Morning Paper

An Ordinary Life

AMANDA PROWSE

LAKE UNION
PUBLISHING

Text copyright © 2021 by Lionhead Media Ltd.
All rights reserved.

Published by Lake Union Publishing, Seattle

www.apub.com

Amazon, the Amazon logo, and Lake Union Publishing are trademarks of Amazon.com, Inc., or its affiliates.

ISBN-13: 9781542017299
ISBN-10: 1542017297

Cover design by Ghost Design

Printed in the United States of America

This book is dedicated to all the young servicemen who died during 'Exercise Tiger' at Slapton Sands, Devon, on April 28th 1944 and to all the incredible Miss Mollys who were at home waiting for them . . .

'The love that asks no question, the love that stands the test,
That lays upon the altar the dearest and the best.
The love that never falters, the love that pays the price,
The love that makes undaunted the final sacrifice.'

—'I Vow To Thee My Country'
by Sir Cecil Spring Rice

ONE

Chelmsford, Essex
December 24th 2019
Aged 94

Her hand shook and her breathing was a little laboured. It was time for Molly to write the letter, just as she had said she would: a promise made in haste, but a promise nonetheless. A task she had avoided through fear, nerves and a worry that she might just get the wording wrong. But enough now – for the love of God, she was ninety-four! The time for putting this off had long passed. She reached for the weighty book entitled *A Study of Flora* from her bedside cabinet. Her slender wrist flexed under the weight of the hardback edition, sending a shooting pain up her forearm.

With the book propped on her raised knees, she selected a sheet of paper from the open sheaf beside her on the bed and carefully unscrewed the lid from her fountain pen.

Holding the pen up towards the halo of light from the bedside lamp, she gazed captivated as the mother-of-pearl inlay shimmered with faint flecks of iridescence that grew no less beautiful with each passing year. The pen had been a gift from her father, one of the few things she knew with certainty had felt the touch of his broad hand; it had no doubt been the instrument via which he let his thoughts tumble from mind to sheet, and all the more precious because of it. She hoped it might do the same for her, a fancy conduit to bring clarity and fluency to a jumble of unexpressed truths that sat knotted in her head like an old ball of yarn, woven of guilt, hesitation and a gut-churning uncertainty. She sighed, finding it far easier to voice the words in her head than to commit them to paper.

Dear . . .

'No, no, no, not "Dear", that's far too formal, for goodness' sake! Start with "Hello" or something more familiar!' She tutted as she scrunched the sheet of paper, crumpling it between her palms before tossing it onto the floor by the side of her bed.

Taking a deep, slow breath, she closed her eyes briefly before opening them again with a welcome sense of clarity. Resting the heel of her palm on the paper, she took her time, forming each word with juddering loops and an abundance of dance on the line. Her heart raced as she wrote the words that had lined her gut and sat under her tongue for decades.

Darling Joe,

Well, they say better late than never and so here we are . . .

Where to begin?

Where to end?

I'm not going to overthink this letter – I paused there for a moment to chuckle to myself. Not going to overthink it? I've been overthinking this letter for decades. I

2

was asked to write it a while ago and I do so now with mixed feelings. Here I sit with the moon peeking through the curtains and the still of the early hours engulfing me and I shall let my thoughts tumble; the circumstances, the explanations, the rationale, feelings and consequences that have been shut away, boxed, taped and shelved for much of my life. And trust me when I tell you that it is a box that has weighed heavily in my thoughts. Weighed heavily in my heart.

Molly let her words flow onto the page and, as they did so, felt the burden of secrecy ease from her shoulders. A quick glance at the clock that ticked on her bedside cabinet told her she had been writing for an hour. She was quite parched. Putting the lid on her pen, she rubbed her knuckles to relieve them of their arthritic ache.

Very carefully she opened the heavy book and placed the unfinished letter between the pages, next to the unopened envelope already hiding there, marked 'Personal Correspondence', and then closed it, placing it by her side on the mattress. She pulled her soft blue cardigan from the corner post of her brass bed. It was snug over her nightgown and provided just the right amount of cosy. Reaching for a tissue from the box on the nightstand, she wiped her eyes, another wonderful facet of ageing against which she had not been pre-warned: the fact that her baggy eyelids, no longer fitting so neatly against her eyeball, could not contain her tears. She wouldn't have minded so much if this were the only baggy, once close-fitting area that leaked, but alas, it was not.

'A quick cup of tea and then I'll finish it off.' She patted the book.

Living alone, she did this. Spoke aloud small words of encouragement or motivation that in another time and another life might have been offered up by a relative or a lover. Not that she keenly felt their absence, having learned over the years to be self-reliant in all aspects.

It might have been the season of goodwill, but she saw no reason to add sparkle and gaudiness to her home, already filled with clutter. The only exception was the rather fragile and misshapen lump of gold-painted, salt-baked dough that had started out in life as a star before age and clumsy storage saw it eroded to this rather ugly nub. Ugly, that was, to everyone apart from her. As was customary, it hung at this very moment from an old branch of pussy willow on her mantelpiece. It was all the decoration she needed.

Pulling back the bedcovers and despite her desire to get the letter finished, Molly took her time. Manoeuvring slowly, as any haste on her part seemed to invoke dizziness, she swung round her skinny legs with their overly large knees until she was sitting on the edge of the mattress. Flexing her toes inside her bedsocks, she stared down at the network of proud purple veins that ran in tributaries over her legs, visible through the thin skin, and tried to remember a time when her pins had been smooth, lump-free and shapely – a long, long time ago, that was for sure. Beauty, she had learned, despite everyone's apparent preoccupation with it, was but fleeting and also relative. It fascinated her how aesthetics seemed to have become the most important thing, remembering a time when the phrase 'it's what's on the inside that counts' was the mantra of the day and when women in particular seemed too preoccupied with all that life threw at them to worry about wrinkles, imperfections and liver spots.

'A different life, different times . . .' She looked at the book with the letters enclosed within and pictured handing it to her son. How would he react? A shiver of nerves ran along her limbs at the very thought. These nerves, however, were shot through with something akin to excitement. As though she was finally going to take her place on the podium, having waited a lifetime for the honour.

In the half-light and clutching her teacup, Molly made her way with caution along the narrow corridor of her cottage, its walls lined with heavily framed works of art, redolent of another life, lived in a four-storey house in Bloomsbury. She walked to the top of the stairs, her slender build enough to cause the floorboard on the landing to creak. The noises of her home were to her a conversation of sorts, a reminder that this little building too had a life, a history and a voice. Her home for life . . . She found it comforting. The very bricks and mortar were not only her haven but also her companion.

. . . *feelings and consequences that have been shut away, boxed, taped and shelved for much of my life. And trust me when I tell you that it is a box that has weighed heavily in my thoughts . . .*

'What else do I need to say?' she asked aloud, revisiting the words of the letter in her mind.

There was a moment when her concentration wandered: her mind fixed on the secrets that lay between the pages of her book and it was in that second that she took a step. It was a movement of mere inches, a small thing, but one that would change the rest of Molly's life.

Time stood still while her brain continued to whir, and Molly knew exactly how things were going to unfold, a minuscule window of warning too brief to act upon. Ludicrously, she clutched the dainty, porcelain cup and saucer, decorated with forget-me-nots, to her chest, as if protecting this was of far greater importance than protecting any of her aged bones. Molly was aware of her feet lifting from the ground as her socks slipped from under her, sending her frail body horizontal for a beat, before she felt the first crack of the back of her head against the lip of the two-hundred-year-old wooden stair and then of every crack on the back of her head against the subsequent twelve steps over which she thumped. There were only two thoughts rattling around in her brain as it shook back and forth, back and forth . . .

The first:

This was my grandmother's teacup! I don't want it to get damaged!
And the second:

I am really, really hurting myself. This may in fact be how I die . . . and this simply will not do. I must finish my letter!

When it was finally over, she found her reaction to be an equal mix of shock and relief. It was a shock that she had fallen and a shock that she had survived; relief came at the realisation that her ordeal was over, all seven seconds of it, before she welcomed the dark cloud of oblivion which now wrapped itself around her.

'Auntie Molly! Oh shit! Oh no – Auntie Molly!'

Molly opened her eyes and saw the jowly face of her great-niece, Frances, hovering over her upside down. As the middle-aged woman lowered her rather bulky frame onto the floor beside Molly, her broad knee came down on the dainty cup and saucer on the floor and crushed it. The same cup and saucer that had once belonged to Frances's great-great-grandmother and had survived two world wars and, miraculously, the tumble down the stairs.

With the crunching sound Molly felt the first jarring bolt of pain, in her legs, arms, ribs, head . . . everywhere! She opened her mouth to speak and what came out was a long, creaking whine of nothingness, like a laboured yawn or the scrape of wood from a barn door unused to opening onto cobbles, a rasp. Nothing more than a dry echo of irritation where her once lubricated vowels had slipped over a tongue loaded with words both whip smart and razor sharp.

The fact that her voice had gone frightened Molly more than the physical pain, the headache, the confusion.

Not only her voice, but apparently her words too, with only a tangle of letters in her brain, like an upturned tin of Alphabetti spaghetti. A muddle from which she could decipher only two words:

Igloo . . . igloo . . . igloo . . . igloo . . . over and over in a pointless, maddeningly frustrating monologue, and then a new addition, which came from nowhere: *paws . . . paws . . . paws . . . paws . . .* And the crazy thing, the *craziest* thing, was that even if she had been able to get the words out, the very last things she wanted to say out loud were either 'igloo' or 'paws', when what she actually wanted to do was shout at the top of her voice: '*My letter, my letter to Joe! I haven't finished it – it's in the book . . . the book on my bed!*'

The urgency of her desire left her breathless and frustrated as again she slipped from consciousness. The offer of dark escape, too tempting to resist . . .

Molly peeped gingerly through her tender eyelids. She hated the harsh overhead strip lighting of the hospital corridor. It offended her senses with its glare, doing nothing to beautify anything it touched, quite unlike the soft lamplight that filled the rooms of her cottage. The place was noisy, chaotic. Busy with preoccupied people coming and going. Her visible bruises, she noticed, sat in clumps, as if someone had inserted bundles of blackberries under her skin. She could feel the swelling of her eyes and face and her head pounded. The only way to keep the intense nausea at bay and to ensure any level of comfort was to lie perfectly still. This was made easier by the plaster cast that encased her arm, the bandages that tightly bound her ribs and the clumpy boot-like contraption on her right leg. It came as no surprise to her that she was more than a little broken. It took all of her energy to move her head, while inside she was shouting, '*There's a letter in a book on my bed – it's for my son! It's very important. Please! I need to get it to him!*', but what left her mouth was a low whine that anyone listening might have mistaken for a howl of physical pain.

Frances was somewhere off to her right, her niece's voice loud enough to break through the fog of semi-consciousness as she chatted on her mobile phone.

'Yep, yep, she's still here, aren't you, Auntie Molly? Hanging in there. Yes, yes, a stroke, apparently. Poor old thing. They don't know if she had a stroke and then fell, or fell and then had a stroke. I've called everyone I can think of and they're all phoning around too . . . I'm just going to go and grab a coffee, actually.'

Molly locked eyes with her and willed her to concentrate, to understand: '*Frances, I've written a letter to Joe – please see that he gets it!*' Her tears fell as what left her mouth was akin to a growl, with the words 'igloo' and 'paws' repeated randomly.

Molly felt the rumble in her gut of utter frustration.

I made a promise!

Growing old had not been something she detested, like some did, but neither had she revelled in it in the way she had heard others do – those irritating souls who liked to repeat their age as if it were a badge of honour or an achievement: 'I'm seventy-four! Can you believe it? I am seventy-four!' Molly thought particularly of Mrs Ogilvy, her disagreeable neighbour.

For her it had been more of a calm acceptance that this simply was how things were and there wasn't a damned thing she could do about it, other than the obvious. Although she did sometimes consider the frail state in which she lived, wondering if it was universal: the dulling of adventure in both palate and music? The desire for soft food, less noise, low light, easy landings and slow movement. Was it the norm: to have taken comfort in her dotage from the familiar, the routine and the predictable? And whatever happened to that thirst for adventure and her curious mind? Spontaneity! When had it all settled?

It would be disingenuous to say that in recent years she hadn't disliked her physical weakness. In her younger days, she could never have imagined a time when what she considered to be a Herculean task – the climbing of a mountain or the chopping of a log – would be replaced by taking the top off the toothpaste tube or the putting on of tights. All of these, however, had become equally impossible for her. It was not only a lack of strength, but a lack of dexterity too, as everything – *everything* – became fiddly and so time-consuming! It drove her absolutely crackers. She was not a person used to relying on others, much preferring to be self-sufficient in all matters.

And surely she was not the only one who felt that her life happened in a blink, with time passing so quickly she sometimes wondered if the whole thing had been some ghastly trick.

'*We are all but dust . . .*' This she spoke in her mind.

Molly felt another wave of unexpected emotion and hated the feeling of hot tears crawling over her temple and along her nose. With one hand in plaster and the other trapped under a top sheet, she realised that to reach her face was not easy. Suddenly the thought of dying without giving Joe his letter was almost more than she could bear.

Is this it? she pondered. *Is this where I die, in this horribly bland corridor?* This was quickly followed by the question: did it really matter? Her life, had, she believed, been an ordinary one and therefore an ordinary death was befitting. This she surmised without the modesty that so many feigned, and with the glorious benefit of being able to stand on the mountain of her years and look back at the path she had trodden. A path littered with pitfalls and rocks into which she had fallen or clambered over, and some of it done with her hand in his, holding her steady, upright, calm. Even after he had gone . . .

Despite her withering body, Molly's thoughts remained exact and clear, which seemed most cruel. She sometimes wished she did not have such ability for perfect recollection, thinking it might be preferable for her musings to dull a little so the reminder of what she had lost might also be blunted. But there was no such luxury for her. Her memories remained sharp and taunting, jostling her from sleep. Not only the bad memories, but the good too, and for those she felt some small gratitude. She could lie in bed and taste a fresh peach placed on her tongue over seventy years since, still sweet in her mouth, making the slippery, tinned, syrup-soaked variety often spooned in her direction most revolting. An insult! And the memory of her lover's palm running over her back beneath the winter sunshine on a stolen afternoon, as they lay close together on a tartan blanket among the ruins of war was, even now, enough to make her weep like the willow beneath which they had sought shelter. His face, captured in her mind like a picture, a particular smile, lips closed, one side of his mouth raised more than the other, his hair flopping forward, his eyes mid-laugh . . . It had always been him.

And now, here she was. Lying alone on a trolley in a corridor, unable to imagine whatever might come next, able to think only about what had gone before: each step, each breath and each day that had led up to that point in time. Her body quite useless now, but oh! The miraculous thing it had done: bearing a child, a boy! *A beautiful son . . .*

She cursed her inability to finish the note she had started, wishing nothing more than to place it in the hand of the boy who had shaped her whole life. She needed to tell him of her history. Her story, her ordinary life, and thus his story, the full truth he'd never known but that she'd promised, finally, to tell him. The truth that now he might never know.

TWO

'Goodnight, Geer, Molly. See you in the morning,' Mrs Templar called from her desk.

Molly raised an eyebrow at her friend. 'Well, she's in a good mood for once!' The two girls laughed.

'Please come for one drink,' Geer begged. 'Oh, don't be a bore, Moll!' She studied her reflection in the shard of looking glass on the back of her locker door. Opening her compact, she patted powder over her nose, forehead and chin, licking her index finger to smooth her shapely brows.

'I don't think so. Not tonight.' It was the last thing Molly felt like after such a long day. Her back ached, she was tired, and in truth was hoping for no more than a wash with hot water, a cup of hot cocoa and to feel the joyous contact of clean, starched cotton sheets against her skin, in anticipation of a good night's sleep. That was unless the bloody Jerries had other ideas and she would yet again be forced to tramp down to the Anderson shelter for the night, where some could snore the hours away, but not her. Once seated inside the corrugated-iron structure she always found herself thinking of her father and wondering what in God's name he had fought for only a couple of decades or so ago in the 'war to end all wars', if *this* was how she and thousands of others were now living: like moles underground, with the scent of the earth filling their nostrils and the sound of the bombs going off overhead. She would think of a poem her father had written, damned if she could recall any more than a line or two:

> '. . . and there in the clearing, somewhere in
>   France,
> I spied two moles engaged in a dance . . .'

This would never fail to make her smile – a happy distraction from the thought of the sirens and the bells of the fire trucks, which were not quite enough to drown out the wailing grief from those who had lost their homes and their loved ones. The Blitz had been devastating to both the fabric of the city and the people in it. She knew they would never forget it. Not that she ever let on to her mother quite how anxious she was, preferring to smile and say, 'Well, here we are – snug as bugs!' before tucking the crocheted blanket around their legs, while her heart hammered and fear made her limbs tremble.

Back in the present, she heard Geer's entreaty once more: 'Oh come on! What else have you got going on? Is Clark Gable popping over again for a corned-beef sandwich?'

Molly looked at her friend and replied without missing a beat, 'No, that's Thursday.'

Geer hooted with laughter. 'Oh please, Moll! Just one! That's all – one measly drink and then you're free to go.' Geer slipped her arms into her blue wool coat and buttoned up the front, looping a silk scarf around her neck, letting the two pointed ends hang down over her shawl collar in the style they had seen favoured by Princess Elizabeth. She fished in her handbag for her lipstick. Red, of course.

There was nothing special about Molly's own face and her body was practical rather than seductive. The thought of being considered even vaguely alluring seemed quite alien to her. She had decided long ago that her lack of bosom might be just the thing to help her gain traction in the world of diplomacy, which was very much the domain of men.

'I don't think so, Geer. I haven't had a good night's sleep in an age.'

'Yes, dear, we're all exhausted – that's wartime for you! Herr Hitler and his chums can rob us of street lighting, stockings and all the lovely men who are withering on the vine in some godforsaken bunker, but we absolutely cannot let him stop us having fun. Please come with me – it's nearly Christmas! Plus I've told my brother all about you. He does like a clever girl.' Geer grinned to reveal her enviable dimples.

'Oh God, no!' Molly felt her spirits sink even further. The very worst aspect of being set up with some 'terrific guy' was when he saw her for the first time and all of his hopes and all of his fantasies of meeting a Jayne Mansfield type trickled from him so obviously that she could almost see them pool on the floor. It certainly carved away at a girl's self-esteem. 'I'm in a crumpled blouse and my hair is a bird's nest. I have ink-stained fingertips and creases in my skirt.' She pulled the olive and mustard tweed material of her tapered skirt, trying and failing to smooth the material.

'Darling, he's been living with a gang of chaps in a bunkroom who no doubt have smelly feet and snore like billy-o! Trust me, the sight of a gorgeous girl while he's home on leave for a day, and one who can hold her beer to boot – I can guarantee the last thing he'll be thinking about is your inky fingers or your lack of pressed clothing.'

'Night, Molly. Night, Geertruida!' Marjorie brushed past them on her way out. She liked to use Geer's full name – a nod to her father's Dutch heritage. It put a level of formality into their interactions, highlighting their different status as colleagues in the translation department of the Ministry of Information. Their work here was classified, and both Marjorie and Molly were senior translators, with a bigger wage and a higher level of security clearance, although it would have been unthinkable to Molly herself that she might pull rank on any of her work chums.

'Night, Marjorie!' Geer called out as the other girl dashed along the parquet flooring of the corridor on the fifth floor of the building in which they all worked, translating and typing missives, notes and pamphlets, often in triplicate with the fiddly carbon paper pressed between the standard-issue watermarked sheets.

This was a job for smart girls – ones like Molly who had excelled academically and fallen through the net of domestic bliss that had failed to catch them as they fell from education. Not that Molly was fussed. Unlike her sister, Joyce, or her mother, for that matter, she didn't want to be caught – not while she was still trying to figure out the kind of marriage she wanted or indeed if she wanted one at all. There were two things of which she *was* certain: first, she wanted a career of her own, and second, she knew that to be stuck at home darning and cooking for a man, or worse, beholden to the needs of some wailing child, was not for her. It wasn't that she didn't respect the lives of her sister, mother and most other women with whom she came into contact – indeed she sometimes envied them, doubting that they had the same mental itch that made it hard to think about settling down, and then having to justify her nonconformist views on the topic. But the thought of being tied to the house and enslaved to domesticity was horrific.

When she originally applied to work for the Foreign Office, she'd been informed that this role was a stepping stone into other governmental departments – most definitely where her sights were set. The plan was to make her mark while translating and after the war, having earned her stripes, figuratively speaking, she would apply for a role in diplomacy. This request had been stamped all over her application form, with emphasis on her outstanding language ability, something she had excelled at in school.

It was only after having been in the role for the last year or so that eighteen-year-old Mary Collway (Molly to everyone who knew her) understood why their work was secret. She had translated propaganda posters from Germany, transcripts of conversations and notes from the enemy, intercepted and squirrelled away until they fell into her hands. She had quickly gone from wishing she was more directly involved in the war effort to realising that by providing understanding of the enemy's written materials and conversations, she was indeed doing her bit. Molly had translated direct orders from Berlin to destroy food-supply ships in an effort to make England and her allies starve. Evasive measures had been taken and this had been in no small part down to the work she had done.

She thought now about the cold cut of pressed brawn and pickles that awaited her at home, no doubt already on the kitchen table with a linen tea towel thrown over the top of it for preservation. She then pictured her mother, or rather the angry, critical shell of this woman who used to be her mother, wandering from room to room as if in search of something – or someone, who would not be coming home. Molly remembered when this veil of despair had descended: the day they had buried her father. It was as if, when the final clods of earth banged against the engraved plaque on the lid of his polished wood coffin, her mother knew she didn't need to pretend any more, not now the very worst thing had happened.

15

Molly drew breath. Even the thought of having to find her bright voice and holler 'Hell-llooo!' as she stepped over the shiny brass step of their Victorian terraced house on Old Gloucester Street, Bloomsbury, was almost more than she could stand.

Unlike her mother's beloved brother Max, who had been blown into a thousand pieces by an artillery shell at the Battle of the Somme, her father had survived the Great War, only to find his life blighted by two things: the memories that haunted his nightmares and his wheezing lungs, which had been irreparably damaged by the noxious mustard gas he had breathed in in the trenches. It was as though he had been spat out far from the battle zone and landed in his chair by the fire in his study, his face pinched, eyes hollow and with a lift to his nose as if the very scent of death still lingered. Her father thought he had been one of the lucky ones, dodging the bullet with his name on it, while those around him fell like dominoes in a line, the first having been pushed by the sharp finger of the Hun. The truth was, however, that he had not dodged it, not at all. His bullet had merely been delayed, delivered slowly. It had taken years for him to finally drown in his own bed without so much as a drop of water within reach.

'Come on, Moll! Don't let a girl down!' Geer whined again.

Molly sighed. 'All right then, one drink. And I mean it, one.'

'Come on – we need some fun after today!' Geer linked arms with her friend and the two swept along the corridor with their gas masks nestling in khaki canvas boxes slung across their bodies. 'You're going to love Johan. He's an absolute hoot!'

'Is he? Oh good,' Molly offered sarcastically as they made their way along the street with the chill of winter turning every breath crisp, heading for the Army and Navy Club in Pall Mall.

'Who knows, we might feel a bit of that old Christmas spirit!' Geer said.

'Darling, it's two weeks away and you obviously didn't get the memo: Christmas is cancelled again this year. Bloody war!'

'Yes, bloody, bloody war!' Geer shouted.

The girls huddled close together for warmth as they walked. Molly had got used to travelling at dusk without the comforting glow of streetlamps or the golden light pooling on the pavements from people's homes, her eyes now far better attuned to a world where windows were darkened with heavy blackout curtains or cardboard and paint to hide signs of life from the enemy. Crews of fire watchers gathered on corners, guarding hand-pulled carts with water pumps and extinguishers, in wait for the sudden siren that signalled incendiary bombs or the urgent cry of 'FIRE!' that would send a shiver through to Molly's very bones, knowing it meant devastation for great swathes of the capital's residents, rich and poor alike. Hitler's bombing raids were indeed the great leveller, in every sense.

Nearly every man on the street was in uniform: both those walking with a straight back and a meaningful stare, working on home soil to keep the nation safe, and those giddy, lopsided, leaning on a mate, no doubt home on R&R, wearing the cocky grin of the inebriated and with a soggy Woodbine hanging from their lower lip and a hat or beret askew. Girls not unlike her and Geer, similarly dressed in winter coats and sturdy brown shoes, tripped along the pavements arm in arm, always in twos or threes: the days and nights of feeling safe to wander the streets alone were a dim and distant memory. Her world, like everyone else's, was thoroughly changed, and the speed with which that change had happened was the most terrifying thing. It felt like mere weeks between the day her friends went from whispering the word 'war' and wondering if it *could* happen again to picking their way through rubble-strewn streets and turning up for jobs deemed unsuitable for women – unsuitable, that was, until all the men had grabbed a tin hat and a gun and gone off to do their bit, when suddenly they were very much in demand. Not that Molly was moaning about *that*.

She would never admit to feeling cheated, not when there were so many suffering, so many fighting.

'Evening, darlin'!'

Molly heard the call from one of the only unaccompanied women in the street, a street worker loitering between a shop doorway and the edge of an alley, with smoke curling from a cigarette and the cloying scent of cheap perfume hanging around her in a pungent cloud. The darkness was kind to her trade, hiding the grimy, age-etched face of the poor woman, who, like everyone else, needed to put food on the table.

'I was chatting to Beryl in the ladies earlier,' Geer said, pulling her close. 'She reckons Marjorie's chap is back home tonight.'

'I didn't know Marjorie had a chap.'

'Nor me – she's a dark horse, that one, don't you think?' Geer raised her eyebrows. 'But according to Beryl, she caught her reading a letter in the stationery cupboard and then squirrelled it away in her bra when she heard Beryl come in. How sweet is that!'

'Terribly. And it does explain her eagerness to get away and her unusually pleasant demeanour over the lunch table.'

Molly didn't have a fella of her own. This was at times an irritation, as she was keen to explore sex, wanting to unravel the great mystery of the physical, but sadly this adventure, too, would have to wait to launch, as all the eligible men were busy fighting. Unlike most girls of her age, she did not see her virginity as the jewel in the crown, nor was it a chip with which to bargain. Within the walls of their Bloomsbury home, sex and all its vagaries were completely taboo. Molly had once been on the receiving end of a stern stare and a not so subtle tut when she had casually mentioned her menstrual cycle. A crime she had dared not repeat, keen to avoid her mother's censorial gaze on all matters physical.

'She never really chats, does she, Marjorie?' Molly found Marjorie either quiet and thoughtful or, on occasion, spiky and intense. There didn't seem to be much space in her for fun or friendship.

'I think she feels a little out of place, truth be told.' Marjorie's strong cockney twang was in stark contrast to the rounded vowels of the other girls. 'And I don't think she has an easy home life.' Geer kept her voice low.

'In what way?'

'Oh, you know, she's from the East End.' Geer pulled a face. 'One of six, apparently, and I heard a rumour there's only two of them bringing in a wage. Her mother was French and died when she was young, and the father took to drink, by all accounts.'

'Good Lord . . . Think I would, too, if I was left with six kids!' Molly sighed. 'She's a bloody good translator, though – thorough. And if she's half French, that explains her fluency.'

'Well, I hope she has a nice time with her fella.'

'How could she not?' Molly winked and they both giggled. 'Any news from Richard?'

Richard, Geer's beau, a friend of her cousin, was currently serving in North Africa. He was a wonderful letter writer. With his gift for penmanship, Molly loved to hear his second-hand protestations of devotion and the small snippets he was able to share of his life on deployment in such a hot, barren place. She was fairly certain that the poor chap would have been mortified to know his declarations of love were shared across the polished mahogany of the dining room, not that he would ever find out.

Geer had a knack for mimicry and storytelling and it always felt like listening to a good play on the wireless when one of Richard's long letters arrived. Molly felt she got almost as much from the post as Geer herself. It wasn't only the lovey-dovey content of his correspondence that was so thrilling, but also the glimmer of excitement it offered. Any news from the front stirred something inside that felt awfully similar to envy.

Despite her reservations, Molly felt the first burble of excitement as she and Geer trotted up the steps of the Army and Navy Club, as the strains of Glenn Miller's 'I've Got a Girl in Kalamazoo' drifted from behind the satinwood doors of the ballroom.

Geer shrugged her arms from her coat and threw it playfully at the cloakroom attendant with a grin, jiggling her shoulders, as if the dancing simply could not wait. Molly took her time, happy to be in the warm, as she pushed her scarf down into the empty sleeve of her coat for safekeeping, still unsure if coming along at all was a good idea or whether maybe she should make her apologies right now and run home to that slice of pickled brawn.

Suddenly the ballroom doors opened. Molly looked up and her eyes widened as her stomach flipped. She had never felt this strange surge of desire in all of its forms. It was like a magnet that drew her to him and him to her, so powerful it could only alter her course that evening and for the rest of her life.

She saw only one person and he was looking at her. He smiled and there was a sudden strange flutter of recognition in her chest, as though she already knew him.

As though she had always known him.

As though she'd been waiting for him.

'Joe!' Geer ran forward and threw her arms around her brother's neck, pulling him close. Johan beamed and kissed his sister on the cheek, his fair hair flopping over his eyes, which never left Molly's.

Everything she thought and everything she wanted became scrambled in her head, wrapped in an unfamiliar band of self-doubt. She stood still, suddenly not quite sure how to walk, where to place her feet, in which direction to cast her eyes or how to position her hands. Ridiculously, she wished she was wearing a clean blouse or even her tea dress, the teal one with the wide belt, and wished that she, too, had bothered to put on lipstick, like Geer. And curiously and selfishly, she also wished that Geer was not there at all.

'You look skinny,' Geer said, pinching his face. 'Come and meet my friend! She's absolutely marvellous! A whizz of a linguist, speaks three languages and beats me at cribbage every time.' Geer grabbed Johan's hand and pulled him towards Molly, whose heart raced.

'Molly, this is Johan, my big brother, and Joe, this is Molly.'

'Marvellous Molly, I believe.' His smile was wide and easy.

He reached out to shake her hand and, as he did so, one of the brass buttons on the front of his tunic came loose and clattered to the floor, coming to rest by the toe of her shoe. Molly bent down and gathered up the small thing, which bore the stamp of a naval crest and a knot of rope on it. She held it out in her palm.

'Your . . . your button.' She cursed the wobble in her voice.

Johan reached out, but instead of taking the shiny button he closed his hand around hers, trapping it inside. 'Keep it as a good-luck charm.'

The heat from his hands warmed a place deep inside her that she was quite unaware had been cold.

'Thank you, I will.'

'Now then,' Geer said, clapping her hands, 'you take Moll for a spin on the dance floor while I ask a nice young gentleman to help me with the beers.' And with that she strode towards the bar, her fingers snapping in time to the tune as she went.

Johan was slow in removing his hand from hers. 'A dance then, Marvellous Molly?' He took a step closer and she breathed in the scent of him: a heady combination of cigarette smoke, hair oil and musky cologne.

'I . . .' What did she want to say? '*I'm not the best dancer . . . I would love to dance . . . I feel nervous and excited all at once . . .*'

Johan crooked his arm while her thoughts and mouth tried to catch up and she slipped hers through as they walked hip to hip towards the dance floor.

'You know, Marvellous Molly, I should tell you now that if you don't immediately say no to a dance, I will always assume it's a yes.'

She smiled. Nerves and apprehension robbed her of the ability to speak clearly and openly the way she did each and every day. It was bonkers! She so wanted to present the best version of herself to this man, her smartest self. Molly coughed to clear her throat, as a new song began to play, 'I'll Be Seeing You' – the deep, melodic tones of Billie Holiday masked the crackles and scratches of the record.

Johan pulled her close to him and she trembled from top to toe. He raised her hand and she rocked slowly against him in time to the music, with her head coming to rest beneath his chin, the button still held tightly inside her hand, inside his.

'Do you prefer Johan or Joe?' she asked, having heard Geer call him by the shortened nickname.

'If it's coming from your lips, Marvellous Molly, I really couldn't care less,' he said, squeezing her hand.

'Please don't call me that; I'm not in the least bit marvellous.'

'Are you calling my sister a liar?'

She heard rather than saw the smile softening the question, and felt an answering one on her own lips. 'No.' The mournful lyrics and soft harmony spun them inside a web on the dance floor . . . The words were haunting, carrying a message of love and hope. It seemed as though they were the only two in the room. Molly felt a heady and unexpected surge of sexual attraction for this man, a low, grumbling desire in her gut. It was a powerful force that left her weak at the knees. Curling her fingers tightly against his, she instinctively wanted to reach up and touch his face, although it seemed inappropriate, given they had only just met.

'In that case, I shall call you M – and everyone will think it's short for Molly, but you and I will know differently. M for "marvellous".'

'Johan . . .' she whispered, too quietly for him or anyone else to hear, but simply for the joy of hearing his name leave her mouth.

Across the room, Geer held up three bottles of beer in her hands by the necks and, with a cigarette between her teeth, smiled, jigging up and down on the spot, as if she might be just as delighted with this turn of events as Molly herself.

Johan pulled her closer. 'Don't look at her, M, don't give her the satisfaction of knowing that for the first time in her life she's done something I wholeheartedly approve of!'

'Why, what's she done?' she asked, unashamedly fishing for the compliment.

'Isn't it obvious?' he asked, pulling back just enough to hold her gaze. 'She's got us beer!' And he laughed and she laughed too. This funny, handsome boy who had her all of a dither.

Molly put the key in the door and cringed at the sound of it closing loudly. She was certain the slam would wake her mother.

'Is that you, Molly?' her mother called out, bang on cue.

'Go back to sleep, Mum!'

'Surely you're not just coming home? It's after midnight!'

'Of course not.' Molly pushed her back against the front door and closed her eyes, dizzy with a little too much beer and the feel of her hand inside his as they danced. 'I was just checking something.'

'What were you checking?' Her mother was irritatingly tenacious.

'I thought I heard something – an animal.' She shook her head. Was that the best she could come up with?

'Well, make sure you throw the bolts top and bottom!'

'I will, Mum. Night night.'

In her room, Molly washed her face and slipped into her night-gown, but then lay in bed, quite unable to sleep despite dancing for more hours than she cared to remember. She looked up at the sliver of moon visible through her window and wondered where Johan was at that very moment and whether he might be looking at the same moon.

She quietly hummed the tune they had danced to and it had the power to put her back in that moment, in his arms.

Was this how it started? Was this the feeling that made women want to slip into white frocks and give up their ambition?

'Don't worry, Moll, there's someone for everyone!' her older sister had trilled just recently while trimming crusts from cucumber sandwiches and warming a pot for the tea.

Joyce, by the age of seventeen, had swept up the aisle with Albert, quite possibly the most boring man on the planet. Her sister was content to stay at home and fill her time running the carpet sweeper over the rugs and making crumbles in the winter, salads in the summer and cakes on a Sunday. Molly had decided she would rather be an old maid than settle for someone like Albert and their ordinary life in a neat red-brick house in Tonbridge, Kent.

But Molly loved Joyce and didn't wish to insult her sister or her lifestyle, so she chose not to say that if marriage meant doing little more than baking, polishing scuffs and scratches from dark wood and washing, starching and pressing white table linens or shirt collars without breaking a sweat, she'd rather remain an old maid with a career in the Diplomatic Corps or the Foreign Office.

But suddenly it felt as though everything had changed. Maybe Joyce was right.

For the love of God, slow down, Molly! These thoughts were as terrifying and alien as they were wonderful. The idea that he might be feeling the same, thinking the same, made her grab her pillow to squeal silently into the feathers and drum her heels against the mattress.

When she removed the pillow she saw her mother standing at the end of the bed.

'Jesus, you scared me!' Molly laughed.

Her mother stared at her. 'What on earth are you doing, Mary Florence?'

'I was having a dream . . .'

Her mother shook her head and muttered under her breath as she left the room, but Molly guessed it was something along the lines of 'Lord, give me strength . . .'

Not that she cared. In fact, she felt so giddy she nearly confessed that maybe her mum and Joyce might be right about this whole marriage malarkey. Instead, she smiled and called out into the darkness, 'Goodnight, Mother dearest!'

THREE

'So you like him?' Geer asked casually over lunch, as she dunked a biscuit into her tea, a habit Molly found quite disgusting.

'I don't . . .' She shrugged, swallowing the uncharacteristic impulse to let her feelings gush.

'You don't like him or don't know if you do?' her friend prompted.

'I don't know if I should say. I mean, you're his sister and, to be honest, it all sounds faintly ridiculous.'

'Of course you can say, no matter how ridiculous!' Geer rolled her eyes. 'I'm your pal, and I'm in the perfect position to pass on any messages and act as go-between.'

'You'd do that?' She couldn't help the note of excitement in her voice.

Geer grinned, nodding frantically, then dipped her biscuit into the hot dark brew again before lowering the whole soggy mess into her mouth.

'We've only met once, but I can't stop thinking about him,' Molly confessed in a lower tone, wary of anyone else at the lunch table overhearing. 'It's as if every thought I have and everything I see now has to pass through a Johan filter.'

Geer widened her mouth. 'I am honestly trying my very hardest not to say that it's fast work!'

Molly sighed. 'I know, I know, and if you were saying that to me, I'd be taking you to task and telling you to pull yourself together.'

It had been mere hours since Geer had introduced Molly to her brother at the Army and Navy Club, hours that felt simultaneously like months and mere moments. Molly found herself distracted at work, the direct result of a whirring brain and as yet no word from the object of her desires. For the first time in her life she felt unbalanced, thrown by her own thoughts. The plan in her head of forging ahead with her career, undistracted by love, was now a little frayed at the edges and, she feared, with the right words of encouragement from Johan, might unravel altogether. And it was all based on no more than a single evening of dancing and an exchange of smouldering looks. She reminded herself not to be so silly: this was, after all, a fledgling thing and might never get off the ground. The words sounded sensible in her head, but her heart, it seemed, had no intention of listening. All she wanted was contact with Johan, and when Geer had asked about her feelings for him earlier this afternoon it had been almost embarrassingly welcome to say his name.

She had nodded, lips pressed together, swallowing the joy that threatened to burst from her. And so she had waited . . . and still she was waiting.

'He did say he'd be in touch.'

Geer grinned. 'Yes, Molly, so you might have mentioned once or twice.'

'What am I supposed to do, just wait?'

'That's exactly what you're supposed to do, darling.'

She rubbed her face. 'Waiting is driving me bonkers! I'm impatient and I've never felt that way before.'

Geer smiled warmly at her friend. 'I know I've been ribbing you, but I'm genuinely delighted that you like the boy. He's a wonderful human. I mean it. He's one of the good ones.'

'Back to work, ladies, please!' Mrs Templar, the supervisor, coughed and tapped her wedding ring on the doorframe of the dining room.

The girls put their teacups on the sideboard and made their way back to the office. Molly had a smile on her face, and willed the hours to pass quickly, keen to hurry home just in case a letter might be waiting.

'I'm exhausted.' Molly yawned as she reached for her coat at the end of the day.

'Me too,' Geer said, yawning into the mirror of her powder compact. 'Got to look our best in the morning, though – it's nearly Christmas!'

In the bottleneck of people trying to leave for the day, Molly held back in the foyer. Despite the early hour, night had fallen. The smoky air was cold, crisp, and she longed for the day when the faintest hue of pink would sit on the horizon, promising the warmth of summer, tantalisingly only a half a year or so away, when, God willing, this whole awful war might be over. A summer free of war – now that really would be something: boat trips, plump berries, green salad pulled from the earth and thin cotton frocks. Fresh shellfish and trips to Brighton, where, hopefully, the beach would have re-opened, finally cleared of the ugly barricades, mines and barbed wire. It was hard to remember the summers she used to enjoy in this highly strung world the colour of mud, where fun was in short supply and stomachs rumbled with lack of food, in anticipation of bad news or both.

She heard Geer shout some way ahead of her in the throng.

Molly finally made it through the mass of heavy coats and hats, then came to a stop on the top step beyond the doors, gazing towards the postbox in front of the building where Geer stood, looking quite invigorated, with her arms looped around the neck of a very handsome naval lieutenant.

'Johan!' Molly mouthed, and excitement exploded inside her like a firecracker, all traces of fatigue entirely extinguished at the sight of him. He looked up, caught her eye and saluted.

'I just need a minute! Back in a sec!' Molly beamed at him before turning and making her way, elbows and all, back through the very crowd she had only just been so keen to pass, ignoring their tuts as she ran up the wide staircase to the ladies' lavatory on the first floor. With her heart pounding, she stared at her reflection in the mottled looking glass over the china sink.

'Oh my God! Get a grip, Molly!' She fanned her face with her hands before leaning on the edge of the basin. The lavatory door opened and Molly was as surprised as she was embarrassed to see Marjorie exit the cubicle.

'Don't think God'll help you with your nerves.' She sidled past Molly to wash her hands under the cold tap. 'Milk of magnesia might be better.'

Molly laughed. 'Marjorie, I don't know what's the matter with me. I seem to have lost my head a little. It's this chap I've met – Geer's brother, actually – and he's here, he's . . .' Molly knew she was babbling.

Marjorie wiped her hands on the loop of towel that hung from a roller on the back of the lavatory door as if she hadn't heard or wasn't paying attention. She pushed her glasses up onto her nose and buttoned up her mackintosh. 'You shouldn't be nervous. Anyone would be lucky to have you interested in them.'

Molly felt touched by the unexpected vote of confidence. 'Do you think so?'

Marjorie reached for her shoulders and turned her towards the mirror. 'You take a good look and like what you see. It's important. It's hard for people to love you if you don't love yourself.'

'I *do* love myself. It's just that . . . I guess . . . I know I'm not one of the pretty ones, and it's not bothered me too much before, but I want him to like me back,' Molly admitted.

'He's here, isn't he?' Marjorie smiled at her and left the small room.

Molly again studied her reflection in the glass, and for the first time she could remember, she did like what she saw. Her eyes had a certain sparkle, her blemish-free skin was bright and her tawny hair, while not neat, hung in soft tendrils around her face, which looked, if she dared use the word, alluring. It startled and concerned her how much his opinion of her mattered. It was a novel feeling and a new vulnerability that she was wary of. She was a girl old enough to know what she wanted, on the threshold of womanhood and all that it promised. Emboldened and with her heart pounding, she finally left the safety of the lavatory.

'There she is!' Geer yelled. 'I told Johan you'd probably scarpered, run away via the back door!'

Outwardly composed and smiling, Molly hid the giddiness that threatened to burst from her. 'I didn't know there even was a back door,' she laughed, 'or I might have.'

'Hello, M.' Johan stood leaning against the postbox, gazing down at her with such intensity she knew it was longing, and all she could think of was that she never would have imagined someone as beautiful and incredible as him looking that way at someone like her.

'Hello, you.'

'I was wondering if you might like a walk?' He smiled that wide, easy smile that was even better than it had been in her memory.

'I would like that very much.'

'Right, that's enough!' Geer screwed her eyes shut and shook her head. 'I refuse to play gooseberry and will leave you two young things to it. Just take care, Joe, and happy Christmas. God, how I long for better times!'

'Me too.' Johan hugged his sister warmly.

'And come home again soon, won't you, darling?' She kissed her brother on the cheek and paused only to squeeze the hand of her friend. Molly noted that neither she nor Johan had asked Geer to stay.

'I thought the Embankment?' He seemed a little nervous, buttoning up his woollen coat over his uniform and crooking his arm, through which Molly slipped hers as though they had done this a million times before and not merely once. Her frisson of joy as they made physical contact was more than she could describe.

'Lovely,' she murmured, falling into step beside this man in naval uniform. 'This is quite a surprise. How long are you . . .?' She couldn't bear to discuss him leaving, but wanted to know how much time they had.

Johan looked at his wristwatch. 'I have exactly fifty-four minutes with you.'

'Fifty-four minutes? Could you be any more precise?' She laughed.

'You may joke, M, but I'm a stickler for getting the time right. It's important when it goes so quickly.'

'I guess so.' She liked his quirkiness.

'Actually, it will now be fifty-three minutes before I need to rendezvous with the car taking me back to . . .'

'Back to where?' Her question was automatic and they held each other's eyeline.

'Back to the coast from whence I have come.' He gave a wry smile. 'I often wonder if after the war we will all be so used to talking in code and withholding information that we might forget altogether how to speak plainly. Can you imagine: "Would you like a cup of that dark brew made from leaves freshly plucked from Assam?" – "My dear, you can just say the word 'tea' these days!"'

Molly laughed, the feeling like little bubbles of air floating up inside her. '"The coast" is vague enough, don't worry. Although if I had to guess, I'd say it's probably a coast somewhere in the UK as you're driving there.'

'A clever deduction, Miss Marple, and, yes, you're right. I'm going down to Devon.'

'Devon!' she laughed teasingly. 'Come on, Johan, what on earth could be that important to the war effort in Devon?'

His smile made his top lip and thin moustache hitch up at one side. He was to her quite beautiful and yet again there was that fold of longing in her gut. 'Now I really should not have said that, so keep mum.'

She drew a cross over her heart.

They both chuckled at the absurdity, leaning in so that their arms and hands were as close as could be. Their hips and thighs bumped as they strolled, sending electrifying pulses of desire coursing through her body.

'I hope Geer doesn't think we're frightful, not asking her along.' She thought suddenly of her dear friend with the tiniest pulse of guilt.

'She'll understand. And I really don't want to waste our' – he again looked at his watch – 'fifty-one minutes talking about my sister.'

'So what *do* you want to talk about?' she asked as they headed towards Horse Guards Parade.

Johan placed his free hand over the one he had captured under his arm, his tone level. 'I want to talk about you, Marvellous Molly. I want to say that you have been in my thoughts, and I wanted nothing more than to tell you that and to see you in the flesh, just to make sure.'

'To make sure of what?' she asked, unable to wipe the smile from her face as his thoughts echoed her own. There was something quite incredible about the thought of her feelings being reciprocated.

'To make sure that you really did make me feel how I remembered and to make sure your eyes actually are this big and your face just . . .' He shook his head and looked away, as if it was all a little too much.

'Just what?' She swallowed, her mouth a little dry.

'I like how smart you are, M, how direct. You're not coy or false. You seem steady and . . . as I say, I just wanted to make sure.'

'And was your first assessment correct?' she teased. 'Have you made sure?'

'Yes, I have.' He raised her hand to his lips and kissed her fingers. 'We have so little time, so let's get down to it. Questions,' he bellowed. 'I have so many questions!' He spun in a circle on the pavement, as if dizzy with all the things he wanted to ask.

'You can ask me anything!' she breathed as they slowed their pace.

'Right.' Johan bit his bottom lip and seemed to consider where to start. 'Your parents. Tell me about your parents.'

'Well, Papa was a bank manager before enlisting and becoming Major Lindsey Arthur Collway. He died when I was very small. He was badly wounded in the war, suffered terribly, and never truly recovered. I didn't know what he was like before, but in my mind

I steal the memories told me by my big brother, David, and my sister, Joyce, and I make them my own. It helps.'

Her brother had told her often how their father would sit in a chair by the fire in his study, his face animated, eyes bright, moustache twitching to conceal laughter, foot tapping on the rug, as David and little Joycey gathered around his feet in the parlour. Their mother rapt – a plain woman ordinarily and yet on these occasions, by all accounts, quite beautiful in the candlelight. Her hands, consciously or not, would clasp over her heart as if to witness such joy and tenderness in her own home between those she loved was almost more than she could bear.

Molly's own memories were very different, with her father a shadowy figure resting upstairs. A world away from the man who before her birth had penned poems and ditties for his older children, always far funnier in the telling than when she read them alone as an adult. One memory came to her now, of one Christmas when she was no more than five or six. With her father asleep upstairs, a tree had been decadently festooned with pom-poms, which she and her older sister Joyce had made in a variety of colours, as well as old family baubles depicting Nativity scenes. These were made of the thinnest glass that splintered almost to nothing if dropped, leaving piles of glittery Christmas dust on the wooden floors. It would fall between the cracks of the floorboards and David, her big brother, would whisper to her that it meant a little bit of Christmas magic lurked in that room for the rest of the year. She had loved this idea.

Molly also pictured herself ripping the brown wrapping paper from her present to reveal a china-faced baby doll with rosy red cheeks – and how happy and excited she had been at the sight of it. Her mum had been smiling, her sister Joyce similarly engrossed in freeing her own gift, a doll with long hair. Joyce, however, had rather frivolously tossed the wrapping paper in the air, from where it had landed over their mother's face. Molly and her siblings had held their breath. Christmas for one beat was sucked out of the room and replaced with nervous apprehension as to how their mother might react. She had sat very still on an old embroidered nursing chair that lived in the corner of the room and pushed the paper to the top of her head before pulling a funny face that sent David into gales of laughter. Taking his cue, she and Joyce had joined in and, just like that, the festive spirit was back. It had been the very best day she could wish for. She smiled now at the memory.

Her brother's glorious descriptions of their father were immensely precious to her and so detailed that time had helped fuse his stories with her dearest wishes and Molly had almost convinced herself that she had been present for all of them.

'Yes. It helps me to picture him before he was so broken – it makes me feel less alone.'

'Alone?'

'Yes.' She took her time, this not being something she ordinarily shared. 'My mother is distant. My brother and sister have their own lives, of course, and I seem to be . . . waiting.'

'What are you waiting for?' His tone was direct yet soft.

You. She swallowed the desire to say this and shrugged instead. 'Waiting for my life to start, I suppose. I thought my career would be a bit more advanced. I want to join the Diplomatic Corps or the Foreign Office and travel the world.'

'A career girl, eh?'

'Yes, very much so.' She held his eyeline, happy that he did not balk at her modern ideas. 'I don't always quite fit, Johan, with what is expected of me.'

'And what is expected of you and by whom?' he asked sincerely.

She pictured her sister. 'I guess there's an expectation within my family and society . . .' She let this trail. 'It seems to be that my goal should be to get up the aisle pretty sharpish and start reproducing, whereas what I want to do is—'

'Use those languages Geer told me about?' he interrupted.

'Yes.' She smiled, happy that he had remembered. 'Not that I don't want all that other stuff, but—'

'You want both.' Again he finished her sentence.

'Maybe I do. Do you think I'm mad or selfish or foolish?'

He shook his head. 'None of the above. I think you are unique and a woman to be taken seriously. You don't yearn simply for domestic bliss—'

'I just want bliss!' It was her turn to interject. 'Domestic or otherwise!'

'Amen to that.' He ran his fingers through his long, fair fringe, which had broken free from its oiled bounds and hung momentarily over his face. She captured his expression in her mind's eye like a photograph.

'The war has rather put a halt to things, changed the course for many people; not just me, I know, but it doesn't mean that I resent it any the less. I guess I'm just not living the life I thought I would,' she admitted.

'Are any of us?'

'I suppose not.' She caught the flicker of sadness in his eyes. 'Some days I want to scream at the world, furious at the mess we're all in and because my father thought he was fighting to make a difference.'

'I am furious for your papa.' He nodded sincerely, suggesting that he too was a man who had experienced the darker side of battle. 'And your distant mother – tell me about her?'

'Her name is Elizabeth – Betsy – and she's . . .' Molly struggled with how best to describe her mother's outlook on life. 'She's angry at the world and I know she misses Papa, but it's as though she's stuck somehow. Stuck in grief and disapproval and I suppose, if I'm being honest, not always the best company.'

'That's bad luck for her.' She liked his humanity, the lack of scorn. 'And bad luck for you, I'm sure.'

'It is.' Molly felt more than a little guilty for not saying something kinder.

'And David and Joyce?'

She smiled, ridiculously happy that he had remembered their names. 'Joyce is married to Albert, who's a very steady sort of man.' She decided not to offer anything more negative. 'He works in the energy sector. They live in a nice house in Tonbridge, and Joyce fusses, but is a darling and she loves me, that much I do know. She's kind and gives people the benefit of the doubt, is never cruel and always thinks things will turn out for the best. I want to be more like her. She's unflappable, reliable, organised and the exact opposite of me!'

'So you're flappable, unreliable and disorganised?' He raised his eyebrows, as they made their way to the Embankment and came to rest at a bench overlooking the river.

'I think I'm pretty reliable,' she offered, making no attempt to deny the other two.

'And David?'

'He's in the army like our father was, but as a medic. He's overseas; we don't know where. Somewhere hot. And his wife, Clara, a rather sweet and submissive sort of girl much of the time, is with their adorable little daughter, Clementine, down at her parents' place in Dorset. They visit us in Bloomsbury occasionally, where Clara reverts to a child herself and sits with misty eyes and a handkerchief pressed to her nose, as if she's really the hardest done by in all the war, while my mother chases Clementine around the garden. Clara is on occasion hardly what one would call a coper.'

Johan laughed. 'Poor Clara.'

'Yes, poor Clara. And between you and me: poor David! I get the impression that no matter how this war pans out, he'll be in deep trouble for abandoning her. Clementine is very quiet – I rather think she's sensing her mother's unhappiness.'

'Indeed. Children need to feel safe, don't they? Need to know there's a steady hand on the tiller, otherwise it's not fair. Poor little mites.'

Molly felt her stomach bunch as Johan expressed such sweet concern. She sat on the bench and he took up the space beside her, their legs touching as they looked out over the murky water and the cluster of vessels cluttering up the Thames. It was unbelievable to her that this was only the second time they had met.

'Okay. So now tell me about your family.'

'Well, Geertruida you know, of course. My father, as you also probably know is Dutch, a physician. He came over here to work and fell in love with my mother, a nurse – how clichéd is that? She is also a career woman and carried on working after we were born, fully supported by my father, of course. I think that's how you thrive as a couple, don't you? By not squashing the other's hopes and dreams?'

Molly nodded. His words made her so deliriously happy it was a struggle in that moment to speak.

'They settled in Hampshire, where I grew up. He's working in London, staying here, so Mum's pretty much abandoned too, but she doesn't seem to mind and he gets home when he can. What else to tell you? I have a dog.'

'Oh, you do?' She liked the idea of a dog very much. 'What kind?'

'She's a golden retriever called Dixie and she's my most loyal friend. I miss her as much as I miss my parents when I'm away – is that wrong?'

'Not to Dixie.' She smiled, liking the softness to his nature and his openness too.

'Probably not. I talk to her, but that is strictly between you and me. I don't tell people that.'

'Your secret is safe with me.'

Two RMPs walked past, hands behind their backs and in step. They had guns in white holsters over their shoulders, red bands around their hats and shiny black shoes.

'Evening, sir, madam,' one of them nodded in greeting.

'Evening,' Johan answered, reaching for his cigarettes. He shook two out into his palm from his cigarette case and offered her one. She raised her hand in decline, watching as he popped it back into the case and lit his with a match, taking a good long draw and blowing the smoke out into the evening air.

'I feel that time is ticking by and there's so much I want to say to you,' Molly said boldly, 'but mainly I want not to have to say goodbye to you in whatever time we have left. It feels like the most enormous pressure to make every minute count.'

'I don't want you to feel under pressure. I want you to enjoy my company.'

'Very well then. And I do.'

'I'm glad.' He took another drag. 'I don't want much in life, Marvellous Molly. I don't want a castle or pots of gold. I want simple things: home-grown apples, a comfortable chair, enough firewood to keep the chill at bay and a glass of beer on a Friday after a good working week – and of course someone to share it all with.'

'I want the same, but I'd swap beer for tea, I think, if it's in front of the fire.' She smiled at him. 'I want that same feeling of satisfaction at a job well done, and I like the idea of sharing chores with someone.'

'A partnership,' he surmised.

'Yes.' *Exactly!* 'A partnership.'

They were silent for a beat as if this new level of openness so in sync was to be savoured.

'I've always worried that I'm not very exciting,' he confessed finally. 'I want routine, the ordinary.'

'I think you're exciting,' she whispered.

'I'm really not. And I don't want you to be disappointed . . .' His face coloured.

'Disappointed?' She let a small laugh escape.

'Yes! You're so accomplished and fabulous and . . .'

'I could never be disappointed. I think you are . . .' She struggled to find the words. 'I think you're wonderful. I haven't been able to stop thinking about you, not for a second. It's quite thrown me.'

'That is such a compliment.' He turned to face her and they held hands, gazing at each other like lovers. 'So what is happening here, Marvellous Molly?'

'I don't know.' She lied because she *did* know, but lacked the confidence to say. This felt like falling, like diving into the joyous abyss that she had been wary of and intrigued by for so long, and now even the thought of it was intoxicating. There was very little doubt about it – she was thoroughly smitten.

'Can we meet again? In a few weeks? I have a day, possibly two, at the weekend and then I'm afraid I will be away for some time.' He lifted her fingers to his mouth and kissed them. 'And I think going away would be a whole lot easier if I could see you before I left.'

'I would like that very much.' Her voice was steady in the face of his words, which were so big she thought they might swallow her whole.

'Happy Christmas, M.'

'Happy Christmas, Johan.'

Molly walked home in a bit of a daze. Her stomach jumped with pure joy when she recalled that there were plans afoot for her to see him in a few weeks' time!

'That you, Molly?' her mother called from the scullery.

'Yes, it's me, Mum!' she called back. 'Who else would it be?' she whispered under her breath as she shucked off her coat and hung it on the coat stand.

'You're a little late.'

'Yes, I met a friend and we went for a walk.' She smiled again, feeling the warmth in her palm from where his hand had rested before he jumped into the car and waved through the window, which he had rolled down before shouting, 'I'll be seeing you!' as it spirited him away. Molly had thought she might explode. He had remembered their song. *They had a song!* Despite her dismissive nature when it came to romance, she was being swept along on a wave more powerful than her resistance and she rather liked it.

Her mother appeared in the hallway. 'What friend?'

Molly refused to let her mum's sour expression suck the joy from her bones. 'Oh, a boy – a man, actually – called Johan. He's the brother of Geertruida; you remember her, of course?' Geertruida was not easily forgotten.

'I do indeed.' Her mother pursed her lips as if her tone alone was not enough to convey her disapproval. 'I'm conflicted, I must confess,' her mother sighed. 'It's wonderful that you are finally seeing sense and spending time with a potential suitor, but is that *Dutch* boy really the best of the bunch?' The way her mother said the word 'Dutch' was heavy with connotations too unpleasant for Molly to voice to herself.

'In fact,' Molly added brightly, 'I'm seeing him again in a few weeks. And I'm very much looking forward to spending some time with him.'

'I see,' her mother commented, and drew breath, as if she wanted to say more.

Molly, however, scooted past and up the stairs. Not even her mother's whiff of disapproval or lack of enthusiasm could dull the bubble of happiness that filled her from top to toe.

FOUR

Near Alresford, Hampshire
January 1944
Aged 19

'You're going a bit fast!' Molly giggled, a little thrilled and a little terrified as the car zipped along at pace. She tucked the thick tartan blanket over her legs and placed her hand on her head, loath to lose the silk headsquare knotted beneath her chin, not with such things so hard to come by. Case in point being her woollen stockings, which she had darned at the toe as best she could. Like everyone, she was schooled in the art of 'make do and mend'.

'I know!' Johan threw his head back and laughed as the fancy sports car wove its way along the winding road, beneath the canopy of trees in the rural county of Hampshire, with its acres and acres of farmland, twisting lanes and quaint pubs.

It felt good to be breathing the clean air, wonderful not to have every aspect crowded by buildings, people and rubble. She could think more clearly away from the din of the city – and what a miserable din it had become, as if war had erased all the colour from the world. It was easy in this moment, just for one second, to forget they were at war. She tilted her head back, letting the bitterly cold winter breeze glance her skin.

'How much further?' she called over the roar of the wind and the whir of the engine, which rose and fell as Johan cranked through the gears.

'To Alresford? About another twenty minutes, but we're going on a slight detour!'

'A detour? Won't your friend be missing his car and won't your mother be expecting us?'

'Hardly! Dougie's flying a plane right now – a machine much bigger than this little beauty to worry about!' He patted the dashboard and laughed again. 'He keeps the old girl bedded down in the stores under several blankets and talks to her as if she's his special lady friend. I told him I needed to impress a certain person and he threw me the keys. I thought, what better way to introduce you to my mother than to do so in style?'

'I see.' She folded her arms. 'And how many times has he thrown you the keys before?'

'Never.' He shook his head vigorously but kept his eyes on the road. 'Never. And don't worry about my mother. I told her I'd be there at some point but that there was a chance we might bail; she said she just wanted me to be happy. She's married to a Dutchman, remember, and neither of them have that British stiff upper lip or concern over doing things the right way.'

Molly didn't know whether she should be relieved or concerned that she might not get to meet Johan's mother, but could not care less either way. Time with Johan was like being under a magic spell, as if they created a bubble where the rest of the world and all its rules melted away and where the ache of war didn't shadow their every move. She forgot the rumble of hunger in her stomach, her duty to her mother, her workload, her ambition and even the sad, hollow feeling at the fact that she and Johan had only a measly twenty-four hours together before he was due to head back down to his jolly secret role in Devon. He had written her brief notes in the weeks since she had last seen him, only ever mentioning the wide sweep of beaches close by and the settle of rose gold on the water at sunset but, as was par for the course, never mentioning his work.

'I must confess to feeling a little bit relieved that I might be delayed in meeting your mum. I'm more than a little nervous. Supposing she doesn't like me?' She tried to imagine the reception her own mother might give Johan.

He shook his head as if the very idea was preposterous. 'I told her you're a linguist and she was very impressed. Don't be nervous. How could she not love you, M? And anyway, I'll be right by your side.'

And strangely, with no more than these words for encouragement, she felt her anxiety ease. Geer had of course been delighted at the mutual admiration between her brother and her friend; it was a girl's dream if not to have a hand *in*, then at the very least to approve *of* her beloved brother's choice of partner.

'The more I see of Johan, the more I like him, and that's never happened to me before, in fact it's usually the opposite,' Molly told her friend over a shared corned-beef sandwich one afternoon. 'I thought I was immune to all this emotional stuff – turns out I'm not.'

Geer spoke through her mouthful. 'A girl would be lying if she said she wasn't the tiniest bit . . . what's the word I want? Not *jealous*, exactly, but I guess a little put out. It's only when I think about the reality of being usurped in Joe's affections that I feel a little miffed, but honestly, Moll, if I had to pick someone to knock me from that pedestal, it'd be you. You're two of my very favourite people in the entire universe.'

'Geer, I do adore you.'

Geer grinned. 'Well, it's hard not to! I am entirely adorable.'

Molly closed her eyes briefly, feeling the warmth of winter sunshine on her face and inhaling Johan's cigarette smoke, which spiralled from the open-top roof of the green MG TB Midget with its tan leather interior.

'Here we are! Damn nearly missed it,' he shouted from behind his cigarette.

The car slowed and bumped along as Johan turned down a narrow track all but obscured from the road. Ancient willows lined the path and sat clustered around a small clearing with one side open to a narrow stretch of river. Johan killed the engine.

'Oh my, this is beautiful!' Molly untied the knot at her chin, flung the scarf onto the seat as she wriggled free of the rug and left the MG, running the few steps over the grass to the riverbank. She stood, transfixed by the sight of the water gurgling over a small weir, where sun diamonds danced on its surface, all in the shadow of a larger willow that wept into the water, its long, delicate fronds, devoid of leaves, dipped into the depths below. Johan stood watching her, smiling, as he discarded his gloves in the vehicle and pulled down his wool tunic, now with the button replaced.

'This is a special place for me.' His voice was low. 'It's where I come to think, and I wanted you to see it. It felt important to me. I first came here with my dad when I was small and we used to play at fishing. I had a bamboo stick with a piece of string tied to the end. I'd sit for hours on the bank, dangling that string into the water, desperate for a fish, while he read a book. It was only when I was older that I sussed that I was never going to catch anything without bait and a proper rod!' He laughed now. 'More recently I come here with Dixie and throw a stick in the water for her, which she really loves.'

Molly felt honoured and delighted that he wanted to share this with her and slightly envious not to have similar memories of her own father. Johan walked forward and ran his fingers lightly along the hairline at the nape of her neck.

'I love every second I get to spend with you in the present, every second, but I also can't help but picture a future' – he paused, letting the enormity of his declaration sink in – 'a future with you.

And I want you to know that over the past few weeks, it's been those thoughts that have got me through the darkest or coldest of nights.' Molly felt her gut leap at the idea, knowing she would recall these words when her own nights were dark or cold. 'Does that thought make you happy or . . . or shock you . . .?' he fished, stuttering with nerves. 'I know it's all very sudden.'

Molly swallowed, barely able to get the words out over the enormous lump that had lodged itself at the base of her throat. 'It makes me very happy, actually,' she managed, her voice quiet but steady. His face lit up at her response. 'I liked what you said before about relationships being a partnership. That's what I want too: equality, conversation, support and love . . .'

'Yes.' He leaned closer to her. 'We could live in a cottage in the country,' he continued now with enthusiasm. 'And we could sit in front of roaring fires with full stomachs and a good brandy and you can knit me socks while I read the paper.' He grinned.

'Or you could knit *me* socks while I read the paper, Mr de Fries . . .' She stood her ground and he laughed.

'I'm teasing you, my thoroughly modern girl. I'd happily knit socks for you if you show me how . . .'

He kissed her then and her whole body softened with longing for this man, his touch, his skin, his scent.

'God, Johan, we hardly . . .' she began, almost breathless as he kissed her again on the mouth, 'we hardly know each other – how' – he kissed her again – 'how is this . . .?' Molly drifted off as her knees collapsed and she became quite breathless.

'It's wartime,' Johan said with sincerity, cupping her face in his hands and gazing deep into her eyes. 'And that changes everything – *everything*. Time is compressed and time is stolen.'

'Yes. Yes, it is.' She thought of the interminable hours she had lain awake, listening to the tick of her bedside clock, wondering where he was and when, oh when, she would get to feel his mouth against hers again . . . and she thought of the Davenport boy, Anthony – three doors along from them on Old Gloucester Street – for whom time had been stolen away. He would forever be twenty-three, and his poor mother, who, in receipt of a telegram only last week, had grown old overnight and now carried an expression that told the world she wanted nothing more than for time to stop. This thought of death made her want to grab life. She pressed against him, seeking his mouth with hers as her fingers stroked his neck.

'Are you' – he pulled away from her – 'are you sure, Molly, this is what you want? Because I'm happy to wait. I don't want to pressure you or . . .'

She silenced him again with a kiss. 'I have never been more sure of anything in my life. You are exactly what I want, Johan.'

'Wait here!' He kissed her hand before running to the car to retrieve the thick tartan rug she had discarded. He took great pains to lay it neatly beneath the willow before sitting down and patting the space beside him. Molly kicked off her brown brogues with the sensible square heel and wriggled her stockinged toes against the chilly grass, not that she minded. She hoped he wouldn't notice the clumsy seam along her stockings.

What came next required no discussion, no thought or pream-ble, the two laughing as they fumbled through a jumble of clothing, lost in the beauty of the moment and revelling in the respite from the uncertainty of war: the misery, the sirens, the rationing, the destruc-tion and the loss. This act was the very opposite. It was everything good: joyful, abundant, generous; and it brought light – light and joy – to two people, equals who had found something bright and beautiful at a time when the world felt shrouded in darkness . . .

Afterwards, Molly lay against him, huddling her coat around them both and seeking warmth from his body, entirely without regret, enthralled at the sensation of her lover's palm drifting over her skin beneath the winter sunshine. It was quite hypnotic. This had been her first time and she knew there was no other place she could have envisaged that would be more perfect. They were happy, content and quiet, listening to the sound of water burbling over the rocks and the beat of their hearts keeping time. They might have dozed a little, she couldn't be sure, but certainly the temperature seemed to have dropped even further and all thoughts of rushing off to meet Mrs de Fries had flown from her mind. Johan eased up onto his elbows and lit a cigarette. Molly propped her head on her hand and drank in his handsome profile. She felt changed and was grateful for it, glad to feel connected in this way to another living soul. She presented him her happiness, handed it to him like a neatly wrapped thing, and for a woman determined to be in charge of her own destiny, it left her feeling vulnerable and hoping – no, trusting – that he would only do good with it.

'Tell me the world isn't always going to be so mad,' she whispered.

He took his time in responding, taking deep drags of his cigarette, his free arm lying alongside hers. 'It isn't always going to be so mad.' He spoke with a calm conviction that she found immensely comforting. 'I promise you that.' He kissed her face. 'If I think about the future, I picture a generation of young men who don't know what it's like to put their hands over their ears to quiet the explosions, who have not seen their blood or that of their friends running into the earth of which they will forever be part. I don't want them to know what it's like to have to say goodbye to the things and people they love with every fibre of their being, knowing it might be for the very last time. And then to have to erase those things and people from their minds and switch to fighting mode just to enable them to get through the next hour and the next and the next . . .'

'Oh, Johan.' His words made her want to weep. She laid her face on his chest and let her tears fall into the cotton of his shirt. 'I want it to be over soon.'

'It will be, darling. It will, and we can all sigh with relief, no longer in a world where some of us are the lucky ones, unable to hold the gaze of those who loved the unlucky.' He let out a deep breath. 'It is so bloody unfair.'

'I need you to be one of the lucky ones, Johan,' she whispered fiercely. 'I *need* you to be one of the lucky ones. I can't possibly conceive of—'

'You don't need to.' He leaned over and kissed her hair.

'I know you said you'll be away. Are you . . . are you going abroad?' She knew not to ask specifics.

'No. No, I'm not. I'm going to be out of contact, but boringly safe – an exercise no more, off the Devon coast. Does it get any safer than that?'

The tight band of anxiety loosened across her chest. 'I know you need to do your duty. Just do it well and know that I'll be waiting for you.'

'That means the world to me, M. And when I come home, it'll be to a world where soft pads of reason have replaced the spikes of hatred, and I can't wait for those kinder times.'

'God, me too.' She nodded. 'I want to live in a world like that.'

He took a slow breath. 'I want to live in a world like that with you.'

'You are . . .' She paused, sitting up to look him directly in the eye, every word inadequate, thin in response to the strength of her feeling.

'I am what?' He fixed her stare, searching.

'I hardly dare say.' She lowered her chin, the intensity of his gaze almost too much.

'Well, that's the other thing about war – it makes you bold. It made us wonderfully bold.' He smiled mischievously, touching his fingers to her décolletage where the cool wind brushed her skin. She knew she would carry the act of their union close to her heart, a precious, glorious surprise of a thing.

Johan too sat up, their legs a lovely jumble. He put a finger under her chin and raised her face until she had no option once again but to stare into his beautiful eyes, the exact colour of amber.

'I love you, Molly. Be in no doubt – I do. I love you. I want to hold you tight and set you free. I don't want you to be lonely and I don't want you to live how you're *expected* to. I want you to live how you want to.'

Hold me tight and set me free . . . His words were the sweetest music that filled every gap of loneliness and halted each beat of doubt inside her. In that moment she saw her life stretched out before her, her *whole* life, spent with Johan by her side in a plentiful world full of colour and laughter and freedom, as equals. A partnership.

'So come on, don't leave a chap waiting – now would be a very good time to tell me if my feelings are reciprocated or if I'm very awkwardly barking up the wrong tree.'

'I love you, Johan. But I think you know that, don't you?' she said clearly.

Johan took both of her hands into his and raised them to his lips, kissed them gently and tucked them against his chest. Another wave of longing swept through her body and she wanted nothing more than to fall against him again, skin to skin.

'I do know that, Miss Molly Collway, I do.' He kissed her full on the mouth.

Molly finally pulled herself away. 'We need to get to your mother's house; she'll be expecting us.' Her tone was less than urgent and she made no attempt to move. There was something about the way he looked at her . . . It would have been hard to describe the effect it had on her, but it felt like coming home.

'I have no intention of sharing you with anyone this afternoon. Mother will understand. I'll write to her this evening and explain. We need to grab every second, M, grab every second and live in it.'

FIVE

Her guts quaking with nausea, Molly stared at Dr Cooper, the black-haired physician in Soho who had tested her pee sample from the previous week. He flicked ash from the end of his cigarette into an overflowing brass ashtray on his desk. His fingernails were overly long.

'Your test came back as positive. You're pregnant.'

He spoke in a cool and professional manner without any hint of emotion or judgement, as one would expect of a medic, and yet his words were of such magnitude that it took her a second to process them. The news did not come as a surprise but was no less shocking for that. At nineteen, she knew her body well enough to understand what was going on.

Molly thought about the day she had been interviewed for her job, keen to press on the board of men asking the questions that she was a reliable pair of hands, most unlike her counterparts, who would, when the right chap came along, be content to stay at home darning and cooking for a man, or worse, be beholden to the needs of some wailing child . . . Her stock phrase. And yet here she was. Strange that this should be her first thought and not how her mother or her love might receive the news.

She let the news sink in as her eyes wandered over the greasy desktop on which sat what she assumed to be the doctor's lunch, a stinky fish sandwich that smelled past its freshest. The oil had leached grease onto the brown paper in which it was wrapped. Her nose twitched in revulsion and her stomach heaved. It was almost impossible to imagine herself pregnant even, though it was clearly the case. But until it had been confirmed there was still the smallest chance that she might have been mistaken. This shock was diluted a little when she considered the father of this baby: Johan, quite possibly the one person in the whole wide world with whom she would actually be happy to undertake this particular adventure. She allowed the smallest frisson of excitement to ping around her veins.

Dr Cooper blew smoke into the room and she wished the window were open. 'I'm assuming this is not a planned pregnancy?'

'No.' She shook her head, resenting the question despite its accuracy. She held his gaze, already feeling a little guilty that the seedling that had taken root in her womb might hear such a thing. What did it look like at three months – *could* it even hear, feel? These very questions formed a bond of sorts that she had not expected at this early stage.

Dr Cooper licked his lips, narrowed his dark eyes and stubbed out the remainder of his cigarette. 'As is the case for the majority of young women I see here.' He gazed at the walls, where paint in a dull shade of ochre peeled in damp patches, as if to suggest that no one who had planned a pregnancy would be visiting this backstreet clinic in Berwick Street with no nameplate on the door. 'It might interest you to know that, for a reasonable fee, such matters can be taken care of in a room across the corridor, no questions asked, payment in cash. I have a nurse.'

Molly kept her composure while her mind recoiled in horror. It was one thing to choose to visit this anonymous man rather than Dr Venables, who her mother knew socially and who was less than discreet, but quite another for him to assume . . .

'That is of no interest to me.'

'Well' – Dr Cooper clasped his hands on the desktop and said with a faint smirk – 'if you change your mind, you know where we are, although I should warn you that as time advances, the price of the procedure rises in direct proportion to the risks for us all.'

At this reference to the illegality of his business, Molly practically ran from the premises, keen to put as much distance between her and the grimy place as possible. Not that she would be able to hide her state for ever, but she'd feel more inclined to tell the family doctor once she had spoken to Johan. Then at least when she sat opposite the man who had delivered her she would have some semblance of a plan.

Johan's face, his sincere open expression and his heartfelt words, *'I love you, Molly. Be in no doubt – I do. I love you . . .'* was enough to buoy her up and allow her to think that fledgling though it might be, this was going to be one hell of a partnership.

'Darling, it's a terrible line, can you . . . can you hear me?' Molly banged the receiver against her palm and then shook it, hoping this might help clear whatever blockage she suspected was blurring the call. *Oh, Johan, hear me! I need to hear you.*

'I can barely . . . It's . . .' His voice fractured and stuttered between the silences. The connection was terrible, faint and crackling. 'I'm going . . . for a while . . . Nothing to . . .' and then he was gone. And even though she knew this, Molly pushed the phone against her face, her eyes squeezed shut. *Please, Johan, please be there. Please . . .* She offered up the prayer to no avail. The call was no longer connected and pip-pipped irritatingly in her ear. Her legs shook as she put the receiver into the cradle and stood for a second to compose herself, wiping her top lip, which felt a little moist. She steadied herself against the edge of the green-leather-topped bureau, smoothed the folds of her pin-tuck silk blouse over her chest, and hooked a loose tendril of hair behind her ear before walking determinedly from the room. Marjorie had, as requested, been keeping watch outside one of the few offices with access to a phone and an outside line.

'Thank you so much, Marjorie. I do appreciate your discretion.' She let a small smile form in thanks for her colleague having done so without asking any questions, particularly, *'What is so urgent you need to sneak a phone call during working hours?'* Not to mention, *'Why did you ask me to keep watch and not your pal Geertruida – when the two of you are usually joined at the hip?'* Molly dared not confide that since she and Johan had failed to turn up at Alresford for afternoon tea, Geer had seemed disinclined to discuss the budding romance. Molly felt a little sheepish and was uncertain as to how she might justify their absence without risk of disclosing what had happened, and so she remained silent, hardly able to confess that they had been cavorting on a rug in the winter sunshine. Not that there was any real awkwardness, they were far too close for that, but it was as if lines had been drawn that neither wished to venture over.

'Discretion is important. We know that, don't we?' Marjorie held her eyeline, while clutching a foolscap file.

Molly nodded. 'Yes, we do.'

'You all right, Molly?' Marjorie asked carefully.

'I'm fine! Perfectly fine,' she replied, with more of a snap than she'd intended. It was part of her armour: remaining calm and unflustered. The thought of being viewed in the same vein as Clara, her sister-in-law, with her tendency to fall apart, was mortifying.

'It's just that—' Marjorie bit her bottom lip and looked to the heavens, as if searching for the right phrase. 'I suppose what I'm trying to say—'

Molly stared at her and her heart raced.

'I suppose what I am *trying* to say' – Marjorie reached out and squeezed Molly's arm in an unexpected and uncharacteristically affectionate display – 'is that you know where I am if you need me, all right?'

Molly nodded stiffly at this girl with five siblings, this girl who had probably lived a far less sheltered life than herself and who just might recognise the signs of pregnancy more easily.

'Thank you, Marjorie.' Molly gave her a brief smile before heading down the corridor and back to the office, trying to concentrate on the mountain of correspondence that needed translating and typing in triplicate, rather than the frustration of not being able to speak to Johan.

At 5 p.m., Molly went to gather her coat from her locker. It had been a long day, made even longer by her frequent need to visit the bathroom and her slight jump every time she thought of Johan, still ignorant of the situation in which she found herself – in which *they* found themselves. She was a little chilly and pictured sliding into bed with a hot-water bottle to bring rest to her weary bones.

'How about a cheeky snifter on the way home?' She was suddenly conscious of Geer standing next to her, winding her scarf around her neck. 'We could nip into the Ritz and drink something lovely! Oh come on, Moll! It'll perk us up. You look disgustingly pale and today has been bloody dull.'

Molly shook her head. 'Not tonight, Geer. I promised Mum I'd get home,' she lied. 'Plus I'm all done in.'

'I know, just plain exhausted, you poor old thing!' Geer rolled her eyes. 'Well, in that case, I shall have to go on my own and try and get some rich old man to buy me a drink.'

'Money isn't everything, Geer! Why don't you go off to Soho and find a poor artist to spend the evening with?'

'Oh God, no! I'd rather be with a rich man I didn't like than a poor one I loved!'

'Geer!' Molly couldn't hide her disapproval.

'I'm joking! God, your face!'

'Anyway, what would Richard say?' she asked in mock disapproval.

'Well, he'd fly into a rage, of course.' Geer leaned towards her and whispered, 'But I quite like the idea of him showing that he's jealous – a girl likes to be fought over, you know. Plus he's never going to find out, is he? Don't let the bedbugs bite!'

Molly laughed as her pal skipped along the corridor, blowing a kiss and then waving over her shoulder as she disappeared from view. Molly placed her hand on her stomach and thought of Johan. She replayed the few words she'd been able to make out from their conversation earlier and filled in the blanks, finding it strangely reassuring:

'I can barely . . . *stand to be away from you, darling M!*'

'It's . . . *been far too long.*'

'I'm going . . . *to come to London this weekend and take you to the Army and Navy Club for a gin and a twirl on the dance floor and* for a while . . . *we will think of all the good things that are going to come our way once this damned war is over.*'

'*You have* nothing to . . . *worry about, my love. Nothing to worry about. Everything is going to work out splendidly!*'

And to think that, at that very moment, he had no idea she was carrying his child. Tonight, however, that would all change when Molly put pen to paper, writing the letter that would tell her beloved of the news, which could not be kept secret any longer. She had considered informing him over the last few weeks, but had wanted to make absolutely sure of the situation before she concerned him. Dr Cooper had certainly done that.

After dinner, having politely refused her mother's offer of soup, Molly rushed to her bedroom, happy to remove her clothes and slip into her nightgown, rubbing at her breasts, which were already sore and felt a little heavy, even when there was no visible difference to her body at all. Her boyish frame and flat chest were her greatest allies in being able to keep her predicament secret.

Molly took a seat at the small leather-topped bureau in the corner of her bedroom. She unscrewed the top of her fountain pen and held it up towards the halo of light from the lamp on her desk, watching entranced as the mother-of-pearl inlay shimmered with faint flecks of iridescence. It was beautiful. This pen was one of her most treasured things and had belonged to her father. What on earth would he have made of such a missive, she wondered – a whole world away from ditties about Brussels sprouts and dancing moles?

Molly bent over the desk and let the scratchy nib of the fountain pen dart fervently over the page.

> . . . and so that's it, my love. I am with child – our child. I so wish the news could have come from my mouth into your ear and then my lips could have touched yours, but this is the next best thing, a letter. Can you believe it, my darling? Johan, truly I alternate between joy and delight at such a thing and then more than a hint of nerves at what might be your reaction to this news. I have nothing to go on, you see, but our spoken trust, in which I do have the utmost faith, but the sooner I hear that you're happy, the happier I shall be as a consequence. How I wish I

could hold you, feel you, see you . . . I would like nothing more than to lie against you and hear you whisper into my hair that there will be a time when we will live in a world where you come through the door each night and take me into your arms and that after supper we will waltz the way we did at the Army and Navy Club to music only we can hear, my hand in yours . . . Oh my darling, I can't wait for it all to be over so it can all begin. I hate this bloody war! I hate our separation. Keep safe. My love. My only love . . .

She wrote the words, stopping occasionally to tap the fountain pen on her bottom lip or to roll the precious brass button in the palm of her hand, a treasured talisman that she often held to her mouth or ran over her cheek. She had found a little walnut box in which to keep it safe, polished and with a delicate inlaid surface; this too had once belonged to her father. A knock on her bedroom door made her jump, and Molly pulled the top sheet over her words and turned the writing pad face down. Her mother walked in.

'I don't know what's wrong with you, Molly – you're either darting out of the door or are cloistered away up here. And you're in your nightclothes already!' Mrs Collway knitted her brows.

'I am indeed.'

'God does not look kindly on the slothful.'

Molly nodded, as ever, finding her mother's God-based admonishments tedious, to say the least.

'Anyway,' her mother said, softening her tone, 'I thought you might be interested to know that I've received a letter from David.'

'Oh, that is good. How is he? What's his news?' Molly loved her brother and was keen to hear how he was faring.

Her mother reached into the pocket of her cardigan and waved the yellowed envelope in front of her. 'Lots of words saying nothing

– the usual. No news to speak of and all a bit too vague to be of any real interest. He seems to think that filling pages is more important than sending anything of note. But lovely to hear from him, of course.' Her smile was fleeting.

Molly thought of her brother, who, since their father had died, had taken his responsibility as the man of the house seriously and might well want to spare his mother the full horror of his war. 'Well, no doubt his letters are censored, or maybe the war has turned him into a man who's selective with what he shares. He might take after Papa in that respect.' The words left her mouth before she'd had time to properly consider them, before she'd had time to remind herself that any perceived negativity directed towards her father would be seen by her mother as a personal attack as well as an assault on his memory, and so would invite a frosty monologue from her remaining parent, who saw herself as the true victim in the whole terrible debacle of her husband's premature death.

'You make it sound as if my husband was a sour man, and he most definitely was not!' Mrs Collway spat. 'And please do not confuse someone who has the horrors of war playing heavily on his mind with someone who is merely secretive.' Her chin wobbled.

'I don't, I really don't, I—'

'Good, because I shan't allow it. He worked hard for us at the bank for all those years. Just ask Mr Mason—'

Mr Mason lived in their street with his plump wife and had been a junior colleague of her father's, taking over his role when her father was deemed unfit to return to work. The idea of going to ask Mr Mason anything was almost comical, a man with whom she had barely exchanged a sentence.

'And then he gave his youth to that damned war and worked hard when he thought it was all over!'

'I know, I know he did, and I didn't mean—'

'Life might come easily to you as you sleep soundly in the house he provided for you and you enjoy the luxury of a job in an office – an office in London! And it might be wartime, but our hardships are minor in comparison. Can you imagine—?'

'Living in mud, Molly, for months and months! Mud! That is what Papa and Uncle Max endured, with sights and sounds around them that no man should have to see . . .' Molly said the words in her head while her mother drew breath.

'Living in mud for months and months! That is what Papa and Uncle Max had to put up with, with sights and sounds around them that no man should have to see—'

'I know, Mummy – I do know.'

'And' – her mother was not done. She stowed the letter back in her cardigan pocket and jabbed her index finger in Molly's direction – 'your brother might be a medic and doing great things for the war, but he would do well to remember what Papa sacrificed and how he suffered when he was home, taking years to draw his last breath with his nights disturbed and his lungs failing.' Her tears came right on cue, and Molly watched as she unfurled her lace-edged handkerchief and dabbed it beneath her eyes before wiping her nose. She was struggling to see how David had ended up being blamed for whatever offence had been committed. Her big brother would have laughed at this fact, the way he used to when she watched him smoke out of the attic window and taught her swear words, which she would then repeat verbatim as he recoiled in laughter, one of her favourite memories of him.

'Bugger off – that's a bad one.'

'Bugger off!' Molly would repeat, while David howled until he cried.

As was customary, her mother ran out of steam and left the room, slamming the bedroom door behind her. Molly watched the small mirror that hung above the chest of drawers in the corner list to the left in reaction to the impact.

She looked longingly out of the window over the higgledy-piggledy rooftops of London, hoping that tonight there would be no siren, no bombs, nothing to disturb her sleep, as she was tired. A big moon hung in the sky and stars twinkled. She pictured David, a nice man, a good man, who she hoped was indeed eating well and sleeping well. *God bless you, David, wherever you are. Come home soon. Come home safely to little Clementine and your Clara – God knows she needs you. Come home and meet this wonderful man I've fallen in love with, and come home and meet my little one . . .*

With her mother finally silent and in bed for the night, Molly took her fountain pen in hand and finished the letter with a flourish.

And so, my darling, I'll be seeing you . . .

With love

M x

On the back of the envelope she wrote 'Personal Correspondence' to ensure it was placed directly in Johan's hands and not read out in dispatches. God, the very thought! In simply writing everything down, it felt as if a small weight had lifted from her shoulders.

Molly fell onto her single bed with its walnut headboard and popped on her cosy old bedsocks before climbing beneath the cotton sheets softened with age, loving the feel of them against her chilly toes. She placed her hand on her still-flat stomach, where nerves and excitement mingled, and let her mind drift as sleep claimed her.

◆ ◆ ◆

It was a bright day, which made her walk to work pleasant. Her breakfast egg filled the gap left by her lack of supper. Her navy beret had found the right jaunty angle on her head and the air was still. The temperature promised much for the weekend. Perhaps on Sunday, after attending a church service with her mother at St George's in Bloomsbury, she might take a walk along the Embankment, replicating the steps she had taken with her beau and hoping the echo of their interaction might linger if she looked and listened hard enough. How she missed him. And how she longed to know his reaction to her news. She decided to invite Geer along for the walk and then they could possibly go for a cup of tea. Not only did she enjoy the company of her friend, she was also keen to hear any snippets about Johan that might have made it to the ears of the family. Plus, she thought with no small thrill, she would soon enough be able to confide in Geer about the baby, and how wonderful would that be? It was hard not telling her, but the last thing she wanted was for Johan to hear this monumental news second-hand, or even worse, third- or fourth-hand, but not being able to talk to Geer openly felt akin to lying and didn't feel right either. They had few secrets between them.

It was a strange thing, but despite the situation which some in her position would have described as desperate if not hopeless, Molly felt mostly joy. She was nervous, yes, and unsettled at times, but Johan was right, this was war and it changed everything. *Everything.* Time was compressed and time was stolen. Normal rules did not apply.

Molly reached into her bag for the letter and was about to pop it in the postbox outside the office when Beryl, one of the girls from her department, walked up to her. She was a big-boned girl with huge feet and a cumbersome manner.

'Morning, Molly!'

'Oh!' She popped the letter back in her bag, ridiculously aware of its contents. 'Morning, Beryl.'

'Are you coming in?'

'Yes, of course.'

The two walked into the lobby, opened the concertina-like cage of the lift and rode up to their floor. She felt the weight of the letter in her bag, hoping that Geer wouldn't see it and become inquisitive. Thankfully, it was safely deposited in her locker by the time Molly had poured a cup of tea from the urn and was seated at the wide table waiting for her friend. Two old men from the policy department whom she had seen before sat in the leather wing-backed chairs by the window, both smoking pipes and nodding seriously as the discussion turned to recent events. She wished, not for the first time, that her baby was being born into a different kind of world, taking comfort at least from the fact that it would not always be this way.

The clock on the wall showed five minutes past eight and there was still no sign of her friend. She wondered what Geer had got up to at the Ritz the night before. Surely she had not made good her promise and let some rich old man buy her cocktails? Or maybe Richard had written a letter so beautiful that Geer was too busy reading and re-reading to bother with work. Highly unlikely, though. Her mouth curved at the thought of the lovelorn Richard, who wrote such loving correspondence, and again she pictured the envelope, which she would now post after work.

Mrs Templar opened the door of the dining room and made a show of looking at her wristwatch and then the clock on the wall. 'Time, ladies, please!'

The girls all placed their cups and saucers on the long, narrow table next to the urn for the char lady to clean and put back, ready for their break for elevenses. They walked in an orderly fashion to their desks. Molly glanced along the corridor, half expecting to see

Geer come running in with her coat flapping, stockings twisted and hair a mess. But it was Marjorie who walked briskly into view. Their eyes locked and Molly thought about the last patchy phone call, and just like that she remembered the frustration of those few snatched words and missed Johan terribly. Suddenly all the good about the day, her perfect egg and the clement weather, was wiped out, leaving her with a hollow ache that she knew only seeing him and talking to him could possibly mend.

The lunch table was strangely subdued without the endless burble of Geer's chatter. Molly considered the possibility that her friend might be sick and mentally sent her wishes to get well soon.

Mrs Templar approached Molly during the afternoon tea break and said matter-of-factly, 'Miss de Fries has not made contact today.'

'Oh?' Molly wasn't sure quite how to respond.

'I assume you have no knowledge regarding her absence?'

'I don't. I'm sorry, Mrs Templar, but if I hear anything—'

'Yes, if you hear anything, then please do ask her to report to my desk first thing in the morning.' The woman walked briskly away and, even though it was nothing to do with her, Molly couldn't help but feel that she had in some way done something wrong.

It was drizzling slightly when she stepped out onto the pavement after work, a blessing not only for all the home veg growers who would welcome a spot of rain, but especially when clouds helped obscure targets on the ground in the event of a bombing raid. Molly looked left and right, before kissing the envelope. She let her eyes linger on the side of the postbox, on the spot where her love had surprised her, leaning there and looking so very handsome.

She decided on the spur of the moment to go and visit Geer, thinking that if she was poorly, the least she could do was make the girl a cup of beef tea and regale her with Mrs Templar's extreme displeasure at the situation. It made her smile, knowing her friend would find humour in it. In the same way they had enjoyed the retelling of Mrs Templar's reaction to Geer's brand-new red lipstick a few months earlier, when the woman's thin top lip had practically curled as she stared at the carmine slick on Geer's full mouth.

'*Garish! That is the word that comes to mind, Miss de Fries – garish!*' Even the poker-faced Marjorie had had to stifle her laughter.

'You walking this way?' Marjorie's voice distracted her and Molly swiftly tucked the letter back in her handbag, guilty that she had lately been thinking mocking thoughts of her.

'That's right.' Molly broke into stride alongside her. 'I'm off to see Geer, actually. It's not like her not to turn up without a word.'

'Well, there was no bombing last night so at least you know she was safe from that.'

'Yes, absolutely. How are things in your neck of the woods?' Molly asked, grabbing the branch of friendship Marjorie had extended since that evening in the lavatory when she had been riven with nerves.

'It's . . .' The other girl drew breath and adjusted her glasses. 'It's bloody awful, actually.' She paused. 'Absolutely bloody awful. Only a couple of miles from here as the crow flies but feels like a world away from up west.'

'Is there anything I can do?'

Marjorie exhaled. 'Nothing anyone can do till it's all over.' She clicked her tongue against the roof of her mouth. 'You still keen on Geer's brother?'

Molly nodded. 'Yes, keen and, erm . . .' The urge to tell someone was almost overwhelming, but if she told anyone other than Johan it would be Geer. 'Keen to hear from him.'

'Things have a funny old way of always working out, Molly.'

'Yes, I guess they do.' She concentrated on placing one foot in front of the other, wondering if Marjorie was letting her know, as subtly as she could, that she could tell she was pregnant. The two went their separate ways at the top of the road, both looking back at the other before turning out of view.

◆　◆　◆

The grand house in Eaton Square Gardens where Geer lived was run by the formidable Mrs Duggan, who had let six of her seven bedrooms to young unmarried women like Geer, whose parents paid monthly for board and lodging.

'It's a house of glorious chaos!' Geer had beamed.

The landlady was fierce when it came to noise, wasting soap, using any more than the bare minimum of toilet tissue, and anyone who forgot to keep the blackout curtains drawn after dark. When, however, it came to courting, sharing cosmetics, washing stockings in the sink and hanging them to dry over the tub or the consumption of alcohol, Mrs Duggan turned a blind eye and was even described by her tenants as 'exceptional fun'.

Molly removed her beret and gave it a good shake, watching the droplets run down onto the Belgravia pavement. She raced up the steps to the front door and let the heavy lion's head knocker do its job. It was a minute or so before the door slowly opened and Mrs Duggan stood on the top step. Her face was pale, her expression not the welcoming smile that Molly had previously seen.

'Hello, Mrs Duggan. How are you?'

The woman stared at her wordlessly.

Molly smiled more brightly, trying not to be put off by the landlady's odd manner. 'I was hoping to see Geer. I'm sure you know she wasn't at—'

Mrs Duggan shook her head, cutting her off mid-speech. 'Yes, dear, I do know.'

'Can I see her? She's not poorly, is she? There have been some rather rotten tummy bugs going around. My own mother's gone for a tonic only today.'

Mrs Duggan took a deep breath and leaned on the doorframe. 'No, dear, not a tummy bug. But she, erm . . .' The woman coughed and took a step forward, her tone and the tilt of her grey head most conspiratorial. 'She's had some rather bad news.'

Molly stared at the landlady and wasn't sure if she had spoken or simply thought the words: *What bad news?*

Either way, Mrs Duggan answered. 'All rather sudden, but she's gone home to Hampshire – caught the early train this morning. I can't recall exactly where the family home is—'

'Alresford.' Molly filled in the blank.

'Yes, that's it, Alresford.' The woman drew breath. 'Well, she's at home with her people and I don't know when she'll be back.'

'With her people . . .? Why . . .? What's . . . Has something happened? What bad news exactly?' Molly asked quietly, as if she didn't really want to know, while desperate to quieten the terrible scenarios that had started to race around her head.

'Very unexpected,' Mrs Duggan said, biting her bottom lip. 'It concerns her brother, Johan. Circumstances are all a bit murky and we don't really know quite what happened, but he's been killed. Her parents got the telegram late yesterday. A terrible business.'

Molly made a strange noise, a bit like a nervous laugh and a bit like a yelp of pain. Everything seemed unreal and her legs suddenly buckled beneath her. Mrs Duggan's voice echoed through the ringing of her ears, and Molly welcomed the darkness that enveloped her as she plunged headlong through the woman's front door.

◆ ◆ ◆

'Goodness me, what a to-do.'

Molly, with her eyes closed, recognised her mother's voice as she was guided from the kerb and into the house. She grasped her mother's hand – something solid to reach for in the dark fog of shock in which she stumbled.

'I paid the cab.' Mrs Collway's tone was one of displeasure. 'The driver said he'd come from Belgravia. What on earth were you doing over there?'

Molly spoke quietly, her voice thin. 'I was . . . I was visiting my friend Geer.'

'Yes, I know the one. Dutch.' Her mother uttered the last word as if it might be some kind of affliction.

'But she wasn't there.' Molly's tears fell and she let them. 'She had to go home because her brother . . . her brother . . .' Her sadness threatened to consume her and stoppered the words in her throat, which felt narrowed and raw. 'He was killed, Mum.' She gave voice to the monstrous words that refused to sink in. *How can it be possible? You're one of the lucky ones, Johan, you told me so – you said you were safe, safe and sound in Devon . . .* Instinctively she placed her free hand on her stomach.

'And he's the chap who took you for tea some weeks back?'

Molly nodded through her tears.

Yes, the most perfect day, when we lay on a blanket under a weeping willow . . .

'Goodness me, you seem awfully sad about someone you barely knew,' her mother tutted. 'These are tough times, Mary Florence, and they call for resilience. I mean, there are of course exceptions – poor Mrs Davenport is still bed-bound, but that I understand: Anthony was her only son, after all. And as hard as it is and as sad as it is for your Dutch friend, you need to toughen up. We're fighting a *war*! This is what happens, and it happens to us all.' She looked at the portrait of Molly's father on the wall in his best suit, seated at a desk and with the fountain pen that would become Molly's poised in the air and ready to write.

Molly extracted her hand from her mother's clasp and gripped the banister. 'I'm . . . I'm going to bed.'

'You don't want supper?'

Molly bit her tongue to stop the furious tirade from flying from her mouth. *Supper? Supper? He's dead and you want to know if I want fucking supper?*

It felt easier to ignore her. Molly trod the stairs with leaden limbs up to the landing and then trudged slowly to her bed, which she fell upon, still in her damp coat, with her beret askew and the brown brogues tied on her feet. Her heart physically ached, her thoughts tumbled and her eyelids felt raw and heavy. Tears slid down her nose as she wept. Her crying left her breathless, her sorrow was all-consuming.

The realisation that she was now truly alone and pregnant sent a bolt of panic through her very core, followed by a very real fear. She had been counting on Johan's love and support. It was hard to open her eyes, trying to kid herself that there was the faintest chance that she might wake to find the whole thing had been some ghastly nightmare. *I need to make a plan. I need to stay afloat. I need to figure out how to make this work! But, oh my God, it hurts!* Molly knitted her fingers in the sheet as if she were physically holding on not only to her bed, but also to reality.

She finally drifted into an exhausted slumber in the early hours, until her mother woke her by popping her head around her bedroom door.

'You're going to be late for work, Molly.'

'I'm not going,' she managed. 'Not today.' Her eyes were swollen and her voice no more than a croak offered from the depths of her pillow.

Her mother tutted, and no doubt Mrs Templar would too when she noted Molly's absence, but that was too bad. Molly's whole world had been turned upside down. The wonderful future she had seen, spent with Johan by her side in a plentiful world full of colour and laughter and freedom . . . Only now did she realise how very much she had wanted it, which in itself was almost more than she could bear.

Her mother closed the door.

Molly rose slowly the next day with the grit of sadness behind her eyelids and a deep hollow ache in her gut. It had been another fretful night of broken sleep, and she wanted nothing more than to stay in bed and pull the blankets over her head, but that was not an option. Not only was Britain a nation at war and she had a job to do, but also she knew that in her current predicament she would need a steady income and must save what she could until her confinement, when her wages would stop. There was barely time to pay heed to the physical weight of grief she now carried, as the survival of this child was down to her and her alone. This thought was sobering and terrifying in equal measure.

'I can do this – I can – I can do this,' she repeated with every step of her journey, hoping it might strengthen her resolve and distract her from the despair she felt every time she pictured the beautiful man she had lost. She laid her hand on her stomach and walked slowly along the grey streets of London, struggling to put one foot in front of the other without stumbling, feeling a little as if she was floating and thinking for the first time of the letter she had written and which still sat in the bottom of her handbag. How cruel it seemed that he would never know his child or even of its existence. Her future had turned to ashes. The lightness she had felt – that perfect bubble in which she had found herself when in his company – was nothing more now than a memory. He was gone for ever . . .

She shook her head and quickened her pace; she had a job to get to and money to earn.

Mrs Templar was kinder than she had expected, assuming no doubt the reason for her distress was that her best friend's brother had been killed. And she was of course right, in part. None of the other girls in the department spoke to her, and she understood. In these critical times, sadness and desolation were contagious and every single one of them had reason to cry, but keeping it at bay was absolutely necessary to survive day to day. Their looks, however, were knowing and kind and their tones hushed. Molly poured a cup of tea from the urn and forced it down before taking a seat at the big table. Marjorie pulled the chair out next to her and sat down, and without saying a word placed her hand on Molly's arm, and the slight pressure of it was a comfort. The two remained in this position until Mrs Templar called them through to take up their seats.

'It'll all be okay, Molly,' Marjorie whispered.

'Thank you . . . my friend,' Molly managed.

Mrs Templar cornered Molly as she made her way back to her desk. 'I spoke with Geertruida's landlady today. She confirmed that Geertruida won't be returning to work and will remain with her mother, which is unfortunate but of course understandable. I believe she's only returning to London today to gather her things. I was hoping you might pass on my sincerest condolences when you talk to her next.'

Molly nodded. 'Yes, of course.' She was reeling from this added news that her friend, her dear, dear friend, would not be returning to work. If Johan's death had not already soaked up all of her sadness, she knew this would have been the biggest blow. At the end of the working day she made the decision to visit Geer, knowing that once she had returned to Hampshire for good, visiting would be a whole lot harder.

It was hard to believe that it had only been two days since she had last set foot in Eaton Square Gardens. Her pulse raced as she recalled being bundled into a cab and sent home to Bloomsbury with the shock of Johan's death ringing in her ears. It was still almost impossible to think about him without wanting to give in to the tears that were always under the surface, but whenever she felt this way, a quick rub of her stomach, a reminder that she needed to be strong, kept her emotions in check. Molly didn't know exactly what she wanted to say to Geer, but trusted their friendship enough to imagine that the words would flow.

Mrs Duggan opened the door and recognised her, of course. Her smile was brief and sad, no more than a cursory twitch at the sides of her mouth. 'I shall go and call Geertruida, dear. Do come in.'

Molly stood in the hallway of the grand house, gazing at the hands of the grandfather clock, wishing, wishing she could have had more time with Johan . . . She heard feet on the stairs and turned to see her friend.

'Oh!' she gasped. Her heart swelled and her tears broke their banks at the sight of this girl who had lost her brother, her eyes swollen and raw from crying. Molly noticed for the first time how much she looked like Johan, a fact both wonderful and unbearable in equal measure. Molly rushed to her, taking her in her arms and holding her fast, but Geer remained stiff, upright.

'Geer!' Molly sniffed. 'Oh my goodness, Geer! I don't know what to say; I don't know what to do. I can't believe it – I can't! I am so very sorry, sorry for you, sorry for us all. And you were right – he was a wonderful human, more wonderful than I can say. One of the good ones! And your poor, poor mother. I can't imagine what she's going through, and poor you. Oh God, Geer, I just can't accept that it's true.'

Her friend pulled out of her embrace and looked over her head towards the front door. 'My brother had two opportunities to see his family.' She paused to clear her throat, swallowing as if it were lined with glass. 'The first one he spent with you, walking on the Embankment. And the second time' – she paused as if the words were too hard to say – 'the second time he told my mother he would be home for tea, but he never turned up, because he was with you.'

Molly lowered her arms and stared at the other girl, whose tone was sharp, her words stilted. Suddenly they felt like strangers to one another.

'But you . . . you left us alone. You said you didn't want to play gooseberry, and we . . . we—' She paused, having been about to say, '*We were glad of it; we were grateful,*' but decided against it. 'And that weekend . . . we ran out of time, Geer!' Molly pictured lying on the tartan rug with her head on Johan's chest while the spark of life took root in her womb. 'He said your mother would understand and that he'd write to her immediately, and—' She ran out of puff.

'You took that from us,' Geer spat, ignoring Molly's words, as her own tears now pooled. 'My mother waited for him on that Sunday, waited all afternoon. She . . . she had baked a cake and he never arrived. You took that last day from her. You took it from us! And I will never, ever forgive you for that.'

Molly shook her head and tried to compose herself. Her friend's words were like daggers that lodged in her heart. It was a confrontation she had not expected, could never have imagined, but then, if life had taught her anything over the last few days, it was that you never knew what was around the corner and how quickly everything you thought you could rely on might disappear.

'I'm sorry, I truly am. I would never want to hurt your mother, but we had no way of knowing.' She let her head fall to her chest, thinking of all the things she might have said *had* she known. 'But trust me, Geer, when I say that it was a wonderful, precious day for us.' She cried again at the thought of the promises made in the sunshine. 'I . . . I loved him, you see, and he loved me and we, we talked about his dog, about Dixie, and . . . he took me to his special place,' she gabbled.

'Love?' Geer laughed loudly, cruelly, dismissing her words. 'You met him a couple of times – that's not love! How can it be? Love is what families have: love is how my mother felt about the boy she gave birth to, and love is what I, his sister, felt for my big brother, so don't talk to me about love.'

'But it's true!' Molly hated her pleading tone. 'It *was* love, and I have something to tell you.' She placed her hand on her stomach and took a deep breath. Geer stared at her hand, which moved slowly over her flat tum. 'I never got to tell Johan, but—'

'Don't you dare! Don't you *fucking* dare!' Geer spat. 'You think that would help? What do you want from us?'

'I don't want anything from you!'

'Good, because you are not and never will be welcome. You have done quite enough!'

'But, Geer,' Molly faltered, shock making it hard for her to think straight, 'this is Johan's baby!'

'No, it's *your* baby, Molly – yours. Just let us be!'

'You don't mean that – you can't . . . This child, it—'

'What don't you get?' Geer rushed forward and opened the front door. 'Don't talk to me about it because it's nothing to do with us. You think we can handle that on top of losing him?' Her face crumpled at the words. 'In fact,' Geer said, tucking her hair behind her ears and wiping the residue of tears from under her eyes, 'don't ever, ever talk to me again.'

Molly couldn't have spoken even if she had wanted to. Shock and grief sat like a physical plug in her throat, rendering all speech impossible. Her tears fogged everything. She fled as the door slammed behind her, keen to put distance between herself and Johan's sister and, right on cue, felt the first kick of her little one in her stomach.

'Oh – oh my darling! And oh my baby!' she murmured, crying harder now as she looked back to the house where, in another time and in other circumstances, she would have been running to share the good news with the girl she so loved. Her dear, dear friend . . .

SIX

Molly put her hands in her coat pockets and watched her elegant sister walk towards her across the road. Joyce stood out as a classy beacon against the dull background of London at war, as army trucks with roaring engines trundled around them. Joyce's neat heeled shoes showed off her slender ankles and her camel coat hung beautifully on her frame. Her hair was set with a side parting and fat waves that fell around her neck. Her eyebrows were plucked and arched and her lips painted red. She looked beautiful.

'Well, I must say this is all very cloak and dagger, not that I'm complaining.' Joyce beamed. 'It's been rather exciting, wondering what it was you couldn't possibly say on the telephone! Of course, Albert wouldn't let me take the train. The railways really are such a nightmare at the moment – he insisted on driving me up. He's parked over on the Mall, no doubt having a not-so-secret smoke of his pipe. I hate the ruddy smell; he's supposed to be cutting down.' Molly reached for her big sister and wrapped her in a hug. 'Hey! What's up, darling? This isn't like you.'

'Thank you for coming into town.'

'That's how it works, kiddo. You need me, you call me and I come to you. That's how it has always been and how it always will be – you know that, don't you?' Joyce gripped her clip-topped handbag in one hand and with the other moved stray wisps of hair from Molly's face and softly ran her finger down her cheek.

Molly nodded. She did know this: the proof being that she had made the phone call only yesterday and her sister was standing in front of her right now.

'You look exhausted, pale. And I'm assuming that whatever it is you need to say you want kept from Mother, otherwise we'd be meeting there, of course. I've been racking my brains, trying to—'

'I'm pregnant,' Molly interrupted, knowing that if she didn't just say it out loud, it would get stuck in her mouth or buried under a pile of other words and pleasantries, and there was no time for that. 'I'm pregnant,' she repeated, wondering if her sister's silence was because she might not have heard correctly.

'Good Lord!' Joyce blinked. 'I was *not* expecting that.' She took a step forward and pulled Molly again into her arms. The two were silent for a beat, letting the enormity of the situation wash over them, standing still while soldiers and airmen, messengers, military police and the public raced around them in a hurry to get to wherever it was they were heading.

'Are you sure?' her sister whispered.

Molly nodded her response against her sister's neck.

'Oh, you poor love. How far gone are you?' Joyce pulled away to study her face better.

'Around five months.'

'Gosh, you don't even have a bump! Not really.'

'It's my build, I suppose. I can feel it, though.' She smiled at her sister, the two sharing the intimate detail of this bittersweet situation.

Joyce took a deep, slow breath. 'I don't know where to start.' She looked towards Buckingham Palace. 'How you have kept this to yourself?'

Molly shook her head, as if in horror at the very idea. 'I don't really have a choice,' she said ruefully. 'Mum's bound to be a little upset when she finds out.'

Joyce huffed at the understatement.

'And I can't risk losing my job,' Molly continued. 'I need to save as much as possible and work up until the very last minute so I have enough to see me through my confinement and then to pay for childcare when I go back. I've done the sums and I think I can do it, just about.' She ran her fingers over her brow; the words were logical, smart, but she knew the reality might be far more challenging.

'But will they keep your job open? You know how employers are about these things. It's hard enough to keep a job if you get married, let alone . . .'

'I know, but I don't see why they shouldn't. I'm good at what I do, fast and accurate, and I work hard.'

'And you'll stay in Bloomsbury?'

'Initially, yes. I don't have too many options; housing is hard to come by as it is at the moment, without adding the unmarried mother element to it. I know many landlords wouldn't entertain the idea. But eventually, I want my own place, of course I do.'

Joyce nodded. 'And what kind of childcare?' she asked, her gaze steady.

Molly bit her lip and wished she had a more concrete solution. 'I'm hoping Mum will be on hand. I have this image I cling to of her seeing the baby and any disapproval being swept away, and she can look after it while I'm at work. I can pay her extra on top of my board and lodging contribution, and that would be welcome, I know.'

Joyce averted her eyes as if not so certain of their mother's likely reaction. It was unnerving.

'Or I'm thinking maybe someone we know, a family friend or neighbour. It's at times like this we all must pull together, isn't it?'

'Yes, dear, but pulling together because of circumstances created by war and pulling together for something like this . . .' Joyce shook her head. 'It might be harder than you think. People can be very judgemental.'

'Are *you* judging me, Joyce?' Molly's voice cracked at the thought, conscious as she was of how others would view her single status when pregnant.

Her sister reached for her hand and held it tightly. 'Oh, my love. No. But I can't pretend I'm not a little fearful for you.'

Molly appreciated the truth.

'Do you have a boyfriend? I mean—' Joyce faltered at the delicate nature of the topic. 'Where is the father in all of this?'

Molly took a sharp breath and did her best to keep her voice strong. 'He was someone I loved very much. His name was Johan, and he died, Joyce. He was killed.'

'Oh my goodness!' The bloom of tears in her sister's eyes was reassuring and welcome. 'That's terrible.'

'It *is* terrible.' Molly gave a dry laugh. 'He didn't know I was pregnant. I wrote to him but never sent the letter. I've hidden it in my wardrobe. And then, just like that . . .' She shook her head. 'A lovely future that felt within reach turned to smoke. I'm scared, Joyce.'

'Of course you are, dear.' Her sister nodded. 'I wish I could tell you it will all be fine, but I think you're in for a rough time.'

This much she knew already.

'Are his people in contact? Do you know the family?'

'You remember my friend Geer?'

'Yes, of course! Loud and fabulous.'

Molly winced, feeling the loss of her friendship acutely. 'Johan was her brother. But since he died . . . We've fallen out and she doesn't want to speak to me and has made it plain that neither she nor her parents want anything to do with me or the baby.' It was a state no less painful to consider, no matter how many weeks had passed.

'They'll be in shock and grieving, of course.'

'Yes.'

'And you, my poor little sister, you must be shredded. Grieving and pregnant.'

'I am, Joyce.' Her bottom lip quivered but she managed to swallow the threat of tears. 'But actually, being responsible for this baby means I need to keep it together. I can't fall apart. I have too much work to do and too many things to plan. It's all on my shoulders.'

'It is. But if any woman I know has the strength to get through this, it's you. You're smart and sensible and you can do it.'

'I don't feel terribly smart or sensible right now.' Molly felt, as she did on occasion, the flicker of resentment that her life plan had been thrown so wildly off track. Not only by losing Johan, but also, she had always seen herself stalking the corridors of the Foreign Office, and now? Her ambitions were, if not thwarted, then certainly a little dented.

'I do think you need to tell Mum. Sooner rather than later.'

'I'm waiting for the right time. I practise telling her in the middle of the night and it's easy in my head, but then I see her and I fold. It's a lot harder than I thought.'

'I bet.' Joyce exhaled as if the thought was scary enough. 'What do you need from us? What can we do to help?'

Molly noted the way Joyce spoke for herself and Albert, for their partnership . . .

'Nothing right now, but I already feel a little better because you know about it. I feel less alone.'

'You're not alone, darling. I'm in Tonbridge, not that far away, and if you need me, get word to me and I'll be there for you always.'

'Thank you, Joyce.' Molly welcomed the slow hug her sister wrapped her in.

I want to hold you tight and set you free. I don't want you to be lonely . . .

'I do love you, Little Moll.'

'I love you too.'

Joyce had sent Molly a wrapped package tied with string; in it was a housecoat she had made. Their mother had been delighted to run her fingers over the peach quilted material, modelled by Molly, with the wide tie belt and the patch pockets edged in grosgrain ribbon in a darker shade.

'Well, isn't she a clever old stick?' From her puffed-out chest and lifted chin, it seemed Mrs Collway took no small credit for her older daughter's ability with a sewing needle. Molly thought it was funny she had never seen her quite so pleased about her own proficiency for languages or her promotion at work last year.

'She really is.' Molly had smiled, but not for the reason her mother might think. For, opening the package in the confines of her bedroom, as per the written instruction on the outside, Molly had unfolded the housecoat to find six nappies, two darling night-gowns and a small cardigan in lemon with the tiniest matching booties imaginable. It had made Molly's heart sing as well as filling her with a cold dread, as the clothes somehow made her pregnancy real and were a reminder of how little she knew about motherhood.

She held the little booties in her hand and tried to imagine the baby feet that might fill them.

Molly was now a little under eight months pregnant. In her head the idea of keeping her situation secret made a little bit of sense in a world that did not; she was certain that when her mother did find out there would be hell to pay. Quite what that hell might look like she wasn't sure, but of one thing she was sure – it would be loud and accompanied by tears. Keeping her confinement under wraps enabled Molly to carry on working and earning, adding to the savings that were growing slowly and steadily in her savings account. This money was, she knew, her ticket to a smooth transition from single girl to working mother. Molly knew enough to understand that without a ring on the third finger of her left hand, the corset she was about to put on stopped the inevitable looks and judgement from anyone she encountered and the predictable conversation, which she did not want to have. Geer's reaction the last time she had seen her lived on in her mind.

With the changes in her form becoming harder to hide and her mother's consternation at the fact Molly was avoiding her, Molly knew it was only a matter of time before she was forced to come clean. Following Joyce's sage advice, she had on a couple of occasions earlier on in her pregnancy prepared to broach the topic, once as her mother was warming the large metal pot for tea, but faced with her disapproving frown as she complained about 'the lack of flour in the shops', how she craved 'tinned sardines' and the fact that 'her teeth felt loose in her gums,' among many, many other moans and ailments, Molly felt that the moment had passed. It was *starting* the conversation that she struggled with, and with a fellow female who had in the past shot her down and made her feel mortified for having been brazen enough to mention her periods. If she had to think about her future, the one vastly altered now from the picture Johan had painted, she saw the nursery on the first floor restored and imagined her mother putting the baby in the old family Silver Cross pram and wheeling it up and down the streets of Bloomsbury with pride. It was not, of course, the life she had wished for, knowing that without Johan by her side her happiness would be measured, but she would not give up on this child – she was determined to make the very best life possible for it.

'For the love of God, Molly, you have to tell her – and soon!' Joyce had instructed over the telephone when Molly called her from the office.

'I know!' she whispered. 'I have in fact decided to tell her tomorrow night, as I'll be finishing a little earlier, and we can sit down at the dinner table and talk calmly, I hope. I've been practising it in my head.'

'Well, amen to that! I'm on hand should things get a bit . . .' Her sister faltered and Molly could only sigh.

'Joyce, I am one hundred per cent sure that things will get a bit . . .'

'Well, I'm nervous for you.'

'You're not helping!' She ended their call and couldn't help but smile briefly at the thought of her sister, who was on occasion a little too truthful.

Standing in the bathroom in her underwear, Molly looked at her limbs, which had gained no weight. Her narrow shoulders, neat, contained bump and slightly rounded breasts meant that from behind she didn't look any different. Right now and turned to the side, there was, however, no mistaking her condition, although she was still very small. Her sadness at losing Johan and Geer had not lessened, but her main preoccupation had been avoiding her mother. This she managed by leaving early and coming home late, and then making her way upstairs to bed the moment she put her key in the door. When necessary, she conversed with her from her bed and in her nightgown; the smocked, high-necked design hid her changed body. Her mother thought her petulant and asked repeatedly how long she intended to sulk for. Molly had no answer and would sink down onto the mattress, giving her mother even greater reason to believe that she was acting like a moody teenager and not a woman on the verge of motherhood. She had registered at the maternity unit at the nearest hospital, leaving blank the line which asked for 'Husband's details'. She had pushed the form across the counter to the attendant nurse, who had stowed it quickly, as if embarrassed on her behalf by her single status. Molly had stood tall, her chin held high.

She cringed now a little to think of the encounter, smoothing her underslip over her form as she fastened the amber-coloured clip in the side of her hair to hold back her wayward fringe. Next, she captured the back of her locks in a net before twisting and smoothing it into a neat bun at the nape of her neck. She cleaned her teeth, patted a liberal amount of Yardley lavender-scented talcum powder under her armpits and into her cleavage, and then patted her face dry with the peach-coloured hand towel that lived on a small woven chair by the side of the sink. She ran her fingers over the little basket of flowers someone had embroidered in one corner, possibly her grandma or Joyce – and why not? It made sense: Joyce was exceptional at everything else, so why not at prettifying the hand towels too? She smiled at the thought of her beloved sister and only ally.

Bracing herself against the sink, Molly breathed in and fastened the girdle around her waist, as she had done every morning for the last few weeks. Wrangling with the contraption, sweating and quite light-headed, she dragged the wide band around her midriff to marry up the reluctant hooks and eyes as best she could, then staggered against the ancient towel rail, gripping it to regain her balance. Taking a deep breath, she whispered to her baby, 'It's okay, little one, you're fine, you are safe and sound. It won't be for long . . .'

She closed her eyes and let the tears gather at the ends of her long lashes as she thought of Johan and all that he would miss, and in turn of all that she would miss – all *they* would miss . . . It bothered her to have to girdle her child, confining its movement. She had read up about women in the past who had been corseted and restricted during pregnancy, and the one big advantage she had was that her bump being so small meant the baby was tightly confined in any case. It did little to allay her concern. Slowly she straightened and pulled her sweater over the girdle and put on her skirt. Again she looked in the looking glass, running her finger under the dark bruises of fatigue that sat beneath her eyes.

'Johan . . .' she said, touching her belly, 'I miss you.' She cursed the tears that were never very far away. 'I miss you so much!'

She sniffed up her tears as she thought now of her mother and how she wore her grief like a cloak that at times covered them all, knowing this was not the future for herself. The difference was of course that her mother had had years and years of memories of times spent with her father, whereas Molly had only seen the man she loved on three occasions, just three. No more than eighteen hours in total. This small number, she knew, would diminish her loss in the eyes of others, but she also knew, *knew* without a shred of doubt, that it had been real and it had been love.

She had very little detail about his death, but had heard, courtesy of Marjorie, who she assumed must have been in contact with Geer, that her beloved had died in a training exercise on a beach, with an unconfirmed suggestion that it had been friendly fire, not that she could see anything friendly in it. Regardless, she was in no doubt that he had died because of the Nazis. Without them and this whole bloody war, he would be by her side and she by his, sitting in front of an open fire, Mr and Mrs de Fries, preparing for the birth of their baby. The precise way in which he had died seemed almost secondary to her, the result being the same. It was, however, almost unfathomable that her colleague might know more about the passing of her great love than she did. And this in turn made her think of this child that Johan's family would know nothing of. She understood their anguish, but quietly hoped that it might not always be the case. The pain of his loss sat like a small stone beneath her heart that dug in all day and meant she carried a pain in her chest that was sharp and physical.

Molly stood up straight and let her body settle into the new and uncomfortable garment. After a minute or two she got used to it, providing she kept her breathing shallow. The one small positive in the estrangement from her best friend was that in not having to face Geer, she avoided the only person who would most definitely have noticed the subtle changing shape of Molly. Who was she kidding? It was no relief at all.

Don't think about it. Keep going. Don't think too deeply. Keep going.

Molly wiped her eyes, pinched her cheeks, painted on a smile and made her way down the stairs.

'Bye, Mum!' In what was now a practised routine, she stood on the doormat and called up towards her mother's bedroom, timed carefully so that if and when she opened the door of her room, Molly would already be somewhere along the pavement, clomping her way in her brogues to work.

The elderly newspaper man on the corner of Russell Square was giving his usual street cry of '*Stand'd!*' as he stood with his flat cap pulled low on his brow, a rolled-up paper in his hand and the obligatory cigarette hanging from his bottom lip. 'V2 hits Chiswick! Three dead! Read all about it! Get your *Stand'd* 'ere!' She listened to his shout of the headlines and her stomach knotted at the words that, no matter how familiar, still had the power to shock and leave her feeling utterly dismayed.

This bloody war! Her thoughts raged and she felt the confined kick of her little one in response.

'*It's all going to be fine, little darling. Don't you worry about a thing. It's all going to be splendid.*'

She thought again of the three poor souls in Chiswick who had perished, and their relatives, possibly fighting abroad, and who were about to be dealt the lowest blow: that while they were out of the country, dodging Hitler's bullets to keep those they loved back at home safe, those they loved had been killed by one of his ghastly bombs. It was the cruellest twist. And one she and the de Fries family understood better than most.

Marjorie approached the building on Malet Street from the opposite direction.

'Good morning, Molly.'

'Morning.' She raised her hand in a little wave as they met by the front entrance steps. Her colleague was starting to feel like quite a close friend these days.

'You look . . .' Marjorie paused, eyeing her colleague before looking away, as if uncertain as to whether to give voice to her observations.

'I look what?' Molly ignored the quake to her knees; they felt as if they might give way.

'Tired. Very tired.' There was a moment of silence when something passed between them – acknowledgement, understanding, empathy? Molly could not have said for sure, but the soft expression on Marjorie's face was one from which she took comfort.

'I *am* tired,' she croaked.

Marjorie nodded. 'I was thinking back to that day when I came out of the ladies and you were so excited—'

Molly swallowed the lump in her throat and let her eyes graze the postbox on the pavement that had known the weight of her lover's touch, where maybe his scent still lingered, molecules of him. She resisted the temptation to throw herself around it, knowing it was ridiculous.

'I can't imagine what you're going through. And I know there are no words, but I want to say that things will get better.'

'Yes,' she whispered. 'I have to believe they will. Life goes on.'

Marjorie took a step towards her. 'We all walk the same path, Molly. All of us. We all trip, but more often than not we are so focused on looking ahead that we don't notice the stumbles of those around us. And we all keep plodding on, because what's the alternative?'

'I don't know,' Molly answered truthfully. 'I'm too busy plodding!' She gave the brightest laugh she could muster.

Marjorie again gave her that intense stare. 'You know where I am.'

'Thank you, Marjorie,' Molly said, and meant it. The two exchanged a knowing look that was kind and connecting, before Molly followed her friend into the building.

She had felt a little out of sorts all day, with a niggling pain in her lower back and an uncomfortable pulse in her womb. She put it down in no small part to dreading the conversation she was to have with her mother that very evening.

'Everything all right here?' Mrs Templar asked the question while looking over Molly's head, but she was in no doubt that she referred to her and her alone.

'Yes, thank you. Bit of a tummy bug,' she added for good measure.

'Milk of magnesia,' Mrs Templar offered, as she tapped the desk with her pencil and walked away.

Marjorie caught her eye from across the room and gave a subtle wink. Molly smiled, wondering if milk of magnesia was actually the cure to all ailments both physical and mental. She thought, if this were the case, she might need a very large bottle indeed. Her work, she knew, had been slow and her error rate higher than normal recently. She couldn't wait to get home and release her stomach from the darned girdle, her fear growing daily of how it might be affecting her unborn child.

She walked home slowly, stopping every so often to rest against a wall or to lean on a lamp post and catch her breath. She put her key in the door.

'Is that you, Molly?'

For the love of God! 'Yes, it's me!'

'There's potted meat and crackers on the kitchen table,' her mother called from the parlour. 'I'm listening to the wireless!'

'Righto!' Molly kicked off her shoes and forwent the potted meat and crackers, as the pain in her back was suddenly ferocious. She crept up the stairs, glancing at the parlour door, where her mother no doubt sat with her darning pile and a crackling wireless.

'It's a wonder to me sometimes that we live in the same house – you disappear morning, noon and night! It's as if I live quite alone,' her mother called out.

Molly paused on the stair. 'Well, during the day I'm at work and in the evenings you're not alone, Mum, because I'm at home. And right now I'm tired – but I am, as ever, just upstairs if you need me.'

'Yes, but upstairs or not, when you're sleeping sound enough to ignore a doodlebug, you're not much company.'

Molly's face fell. 'I can't help that I'm sad, Mum.'

'Oh, and here we are again – back to the Dutch boy, no doubt.'

Molly shook her head, too weary and uncomfortable for the fight.

She closed her bedroom door and stretched out her lower back, shutting her eyes in a moment of pure bliss when the corset pinged to the floor. She then spent a good minute or more rubbing at the skin of her abdomen where the firm edges had cut in.

'There you go, little one, have a good wriggle.'

After taking deep, unrestricted breaths, Molly climbed between the sheets in her nightgown. She didn't care how early it was. Her body needed rest. It was now customary that she lie on her side and let her mind run free, with everything she had kept pent up during the day. Her grief was quieter now, but each night felt as raw as that first time when she had smiled and banged the lion's head knocker on Mrs Duggan's door.

'. . . *Very unexpected . . . It concerns her brother, Johan. Circumstances are all a bit murky and we don't really know quite what happened, but he's been killed. Her parents got the telegram late yesterday. A terrible business . . .*'

Only an hour later she woke with a start and a grumbling ache in her pelvis.

No no no no! Her instinct told her that this rude awakening was nothing good. And then it came, sharp and fierce: a searing pain that felt like a knife in her gut, but working from the inside out. She put her hands between her legs and felt the soaked mattress and nightdress.

'Not yet, no – it's too soon, too soon! Oh my God, oh dear God!' she said into the ether.

She must have yelled or screamed out because she heard her mother call up from the parlour. Ignoring her, Molly hauled herself out of bed before staggering along the hallway to the bathroom. Her bare feet were sticky on the linoleum floor as she locked the door. Instinct told her to squat and this she did, holding on to the side of the tub for support. The position offered momentary relief. She was sweating, her hair loose about her shoulders, stuck to her face and forehead. Without warning and more quickly than she would have anticipated, wave after wave of pain rippled through her and it was all she could think about. No sooner did one wave calm and she found a second to catch her breath than the next one started, building to an almost unbearable crescendo. And pretty soon, all the waves rolled into one with no glorious moment of relief in between when she could catch her breath.

Molly became aware of the sound of her mother stomping up the stairs.

Oh please, please go away! Just go away! she prayed, to no avail.

'Aargh!' The shout surprised her. Her body doubled with pain that was cutting and unexpected in both its ferocity and duration. Her mother banged on the door.

'Molly! Good Lord above, what is going on in there? With all this crashing, bashing and shouting I can hardly hear the wireless. Molly? Molly, answer me!'

She wished she *could* answer, wanted nothing more than to tell her mother she was fine, to find a tranquil voice that would allay her mother's fears and send her scurrying back to the parlour and her wireless. Some part of her brain also registered that to speak calmly would soothe her baby, convinced that to hear this level of distress would do it no good at all.

'Aaaaaaah!' She hadn't meant to shout out again, hadn't intended to make a peep, but it was beyond her. Her reaction was as visceral as it was overwhelming – her body's natural response to the sensation of being torn apart. 'Mum,' she managed between tight breaths, panting like a dog, 'Mum . . . go . . . go . . .'

Again her mother banged hard on the door. 'Unless you unlock the door right this very second and let me in, I will have to take action. Talk to me, Molly! For goodness' sake, talk to me – are you ill?' Her mother's voice had gone up an octave.

Molly gripped the side of the tub and bore down, gritting her teeth as the sweat poured from her, and the low, growling noise she made was almost primal, drawn from deep within. She was lost to the pain over which she had no control. Her mother's next words barely registered.

'I don't know what's going on in there, but I don't like the sound of it. I'm going to fetch Mr Mason to come and barge the door down!'

There was a brief lull, a pleasant welcome moment of silence that wrapped Molly. A chance to breathe, she hoped, but before she had time to gather her thoughts came a further strong contraction, followed immediately by another, so fast and so intense they took her breath away, leaving her suspended on a crest of pain so acute, so all-consuming, that she felt she was hovering above the floor, above reality, lost to this intense and unnatural feeling that was such an immense shock to her body and mind.

The baby came quickly then. And the surprise of it was enough to make her sob. There it suddenly was: a slithering, damp little thing that looked to be all arms and legs. No more than a couple of pushes really and there it was – *he*, there he was – delivered into her own hands, fresh with blood and more liquid than she would have expected, but then she hadn't known what to expect. She had read a book and knew enough about the rudiments of pregnancy, but no book could ever have explained how this felt, the brutality of it, the raw pain, and yet at the same time how wonderfully invincible it made her feel to have come through it.

'Oh . . . oh!' she managed through her tears as she gripped her little boy tightly with one hand and reached for the towel in which she wrapped him. He screamed – yelled! It was loud and violent and she understood, wanting to yell at the world too!

Molly, feeling quite light-headed now, sank down onto the bath mat and leaned against the side of the tub. It was shocking what she had been through, but she was at the same time euphoric. With trembling limbs she held her baby, kissing his squashed little face and taking in every bit of him, not at all alarmed by the umbilicus that still connected her to this beautiful, beautiful boy.

'Oh, Johan!' She looked towards the window and up at the shadowy moon. 'Johan – your son, *our* son!' Her tears were hot and splashed down onto the face of her boy. He raised his little fist and batted at his cheeks, eyes screwed shut as his wailing stopped, and then he looked up towards the ceiling with the milky gaze of new, unfocused lenses, a tiny new human. A wonderful thing!

'My darling, my darling, my darling . . .' She spoke to the man who would have been her husband had the war not spoiled absolutely everything. 'My heart, my love, we have a boy. Joe, his name is Joe. Of course it is – Joe, after his daddy.'

The bang was loud and unexpected. Molly jumped as the wooden door flew open and hit the wall with force, thankfully missing both of them. With the instinct of a new mother, she cradled her child to her chest with her hand cupped over his soft little head.

'What in the name of God our Father?' It was her mother's turn to shout now.

The brawny Mr Mason stood in his shirtsleeves, staring open-mouthed, eyes wide. She saw the slight smile form on his lips and the crinkle to his eyes, which had misted with tears. Molly's eyes met his and they shared a look that was brief but knowing – as if both for a second in the midst of this foul and ugly conflict were reminded of all the good that remained in this world.

'May God forgive you!' The snarl on her mother's lip was the exact opposite. 'And in my house!' she yelled with a hand at her throat, as she gasped for breath. 'In your father's house!' Her mum shook her head and plugged her small mouth with her white knuckles. Molly was glad, hoping the bony gag might stop more of the bitterness escaping, already wary of what might reach her son's ears and how. She had no energy for confrontation, was barely able to remain propped against the side of the bath.

'Should . . . should I call the midwife?' Mr Mason asked softly, as if he at least were wary of volume around newly hatched ears.

'Midwife?' her mother spat, as if he had asked if he should fetch Herr Hitler himself. 'I'll have no midwife step over my threshold. As if the situation isn't bad enough! A midwife would find much tittle-tattle in this, I'm sure. I don't think such a thing has occurred before in Old Gloucester Street.' Her chin shook. 'I mean, it might be expected in Islington or Bow, but not *Bloomsbury!*'

Molly looked from her mother to Mr Mason, who looked to be, like her, a little lost for words. She had given birth unaided to a beautiful, beautiful boy and yet his grandmother was more interested in the moral reputation of the area.

'We need to cut the cord,' Molly said softly.

'My sister has . . . She's . . .' Mr Mason began, hesitant and clearly aware of couching his words in a way that would not offend Mrs Collway.

'Is she . . .?' her mother began.

'Qualified?' Mr Mason cut in. 'Not exactly, no, but she's a mother to three and has some medical training.'

'I was going to say discreet.'

'Go and fetch her, please,' Molly said firmly, while cooing her love and holding her son close to her breast.

Mr Mason dashed down the stairs, leaving the two of them in an atmosphere thick with all it tried to contain. Molly stared up at her mother. 'He's beautiful, isn't he?' She opened up the towel to give her mother a better view.

Her mother looked away, seemingly without any inclination to look at the face of her first grandson. 'Whose is it? Do you know?'

Molly drew a sharp breath. The pain of her mother's insinuation was actually greater than the ache in her bones and the throb of her muscles that had just delivered this wondrous child.

'Of course I know! His father is Johan de Fries – Joe. Geer's brother.' She flinched at the mention of the two people whom she knew would have made this whole event bearable and with whom she would have loved nothing more than to share the moment.

'Oh well, that's just marvellous.' Mrs Collway threw her hands in the air and sought help from the heavens with a heavy sigh. 'Well, there's no chance of him rectifying the situation then, is there? I suppose I should be thankful that your poor father's not here to bear witness – whatever would he say? After all he sacrificed, all he did to build a respectable life for us here!' She shook her head. 'And what on earth will the neighbours think? How *could* you, Molly? How could you?' And then came the tears.

Molly snuggled her boy to her, shutting out her mother's words and doing her best to stop them from reaching the ears of her son.

'I'm assuming, Mum, that you're in shock, and I understand.' She wiped the tendrils of loose hair that had stuck to her forehead with sweat. 'It's a lot to take in, I know it is. But look at him! He's perfect and he's mine. Would you like to see him or hold him?' she asked as she cradled him to her, his damp head now resting under the crook of her chin. Confident that if her mother peered into his beautiful little face, she too would fall under his spell.

'I don't need to see him to know what I think: he's a bastard and under my roof!'

Molly swallowed these words, which scratched down her throat like shards of glass.

'I . . .' She searched for a response that was reprimanding yet conciliatory – an impossible task that rendered her mute.

'There *will* be a solution.' Her mother blew her nose. 'I don't know what, but there will be one.' The lady turned on her heel and made her way down the stairs, gripping the banister.

Molly felt a shiver of terror in her gut – *a solution* . . . She slumped further down against the side of the bath as the front door banged shut and she heard voices: Mr Mason and his sister, no doubt come to disconnect her from her baby boy.

'You're wonderful, little Joe. You are so incredibly wonderful. A gift.' She kissed his downy cheek and inhaled the scent of him, a glorious smell that reminded her of baking.

'Happy birthday, little man – happy birthday.'

SEVEN

Bloomsbury, London
August 1944
Aged 19

Molly had been a mother for two weeks, living in a bubble of her making. She took more joy than she could ever have imagined from simply feeding her son, holding him, singing to him and cradling him in her arms, loath to let him out of her sight even for a second. She cringed to think of how she had resisted the pull of motherhood for so long, lamenting the idea of getting stuck with a wailing child when, well, the reality was that even Joe's cries were sweet to her. She was certain the novelty of this perfect little human who took up every second of her day would never wane.

Communication with her mother was rudimentary at best. The only time she had left Joe was for the twelve minutes she walked to the telephone box in the next street to phone Mr Jenkins, who ran her department, leaving a message for him with the switchboard that she was sick. The half-truth seemed the best option, worried as she was about being dismissed. Her mother had silently nodded her agreement to watch him as he lay sleeping in Molly's old crib, now in the parlour and within warming distance of the fire on a cool night. She and her mother lived side by side, keeping as much distance between them as possible, her mother's face always drawn and grey, her expression fraught. They ate in silence, bowls of soup slurped noisily when there was no other sound to dilute it and cups of tea sipped with tight mouths and straight backs, with the occasional sigh from her mother if Joe interrupted by daring to cry. Molly had stopped trying to force any engagement on her mother's side and was torn, certain that her parent did not deserve to feel the wondrous weight of her grandson in her arms and yet hoping that she would nonetheless consider caring for Joe while Molly worked. She hated feeling beholden to her and how duplicitous it made her actions.

'Here's the thing, Mum,' she tried one evening after supper, laying her forearms on the table. 'I know how upset and angry you are with me, but he's here and he's your grandson. He's a darling little thing and we need to find a way to make this work! I *need* you, Mum. I have never needed you more.'

Her mother wiped her mouth with the starched linen napkin that had been resting on her lap and rose from the table. 'You *think* you know how upset and angry I am with you, but you have no idea. You have no idea what you've done to me and, worse still, you have no idea what you've done to yourself. And it's the very last thing on top of what I have been through – that I *needed*.'

Joe cried on cue and Molly rushed to him as her mother made her way slowly up the stairs. The coldness of their estrangement made her feel as if there was very little love in the house, turning her childhood home into something more akin to a boarding house, but one where the landlady silently judged her. It made her think of the lovely Mrs Duggan, not that she had time to overthink it, being too consumed with caring for her son and mourning the loss of his father.

Without any word from her place of work, Molly wrote to Marjorie, remembering her words that she would be there if ever

Molly needed her. Desperate to know her position was secure, she certainly needed her now. Taking her father's ink pen in her hand, she tried not to think of the last letter she had written to her love, seated here at this very same table, and which now nestled in the bottom of her wardrobe under the sheets of newspaper placed there to catch the dust. The truth was, she knew, the only way to explain her absence and hopefully keep her job. And something told her she could trust Marjorie.

Dear Marjorie,

You have told me more than once that I could reach out to you, and here I am, doing just that. I ask for your confidence in this matter. I will be absent for work over the next two weeks or so. I have, as I think you may have suspected, had a child and will be confined with him at home – a son, who I have named Joe. I am making provision for his daily care, thus enabling me to return to my role. I would appreciate your discretion in this matter for obvious reasons, preferring that my private life remain just that, private.

Thank you, Marjorie, for everything.

Yours truly and with love,

Molly Collway

She marked the letter as confidential and dropped it in the post.

Joe was only a week old when her sister arrived. Molly, still in bed and with the baby in her arms, heard the tentative knock on the bedroom door. Joyce crept in with her hands clasped to her chest and her tears already welling. She wrapped Molly in a much-needed hug, palming circles on her back and smoothing her sister's hair. It was an act both maternal and sisterly and Molly was glad of it.

'My poor little Moll, what have you been through?' Joyce pulled away and ran her finger over the soft curve of her nephew's cheek.

'Would you like to hold him?'

'Yes! Yes, I would, very much!' Joyce held out her arms and Molly placed her child into her sister's clutches. 'Oh hello, little one! Hello there, gorgeous boy,' Joyce cooed, her eyes brimming. 'Molly! He's perfect, so perfect.'

'He is,' she agreed, overjoyed to feel the warmth coming from her sister as she welcomed this newest family member in the way he deserved.

'Oh, look at him!'

Molly sat back against her pillows and watched her sister as she sat on the side of her mattress. It was nice for Molly to see him from this angle. He looked rangy and beautiful in the embroidered cotton nightgown his aunt had sent.

'How are you feeling?' Joyce asked, while beaming into the face of her nephew and stroking his little hand with her finger.

'Sore, happy, exhausted . . .'

'He's beautiful!' Joyce cooed again.

'He is.'

'Does he look like his dad?'

Molly felt the lump of emotion swell in her throat. 'I don't know. I can't see too much of Johan in him, but then I can't see much of me in him either.'

'I guess they take a while to properly inflate.'

Molly laughed out loud. 'Yes, I guess they do. How did Mum seem to you?' She was interested to hear her sister's take on the matter.

'She's in shock, as you'd expect, really. It's a lot for her to process. You should have told her.'

'Yes. Thank you, Joyce.'

'I didn't mean to moan at you, not today. I'm sorry.' Joyce held her sister's gaze.

'You're right, of course. I should have told her, and I was going to.' She fell silent, realising how flimsy any words might sound in her defence and how her sister was only speaking the truth. Hindsight is, they say, a wonderful thing and Molly could only concur, thinking of how she should have tried harder to broach the toughest of topics; it might have made things a little easier now.

'I was scared of telling her,' she confessed. 'Putting off the inevitable.'

'I can understand that.' Joyce reached out and stroked her arm. 'He's adorable.'

'He is and yet, some days, I feel that I barely get to appreciate him. My mind is racing because we're in the middle of this bloody awful war and I only have money saved for a short respite. I need to go back to work and I thought I'd be doing this with Johan, but now I'm on my own and . . .' She let out a long sigh. 'It's the most wonderful thing that's ever happened to me, and at the same time a horrible mess!' She briefly covered her face with her hands. 'I keep thinking Mum will come round, but the more time goes on, I'm not so sure.'

'Oh my darling! My poor darling. Give her time.'

'I know I can make it work. I just need to find someone to look after Joe during the day.'

'Such as who?'

'Such as Mum, first choice. I've also put the feelers out, responded to a couple of advertisements in the back of the paper – women offering childcare in their homes.'

Joyce pulled a face. 'These are desperate times, Molly, and some of those places might be . . .'

'Do you think I might leave him somewhere terrible?' Molly's voice went up an octave.

'No, of course not. I'm just stating that I think it might be a little harder than you imagine.'

'No, trust me, I do think it's hard. I . . . I was also thinking maybe Mrs Mason?'

'Mrs Mason?' Joyce's expression was one of incredulity.

Molly nodded. 'She's always been a lovely neighbour and was marvellous with me when I was little – she used to babysit me, do you remember? And she's at home, which means that picking him up and dropping him off would be very easy for me. What do you think?'

'I think that's a little random, and rather a leap from babysitting you to looking after Joe full-time, but if Mrs Mason agrees, then why not?'

'Why are you laughing at that?' Molly was curt.

'*Mrs Mason!*'

Molly had no idea why it was such a funny idea.

'Has your work agreed to you going back?' Joyce asked, now composed again.

'No, but I've written to a trusted colleague. I've not heard anything yet.'

'I think it's hardly likely you will. Darling, it's hard enough for women who marry to continue working, outside of wartime, of course, but women without help . . . and an unmarried woman too. I'm worried they wouldn't want you there because of reputation alone.' Her expression was earnest.

'But I'm good at my job. I need to work!' Molly was aware of her tone rising again.

'Well, let's just hope Mrs Mason comes up trumps.' Joyce kissed Joe's face.

'I just remember her as kind and smiley. I liked her looking after me. Mr Mason dropped some clothes off for the baby, a cardigan and a bonnet, which was so sweet of him – obviously, his wife sent them, which means she knows about Joe and doesn't disapprove—'

'Yes, Mum said Mr Mason had been on hand when he was born.' Joyce sighed. 'What about Johan's family? Have you told them that Joe's arrived?'

Molly shook her head, hearing Geer's words loud in her ears: '. . . *Your baby, Molly – yours. Just let us be! . . . What don't you get? . . . it's nothing to do with us. You think we can handle that on top of losing him?*'

'And what is the plan if you can't organise childcare?' Joyce asked softly as she shifted Joe's position in her arms.

'I suppose I'll look for a job where I can take Joe with me.'

'Such as what, for instance?'

'I don't know, Joyce! Great heavens above!' Molly instantly regretted snapping at her sister. 'Sorry, I'm just anxious and trying to figure it all out.'

'I know, darling, and it's not easy to work out what's for the best. Well, I'm glad the Masons have been kind, but a job might be hard to come by. Not everyone will feel the same way. Your life will be difficult. It's hard for unmarried mothers. It's a terrible shame for you, for him, for all of us. Not that I don't love you both – of course I do – but I think you're underestimating how these things are viewed.' Joyce's eyes were pleading, as if this might come as news to Molly and she needed to make her understand.

'Well, it's not a terrible shame for me, because I've got Joe.' Molly reached out and touched his leg. What she chose not to share was that she had a Plan B. If it came to it, she had figured out a possible way to combat the supposed shame of having a baby out of wedlock. Molly had considered the idea of slipping a ring on the third finger of her left hand and stating with more than a semblance of truth that the boy's father had been killed. With so many widows and orphans as a result of this godforsaken war, how would anyone know that the one crucial action of actually getting married was missing in this case?

Joyce lifted the baby to her face and kissed his cheek. He mewled, settled and fell asleep.

'You're a natural.' Molly sniffed.

'I doubt it,' Joyce said with a cough. 'Nothing very natural about it for me. In fact, nature has been my enemy where babies are concerned. We have tried, you know, to conceive, but' – she shook her head – 'it hasn't worked for us. And we now know it *won't* work for us.' Her face coloured.

'Not ever?'

'No, Moll, not ever . . .' Joyce swallowed hard.

'Oh, Joyce!' Molly felt a twist of guilt in her gut that her lovely sister had been denied this most wonderful thing.

'Albert says you don't get all the gifts, and I guess he's right, but it's a gift I really, really would have loved.' Lifting Joe's tiny hand, Joyce ran it over her lips and kissed his little fingers. 'I would offer to look after him for you, Molly dear, but it's too far for me to travel every day, especially after dark with curfews and whatnot.'

'I wouldn't have expected you to, Joyce, but thank you.' Molly thought for the first time how her sister had everything she didn't – a stable marriage, a beautiful home of her own in the suburbs and money in the bank, but not this one thing, a baby, the very best thing . . . Life was so unfair.

'No, thank *you*. Holding him has been the loveliest thing I've done in as long as I can remember. You're very lucky.'

'I feel very lucky.' And in that moment as Joyce handed her back her son, it was the truth.

Dr Venables, her second visitor, had checked on her and her newborn. His officious manner and clipped tone told her he was less than impressed with the fact that she had not confided in him, but that was too bad. He confirmed that her confinement was nearly up and that she would soon be ready to get up and get out, take fresh air and get some exercise.

'And I can go back to work?' she had asked, not that she had had a reply to her letter, as she swaddled Joe back into a crocheted blanket she had found in the linen press on the landing.

The doctor gave a wry laugh, distorted by a snort through his large nose. 'If you think that wise or indeed possible.'

'I do, actually, Doctor.'

'Which?' he fired back at her.

'Both.' Molly stared at him until he looked away and went over to do up the clasps on his ancient leather Gladstone bag, leaving her with Joe. His words, which had been discouraging and laden with hidden portent, still echoed around the walls.

Once Dr Venables had left, Molly decided to ask Mrs Mason outright if she might be interested in caring for Joe when she returned to work. If she was unable to get the Ministry to see sense or even respond, then she would take any other job that came her way. It wasn't as if there weren't plenty of opportunities for a fit woman like her.

Molly waited until she heard the front door close and, confident then that her mother had left the house, made her way down the stairs with her son in her arms. She walked slowly along the street, the warm summer breeze lifting her hair and her spirits. With a brisk knock on the front door of the Masons' house, Molly stood back on the top step, taking a deep lungful of air; it was such a novelty being outside in the bright light: restorative. She smiled brightly and full of hope as Mr Mason opened the door.

'Oh, Molly!' He looked at the floor and for the first time she considered that he might carry some awkwardness from what had passed between them and what he had seen. This only encouraged her to be bold, knowing that if they were to live in such close proximity, it was something they needed to get over pretty quickly.

'Hello, Mr Mason. How are you?'

'Good! Yes, good.' He avoided looking at her directly, which did nothing to instil confidence. 'Would you like to come in?' He gestured down the hallway of his home, but curiously did not stand aside to allow her entry, forcing her to stand with baby Joe out on the step.

'No, no, I don't want to disturb you, but thank you. In fact, thank you for the clothes you very kindly dropped off for Joe and for being there when . . .' – she let this trail – 'and for fetching your sister.' She smiled at the thought of these people, strangers, who had become part of her story.

'Not at all. And you can rely on our discretion if that is what is concerning you.' He smiled and looked from her to her son. 'He's a bonny little fellow.'

'He really is.' She smiled into the face of her boy, both delighted and buoyed up by the compliment. 'I was wondering if I might speak to Mrs Mason?' She peered down the hallway behind him.

Mr Mason gave a hearty chuckle. 'Oh, Molly, I'm afraid not. Mrs Mason has been on the coast in Dorset for some months and will stay there until the end of the war. It's far safer.'

'. . . *boringly safe – an exercise no more, off the Devon coast. Does it get any safer than that?*' These words now rang in her head.

'I see. I had thought maybe' – she paused – 'the baby clothes . . . I'd assumed that Mrs Mason had—'

'Oh, that was entirely down to me. I thought the boy might need them.' He rocked on his heels.

'He did, and . . . and thank you. It was very kind.' She watched as their neighbour looked over her head and glanced along the street, as if embarrassed by her very presence. 'I should probably' – Molly jerked her head in the direction of home – 'I should get him inside. Thank you again,' she offered as brightly as she was able and rushed along the pavement, keen to get back to the safety of her bedroom, where she sat and rocked her baby, mumbling to herself, 'What am I going to do, Joe? What do I do now? How do I make this work?'

Surely there would be facilities in place all over the city for working mothers or orphans or for the many families who found themselves displaced. Tomorrow she would wrap up her boy and take him out into the big wide world, to find a nursery, a crèche, anywhere she might be able to leave him for the working day. Remembering Joyce's disdain for the idea, the thought filled her with worry about the level of care he might receive, but it was better than sitting in the bedroom and struggling.

As night drew in and with Joe bathed, fed and settled in his crib, Molly lay back on her bed and opened up an old exercise book with loose sheets inside of her father's scribblings. Her eyes fell upon his family-famous poem about Brussels sprouts. She read it aloud for Joe's benefit.

> 'Green and round and perfect, the beauty of
>   the sprout,
> Yet it's I alone who love them, causing many
>   a chap to pout,
> "Lord, no!" they yell when presented with a
>   sprout upon a plate.

These are the chaps I favour, knowing if I'm
    their mate –
That sprout will make a leap – from their
    dinner plate to mine and
That my friend is glorious! Rather sprouts
    than fine wine!'

Molly felt her mouth lift in the beginnings of a smile. This funny version of her father she had never got to know.

'And you have a grandson now, Papa. His name is Joe – a cousin for Clementine, David's little girl.' She ran her fingers over his handwriting, talking about the family members he had never got to meet. It made her think again of Johan's parents and she decided to write to them, to offer an olive branch, certain she could get the address from Mrs Duggan, and hoping her words might make them come around . . . Her bedroom door opened suddenly, interrupting her thoughts, and Molly closed the book with a snap.

Her mother's eyes were small and her mouth tight and Molly could tell that whatever it was her mother wanted to say had been cued up and practised on her tongue long before this moment. She reminded Molly of a coiled spring.

'I am quite mystified at your behaviour!' she began. 'Mystified and mortified on your behalf! It seems it's not enough to have ruined your own life and brought shame to my home, but apparently you have seen fit to further humiliate me by parading the bastard up and down the street, as bold as brass for the whole community to see!' Her mother's jowls shook.

Molly ground her teeth at the use of a word so offensive to her ears and looked down at her son, who was miraculously sleeping through it all. 'Don't call him that.'

'Have you no shame? No self-respect? Can you imagine my horror when Mrs Granton-Smythe waved to me from her parlour window? She was surprisingly cordial and desperate to chat. I waited while she ran down her steps with her spectacles in her hand, as if she'd been scouring the street, waiting for me.'

No doubt about it, the frightful woman. Molly kept this to herself.

'She then asked if I was well and if you were well and I told we were – quite well.' Her mother's voice cracked. 'She then proceeded to enquire as to whose was the baby she had seen you with earlier, wandering down the street. I lied to her – as God is my witness, I felt forced to tell a lie! I told her you were minding the child for a friend who was indisposed, but I could tell by the slight smile on her mouth that she did not believe a word of it!'

'I don't care what she thinks.'

'Well, you jolly well should!' Her mother shouted loudly now, and flecks of spittle left her mouth. 'You jolly well should care! And even if you don't, even if you are too far down the route of sin and misadventure to know right from wrong, *I care!*' She yelled again, jabbing herself in the chest. 'I care, Mary Florence! This is my reputation that is at stake. What in God's name possessed you to go out into the street?' She gave her daughter no time to answer. 'You float around like some ethereal creature, revelling in this state, wearing it like a badge of honour, but it is *not* good and you appear to be the only one who can't see just how wicked a thing it is that you have done. You have had a child out of wedlock!' Her mother covered her mouth with a shaking hand as if to voice the fact was almost a sin in itself.

'Why does it matter what some old gossip thinks? Why didn't you say, "Oh, that's Molly's baby" and be done with it, then there's no need for her or anyone to guess or gossip. I think if we look at it positively, it means—'

'You think it's a case of staying positive?' Mrs Collway clearly had not picked up on the tone of Molly's words. 'You still don't seem to fully grasp the situation. You have blotted your own copybook,' her mother said sharply again. 'You will be considered no good, disgusting, loose! And I will be associated with that for as long as you and that child are here! People will question how I have raised you, question my morals!'

'*What* people?'

'People whose opinions matter!' her mother shouted, and Joe shifted, threatening to wake.

'Does it really matter what anyone thinks or what anyone says?' Molly did her best to keep her voice calm while her stomach churned with the reality of her predicament, and her mother's lack of support made everything feel infinitely harder.

'Oh, don't be stupid, girl! Are you honestly that naive? You will be ostracised. How in God's name do you intend to care for him, pay for him?'

'I'm figuring it out. I've made an approach to return to work with a girl I trust and I still have some savings to pay my way. And I was thinking I might wear a ring' – she hoped her mother might be on board with this face-saving plan – 'and say my husband was killed. He *was* killed.' Her tears fell unbidden. *Oh, Johan, my love! I need you. I need you right now!*

'How dare you call yourself a widow when I have lost your father! How dare you compare our marriage to some sordid dalliance!'

'It wasn't a dalliance. And it was not sordid. And I don't regret it.' Molly kept her voice low. The simple truth was that maybe Geer was right – how could it have been love? And then it came to her, an image of his intense gaze offering words of devotion when time was slipping from their grasp. 'I loved Johan and he loved me. And I can do it, Mum. Please. There are plenty of widows and orphans in this city – who would know the difference?'

'Oh wake up, Molly, you're being foolish. You are going to condemn this child to a terrible life. Illegitimacy and infidelity are stains that do not wash off, not ever! As a woman of low moral conduct, what job do you think you might secure, exactly? You are consigning him to a life of scrabbling around for pennies and wondering where his next meal is coming from. Have you been to the East End? Have you seen how people like this live?' Mrs Collway spat.

'But that won't happen, Mum! I'm smart and I can have a career. If we can stay here, just for a bit; if you could see your way to help with—'

'Oh no, my girl! Oh no.' Her mother's chin jutted as she cut her short. 'Be under no illusion that a bastard has any place under this Christian roof. Any place at all.'

'But . . .' Molly was staggered to find that she did not have the words. She thought of the hours spent with her mother at St George's, listening to her recite prayers for the poor and unfortunate and giving thanks for her own very good fortune. Molly stared at the woman as if she were a stranger and knew she would never again set foot in a church.

'If you will not see sense, Molly, I have no choice but to ask you to leave and to take the child with you. I've been generous thus far, but enough is enough. You have a month. One month, and then either you do the sensible thing and give this child up or you get out, both of you.'

'Give him up?' Molly's voice was high-pitched and her heart raced. She jumped from the bed and gathered her son from the crib in which he slept. She held him close, and even the thought was more than she could bear. 'You underestimate me, Mother. You always have. I would never give him up.'

'And you underestimate me. You have one month.' Her mother was resolute.

'Where do you suggest we go?'

'That is not my concern.' Her mother reached out a finger and ran it over Joe's downy scalp. 'Poor little mite, I would have thought—'

Mrs Collway's sentence was cut short by the sudden wail of the siren, which cracked the air. Molly grabbed the crocheted blanket and the counterpane from the bed and raced down the dark wooden stairs towards the back door. Ordinarily, at the sound of the siren, she would walk slowly, taking her mother by the arm and guiding her down the stairs and out of the house with words of reassurance that belied her own fear. Across the muddy back garden and down the rickety steps to the Anderson shelter they would traipse, with Molly doing her best to make the whole event feel mundane. But not tonight.

Tonight, with her son pressed to her chest, Molly took a seat on the makeshift bench along the side of the structure, where she rocked him back and forth.

'Look at us, baby Joe, underground like moles, hiding under the earth, but we will be okay. I will keep you safe, my little one,' she whispered to her child, who slept on, oblivious.

Her mother's foot tapped on the step outside the door, feeling her way. She stared at Molly, her chest heaving, clearly out of breath and furious to have been thus abandoned.

'Is this truly what you want for the boy?' her mother asked. 'This life, but without the security of a home? Give him up, Molly. Let him go to a family in the country – a married couple. There are plenty who would treasure the gift of a baby. It would be the noblest thing to do, the kindest.'

'And just what would you know about kindness?' Molly spat.

The ferocity of her response and the intensity of her stare saw her mother sit down and shrink a little. And Molly was glad, unable to cope with any more of her berating. Not tonight, not when

112

the threat in the skies from the Luftwaffe quite literally hung over them. She imagined what it would be like if an attack came and Joe was in the care of someone else, the kind of facility she had been thinking of earlier, where a woman might have several babies in her care . . . It was a horrific thought. She thought of Alresford, a rural town surrounded by rolling green fields and babbling weirs . . . Was that the solution: to let Johan's family take him, assuming their anger had dissipated, their grief now come under control?

Molly shook her head and closed her eyes, burying her face in her son's blanket. An image of Joyce filled her mind, her lovely sister, who had been denied all the gifts.

The first bang sounded a little way off. Molly shook, trying to stem the tremble of fear in her limbs. Joe started to cry.

'Don't cry, darling. It's okay, sweetie. Don't you cry.' She tried to get him to suckle, knowing this usually calmed him, but not tonight. As the sound of the planes grew louder overhead, so his crying increased.

'Close.' Her mother, whether consciously or not, said the word out loud.

Then came another loud bang, and this time the shelter shook, grains of dirt fell from the ceiling and pooled in dark tears on the makeshift floor. Molly couldn't help the scream that left her throat involuntarily. Her limbs trembled as the lights flickered and went out, and there they sat, in the dark, waiting for the sky to fall in, for the earth to fill the shelter, for the house or falling masonry to crush them dead or for Hitler's boys to score a direct hit and blow them to smithereens.

This was the reality of war. This frightening, fire-filled night of destruction that saw homes destroyed all over the city, families and landmarks wiped out in wanton ruin, was a turning point. The fear Molly felt and the clarity that came with it was like a knife plunging into her chest and piercing her heart, making breathing difficult. She held her son close and tried to take even breaths, tried to recall the words that might soothe him while fighting her own rising sense of panic, remembering what Johan had said, words she now took as advice . . . '*Children need to feel safe, don't they? Need to know there's a steady hand on the tiller, otherwise it's not fair. Poor little mites . . .*' And as a thought crystallised in her mind, she let out a long, low moan, drawn from her very soul.

'Molly?' Her mother's urgent tone floated through the darkness. 'Molly, what in God's name is going on? Are you hurt?'

'Shut up,' she managed. 'Just shut up.'

EIGHT

Molly had spent the last ten days in a kind of subdued panic, having made a decision that was almost too huge to consider. What was the word her mother had used? *Ethereal* . . . That was it and, yes, Molly did indeed feel a little otherworldly, as if living in a nightmare of her own making and only able to sleep if she put thoughts of separation from her son far from her mind.

The night the bombs fell so close was the first time she had experienced white-hot fear at the prospect of her baby boy getting hurt. It was the night things changed for Molly, when she fully understood that she could not keep her son safe here in the city. Her only viable alternative was to give him up, just for a while, until peacetime. With Joe now sleeping and her mother having reluctantly agreed to watch him, she made her way to Eaton Square Gardens. It felt good to be out of the house, to close her eyes for a brief second and concentrate on the feel of the sun on her face as it peeped through the clouds, and not the enormous weight of her heavy heart that felt as if it might drop right through her chest and fall to the floor. She felt different now she was a mother out alone, as if she had forgotten something, overly aware of the perils of crossing the road, the abundance of guns carried by the military police and Home Guard and any loud noises that made her jump. She was now on high alert, knowing she needed to return home safely as there was a little human who relied on her. She knew she would have to get used to this feeling: being apart from her baby.

Don't think about it . . . don't think about it, just keep walking, Molly . . .

Gingerly she trod the steps to tap on the door with the lion's head knocker, remembering the last time she had seen her dear friend Geer and the time before, on that rainy night only months ago when she was to learn the fate of her beloved. She hoped it was Mrs Duggan who opened the door. It was not. The door was, however, opened quickly, in the manner of someone who before a single word had been exchanged was making it clear they were none too happy to have been disturbed. Molly smiled at the woman who appeared, wrapped in a scarlet and gold silk kimono and with a newly lit cigarette in a holder between her fingers.

'Yes?' She was sharp and stony-faced.

'I'm sorry to bother you.'

The woman huffed, as if suspecting this to be a lie.

'I was hoping to speak to Mrs Duggan.'

'Who?' The woman took a long draw of her cigarette.

'Mrs Duggan? I believe this is her house?'

'Oh right.' She looked up, as if recalling the name. 'Yes, prob-ably. Not here, though.' She scratched at her scalp and blew smoke in a long plume. 'She went back to her family in Ireland months ago. There's only three of us here.'

Molly was reluctant to leave, this being her only connection to the de Fries family. 'I was hoping to make contact with someone who used to live here, Geertruida de Fries, and wondered if there was a forwarding address left for post or anything that might help me get in touch with her?'

'No.' The woman shook her head.

'Could you check?'

'No.' She stared Molly in the eye.

'I see.' The two women stared at each other in silence for a beat. It was Molly who spoke first. 'I honestly don't know what to say to you. I've left my newborn son to come here because it's important. Geertruida would have been my sister-in-law and I need someone to help me look after my son, to keep him safe and take him out of the city.' She cursed the crack to her voice. 'It's not an easy thing for me to consider, but there we are and why would you give a damn? And, for the record, I find you rude.'

The woman laughed and seemed to thaw a little. 'Well, I am rude. I'm also working nights and you've woken me up after only forty minutes of sleep. I am therefore rude, exhausted and angry to have been pulled from my bed.'

'Maybe you should put a note on the door.' Molly felt chastened.

The woman slapped herself on the forehead. 'Now why didn't I think of that?' She pointed to a rather crudely written postcard that sat shy of the letterbox, which Molly hadn't seen. It read 'DO NOT DISTRUB WORKING NIGHTS'.

Molly shook her head. 'I apologise for waking you. I didn't think—'

'No, you didn't. And for the record, I do not know Trudy or whatever her name is, and there are no forwarding addresses for anyone, and I've never met Mrs Duggan, and I don't know what to suggest.'

Molly nodded. She turned to walk back down the steps.

'Good luck with your little one and with finding your friend.'

Molly looked back and smiled at the woman, who continued to draw on her cigarette, although her mood seemed to have softened a little. 'Thanks. And you've spelled "disturb" wrong.' She pointed at the sign.

She decided to write to Miss Geertruida de Fries of Alresford, Hampshire, hoping that the vague address but unusual name might give the letter a better than average chance of delivery. It was a simple note, written with her father's pen.

Geer,

Too much has happened and too much binds us for us not to be in touch. I miss you and hope we can find a way to come together, to build a bridge that takes us over all the things that have kept us apart. I have a beautiful son named Joe – your nephew.

I need your help, Geer, help to keep him safe until after the war. There is no one else I would trust with his care: you are his family. I would love nothing more than for you and your parents to meet him. I miss Johan every day, but Joe is a comfort and a small part of him that lives on.

With love as always,

Molly

She had as yet received no reply. And actually her words were not entirely true – there was, she decided after much deliberation and sleepless nights, someone else she would trust with the temporary care of her baby: her sister, Joyce.

She had called from the phone box on the corner. She waited for the operator to clear the line, then blurted, 'Can . . . can you come here, Joyce? I need to see you.' She had swallowed, looking skyward, as if still hoping that some other solution might present itself.

'Of course, dear, what's wrong?'

'I need your help.' Molly cursed the slip of tears down the back of her throat. 'I need you to help me with Joe.'

As the words left her mouth, so did the strength from her legs. She slipped down in the telephone box, her body slumped against the glass door and with the phone still in her hands, reaching up as if in prayer. A loud tapping on the glass from outside caused her to look up. An older lady in a headscarf and with a crocodile handbag dangling from her wrist was looking down to where she sat. 'Are you all right in there? Do you need assistance?' she asked. Molly needed so much assistance it felt easier to dismiss the question with a laugh, while she fought for composure and struggled to her feet.

The country, more specifically the cities, having been battered and bruised by war, was experiencing a shortage of housing. There were not enough beds for all those displaced by the bombing, and some families were still, some years after seeing their homes destroyed, sleeping in the homes of relatives and neighbours or in communal school halls or huddled with their belongings on the platforms of the Underground. These facts, however, did little to help justify her decision when emotion threatened to overwhelm the practicalities of the matter. But it was the simple truth: where could she possibly take her little boy that was safe? She was stuck, unable to work with Joe in her arms and unable to go away and keep Joe safe without a job and, as would be the case very soon, no roof over her head.

Molly was damned if she was going to stay at her mother's house for one night longer than she had to.

In the face of the emotional turmoil she savoured every second with her boy. Shutting herself away from the rest of the world, able only to tend to Joe's immediate needs, changing his napkin, holding him while he slept and feeding him when he woke. And, in truth, when she was able to pretend that it might last for ever, life inside this little bubble she had created was the happiest she had ever been. To wake with his rosebud mouth seeking her breast for food and to hear his snuffles of slumber as he slept next to her was, she knew, a memory she would take to her grave.

Baby Joe was asleep at that very second, quite oblivious in his knitted jumper, leggings and bonnet, and she again could not resist the temptation to lift him to her face and kiss him. He had changed so much in his short lifetime: his cheeks were already more rounded, his nose sharper, eyes brighter and more focused. His hair had also grown a little and now sat in a downy cap on his little head.

Joyce had, as per her promise, agreed to visit. Their telephone conversation had been brief before Molly's collapse, but she had managed to outline her intentions.

'So you've asked your sister to come here?' her mother queried as they ate a thin stew with soda bread at the kitchen table.

'Yes.'

'It's a bit of a way for her to come for a catch-up . . .' Mrs Collway let this trail.

Molly rested her spoon on the side of the bowl and sat up straight. 'I'm going to ask Joyce and Albert to take Joe to Tonbridge, just for a bit, to keep him safe until the war is over. I can then go back to work and save for the day that war ends and I can get him back. At which point, housing, childcare – everything – should be a bit easier to come by.' She kept her voice steady despite the squeeze to her heart at the very suggestion.

Molly knew she would never forget her mother's grin then, displaying her small teeth, and the way her shoulders slumped with something like relief. A baby was, she knew, the missing piece in Albert and Joyce's puzzle and, while he was away, she also knew he would be a missing part of herself.

'You're seeing sense at last! And no one would think twice having seen you out and about with your *sister's* baby. I'm sure even Mrs Granton-Smythe wouldn't question that.' Mrs Collway beamed. 'It really would be for the best.'

Molly stared at her mother and was surprised to recognise her overriding feeling towards her as one of pure hatred.

When Joyce arrived, the two sisters stared at one another, both a little overcome with emotion, bound by the simultaneous sadness and beauty of what was about to occur.

Unwilling to watch her mother's satisfaction as she witnessed their conversation, Molly suggested they speak in her room. Joyce sat on the edge of the bed and was close to tears, as the two held hands and Joe slept on his mummy's lap. They sat this way for a minute until composed enough to speak.

'You want me to take him – that's what you said on the phone,' Joyce managed, her voice small. 'Is that really what you're asking?' There was no doubting her distress, but Molly detected the faint-est glimmer of happiness in the eye of her beloved sister, who had always wanted a baby of her own to hold, and she understood.

'Well,' Molly said, drawing a long breath, 'I don't *want* you to, absolutely not, but I think it's for the best. Just for a while, until the war is over and the threat of bombing has gone. I can't keep him safe here, Joyce, and Tonbridge is safer, isn't it?' Her voice broke and Joyce reached out to move her hair from her face, tucking it gently behind her ear, an act so kind and motherly it was moving.

'It is much, much safer, darling.'

'I thought so. I've lost Johan and I can't lose Joe too.' Molly stared at her boy and found it hard to fathom the depth of pain that the prospect of separation caused. It hurt her physically as well as mentally, but she knew it was for the best. 'I couldn't cope with that, I know I couldn't. There's a reason there are no children around, Joyce – they've all gone to safe places, haven't they: been evacuated?' Her question was rhetorical, but her sister nodded nonetheless. 'And who knows what's going to happen to our country? I want to believe it will end well and end soon, but . . .' She paused. 'I'm afraid.'

'We all are, dear,' Joyce confirmed.

'Yes, and I certainly can't stay here.' Her eyes wandered the walls of her bedroom, remembering the night she came home after dancing with Johan, the excitement she had felt and the first night she had held Joe in her arms . . . This was a room with too many memories. 'I need to go back to work and don't have money for decent childcare. It's not fair on him.' Her voice broke and she held her child tightly to her. 'I'm being brave and trying to do the right thing, Joyce. I've seen countless little ones shipped off to the countryside with their name and address labels pinned to their coats, but inside my heart is breaking.' Molly nestled his sleeping form into her chest and breathed in his scent deeply with her eyes closed.

'I know, darling, I know, but I promise you that for however long he is in our care, we will love him like you would and care for him like you would. I've bought formula for him and aired the little room. We will tell him every day about his funny, smart mummy. And we will write and make the absolute best of it.'

Molly nodded. Her sister's words were cruel to her ears, placing distance between herself and her child, and yet she knew were so sweetly intended.

'Just for a while, Joycey – a few months maybe, and then who knows? Things will be different, the country will be different, and when it's safe and I'm more established in my own place' – she drew breath – 'then he can come home to me.' She turned to her son. 'You can, darling, you can come home to me!' she sobbed, her voice thin and high with distress.

'He can and he will.' Joyce lifted Molly's chin with her finger. 'It's going to be okay, Little Moll. There's just one thing I need to tell you, and it might dictate how long we have Joe for.'

Molly watched anxiously as Joyce swallowed nervously.

'Albert has accepted a job offer as a contractor in Canada, and so the plan is to head over there for a bit.'

No, it's too far! Molly did not want her sister to be any further away, knowing the reason she had managed not to crack until now was because Joyce was on hand when she really, really needed her. 'How . . . how long is a bit?'

Joyce shrugged. 'A few months, a year at most. Albert is quite in demand with his knowledge of the oil and gas industry and we think it'll be good to go somewhere new and reset—'

'Canada? Joyce, that is so far away! When will you go?' Molly felt desolate at the prospect of her one ally in the family leaving her all alone, while wondering how long she would be able to mind Joe before she left, wanting him above all else to be safe.

'We don't have a date yet, but it'll be a while before we leave, possibly not till the end of the war even, so the timing might be perfect in terms of getting this little one back to his mum. I just wanted you to know it's on the cards.'

'I don't know what to say. Canada!' Molly couldn't imagine her life without her sister in it.

'Yes, Alberta, to be precise, where they're exploring fresh oil fields, but we're keeping the house in Tonbridge. It'll be good for his career and it's an adventure, but I shall' – Joyce coughed – 'I shall miss you and I shall miss this little darling.' Again she kissed Joe's head and the sisters locked eyes. Parting, they knew, was not going to be easy.

'Whatever will I do without you, Joyce?'

'I . . .' Her sister faltered and Molly felt a very real beat of fear as the answer felt terrifyingly elusive. 'Would you like us to take Joe today?' Joyce asked softly. 'I assumed that was what you were asking on the phone?'

Molly gripped her boy even more tightly and found it hard to say the words. 'I don't think there's any point in delaying things, as much as I want to.' She spoke sense and yet each word was like an arrow fired straight down her throat and into her gut.

'All right then, my love.'

Molly wanted to explain to her little one just what was going to happen and, selfishly, she wanted to feed him some more, hold him some more, kiss him some more. She knew, however, that she would never be ready to hand him over.

'Just give me a minute with him, Joyce.' Her eyes never left his darling face.

'Of course! Oh, of course! I'll go and have a cup of tea with Mum and tell Albert what's happening.'

Molly was only vaguely aware of the bedroom door closing. She stared at Joe, drinking in every little detail. He began to fret and she opened her blouse to feed her baby, but he wouldn't suckle. She settled him instead by rocking him in her arms.

'Don't you forget me, Joe. Don't you forget that I'm your mum, and know that I love you. I do. I love you more than I ever thought it was possible to love anyone in my whole life and I always will, my little one. Always . . .' She hummed to him softly the tune of 'I'll Be Seeing You', pretending this was any other day and she was simply rocking him to sleep, aware that if she fully acknowledged what was about to happen she might just fall apart. Her tears slipped silently from her nose nonetheless. She pulled out Johan's button from its little wooden box.

'This is my most precious thing, Joe. My most precious.' She placed it briefly in the palm of her son's hand so that it carried his touch as well as his daddy's, knowing this would bring her comfort. It made her smile, the sweet connection between the two people she loved most in the world. 'It might bring you luck, darling. I hope it does,' she cried.

Half an hour later, the door slowly opened. Molly felt her mother's presence in the doorway as she cradled Joe to her chest with both hands, trying not to give in to the temptation to grip him tightly and smother him with hard kisses, wary of alarming him. She could only take very shallow breaths. The pain in her chest was physical, as if her heart hurt. Molly knew that if her mother reached for him willingly for the first time ever on this day that he was leaving, she might actually rage at her. Thankfully, her mother did not.

'You're going to be fine, my darling,' Molly cooed. 'You are going to be just fine. It won't be for ever, baby Joe. It won't be for ever.'

'He *will* be fine,' her mother offered, in a tone softer than Molly had heard of late. She walked over to the window and looked down to the street. 'Albert has started the engine running to warm it up. Joyce will be with you in a second.'

'I . . . I . . . just . . .' There seemed too many words cued up on Molly's tongue. Marshalling them into some kind of order was impossible, along with the rising wave of cold panic that had started in her toes and was now at her chest. She felt as if she were drowning in this moment, the utter horror of it, and the fact that she knew she had to put her boy first and do what was right by him. She coiled Joe against her chest and breathed in the scent of his little soft head, trying to fix it in her memory. He reached out his tiny fingers and laid them against her face and she felt his touch like a sharp thing.

'Oh, Joe! Oh, my little one.' Her words coasted on a fractured breath, accompanied by fat tears on her cheeks, which she cursed, lest they wash away the touch of his tiny fingers against her skin. As she held him tightly, Joe began to cry.

'Shhhh . . . shhhh . . .' she breathed into his downy hair. 'Don't cry, my darling; don't cry, my baby boy; don't cry.' Her voice was high and reedy. To speak at all took every last ounce of her strength. Her sister appeared in the hallway, her face ashen.

Molly stood and watched as her mother bundled Joe's small amount of clothing into the crib and proceeded to haul it from the room. She couldn't help the whimper that left her throat.

'Look after him, Joycey.'

'I will, darling – we will – I promise you!' Joyce was crying quietly too now, but smiled weakly through her tears, trying to make everything a little less frightful.

Molly knew her time with her precious son was running out. These were the very last few minutes and seconds left to her . . . She had to make them count. Her arms shook and her bowel spasmed. *I can't . . . I can't do it . . . I can't . . .* She fought the mental battle, remembering how it had felt when the light went out in the shelter and they had sat there, waiting.

'Don't think badly of me, little one. We're at war, Joe, war! And your wonderful daddy was right: it changes everything. I love you, I love you, I love you, I love you . . . I do, I do. Never forget it.' Her tears clouded everything. Her sobs were noisy and ugly as her sadness spilled from her uncontrollably now.

With one final kiss on his sweet face, she handed her son to her sister.

'I will treasure every second with him, Molly.' Joyce spoke through a face contorted with her own tears. 'I will take good care of him for you.'

Molly nodded and sank onto the chair at her desk, her hands folded in her lap. She stared as her sister fussed over her son, tucking the blanket around him. With Joe in her arms, Joyce walked from the room without looking back.

Their mother reappeared at the door and took a step towards her. Molly bit her cheek to stop from swearing at the woman, who at that moment was a focal point for all of her grief.

'I know you can't see it now, but it's for the best. You have done something brave and selfless. It's best for the boy and best for you – for all of us. It's a solution, Molly.'

'A temporary solution,' she fired.

Her mother turned on her heel and was gone. At the sound of the front gate, Molly felt a jolt of panic. Wanting one last glimpse of him, she jumped up and hurried to the window, scrabbling to open it wide. Leaning out, she watched as her sister, with a look of the utmost distress on her face, turned to look up at the bedroom window from which she now leaned.

'Joyce! He likes . . . he likes to be wrapped and held tightly when he's scared, when there's noise!' Molly yelled, her voice hoarse with anguish.

Her sister nodded, tears streaking her face as she stepped across the pavement to the waiting car, the back door of which stood open. Albert was by her side, his hand placed on her lower back. Smiling a little stiffly, he raised his other hand towards Molly, his eyes kindly, and she was grateful. Molly hung out of the bedroom window, craning her neck to get one last look at her baby boy as the troupe climbed into the shiny black Austin 12. The strength left her as she stared down and her eyes met those of her sister, who had turned to look up at her from the back seat. Clever, accomplished

Joyce, who she knew would do her very best for her baby while he was in her care. Their eyes remained locked as the car pulled away.

Molly closed the window, her heart shredded into a million pieces, her gut newly hollowed out with the loss of Johan all over again, amplified by a deep ache to hold her son.

'I want him back!' she whispered. 'I want him back!'

Reaching into the little wooden box, she again took out the shiny brass button and gripped it tightly in her palm. Her thoughts fluctuated between the scent of Joe and the weight of him in her arms, to memories of Johan and the words of the song they had danced to, cheek to cheek on the dance floor, the first time they had met.

And then, as if floating through the ether, the strangest thing occurred, as if someone had moved the hair from her ear, and she heard a thin voice that was not unfamiliar whisper in her ear:

It will all be all right, Molly. He will come back to you . . .

'He will.' She nodded. 'He will.' Popping the button back into the box, she stood and coughed to clear her throat, galvanised into action.

Marching into the bathroom, she ran a basin full of cold water and stripped to the waist. Working the sliver of coal tar soap into lather she tried not to look at the patch of linoleum where she had given birth and set to vigorously scrubbing herself. She took especial care around her nipples, which were cracked and a little sore, and her breasts, bloated with milk, which she let into the sink, sloshing it away down the plughole and trying not to think too much about the absolute tragedy of the act. Next she cleaned her teeth, before fastening her hair into a loose knot at the nape of her neck and trying not to look at her eyes, swollen from crying. She dressed in her familiar blouse and skirt, the waistband of which was a lot roomier than when she had last worn it, and laced up her sturdy shoes.

Her mother called from the landing as Molly opened the front door.

'Mary Florence? Where are you going?' Her tone was quite shrill.

'To work, Mother,' she called as she closed the front door behind her, marching along the street and making her way to Malet Street, ignoring the swish of Mrs Granton-Smythe's lace curtains, which she caught from the corner of her eye.

The cool mid-afternoon air was reviving and glimpses of blue sky behind the cloud were enough to lift her spirits a little. It was a simple equation: the sooner she got back to work, the sooner Joe would come home.

Have you settled in the car, my darling boy? Are you sleeping now in Joyce's arms? I could come and get you . . . change my mind . . . With these thoughts percolating, she spied the postbox outside her place of work and pictured Johan leaning on it, a man with his whole life ahead of him, all wiped out in a flash. It was a sobering moment; she could not – would not – let that happen to her son. Tonbridge was safer. It was the right decision.

Molly tripped up the stairs and took the lift to the fifth floor. It was quarter past three and time for the tea break.

'Oh hello, Molly!' Beryl said with a wave as she stepped from the lift. 'It's been an age – how are you? Have you been ill? We were all rather worried and Miss Templar seemed more than a little put out, but then she is about most things.' Beryl gave her usual snort of a laugh.

Molly took heart from the fact that her life and all its drama did not appear to be common knowledge. She and Beryl walked along the corridor towards the dining room.

'Yes, I've been ill' – she paused – 'but I'm better now and ready to get back on the horse.'

'Well, it's really good to see you. Welcome back,' Beryl said in encouragement.

Molly walked down the corridor towards the office, just as she had done hundreds of times before. Memories of giggling and plotting with Geer left her a little hollow; she still had not received a reply from her friend.

'Molly!' Marjorie called from the entrance to the dining room. 'Beryl said you were in. It's good to see you.' Molly was happy to see her, aware today, however, that kindness might only encourage the tears that hovered very close to the surface.

The other girl held out her arms and, despite Molly's reservations, they clung to each other for a moment. Molly then coughed and adjusted her collar, trying to restore the level of distance and professionalism that might help her get through the afternoon.

'It's good to see you too, Marjorie.'

There was a moment of silence while the two stared at each other, seemingly waiting for the other to speak.

'You look better, or at least getting better.' Marjorie eyed her stomach and, whether consciously or not, Molly ran the flat of her palm over her waistband.

'I am getting better.'

'Good, good.'

'Did you . . . did you get my letter, Marjorie?' Molly asked, clearing her throat.

'Letter?' Marjorie looked back at her quizzically.

'Yes. I wrote asking for your—' Molly took a breath. 'I wrote to explain my rather sudden absence. But as you can see, my circumstances are different now and I'm ready to come back to work. Right now, in fact. I'll just grab a cup of tea and then go to see what awaits in the "in" tray!' She laughed brightly.

'I didn't see your letter, no,' Marjorie said, shaking her head, 'and I'm not the person to ask about coming back – that would be Mr Jenkins.'

'Very well, Marjorie, thank you. I do know who Mr Jenkins is.' Molly was aware she had snapped: a tightly coiled spring of sadness sat lodged in her throat and it was all she could do not to let it ping from her mouth.

'Well, I'll let you go and find him then.' Marjorie scurried off to the dining room. Molly regretted having been so curt, but there was no time to think about it now, as she knocked on Mr Jenkins's door.

'Come in!' he called.

She took a deep breath and walked in. Mr Jenkins, a small pragmatic man whose round glasses only added to his rather owl-like appearance, was not alone. Molly was surprised to see Mrs Templar standing by the window that overlooked the street.

'Miss Collway.' She almost tutted the name.

'Good afternoon, Mrs Templar.'

'Is that *all* you have to say? "Good afternoon, Mrs Templar", while we were forced to find cover after you abandoned your post so abruptly? Have you any idea of the inconvenience you caused me? You and Miss de Fries both. No matter the circumstances' – she lowered her eyes briefly – 'we're on a war footing and things like that matter.'

'I can only imagine the inconvenience,' Molly began.

Mrs Templar made a harrumphing noise, which did not bode well.

'Do sit down, Miss Collway,' Mr Jenkins interrupted, pointing to the chair in front of his desk. Molly sat.

'I would like to apologise for not coming into work for the last . . .' She paused, trying to figure out quite how long it had been.

'Nearly five weeks!' Miss Templar was more than aware.

Molly picked at the bump of tweed on her skirt, fearful of all she was trying to contain and desperate to get back to work.

'Yes.' The time had passed so quickly . . . 'But moving forward, I'm happy to say that I am able to return to work with immediate effect and would like to remind you that I am a senior translator with heightened security clearance. I am diligent in my work, dedicated and more than happy to make up the—'

'Let me stop you, Miss Collway,' Mr Jenkins offered firmly; his smile nonetheless spoke of kindness, as he nudged his glasses further up his nose. 'It was with regret that we had to fill your position here. I'm sorry, but we were left with little choice. As Mrs Templar quite rightly says, there is a war on.'

'I'm aware there's a war on, sir' – *more than aware, believe you me!* – 'and I want to do my bit: I want to come back to work. I need a job – I need *this* job! It was always a stepping stone for me and if I can't come back, then—'

'I'm sorry, Molly,' he said with another smile, 'it's out of my hands, but if I can put a word in for you with any other department, then I will.'

Molly felt her stomach sink. 'But . . . but, Mr Jenkins, I don't need to retrain or anything like that, which means I can slot right back in and get cracking. My work rate is high, we can get ahead, and—'

'Did you not hear?' Mrs Templar asked sharply. 'There is no role for you here. Someone else has your job now.'

'But—' Ignoring Mrs Templar, Molly looked at the man, still hoping he might look kindly on her appeal. 'Mr Jenkins, I am desperate to work. I—'

'I am sorry.' He picked up a sheet of paper and stared at it. She guessed it was a welcome prop – anything rather than look her in the eye.

Mrs Templar tapped her watch. 'I need to rally the girls. I'll see you out.' She made for the door and Molly rose slowly to her feet to follow her, feeling so out of place, unwanted even, in this building that had been her place of work for the last two years. She hated the embarrassment and awkwardness snaking over her.

'Goodbye, Miss Collway.'

'Goodbye, Mrs Templar.' Molly walked briskly along the corridor, trying to ignore the clicking of heels on the wooden floor behind her as girls rushed to take up the seat behind their typewriter, girls like her who, at the end of a day, had been asked to go for one drink. *Just one! . . . don't be a bore . . .* and in minutes the course of her whole life had changed.

She slowly made her way home and put her key in the door.

'Is that you, Molly?' her mother called from the kitchen before her foot had stepped over the threshold.

No, it's Adolf bloody Hitler! Don't you remember giving him a key too?

'Yes, it's me,' she called, in no mood to talk as she made her way up to her room, where she fell on her bed, cursing at the sound of her mother's footsteps trotting up the stairs. Her mum opened the door.

'Is this it? Is this what we can now expect? You lounging the day away like some drunken wastrel?'

Molly actually laughed, thinking she might quite like to be drunk – a nice escape from her thoughts, which were often intrusive and interminable.

'No, this is not it. I will find a job. But funny as it sounds, I'm still a little distracted by having just today handed over my newborn son to my sister. Do you understand?' Molly stared her mother in the eye and watched her take a step back.

'We all have choices, Molly,' her mother said as she pulled the door to behind her.

◆ ◆ ◆

The siren that woke her was loud and urgent. It was a shock to her that night had fallen, and with a pulse of panic she jumped out of bed and searched for the crib, before remembering that her little one was safe in Tonbridge. And although the pain of missing him was strong, her relief was sweet and instant: justification that her heart would do well to remember. Shoving on her shoes, she grabbed her blanket and fumbled along the corridor, calling for her mother.

'I'm here.' Mrs Collway was right behind her. Her glasses were on and she was holding a Bible, but whether she had been reading it when the alarm sounded or had grabbed it to read was unclear. The two women sat in silence at either end of the bench in the Anderson shelter and listened to the distant thuds and cracks of bombs and the answering fire from the ack-ack batteries across the city.

'It's off to the east,' her mother surmised, her ear cocked.

Molly thought of the poor souls whose lives at that very moment were being taken or destroyed. She pictured Marjorie, who had held her so lovingly earlier in the day and whom she knew lived in that direction, bitterly regretting their charged exchange.

'At least the boy is safe, I expect,' her mother added.

'Don't talk about him!' Molly snapped. Her mother had no right to do so, and to be reminded of her loss in this very place where she had held him tight and kissed his sweet face was almost more than she could bear. She sensed her mother shrink even further away from her in the cramped environment. It wasn't until daybreak that the two wearily made their way inside, where Molly slipped into her nightgown and crept between the sheets on her bed.

Judging from the light peeping through the gap in the bedroom curtains, it was mid-morning when she awoke. Her bedroom door opened slowly and Molly rubbed her eyes as she lifted her head from the pillow. She expected to see her mother delivering a peace offering in the form of a cup of tea, as was her normal way of things, or else mumbling useless platitudes on how best she might 'pull herself together', but the figure who stepped into the room was not her mother and for a second the surprise rendered her silent.

'Marjorie! What are you doing here?' Molly smiled at the sight of her.

'Hello, Molly.' The other girl stood awkwardly at the end of the bed while Molly heaved herself to a sitting position. It was very odd to have her colleague here in her bedroom. 'This is a beautiful house.'

'In some ways,' she whispered. 'Please – please sit down!' She pointed to the chair at the desk. Marjorie sat and pushed her glasses up on her nose. 'I was thinking about you last night when the bombs fell. How are you?'

Marjorie looked out of the window and shook her head. Her eyes held a slightly faraway stare. 'I'm allrightispose.'

'How did you know where I lived?'

Marjorie laughed. 'Personnel records.'

Molly nodded. 'Of course, personnel records. I'm so glad you've come. I wanted to tell you how sorry I am about the way I snapped at you yesterday. It had been a terrible day and—'

'Don't worry about it.' Marjorie flapped her hand.

'I do worry about it. The fact is . . .' She paused, following Marjorie's eyeline and catching sight of two large circles of wet milk on the front of her nightgown. She ran her hand over the damp mess. 'The fact is' – she kept her voice steady – 'I had a child. A son. He's named Joe, after his dad.'

'Geer's brother?'

Molly nodded. 'I sent him away to Kent yesterday to live with my sister. He'll stay with her until the war is over and I know I can keep him safe, but it's hard, Marjorie, harder than I thought, and one of my biggest motivations was to get back to work, earn a living and give us a good life!' She shook her head. 'And so to find out yesterday that there's no job for me . . .'

'Not the best day you've ever had then?'

'No.' Molly gave a wry smile at the understatement. 'So today I will hit the job trail. I'm confident Mr Jenkins will give me a good reference and—'

'That's why I'm here. There might be a job if you're interested.'

'Oh!' Molly's face brightened. 'Oh, that's wonderful! I thought they'd filled the position, Mrs Templar said.'

'This has nothing to do with Mrs Templar.' Marjorie spoke with a hint of amusement in her voice.

'What job? Where?'

'Get dressed, Molly.' Marjorie held her gaze. 'There are some people who'd like to talk to you.'

'What people?' She was already jumping up. A job opportunity was not to be sniffed at.

'People who can help you earn a living and get that good life.' Marjorie smiled at her.

Marjorie pushed open the door of an office on the third floor of the Ministry of War building in Whitehall and beckoned for her to enter. Molly shot her colleague a look, not sure she wanted to walk in to the dimly lit space.

'I'll be right here, waiting for you,' Marjorie said softly.

'Don't be alarmed,' a male voice offered in low tones. 'Do come in.'

The room was sparsely furnished, save for a large mahogany boardroom table with ten chairs evenly spaced around it. The walls were bare and the windows covered with blackout fabric. The voice belonged to one of two men now standing in front of her. Both wore unremarkable double-breasted, pinstripe navy suits and both had neat pencil moustaches and slicked-back hair. At first glance they looked eerily similar, but closer inspection revealed them to be quite different. One was heavier set and it was he who had spoken first, in crystal-cut English. In any other circumstance it would have been quite uncomfortable to find herself in a room with two male strangers, but with Marjorie posted outside the door Molly was both interested and curious as to what they had to say. Her heart beat a little too quickly. This was all rather odd and felt a little shady somehow.

'Do sit down.' The first man pulled out a chair for her, and she sat, noticing the exceptionally shiny black toes of the shoes worn by both men. They walked now to the opposite side of the table and seated themselves. It gave the meeting an air of formality and a distance between them, for which she was grateful. It helped ease her anxiety a little.

'Miss Collway.'

'Yes?' She was pleased with the steadiness of her voice, giving no hint of the nerves that sparked in her veins. This was an unfamiliar situation and she had no idea what to expect.

'Thank you for coming to see us. My name is Mr Malcolm.' The slimmer man was speaking now. She saw his right hand twitch but he didn't offer to shake her hand.

'And I am Mr Greene.' The first man inclined his head.

'Well, this seems all very irregular,' Molly breathed. 'However, Marjorie may have mentioned to you that I am looking for work.' Her eyes had begun to adjust to the low lighting and she could see these two were older than herself, although not that old – early thirties, maybe. Their white shirts were crisp and clean and their ties black. They looked sombre but well fed, without the hollow pockets at neck and cheek that many sported in these times of war.

Lucky ones . . .

'We've been in touch with Mr Jenkins.' This fact gave her confidence – he had indeed said that if he could, he'd put a word in with other departments. Was that was this was all about?

'I . . . I went to see him yesterday, fully prepared to come back to work,' she said slowly, 'but I was told there were no vacancies, and that my position had been filled. I was extremely disappointed. I'm good at my job and—'

'Miss Collway,' Mr Greene interrupted, 'both Mr Malcolm and I are fully apprised of your situation.' It was a relief not to have to elaborate, but also a concern – how and what did they know about her 'situation'?

'Is that right?' She clasped her hands on the table in front of her, feeling more than a little exposed.

The two men exchanged a glance and Mr Greene coughed.

'We have something to ask you.' He leaned forward and met her gaze, his expression earnest, searching.

'What do you want to ask me?' She was aware that she had been holding her breath.

'We have a role for you, an assignment, if you will.'

Her optimism soared. 'What kind of assignment?'

'Here's the thing . . .' Mr Malcolm leaned back in his seat and rubbed his chin.

Mr Greene kept his eyes on her. It was unnerving. 'This is a very different job to the one you're used to' – he paused – 'and it's a request that comes from the very heart of Whitehall. A courier role, you might say.'

'A courier? I don't quite understand.'

'It's very simple.' Mr Greene now picked up the baton. 'It sometimes happens that the country has a need, and it is a matter of civic duty to execute that deed. Never more so than in wartime, but I don't need to tell *you* that, Miss Collway, do I? We were very sorry to hear about Johan de Fries.'

Tears gathered at the back of her throat at the very mention of him, but it was also nice to hear someone offering condolence, as if legitimising her loss.

'How . . . how do you know about Johan?'

'We have our sources,' Mr Malcolm said evenly.

'And we are also very sorry for all that has . . . befallen you,' Mr Greene said softly.

Her heart beat a little too quickly and she could feel the rise in her pulse. He had seen her letter, no doubt about it.

'Who are you exactly?' she asked again, suddenly a little fearful of these furtive men who seemed to know all about her when she knew absolutely nothing about them.

'We are colleagues of yours, if you will.' Mr Greene smiled at her.

'How peculiar. I don't seem to recall seeing you in my department.'

The two men exchanged a look. 'We have agents inside all of the ministries, keeping an eye out, briefing us. It's prudent to do so and you have been brought to our attention.'

The use of the word 'agent' alerted her – what kind of job were they offering, precisely?

Mr Malcolm now turned to face her. 'There's something about those of us who have suffered loss, Miss Collway. We tend to fall into two camps: those who crumple, sink, wither and fade under the weight of the unimaginable pain; and those of us who take that hurt, ball it tightly, put it in the base of our gut and use it as fuel. And when that happens it is a very powerful thing, the *most* powerful. It is an unstoppable force and one that can do good, immeasurable good. So much so that it can change the course of this damned war. Maybe even help draw it to a close, thus ensuring that others, old and young, even the very young' – he let this trail – 'will never have to know the kind of hurt that lives in the gut for a lifetime.'

'What is it you want me to do?' She wasn't agreeing, but Mr Malcolm had sparked her interest. She would do anything, anything at all, to stop her baby, her boy, knowing what this life felt like or, God forbid, having to step into the marching boots of his father and grandfather.

'All in good time,' Mr Greene said quietly. 'We have faith that you are exactly the kind of person who can get a job done and who will do so for the greater good.'

'What do you mean, "the kind of person"?' she asked directly.

'It's a very rare skill set. People who speak a second and third language. People who are smart. People who have the potential to be brave,' Mr Malcolm said resolutely, 'and people who are already broken. People who know what it's like to have to rise up over adversity and take back control.'

'I am not broken.' Molly tapped her fingers on the tabletop. 'I've lost Johan, but I am not broken.' She thought of Joe with a surge of joy at the thought of their blissful reunion and the life she would give him. It was a reason to hold on. 'But I do want to triumph and I do want to take back control.'

'Yes.' Mr Malcolm let the one word ring out and she almost heard the word that followed, unspoken: *exactly.*

When Molly left the room an hour later, having agreed to consider their proposal, Marjorie was nowhere to be seen.

NINE

I am not Molly Collway, I am Claudette Menard, secretary. I am going to visit my cousin in Saintes. I'm married to Benoît. We have no children. I'm quiet, myopic, and très réligieuse . . . She pushed the heavy glasses further up the bridge of her nose, mimicking the habit she'd seen in Marjorie. *I am travelling from my home in Amiens, where I tend my garden and grow vegetables. I'm a good citizen who has handed in her savings in exchange for war bonds with the Banque Nationale de France and I, like every other citizen, want the fighting to be over so my husband can come home from the front and we can start thinking about a family . . .*

'Where are you going?' her mother had asked, surprised, watching from the bedroom doorway when Molly came home from her interview and packed a few clothes, the exercise book containing her father's scribblings and his fountain pen in her suitcase, along with a hairbrush, her lavender-scented talc and the brass button from Johan's naval uniform.

'Away for work, Mum,' she answered.

'What work, exactly? And when will you be back?' Mrs Collway had demanded.

'You will be carrying items into France that would be difficult for us to get into the right hands without interception or with a risk of things going awry if we sent them by other means,' the Major had explained.

'What things?'

'A few small objects and information. That's strictly hush-hush – it's better you don't know, then you can't tell,' he had said sternly. 'But I will tell you that a sophisticated operation by the French Resistance is at risk because a mole is feeding information to the occupying German army. We're getting close to identifying him and have a photograph of the back of his head, but we need to let the powers that be know his identity so they can root him out. A bigger operation depends on it. That's all I am prepared to say.'

'How do I carry these things?'

'Hidden – cleverly hidden.'

'Will I be in danger?' She thought of Joe's sweet face and felt the familiar fold of longing in her gut to hold her boy, aching for the day . . .

'Only if you're caught,' he said honestly.

'What are my chances of success?'

'Well,' he said, taking a cigarette from the pack, 'if you listen and learn and practise your dialect, I would say your chances are good.'

'What should I say if anyone at home asks where I'm going or what I'm doing?'

'Say you have a translation job. The more we can hinge a story on the truth, the easier it will be believed and the easier for you to say it with conviction.'

'It's a translation job. And as to when will I be back' – Molly paused from her packing to look her mother in the eye – 'I won't ever be back, not properly. I've secured digs in St Pancras. I'll visit you in due course, but I don't think I can forgive the position you've put me in. I needed help. Help and understanding, and I got neither and it's shocked and disappointed me, but strengthened me too. In time I hope I'll stop feeling so angry with you, but even then I suspect I will always feel sorry for you. I will always, always, do what is best for *my* child' – she could still barely say his name without a lump of emotion rising in her throat – 'but I wonder, Mum, will you be able to say the same?'

'I . . .' Her mother reached for her handkerchief and dabbed her reddened eyes. 'Mary Florence, I . . .'

Molly snapped shut the catches on the suitcase and walked past her. She trotted down the stairs and out of the front door of the house on Old Gloucester Street, Bloomsbury, without so much as a backward glance.

She had moved her meagre belongings into the damp lodgings near St Pancras Station and spent a couple of nights in the small room on the middle floor of the slightly dilapidated house. It had a comfortable enough bed, a hot plate and sink, which were hers, and she was grateful. Her home for the next six weeks, however, would be a little further afield.

Mr Malcolm had met her off the train in a shiny black car. As he placed her suitcase in the boot, she noted that he was wearing the same clothes as when she had seen him before. 'There's always a small possibility that a candidate might have a change of heart and not get on the train,' he had told her. 'We call it the Waterloo wobble.'

'That didn't even occur to me,' she told him honestly. She'd boarded the train at Waterloo with nothing but determination in her gut – both to do a good job and to earn enough money to provide Joe with a good life.

West Court was an impressive red-brick house with a large duck pond at the front and an imposing tree.

'This is nice,' she said aloud.

'Let's hope you still think so at the end of your training.' Mr Malcolm drew breath through his teeth, which made her smile.

At the end of her course, she had still found the place nice and the skills she had learned more than useful, not to mention her new level of fitness. She wondered what Johan would have made of it all, thinking of him as she learned to zero a pistol in the long corridor down in the wine cellar, firing bullets that hit the backstop on the far wall, the recoil making her wrist flick up. She also spent hours and hours in conversation with a native from Amiens, chatting to the lady, who gave her name only as Belle, as they strolled inconspicuously around the grounds, practising the nuances that would place her firmly as a local. Her daily classroom instruction had been taught her by rote by an army man known as Major P.

'Sleep is your best friend when on public transport. No one wants to wake a tired person – there isn't a man, woman or child alive who can't relate to that kind of fatigue. Don't overly engage, keep things formal, just sleep. Don't evade or stumble or snub, simply respond calmly . . . and then sleep.'

The words of her instruction issued in the makeshift classroom came readily to mind now on the last leg of her train journey to France – into enemy territory. She heard them in Major P's clear voice and they were a comfort.

'Oh là là, qu'il fait chaud . . .' said the old woman sitting opposite. Looking hot and weary, she drew a paper fan from her hessian bag and started wafting herself. On her lap lay a parcel wrapped in brown paper and tied up with string.

'Oui, c'est bien ça.' Molly kept her voice low, quiet and slow, as instructed: better able to control the quaver of nerves and to

concentrate on each vowel sound. She tilted her head to one side against the once plush headrest, fraying through now to the webbing beneath, and closed her eyes. War, she thought, made everything once beautiful tatty. No one had time to think about aesthetics when their very survival was in doubt. It was universal: the damage, the wear and tear and the spoiled. In London, like anywhere else, flowerbeds had been given over to grow food, even in and around Buckingham Palace and the Royal Parks. Buildings that had been shaken by bombs but managed to resist the urge to topple had windows missing, while stucco rendering had fallen away to reveal the brickwork beneath. A number of frontages were supported by giant wooden props set at an angle, and on the upper floors, where the wind whistled through, wallpaper clung in thin strips to what was left of walls, and bathroom tiles could be seen where there was no longer a bathroom. People took short cuts through gaps piled high with rubble and dust where until recently a building had stood. It was just another element of life made ugly by the turmoil of war.

'*Dormez, ma petite*,' whispered the old lady on the train, words offered so sweetly to a stranger . . . It took all of Molly's resolve not to leap up and hug her as she feigned sleep.

'*Remember, there is no time for sentiment. Sentimentality is a distraction you can ill afford. No time to overthink. Even the slightest deviation in terms of agreed timing or route or behaviour can be like pulling a thread that just might unravel an entire garment, or worse, might reveal an entire plan. Do you understand?*'

'*Yes.*'

'*Sentimentality. Going off plan. Letting your guard down. Overfamiliarity. It's in these small details where danger lurks, and remember the danger is not only to yourself but also to others who are relying on you. We are relying on you – do you understand that?*'

'*Yes.*'

Molly kept her ears alert and listened to the announcement of the guard at each stop, as well as the general hum of conversation as the train trundled on. She was relieved when the lady left the carriage, once the train pulled into Cognac. Rough hessian brushed against her shins.

Two more stops. Two more stops.

Opening her eyes, Molly sat up in the chair, trying to hide the start to her limbs and the flip in her gut as she avoided eye contact with the two German soldiers who had taken the seats opposite her and who now sat with legs spread, their MP 40 sub-machine guns resting on the floor between their feet, barrels down, hands gripping the butt, as if it were any old stick. She swallowed at the sight of their weapons, trying to ignore the chatter in their native tongue about some football match, played apparently on an airstrip, and the narrow victory they had stolen in the face of defeat. Again she closed her eyes and let her head fall forward, trying to still her racing heart and wishing the small beads of nervous sweat on her upper lip would disappear. Thank goodness it was a warm day.

'*Walk slowly, decisively, with your ticket and, if necessary, your papers in your hand. Always be a model citizen to avoid drawing attention to yourself and any unnecessary interactions with the police. The fewer people you interact with, the better. Remember, you have nothing to fear. You are Claudette Menard, coming to see your cousin. Leave the station and walk directly along Rue St-Martin and make your way to the Café Hubert. Take a table outside and wait. You will be approached by your cousin Violet, who will make contact. She will tell you what to do next.*'

'*What does Violet look like?*'

'*We don't know, but she'll be wearing a headscarf and will call you her sweet cousin.*'

Molly left the railway station, her ears filled with the sound of her heart clattering in her ribs. Staring down at the cobbles beneath her feet on the winding road alongside the river, she waited for the tap on her shoulder that would blow her cover. A group of prisoners – local men and boys, she imagined – came marching along in the other direction, with one German soldier at the front of the line, one at the rear and two on either side. Their expressions imperious, each walked with his chin up and his nose in the air, weapon raised and readied. Molly felt a sudden intense flash of hatred towards these men, whose armies had decimated her own city, forced her country to its knees, fractured the whole of Europe and taken away her lover . . . They were the reason she was separated from her beloved son.

The Frenchmen's faces, however, were bruised and battered, their eyes blackened and sunk in their sockets over sallow cheeks. Their ragged clothes hung limply from bowed shoulders, their emaciated bodies shrunken by hunger. They had wound makeshift bandages around hands, legs and at least one person's head. The man with the head bandage and a tattered red scarf around his neck briefly held her gaze, his dark eyes imploring, as the troupe limped onward. Molly wanted to give water to each one of these desperate men, with their blistered lips and the downward cast of the exhausted, and offer words of encouragement that this would be over soon, or at the very least that she was thankful for their sacrifice. Instead, she kept her eyes to the front and sang a hymn in her head as a distraction . . .

> The love that asks no question, the love that
> stands the test,
>
> That lays upon the altar the dearest and the
> best . . .

Anything rather than reveal her sympathy in front of the guards who would have no hesitation in using those weapons on a sympathiser. She walked past and heard shouts of:

'*Los! Bewegt euch, ihr Schweine!*'

The loud, guttural instruction sent a shiver down her spine.

The buildings on the other side of the water were ornate, with wrought-iron balconies and fancy balustrades, but even here the fronts were pitted with bullet holes. It was a shock to see the beautiful town so damaged and so very different to the images of French rural life that lived in her mind. She thought of the houses back home, many of which had had their iron plundered for the war effort. Blinking twice, she erased the image of the car door closing, of Joyce's foot lifting as it stepped into the car and how she swept the edge of her coat from the kerb, the last thing to be folded inside the confines of the vehicle that would spirit away her baby boy . . .

Stop it! No sentiment. You are Claudette, off to meet your cousin Violet. You are Claudette, off to meet your cousin Violet at the Café Hubert.

The air along the river was thick with the smell of cut grass. In the nooks and crannies of the low wall separating the road from the drop down to the river, she saw clusters of tiny purple flowers sitting in fine sprays of green foliage. Gazing up at the deep blue sky and with the warm sun on her face, she could fool herself for a moment that this was any other town on any other day and not a place under occupation where soldiers of an invading army could do as they pleased, when they pleased and with whom they pleased – because there was no one brave enough to stop them.

'*I am brave enough . . .*' Johan's words came to her.

'*I picture a generation of young men who don't know what it's like to put their hands over their ears to quiet the explosions, who haven't seen their blood or that of their friends running into the earth of which they will forever be part. I don't want them to know what it's like to have to say goodbye to the things and people they love with every fibre of their being, knowing it might be for the very last time. And then to have to erase those things and people from their minds and switch to fighting mode just to enable them to get through the next hour and the next and the next . . . I want them to live in perfect peace.'*

I am brave enough! She gritted her teeth. *I am!*

Gripping the wooden handle of her rattan bag, she stared at the ground, tucking her recently chopped hair behind her ear. Her locks were now as sharp as the paper scissors would allow and hung along her jawline in a bluntish, straightish line.

'*There we go.*' The man who had volunteered to chop her locks at West Court stood back in the dim light of her bathroom to admire his handiwork. '*Almost professional.*'

'*Are you a barber?*' she had asked.

'*Good Lord, no! I'm a cartographer.*'

'*Well, that explains a lot.*'

She had laughed, and the man cutting her hair had laughed. She knew she would remember this, as it was the first time she had laughed since she had handed Joe to her sister.

And suddenly there it was ahead, just as they had described it, the meeting place. Her gut churned at the sight of it. The Café Hubert was nothing grand or fancy, no Lyons Corner House, but instead had a modest frontage under a striped awning with dark wooden bistro tables and matching bentwood chairs arranged over the cobbles outside the double-fronted windows. There were no tablecloths, just a solid ashtray on each surface and, by the looks of it, the remnants of an afternoon spent drinking. The gilded lettering of 'Hubert' above the bar had faded somewhat.

An elderly woman stood in the doorway, adjusting the waist of her floral apron beneath a fastened-back curtain of green beads. Her arthritic fingers gripped the rim of the dull metal tray under her arm. A limp roll of grey hair sat on top of her head above deep-set eyes, their gaze milky and far off. Creases ran from her nose to her chin, lending her the air of a marionette. She carried a heaviness about her bow-legged frame, as if the world and all that went on in it was more than she could bear, as if the very knowledge crammed inside her head was enough to push her feet further and further into the ground. This Molly could more than understand.

She swept the seven tables with an apparently casual glance. Four were occupied by groups of German soldiers, all loud, all drinking, hollering and banging the tables without any regard to the old woman's underlying melancholy. They threw pastis and dark beer down their blond-stubbled throats from thick-ribbed glasses held in square hands equally used to gripping a gun. At one table sat two older women, crudely made-up and flashing a tantalising glimpse of the tops of their stockings. Molly felt a sudden and curious pang of homesickness for the tarts who haunted the alleyways of the West End. The two women avoided eye contact and she did not judge them, knowing that when you and yours were hungry you made your money however you could, and in wartime you did things you could never have imagined during peace. This was never more true of her own situation – here she was in the west of France, miles and miles from her baby, fighting the fight, doing her bit and hoping in some way to make the bastards pay.

Molly took a seat at one of the free tables, sandwiched between two where soldiers languished. The old woman caught her eye.

'*Un café, s'il vous plaît.*'

Her mouth dry with nerves, Molly tried out the dialect for the first time, hoping she had done Belle proud. The waitress nodded and disappeared inside, before returning with a small white cup and saucer, which she placed on the table. Up close, Molly could see that the woman was in fact not nearly as old as she had suspected but simply sad, broken and a little bowed, enough to age the prettiest of faces.

'*C'est café?*' She stared down at the brown slightly grainy mixture with fascination; a cup of coffee was a rare thing.

'*Oui, si vous voulez, mademoiselle.*'

It was a chicory mixture with goodness knows what else.

'*Merci, madame.*' Molly had found it surprisingly easy to switch to French in her head, translating as she went. Belle's instruction was proving invaluable and, so far, no one had questioned her accent or her intonation. It gave her the confidence to speak fluidly.

'*Je vous en prie.*' The waitress almost smiled.

The Rue St-Martin was wide, with a sweeping bend where the Café Hubert was situated. Opposite was a boulangerie, sadly closed. The windows of a pharmacie had been boarded up from the inside, the jagged stars still visible on the broken glass, the reason for which she could only guess at. The only place open was a boucherie, which seemed to stock nothing but small skinned rabbits and a tray of what could only be identified, according to the handwritten sign, as '*entrailles*'. Molly's appetite, already diminished, now disappeared almost entirely.

It was a strange thing, but having thought about this moment on her journey here, she had felt a heart-stopping fear. And yet here she was, surrounded by German soldiers, this close to the enemy she had previously only seen in newsreels and newspapers. She had of course heard their planes fly over her city while she cowered in the Anderson shelter. Right now, she could have reached out and touched them, had she been so minded. And yet, despite her fear, she felt in control.

Molly knew from the map she had studied that the market square lay further along the street, where the Église Saint-Martin stood proudly on a rise, keeping watch over the pale stone buildings, cobbled streets and shuttered rooms of the town. Right on cue the church bells rang out.

One . . . two . . . three . . . four . . . She was in position and on time. Four o'clock.

Holding her hand steady, she took the cup in her hand and sipped gingerly at the vile and impossibly bitter brew.

'Remember, it's the smallest things that can give you away – turning left instead of right and then doubling back because you don't know the way, when everyone in the town knows the way. The detail. It's all about the detail.' Molly had pored over the maps of Saintes until she knew them by heart, role-playing with Belle until she was able to give directions to just about anywhere in the town if asked.

She swallowed the warm drink and even managed a small smile, like a local who was used to the foul concoction, quashing the desire to wrinkle her nose and splutter. As the laughter of the Germans rang out around her and as per instruction, she settled back in the seat with the rattan bag on her lap.

'Don't let the bag out of your sight. Not for a second. Hold on to it. Grip it tightly. Only hand it over to Pascal.'

'Who is Pascal?'

'He will make himself known and will suggest the bag was a gift from your mother. That's the code. If anyone other than Pascal tries to take it, act nonchalantly and don't arouse suspicion. But do everything in your power not to be parted from it.'

And so she waited, her eyes straying on occasion to the bag as her thoughts pondered on what might lie within, invisible to her eye.

TEN

'Claudette!'

Molly looked up, aware she was being addressed.

'Claudette!' A young woman was calling her loudly from the flatbed of a rickety Citroën truck that drew into the kerb, driven by an unshaven old man in a straw hat. The girl was waving vigorously, but Molly kept her hands firmly on her coffee cup, offering only a small smile in exchange. A wave: that was the kind of thing that could give a person away. The girl in the back of the truck – Molly's contact, no doubt – grabbed a large black bike with a battered basket on the front and dropped it inelegantly over the side, where it clattered onto the cobbled ground. Germans watching with avid interest from a nearby table burst into laughter.

'*Feine Muskeln!*' they called out. The girl ignored them.

Jumping down onto the pavement herself, she rested the bike against a nearby tree and almost ran to Molly's table. Even the whores glanced up briefly. There had been nothing subtle about her entry, nothing at all.

'Fearful people act fearfully. The easiest way to hide is to do so in plain sight. Nothing furtive, nothing whispered.'

Close up, Molly could see they were of a similar age, but 'Violet's' skin was darker, the result of working outdoors in the sunshine, no doubt. Her brows were heavy and her hair almost black, shining blue in the glint of the sun and just visible in snatches beneath the navy cotton scarf tied about her head. She was long-limbed and rangy, with the flat bust and jutting cheekbones of the hungry. Her overalls were the colour of mud and the sturdy boots on her feet looked at least a couple of sizes too big. She rushed to the table, hands outstretched towards Molly and wearing a huge smile of welcome.

'Ah, Claudette, my sweet cousin!'

And there was the code.

'Violet!' Molly rose to greet the other girl. Wrapping their arms around each other in a comfortable hug, they greeted each other with the customary kiss on each cheek.

'It's so good to see you again!' Violet sighed, sinking into the free chair at Molly's table with her legs stretched out in front of her. Her manner was intriguing: calm and relaxed, as if they were meeting in an English pub by the river in summertime and she was quite unaware of the throng of drunken soldiers – the enemy – seated at the surrounding tables.

'You too.'

Violet placed her hand over Molly's on the tabletop and squeezed gently. It was both familial and reassuring and Molly felt a flicker of confusion, pleased to see this new friend before remembering she was a total stranger.

'Are you well? Did you have a safe trip?' Violet asked.

'Yes, good, thanks. I'm a bit tired, but that's only to be expected.'

'Of course. I have to go to work, worse luck – I'd much rather sit and chat with you.'

'Oh, me too, but I do understand.' Molly felt her mouth go dry – was Violet leaving already? Her heart raced – what was she supposed to do now? She had been told to trust the process and that instruction would follow, but her gut leapt in fear nonetheless.

'But I'll see you at Grandma's later?' Violet asked brightly. 'How's Benoît? I bet he's missing you.'

'Oh, and I him.' Molly couldn't help but picture Johan's face drifting into her mind's eye.

'Right, well, I'd better get a move on. We'll catch up properly later!'

'I can't wait to see you.' Molly meant it, looking forward to their reunion, if indeed that was the plan. There was something about Violet's presence that calmed her fears.

Violet jumped up and dusted off her bottom. 'Jacques insisted on picking you up; he thought you might have luggage?' She pointed towards the truck.

'No, just this.' Molly lifted up the large woven bag on her lap.

Relieved to be on her way, she reached for her purse to deposit a few centimes on the table in payment.

Violet walked over to her bike, watching as Molly climbed into the front seat of the truck and slammed the door behind her, placing the bag on her lap.

'See you later, Claudette!'

'Bye!' Molly waved out of the window as the girl cycled away.

She nodded at Jacques, the elderly driver in his straw hat, who carried an overpowering scent of tobacco, wood smoke and body odour. Taking shallow breaths, she waited for her nose to acclimatise. One or two of the soldiers were on high alert, studying their every move as the noisy engine clattered into life and the truck pulled away.

They turned left, rattling through the market square in the shadow of the church, where the front of the mairie was draped in a vast red flag bearing the proud black swastika of the occupiers. This first time she had seen it in real life was enough to make her blood run cold and strike rage into the very heart of her. The truck headed north, following the path of the river, where the buildings began to thin and she again found herself in the French countryside.

'You okay?' Jacques asked, without taking his eyes off the road.

Molly nodded, glad that he seemed a man of few words.

She was immensely reassured at the sight of the farmhouse appearing at the end of a long driveway. Smoke rose from three chimneys standing proud of a traditional catslide roof. The courtyard was busy and parked up with vehicles of various types, dispelling any images of dark and empty chambers where she might be alone with her thoughts. The truck she was now in drew to a halt, parked half inside a three-sided barn. A couple of older men and a middle-aged woman, all in overalls, stood with oily rags, spanners and cans of oil, their heads bent low over engines, while there seemed to be much discussion about the best course of action. It looked more like a garage forecourt than a farm.

'Come!' Jacques jumped from the vehicle with surprising agility and beckoned her towards the house. She followed, feeling the stares on her back of those who looked up from their tinkering. The low wooden door with an iron latch led through to a large square kitchen with a blackened range running along the back wall on which sat a vast cooking pot, the lid askew and its contents steaming. A huge kettle swung from a hook over the range, while a meagre pile of chopped wood lay neatly piled on the flagstone floor alongside. Brick pillars supported a heavy stone sink in the corner of the room. On another wall stood an ancient dresser on which Molly spied a stack of thick china plates and a clutch of glasses and mugs, next to a bundle of cutlery poking from a slightly rusted blue and white tin with the word 'Riz' on the side. Edging the shelves on the dresser were narrow borders of delicate lace the colour of tea; Molly wondered who had made them and when. It strengthened her resolve, imagining a time when something so frivolous and pretty might once have taken priority over fixing vehicles, the housing of 'guests' like her and before the word 'Maquis' would have been part of their hushed vocabulary: a time, she imagined, before a red and black flag had come to flutter over the front windows of the mairie.

A young girl was sitting at the long scrubbed table in the centre of the room, stripping rhubarb leaves from the stalks and placing them in a cooking pot, while the rhubarb itself she chopped into a neat heap on the tabletop.

'There is no need to make conversation, no need to introduce yourself. Try only to speak when spoken to and even then only offer the minimum of information, this again for your sake and theirs. People can't give information if they don't have it.'

Molly avoided the girl's gaze and followed Jacques as he opened one of two inner doors, finding herself in a cool corridor with a stone floor and very little light. It took a second or two for her eyes to adjust. All the doors leading off the corridor were closed and she saw that the main entrance directly in front of her had been bricked up from the inside.

'This way!' He turned sharp right and she saw that the layout of the farm was an L-shape. Here the hallway was wider, but similarly dark. Candle sconces had been fashioned out of old tins and crudely nailed into the walls, on which sat stubby mounds of wax with blackened wicks. There was a strong smell of old dust, damp and a faint lingering scent of fresh lavender. Jacques picked up pace until he came to another door, this time leading to a low, wide room that looked to be part office, part storeroom for discarded furniture. Offcuts of wood had been nailed over the window frames and the floor was no more than compacted dirt, lending the room a dank and fungal odour of secret things blooming in dark corners.

In the middle of the room stood a small, beaten-up sofa. A dark spring poked out from one of the arms and ragged strips of faded red velvet, hinting at a former luxury almost unimaginable now, hung from the horsehair still tightly packed within the wooden frame. Also in the room were a couple of cane dining chairs that had seen better days and a small paint-spattered card table.

'Wait here.' Jacques shut the door behind him and Molly swallowed. How long was she supposed to wait and what was she waiting for? She ground her teeth in impatience.

The door opened with a bang and Molly spun round, relieved to see it was Violet staring back at her, with her hands on her hips and a broad smile on her mouth.

'Hello again.'

'You speak English?' Molly was surprised.

'Well, I should bloody well hope so. Would have been hard to understand me in school if I hadn't!'

'You *are* English?' This thought had not occurred to her at their last meeting.

'A bit,' was all Violet was prepared to say on the matter. She parked her bottom on the edge of the old card table and folded her arms across her chest, seeming to study her. 'I cycled from the café. Took the back roads – only four minutes off my record. Not bad, eh?'

'Not bad at all.'

Violet pulled half of a cigarette from her front pocket, lit the stub and inhaled deeply. 'So how are you feeling?' she asked.

'I guess I was surprised to have such a public arrival,' Molly said.

Violet snorted with laughter. 'It was important you were seen to be arriving. It means no one gives a crap if you pop up again.'

'Of course, yes.' *You dunce, Molly.*

'So,' Violet said, taking another drag, 'I don't know how much you know about what happens next?'

'I've had a full briefing.'

Her instructions had been clear: *'. . . Hand the bag over and then travel back with Violet to the Café Hubert when she goes for her evening shift. A motorbike will take you back to the railway station – and then you will simply do the journey home in reverse. Keep your papers on hand at all times and remember your training.'*

'Okay, good.' Violet rolled the cigarette between her thumb and forefinger. 'And you have the bag, I see.' She eyed the rattan holdall that Molly still clutched in her hand.

Molly nodded.

'May I take it from you?' Violet asked.

'No.' Molly gripped the handle. That was not the code.

'Good girl.' Violet winked at her.

The door opened and in walked a man in his mid-forties. His skin was dark, his close-shaven beard even darker, but his eyes were the colour of caramel. Violet turned to him with a smile that lit her whole face, a smile that came from within. Molly felt a jolt of envy and the memory of being within touching distance of Johan folded her gut with longing, instantly followed by the tightening of her nipples as the desire to feed her little boy pawed at her. She pushed both images from her mind and focused.

'Claudette!' Violet beamed. 'This is Pascal.'

Molly rose to her feet. 'How do you do, Pascal?'

'It's good to meet you.' His accent was heavy.

Violet ground the last remnants of her cigarette into the dirt floor under the heel of her boot.

'Can I take your bag?' he asked.

'My handbag?' she asked.

'Yes. A gift from your mother, no?'

Molly nodded: that was the phrase she had been waiting for. She handed the bag over to Pascal, noticing how he and Violet locked eyes momentarily, and then watched rapt as he took a small, sharp knife from the inside pocket of his jacket and started to cut away the lining. There under the rim of the frame was a flat, sewn pouch, barely discernible from the inner fabric of the bag itself. Pascal cut through the stitches with the utmost care to detach it, and then held it up to the dull beam of the single light bulb hanging in the centre of the room. He smiled at Violet. In her role as a courier, Molly was still unaware of exactly what she had carried all the way from London.

Pascal stared at her for a moment before carefully opening the pouch and placing the contents on the table, including a letter, which he read slowly, the only clue as to its content being a slight twitch below his left eye. Along with this came a grainy photograph, which he studied, holding it close to his face as if to better discern the image, and five small keys, each wrapped in tissue, one of which he opened. His expression was hard to read, his tone deadly serious.

'Thank you, Claudette,' he said.

'You are most welcome,' Molly offered in all sincerity.

The door opened and in walked the woman Molly recognised from earlier out in the barn, still in her overalls and with engine grease over her fingers and all up her arms.

'We have a problem.' She was a little breathless, glancing nervously at Molly. It reminded her of when Mrs Templar would cast an irritated eye in her direction when it was Geer who was in trouble, as if she were guilty by association.

'What kind of problem, Lisette?' Pascal asked calmly while Violet tensed, folding her arms across her chest.

Again the woman looked at Molly and jerked her head in the direction of the door. Pascal followed her out. Molly and Violet were left staring at the door, doing their best to listen as the two outside whispered inaudibly, save for the odd sharp intake of breath and then what sounded like a short, angry curse from Pascal. A minute later he returned alone.

'Bernardine is sick,' he said, addressing Violet.

'Shit!' Violet knitted her fingers in her hair and closed her eyes briefly.

'Yes, shit indeed!' Pascal paced the room, his hands on his hips.

Molly felt like an interloper, an encumbrance.

'What will we do?' Violet asked.

'I'm thinking,' he fired, before coming to a standstill and gazing at Molly.

'She could do it!' Violet stared at Pascal, as if both were on the same page.

'I could do what?' Molly asked, hiding the leap of nerves at just what might be being suggested.

Pascal took up a rickety wooden chair at the little table. Violet stood behind him with her hands on his shoulders.

'I need you to listen, Claudette,' he said. 'We need your help. We can get word to delay your transport by a few hours. If you agree—'

'What am I agreeing to?'

'We have an operation planned for tonight—'

Molly breathed slowly, trying to calm her heart rate. 'What kind of operation?'

'We're going to cause a break in the chain that will impact the Nazis. What you English would call "throwing a spanner in the works". It will cause sufficient delay that could mean freedom for numerous individuals who can take advantage of the opportunity.' He placed one of the five small keys from the pouch in the palm of his hand. 'We are hoping this one small thing will become a mighty inconvenience to Herr Führer.' Molly and Violet stared at the little key.

'How so?' Molly wondered what it might unlock, or the other four like it.

Pascal spoke slowly. 'It contains the thing that will kill General Heistermann.'

Molly had so many questions but as she took a step backwards her calves bumped into the sofa and she sat down abruptly. She had been prepared to make the drop, but this?

'So that's it? I give him the bag and then what?' she had asked.

'Then you will come home. And you will have done more than enough; transporting the bag is not without considerable risk. The less detail you know of the wider plan, Miss Collway, the less you can tell if asked. Do you understand?'

Pascal carefully unscrewed the shaft of the key, which to the untrained eye looked solidly fixed but was easily removed. He tilted the metal case and out popped a tiny scroll of brown film rolled into a tube with a minute white shape nestling inside.

'What is it?' she asked.

'Poison. He eats this and he dies. *Voilà!*'

'How . . .' she swallowed, 'how are you going to get him to eat it?'

'Well, General Heistermann is a glutton. Violet has prepared sweets for the pig for months now; he can't get enough of them. They will be there as always for him at the Café Hubert and Violet will feed him one; he always has two or three.'

'Supposing he doesn't—'

'Here's the thing,' Violet interjected, clicking the side of her mouth, 'you don't have time to worry about the things that can, might and often do go wrong. You have to make a plan and find a way to carry out your orders. It really is that simple.'

Molly nodded, but in truth really couldn't see it was that simple at all. The blood was rushing in her ears and her mouth had gone a little dry. The stakes had been raised. They were talking about murder and this was about as far from couriering as she could possibly have imagined.

Pascal tipped the poison back into the key and popped it in his pocket.

'Bernadine was supposed to be waitressing with Violet tonight in the back room of the Café Hubert, but she can't make it. We need two of you in there, to look out for each other, but also because two girls serving is the norm. It can get busy and we don't want to arouse any suspicions. No one will think it unusual if Violet brings her cousin in for a shift to help out. All hands on deck when needed, and there aren't too many locals willing to work at the Café Hubert. There will be a plate with six bonbons. Violet will offer him one and he will take one, as he always does, but if on the odd chance he does not, she will eat one herself, the one without poison, naturally, and encourage him that way. If he's smart, he may make Violet eat one first, and she knows to pick the one next to the letter C written on the edge of the plate – the gold lettering of the Café Hubert is stamped on all the china. You're quite clear on this, Violet?'

'I am.'

Molly envied the girl's steady composure.

'So I would be waitressing with Violet?' she asked, putting her own thoughts in order, feeling a throb of nerves, but wary also of these two strangers, who could discuss an act of murder quite so matter-of-factly. She wasn't sure what their reaction might be if she declined to help, now that she knew the plan . . .

'The poison acts within a few seconds and death will be quick once it hits his system. At the first sign of it taking effect, you and Violet will shout vigorously for help, throw up an audible smokescreen, while at the same time you get as far away from him as possible and as quickly as you can – get to the edge of the room, keep your back to the wall and head out of the building. You haven't met him yet, but Jean-Luc and I will be on motorbikes and we will carry you both out of danger. In case things don't go quite to plan, Jacques will be on standby at the end of the main street by the river, in the truck.'

'Supposing—?'

Pascal and Violet both shot her a look, a reminder that they did not want to hear Molly 'supposing'.

She closed her mouth. She had been about to ask what would happen if the General did not fancy a bonbon – what were they to do then?

'Think you can do it? Help Violet, serve food and drinks to the pigs?'

'It would be my honour.' She fixed Pascal with a steady look, as if she had done this kind of thing many times before.

'Good, good.' He breathed with relief.

'If I were you, I would get some sleep.' Pascal nodded towards the sofa before standing and turning towards Violet. They were close, facing but not touching, and yet the energy they emitted almost gave off sparks in the gloom.

Molly remembered what it had felt like to have a man look at her like that, and to know that with no more than a glance you could make a promise that bound you like no other. Her very presence here felt like an intrusion.

'*À bientôt.*' Pascal reached out and ran the pad of his thumb along Violet's jawline before sweeping from the room. Violet slunk down on the sofa next to Molly and placed her hand on her stomach. Molly wondered if she was imagining what it might feel like to have a baby nestling in there and felt a sudden punch to the gut. She would do whatever it took to make the world safer for her baby boy, to create a home and get him back.

Sentimentality is a distraction you can ill afford. She heard the reminder in her head.

Violet sighed and pulled off her headscarf to scratch her scalp all over.

'I would love to wash my hair right now, you know – with lashings of hot water and Pears soap.' She continued to scratch her head. 'I can't remember the way it smells, and that really bothers me.'

'I think your hair looks fine.' Molly meant it.

'Thank you, Claudette.' Violet considered her. 'You look . . .' she began.

'I look what?'

'Angry. Others I've met in situations like this are sometimes wired, sentimental or else afraid and edgy, but you' – Violet held her eyeline – 'you just look furious.'

Molly swallowed. 'I have a lot to feel furious about.'

'Okay,' Violet said, patting her leg, 'we are going to divert you from that anger and pass the time!' She lay back on the sofa and closed her eyes. 'So, Claudette, my sweet, sweet cousin, if you could eat anything right now, *any* food you can imagine, what would it be?'

'Oh.' Molly lay back, matching Violet's position, as if they were old friends in a dorm and not strangers with an unthinkably dangerous night ahead of them. Closing her eyes too, she pictured a white, starched linen tablecloth, set with a china pouring jug and a large bowl with a polished silver spoon. 'I haven't had much of an appetite of late, but I suppose if I could have anything, then it would be suet pudding with golden syrup and piping-hot custard.' Her mouth watered.

'So you're a fan of sweet things?'

'Not really, but in the shelter at night I used to think about suet pudding and golden syrup a lot, especially when I got cold, and I'd imagine upending the whole jug of custard, so the pudding would practically float.'

165

Molly could almost taste the food she had eaten before the war, before she had known love and loss so intense it had shredded her heart, robbed her of any appetite and left her looking so upset and angry it was obvious even to this stranger.

'And what about you?' She turned her head to the side and took in Violet's sharp features, her strong nose and bold brows, not pretty and yet beautiful.

'Oh, that's easy. I think about it a lot too, but for me it's not a pudding but a well-baked jacket potato cooked on the fire with butter and salt. The crispy skin, blackened in places, saved until last, when you can put a fresh knob of butter into it, fold it over with your fingers like a crispy sandwich and eat it in two bites – the most delicious thing you have ever tasted, with puffs of fluffy potato clinging to it like little surprises and the butter, melted and running down your chin . . . And to follow' – Violet turned briefly to face her – 'as you've eaten all the suet pudding with syrup and custard, I'd have blackberries, so plump and delicate that it's impossible to hold them without the dark purple juice trickling in a sweet river down your fingers. I'd push them up to the roof of my mouth with my tongue, where they'd burst and fill my mouth with the dark sweet jewel of fruit that is sharp and like nothing else . . .'

The two girls sat in silence, almost in reverence at the delightful memory of favourite foods denied them both for what felt like the longest time.

'Bloody, bloody war!' Violet huffed.

'Yes,' Molly could only concur, 'bloody war.'

'Pascal's right,' Violet said, settling back. 'We should get some sleep.'

What is your real name? How long have you been here? What have you seen? Are we safe? Where are you from? Do you have family? Do they know where you are?

'Is he your . . .?' Molly asked, forgetting one of the rules: *Overfamiliarity. It's in these small details where danger lurks, and remember, the danger is not only to yourself but also to others who are relying on you.*

As if she hadn't asked, Violet tipped her head back and closed her eyes with her arms folded high across her chest.

Johan had been right about how war changes everything. *Everything.* Here, too, time was compressed. Molly was sleeping on a sofa with a girl she had known for less than an hour and yet who felt like a friend. She *missed* having a friend and an image of Geer floated into her mind. And she thought of how she had fallen in love in one evening and then lost both her love and her child in a mere matter of months. Yes, everything was condensed, squashed into a small, hard ball that could fly through the air faster than you had time to catch it, because the clock was ticking in time with the firing of machine-guns and none of them knew when the day might come that would be their very last.

She was jolted from the sleep that had finally overcome her when the door opened a little while later and Lisette came in, bearing two floral dresses over one arm and a shallow basket with a few items of make-up.

'Quickly!' she said, throwing each of them a dress, without too much consideration, it seemed. 'Do you want something to eat?'

'*Non merci, Lisette.*' Apparently, Violet was in no mood for whatever poor substitute might be offered in place of a jacket potato with butter and salt.

Molly shook her head too, not at all sure that food would sit well among the tumble of nerves that churned in her gut.

Lisette shrugged as she left the room, as if it were of very little consequence to her either way.

Molly held up the dress, a green crêpe de Chine pleated frock with boxy shoulders and a nipped-in waist. The pattern was a sprig in the palest gold with darker blue flowers dotted along the narrow branch and, other than the colourway, resembled cherry blossom. Rising to her feet, she held the dress to her shoulders and took in the scent of mothballs, swallowing the sour query as to whom this frock might belong and where they might be now.

'Oh God, I think this is one of my grandma's cast-offs!' Violet wrinkled her nose at her floral shift with a sash belt that looked as though it should sit low on her hips – if she had any, that is.

'Do you want to wear this one?' Molly held out the green number.

'Oh, you're too kind, darling, but I shall look gorgeous even in my gran's frock!' Violet announced gaily, wrapping the fabric around her body.

Molly laughed in spite of her nerves.

'Are you feeling okay?' Violet asked suddenly.

'I don't know how I'm supposed to feel,' Molly whispered back.

'I'm thinking back to the first time I did a job for . . .' Violet let this trail. 'I was scared, excited, petrified, and then numb with fear – which is a whole lot worse than petrified, but actually easier to hide, so that's a plus.'

'And you know this is my first time?'

Violet nodded. 'I noticed the way you didn't wave when I did, didn't acknowledge me until I'd given you the code. That was good.' She spoke as if impressed and it was encouraging, easing Molly's concern that she might be a complete liability as a novice.

'Right,' Violet said, unbuttoning her overalls, 'time to put on our glad rags.'

ELEVEN

Saintes, Charente-Maritime, France
October 1944
Aged 19

Molly gripped the side of the seat as the truck bounced along the lane in the encroaching darkness. It had been quite beautiful, standing in her finery on the edge of the courtyard at the farm, watching the sun dip as the rounded landscape with its abundant vineyards turned a pleasant shade of lilac with an almost fiery orange sky. She wished she could have seen it with Johan, but then she wished many things. Violet had climbed in deftly and sat in the middle of the long seat, rubbing her hands together as if keen to get on with the job in hand. Molly sat next to her, not quite so keen and wary of what lay ahead. Jacques, still in his straw hat, seemed as indifferent as he had earlier, saying little; he was simply the driver, the farmer. Doing his best and doing his bit right under the nose of the Nazis.

Molly's own shorter hair had been brushed, and the rouge that now adorned Violet's cheeks added fullness to her lips. The evening was close and Molly was sweating. Had nerves not made the breath stutter in her throat, she would have asked Jacques if it was okay to roll down the window. The night was dark now, with only the odd flicker of a naked flame dotted here and there in the distance, as lamps and fires flared on homesteads across the once vibrant vineyards. Even under these terrible circumstances, it was a magical place. As they neared the town, she could see it was brighter, with street lamps lighting the way. This was something she was unused to back in the streets of London. Blackouts meant she had become accustomed to trotting over the pavements with no more than a sense of where she was heading, following the route home by judging familiar outlines and on instinct, as much as anything else. Tripping and stumbling over the potholes and uneven paving slabs, which the powers that be had neither time nor inclination to address when their eyes were on a much bigger prize.

Violet exhaled slowly, tapping her fingers on her thighs, the only indication she might be nervous. The truck slowed on the edge of the market square and the flag above the mairie seemed to have grown since Molly last saw it. The crimson flutter of the fabric filled the sky and cracked the air above them. Groups of occupying soldiers stood gathered on the street corners and the intersections of roads and walkways. The two women prepared to jump down from the truck and onto the cobbled street and Molly felt the icy needle of fear in her veins.

'Fear is a state of mind and one you cannot allow yourself to dwell on. Fear can give you away and fear can trip you up, so stay focused and never forget that you are doing something for the greater good. Think about your own personal motivations; remember why you are here and what we are fighting for . . .'

Unbidden, Molly pictured her baby boy and the way it had felt lying next to him in that single bed, the feel of his warm little body next to hers and the complicit nature of his slumber, him trusting her to be the very best custodian of his safety. She balled her fingers into fists. She would, she knew, always remember what she was fighting for: to keep her baby boy safe, to bring him back home to her.

Violet turned to her. 'Fun, remember? We are here to have fun. Life is funny.'

Molly laughed for real at the utter absurdity of the sentence.

No sooner had their feet touched the cobbles than Violet let out a loud laugh, her head thrown back and her eyes closed. She linked arms with Molly and the two tripped along, whispering, giggling and stopping only to twirl in a dance move, much to the amusement of the soldiers, who paused from their smoking, leaned on their guns and smiled or whistled in appreciation. Molly had to concentrate hard on moving her legs, which felt like lead, as if her body was intent on pulling her in the opposite direction of danger.

An old woman in a black headsquare with a large basket over her arm came towards them along the pavement; she was muttering under her breath, her face contorted with anguish. It was an expression Molly recognised, familiar to many in these turbulent times: the face of someone who had had their heart shredded and their hopes smashed but was powerless to seek redress.

'Whores!' the woman hissed.

'Kiss my arse!' Violet's response was fast, fierce and believable. It was only at close quarters that Molly could see the pain in her associate's eyes, belying her cocky response.

Two soldiers within hearing distance laughed loudly. Violet blew them a kiss.

The Café Hubert was busy and loud in the evening. The outside seating area occupied earlier by a few tables and chairs was now far busier – bustling and almost standing room only. A skinny unshaven man with an accordion sat with his legs splayed on a rickety canvas-slung stool, pumping out a mournful tune, his eyes closed and his head tilted. Molly could only imagine that in his mind he was anywhere but here, possibly with his true love in a place with no occupying soldiers . . . These loud and boisterous soldiers were red-faced men with caps askew and unbuttoned tunics.

Swilling red wine, beer and pastis, they grabbed snacks from trays passed around at head-height by a waitress who was pawed from all sides. She didn't flinch, suggesting this was the norm. Molly locked her jaw, knowing she was about to enter the lion's den. She could feel the slight tremble in her limbs. A jolly man with a white apron tied under his ample chest called across the pavement, 'Violet, Claudette, you're late!'

'*Bonsoir, Bernard!*' Violet laughed and quickened her pace towards the café.

Molly felt the eyes of several men upon her.

'*Na, hallo, meine Süsse!*' one of them called. Taking her lead from Violet, she managed to laugh a little.

Bernard led the two of them through the throng and into the café, where it was quieter. A handful of women sat at a tall dark bar with a zinc top, some smoking alone, others gazing into the blue eyes of German soldiers while their hands snaked up the leg of their field-grey woollen trousers and came to rest on taut thighs.

Bernard walked quickly past, seeing nothing, hearing nothing. He opened a low door of pitch pine with a heavy iron latch. Through here were more tables crowded with Nazis, these ones wearing rather grander uniforms adorned with shiny buttons and chains, black crosses and medals, while nearly all of their high-peaked officer's hats now lay carelessly abandoned on the tabletops. The sight was enough to make Molly's blood run cold.

'*If you feel you might be losing your nerve, remember that these are the men who take orders from the very top and who give the orders that mean the loss of British lives, and that's happening every day to people just like you and just like me.*'

A small makeshift dance floor sat at the back of the low-ceilinged room, the air thick with smoke. Music came courtesy of a gramophone which pumped out a scratchy but passable beat, enough to get a few feet tapping, and one officer was even on the dance floor with a young woman – a really very young woman. Molly watched as they spun and spiralled away and then back to each other, arms around waists, cheeks flushed, sweat gathering in damp pools at their backs and armpits and smiles lighting up their faces, as if it were any other dance in any other dimly lit hall in any other part of the world – as if outside this room their families did not spout malice behind closed doors and wish harm on the other. The girl's shoes were too big, buckled up around her slender ankles, her dirty little feet sliding with each step, and it saddened Molly more than she could say.

'*You know, Marvellous Molly, I should tell you now that if you don't immediately say no to a dance, I will always assume it's a yes . . .*'

'Claudette!' Bernard called sharply. He reached for a large tray on a sideboard in the corner and handed it to her. On it lay small parcels of golden pastry that smelled like heaven; she could make out undertones of cheese and a herb that was new to her. Her mouth watered – food like this had never been on the menu at Old Gloucester Street, war or no war.

'Serve our guests,' Bernard instructed her curtly. Molly took the tray and approached a table, watching as the men glanced from the pastries to her face and then back again, their eyes closing briefly in pleasure as they crammed their mouths. Their harsh German staccato and their close proximity made the hairs stand up on the back of her neck. This was the hated sound of the enemy which had blared from the wireless set occasionally at home – the sound of the Führer himself.

'Ah, General Heistermann!' Bernard called his name, as much to alert them to his presence, Molly realised, as to give the big man the entrance he no doubt expected. 'Your table is ready!'

She carried on handing out her dainty morsels, with one eye on Bernard, whose obsequious manner was really quite repulsive. The General shrugged the black leather coat from his shoulders and folded it carefully over the back of his chair, placing his neatly paired gloves in his upturned hat on the tabletop. Bernard beckoned for a waiter to bring a bottle of wine and some glasses. The General called forward a lackey, who poured a little wine and sipped it before swilling the bottle, holding it up to the light bulb and doing the same again. Satisfied, another glass was filled and the General glugged the glass of red before Bernard hastily rushed to refill it. Two officers now joined the General at the table and the three drank, elbows on the table, heads together, deep in hushed conversation. Bernard clicked his fingers and motioned for Molly to offer her tray of food to their esteemed guest.

'Monsieur?' she prompted, lowering the tray, and the General looked her full in the eye. Molly was convinced there was a moment when her heart actually stopped and all the blood left her body.

The General waited for his manservant to test the safety of a pastry before picking one himself with his neatly manicured fingers and popping it onto his tongue. And then he smiled at her and she smiled back.

'*Wie wär's mit einem Tänzchen . . .? Na, hmm . . .*' He clicked his fingers. '*Tu aimes danser?* You like dancing?'

Molly had understood the first time; her German was as good as her French.

'*Oui.*' She knew enough not to refuse. Her voice was not as small, as she had feared. Bernard took her tray and she watched as the General slowly rose to his feet.

'I like your dress.' The General's eyes roved over her body and, despite her fear, Molly understood that playing this part was her way of helping the war effort, her prize being when it was all over and she got Joe back. And if anything *should* happen to her, then at least she knew he would be intensely loved by Joyce and Albert. She thought of the accordion player outside and followed his example, briefly closing her eyes to picture the man she had loved and lost.

'*Merci.*' Her voice was much quieter this time.

Herr Heistermann led her onto the dance floor, his large paw on the small of her back and her hand inside his, waiting for the music to change. She caught Violet's eye and caught the faintest flicker of concern on her face and the tension in her jaw. This was not the plan. There had been no mention of dancing.

'*A good agent will improvise, adapt and overcome, but always with the endgame in mind. Don't forget: the plan is the plan until the plan changes. No matter how many deviations or interruptions are thrust in your path, the plan is always the plan.*'

The gramophone sparked into life and a Schubert waltz filled the room. The General moved slowly and gracefully for a man of his size, whisking lightly across the floor. Molly let herself be guided by the firm hand on her back and the defined movement of his legs. It was agony being held by this man whose comrades had killed Johan, had made the world ugly and unsafe and caused her to be parted from her son. There was, however, no option other than to push the ball of fury and revulsion down into her gut and get on with the job.

She blinked, shutting out the image of the last man she had danced with.

Forgive me . . . Her thoughts flew, she hoped, to wherever her beloved might be.

As if in honour of some unwritten rule or in reverence to the General's status, no one else came to join them on the floor and the two danced alone until the end of the record with the eyes of everyone in the room upon them. Molly felt exposed and conscious of her every movement. As the last notes faded, the General raised her hand to his mouth and she felt the brush of his lips on her skin. She cursed the bloom of tears in her eyes, wanting to erase the memory of the contact, hating that he had kissed any part of her. He was the enemy, a foul and powerful enemy. She knew, however, that to wipe away his touch or release the words of disgust that trembled on her tongue would at the very least be provocative. The Walther P38 in his holster seemed to catch the light, a reminder that it was only the twitch of a finger away and that he would no doubt have little hesitation in aiming it at her.

'Never underestimate just how dispensable you are. To all parties. It simply has to be that way.' The Major's words had had a profound effect on her, so low was her mood, with her own expectations of happiness so entirely shattered that the prospect of being dispensable hadn't frightened her at all, in fact quite the opposite. It was, as ever, only the thought of reunion with her son that kept her fighting day by day.

General Heistermann appeared moved, clearly misunderstanding her brief flash of emotion, and he smiled at her.

'What is your name?'

'Claudette.' She kept her eyes on the floor.

'Claudette,' he repeated with an unexpected softness to his tone, clicking his heels with a slight bow.

Evocative of everything Molly hated, this was enough to galvanise her into action. She gave a half-curtsey based on little more than intuition and then crossed to the sideboard at the rear of the room to collect a carafe of wine. On the way, she passed Violet, who now held a small white china plate in her hand, the edge rimmed with two gold lines and the words 'CAFÉ HUBERT'. The two barely exchanged a glance.

Violet held the plate aloft and walked jauntily to the table where Heistermann and his cronies were again reaching for the wine. Molly remembered her instructions and made her way slowly to the table by the door. Bending forward to refill the glasses of the officers who were seated, she felt the man to her left slide his hand up the back of her leg. It came to rest at the top of her stockings. Her instinct was to yell at him, to punch and snarl, but instead she played the coquette and slapped the man's hand.

'Naughty!' she giggled.

The men at the table laughed. Herr Heistermann glared in their direction and the officer removed his hand and sat up straight. The wave of gratitude she felt towards the General was conflicting and momentary, quickly crushed by the rocks of hatred that lined her gut.

Only time could offer any clarity as to what happened next. Time and the careful piecing together of each small fragment of information that she would gather from the furthest corners of her memory, rebuilding events until she was certain she had correctly laid it out in her mind, like a jigsaw that revealed the picture only when finished. And how she *wished* it had been a puzzle, quickly dismantled, easy to forget and shut away in a box. Now, alongside the faces of her beloved boys, Johan and Joe, Molly knew she would forever see the interior of the Café Hubert and what followed. The whole frightful thing unfolded in less than three minutes. Three short minutes that would change lives for ever. But that, she knew, was the nature of war.

V2 hits Chiswick! Three dead!

Violet bent forward. Molly noticed how she had unbuttoned the top of her frock to reveal a healthy glimpse of bosom.

'Good evening, Herr General.'

'Ah, Violet, and how are you?' He smiled at her trustingly.

'Awfully well, thank you!'

'And what do you have for me tonight?' He grinned, his eyes bright, as they passed over her delectable sugar-coated candies.

She held her plate towards Herr Heistermann, who without any further prompting reached for a sweet, one of five pre-loaded with the poison Molly had brought from London. Instead of putting it straight in his mouth, he waved it in his fingers as he chatted to his colleague, labouring a point before calling to his lackey to come and take one. Violet appeared perfectly cool, but her fake smile was telling. She watched as the lackey took a sweet, and tried to hasten things by selecting the one that was untampered with, popping it into her mouth with sheer teasing audacity, chewing slowly and closing her eyes momentarily as she swallowed. The whole display was enough to make anyone want a sweet. The men at the table and the lackey laughed at her impudence.

Molly watched the lackey bring his own sweet to his lips. Her hands were shaking and time seemed to run slow as she watched him slowly, slowly . . . Suddenly there came a loud shout from beyond the pine door, followed immediately by more yelling, screams from one or two of the women and then gunfire. Molly felt her heart leap in her chest; her fear was like a note in her mind – high and shrill. Driven by instinct, she jumped back against the wall, next to the door and its heavy brocade curtain, as every soldier in the room jumped to his feet, quickly and instinctively reaching for his firearm. She wanted to make a run for it, but all her movements seemed to drag through a thick treacle of fear. She watched as the lackey dropped the sweet to join men from the nearby tables in a protective ring around Herr Heistermann. Violet seemed to have frozen, the plate of bonbons still in her hand.

The door to the back room slammed open, missing Molly by inches. Her legs almost giving way beneath her, she was rooted to the spot, fighting an overwhelming desire to urinate.

Two German soldiers came into the room, dragging what she took to be a weighty sack. Only when they dumped their cargo and Molly saw it hit the deck face down, arms which in life would have been raised to protect the face before it smashed onto the flagstones lolling at the sides, did she realise it was a body.

The leg lay partially shattered, revealing the pale gleam of bone; the set of the leg was so odd it made her gut churn, but not as much as the back of the head, which was a red, gooey mass. Molly found it hard to look away.

The soldiers were shouting loudly and, in the melee and with her mind reeling in shock, she found it hard to decipher some of the words, but one was clear enough:

'Resistance!'

The shouted word made her bowels turn to ice. One of the officers hooked his foot under the body and kicked it over until the face was visible.

The breath caught in Molly's throat. She looked immediately from the body on the ground to Violet, still motionless in the middle of the room, as she too stared down at the body and the unmistakable handsome face of her beloved Pascal.

Oh, dear God, no! No no no!

Molly remained frozen. Her heart told her to go to Violet and take her in her arms, but a small voice of reason was telling her not to give herself away. As far as anyone knew, she was not involved here, did not know this man. Violet seemed to sense her stare. She looked up and for no more than seconds she and Molly locked eyes across the room, as both understood in that moment that, although friends for the briefest time imaginable, they were now powerfully and irrevocably linked by this event.

The Nazi officers began to rally, running from the building with weapons raised. The General, back in his hat and authority restored, barked orders. One of the soldiers grabbed Bernard and threw him to the ground, hitting him full in the mouth with the butt of his gun. Molly saw two little white squares tumble from his bloodied mouth and roll along the floor. Bernard's teeth: a small part of him that was to be trodden underfoot in the panic that now ensued.

Violet gazed on the face of her love and let out a cry of distress. Herr Heistermann lifted his pistol and aimed it at her.

No! Molly shouted in her head. 'Herr General!' she called loudly and, miraculously, he looked in her direction, his expression quizzical, as the muzzle of his gun drooped. It was barely an instant, but that was all that was needed.

Almost in slow motion, Violet grabbed two of the sweets from the plate. Molly watched as she threw them in her mouth, powerless to stop her. Knowing that to intervene now would only make things worse, further muddy the chaos, not to mention her overriding thought that she had a child who relied on her survival.

With Herr Heistermann now being bundled out of the back door, Molly remembered her training and planned for her exit.

'You are much harder to hit if you drop and keep low, out of sight, out of range, behind objects or walls or cars. As low as you can, but always moving towards the exit or a safe place to wait it out.'

On her belly, she slid under the curtain and out of the door, crawling behind the high bar in the main room, where she rose up onto her hands and knees. She kept going, head down, picturing the truck with Jacques in it, waiting for her, and thinking of Joe, who needed her to arrive home in one piece. Her body moved deftly now, but in her head she flinched, as if expecting to feel the sharp crack of a bullet against her bones any second, or the rough grip of a leather glove on her skin. She shook her head in an effort to remove her last image of Violet, who, having bitten down hard on the bonbons, had thrown her head back and fallen to the floor, landing on top of Pascal. The sounds she had made were ones that Molly knew would haunt her always.

Somehow she made it outside, slipping out into the darkness just as everyone else was dispersing or trying to get inside the building. Every second she survived felt like a small triumph, and as her adrenaline soared so did her courage and this gave her a strange sense of calm. Standing in the shadows behind the shutters of the frontage, she looked down and spied the older woman who had served her only that morning, coiled into a ball with her hands over her ears, her knees up to her chest and her eyes screwed up tight.

Molly bent down and touched her shoulder, feeling every inch of her tremble.

'You're okay, you're going to be okay. When you can, get as far away from here as possible. Go home.' The woman looked up at her with eyes as big as saucers and nodded.

Molly scanned the pavement ahead of her and noticed Pascal's motorbike lying on its side, abandoned. She swallowed the sob in her throat – this was not the time for emotion; she needed to keep her wits about her and stay focused. She noticed suddenly the other motorcyclist: Jean-Luc, sitting astride his bike. Their heads close, he was chatting to a German soldier, who gave him a cigarette. Jean-Luc patted the soldier in return, a backslap that was friendly, jovial, congratulatory, intimate even, and in that split second she knew where she had seen Jean-Luc before, and her heart beat quickly at the realisation. He had been one of the marching men she had seen when she left the station earlier in the day. He had been wearing a red scarf around his neck, a bandage on his head; she remembered his imploring dark eyes . . . but he hadn't been a prisoner at all! He was Jean-Luc, part of the Maquis, trusted by Pascal, and also, she now knew, the mole.

Molly felt sick. It had all been a trap set by Jean-Luc – Pascal had never stood a chance. She looked down the road in the direction of the station and took a deep breath, ready to run to Jacques in the truck, but something stopped her. The information she had was useful, vital even, and so she stood with her back against the wall. Her heart beating in her ears, she then slipped back into the bar and, dropping down, spied the unshaven accordion player of earlier, ducked down at the other end of the counter. He turned and did a double take, before scooting across the broken glass towards her.

'What in God's name are you still doing here?' he said in perfect English, in an accent not dissimilar to her own, which surprised her.

'I know who the mole is. Jean-Luc! I saw him this morning being marched with the prisoners by the Nazis, but he's out at the front now with them – friends!'

'Go! Get out of here – run run run!'

Even as she shuffled back towards the door a Nazi officer grabbed the accordion player's wrists and hauled him out from behind the counter, throwing him to the ground in the way they had with Bernard.

'Know when to take orders. They may come from the most unexpected sources, but you will know when they are to be acted on. Never question them. Simply do as you are told. It could mean the difference between life and death.'

And so she ran.

Still terrified that this was the night she might die, she ran in the shadows, staying within the line of trees or using the shade of buildings to make her way to the top of the main street. Her body sagged with relief at the sight of Jacques' truck parked up at the end of the main road a little way out of town. She banged on the door with the flat of her palms and climbed in with lungs that felt as if they might burst from her ribs. Jacques, she noticed, had removed his straw hat and was weeping silently.

'My son!' he sobbed. 'My Pascal!'

Molly reached over and wrapped the man in a brief, tight hug before slumping down in the front seat, her hand resting on the worn leather where only an hour ago Violet had sat, looking beautiful.

At the drop-off point, she and Jacques nodded a tearful goodbye.

Quite overcome by all she had seen, Molly slept on the train, exhausted, as if her body had needed to switch off. And before she knew it, as day began to snake over the horizon, she was running towards the light aircraft, barely visible in the half-light. The sound of the plane engine as it rose high into the sky was something she would never forget.

It was intensely cold in the plane. She huddled inside the sheepskin jacket the pilot had thrust at her with the command to 'put it on'. He had then remained silent throughout the journey, but when she touched down on the Kent coast Mr Malcolm was waiting in his customary coat and hat, with a cigarette in his mouth and his hands thrust deep in his pockets.

'Welcome home, Miss Collway.'

He handed her a blanket, which she wrapped around her shoulders before trembling in the back of the jeep all the way home to London.

Molly climbed the stairs of her digs in St Pancras and fell into bed, still wearing the pretty dress she had put on in the old farmhouse on the outskirts of Saintes. The same dress in which she had danced with the General. Finally her tears came and her body shook, clinging to the bedclothes and trying to stop the sensation of the earth trembling beneath her. She cried for Johan and for her baby Joe, of course. But now she cried also for Violet and for Pascal, recalling the way he had run his thumb along the jawline of the girl he loved and how he had looked at her! Molly cried at the horror of seeing his bloodied body lying slumped on the floor; and the last look Violet had given her before biting down on the poison; and then the sight of Violet's face, head thrown back, before she toppled . . . The poison Molly had carried to her in France. The key. She herself had been the key and the task had been given to her because she was just what they were looking for: someone almost broken.

TWELVE

'It's so good to hear your voice!' Molly stood in the telephone box and could tell Joyce was smiling down the phone. It made her smile too. She was glad to be back on home soil. In the week since she had returned, the events that had occurred in the Café Hubert seemed more and more surreal. She buried them and it was only when nightmares yanked her from sleep that she was forced to relive the heart-racing horror of what she had seen.

She had walked the route to Whitehall for her debrief with Mr Malcolm, Mr Greene and a Mr Markham, looking at the people she passed in the street, ordinary people like her, all going about their business as best as they could in this time of war, except that she now carried a secret on her tongue and in her thoughts. She had been at the very heart of the conflict, smuggled poison, danced with a Nazi general and seen a shot man thrown to the floor like mere detritus . . . She would have been hard-pressed to explain exactly how, but she knew she had come back changed, a little hardened maybe to the world around her and with a newly reinforced perspective on the capacity of mankind for wickedness, if that were possible. It strengthened her resolve to get Joe back, to keep him close, safe.

'How's he doing?' she asked, the phone gripped close to her face, ignoring the smell of stale tobacco, no doubt from the breath of the previous occupant, and aware of the background growl of army trucks noisily trundling along the road behind her. She concentrated on Joyce's voice, not wanting to miss a nuance, a breath, when hearing about her baby boy.

'Oh, Molly, he's so sweet, so lovely and growing fast!'

'I bet.' She swallowed to push the arrow of envy back down in her gut, lest it should rise up in her throat and force misplaced words of pure jealousy onto her tongue.

'I was cooking yesterday and he started to fret so I lifted him from the crib and he licked my finger, which had some lemon juice on it – his little face, Molly! He cried! But then, after I'd settled him, he grabbed my hand and went back for more, can you believe it? Albert says he's going to love a good gin and tonic when he's older.'

Molly tried to laugh, but the thought of him crying and, worse somehow, being comforted by someone other than herself was hard to hear. Not that she wasn't grateful to her sister and brother-in-law – she was, immensely – but still she felt the desperate need to hold her baby and to remind him that she was his mum.

'And he took to the formula milk okay?'

'Oh, absolutely. He guzzles it, no problems whatsoever.'

'That's good.' She was delighted that her boy was thriving, but felt also the bite of redundancy at her throat – happy that he was doing well without her, while at the same time hoping that he might when reunited be reminded of the breast that had fed him. 'I do miss him, you know.' She bit her lip.

'Of course you do, darling. And he misses you, as do I. Not much longer now.' And just like that, sweet Joyce knew what to say to bring comfort and reassurance.

'Yes, not much longer.'

'Where are you working? What are you up to?'

'Starting a new, erm . . . a new assignment, immediately. So all good.'

'Righty-ho. Well, take care of yourself, Little Moll, and I'll take care of your little man.'

'Love you, Joycey.'

'And we love you!'

'Can you put him on the phone?'

'Yes, of course! Hang on a mo'!' There was muffled background noise and then came the unmistakable sound of Joe's sweet burble and his snuffly breathing.

'Hello, darling! Hello, Joe!'

His wail was loud and instant.

'Sorry, darling, he's not that keen on the phone, it would seem.' Joyce smoothed over the cracks.

Molly hung up, determined to get him back as soon as was possible. No matter how necessary, she could see this separation was damaging to their relationship. And she didn't like it one bit.

The debrief led by Mr Markham had been intense and detailed until she felt quite irritated at the prospect of going over it yet again.

'Did you see Jean-Luc make contact with any of the soldiers as they were marched out of town that morning?'

'No.'

'And Pascal never raised his suspicions to you about Jean-Luc?'

'No.'

'Did Pascal or Violet mention that Bernadine was in a relationship with Jean-Luc?'

'No, but I guess that would explain why she cried off that evening, if she knew something was afoot.'

'So you believe Bernadine had prior warning and was maybe allied to Jean-Luc?'

'No, I'm not saying that. I don't know her and I don't know them. I never met her.'

'Could we just go over it again?'

'Yes, of course.' She kept her composure and sipped at her tea.

It did nothing for her mental well-being to keep reliving every small detail of such a harrowing experience. On day two and with a different approach altogether Mr Markham asked her directly, 'How do you think you coped with the role in Saintes?'

'I think I coped well. I improvised and was adaptable and did what was asked of me.'

He nodded and looked briefly at Mr Malcolm and Mr Greene. It unnerved her and made her feel judged, as if she had not done as well as she had thought.

'How have you been sleeping since you got back?'

She met his gaze, hoping he didn't catch the fear that must surely have flickered over her face. 'I don't sleep well, but that was the case *before* I went to France and will probably be the case for a while now I'm back.'

'I see.' He lit a cigarette and flicked out the match with his thumb and forefinger. 'Would you be interested in undertaking another job?'

'Similar to . . .?' she started.

'Yes, similar to but not the same. Again in France – Paris, to be exact.'

Molly sat up straight and folded her hands in front of her on the tabletop, feeling the pull in her gut to hold her boy. 'The thing is, Mr Markham, I want to work. I *need* to work and I want to do what I can for my country, but I am also mother to a baby boy.' She felt simultaneously emboldened and proud to be voicing it out loud.

He nodded, as if this was not news to him.

'And I would prefer not to be put at risk in such an obvious way. I know there's danger in simply walking down the street in London at this time – who knows what's around any corner. We are, after all, at war.'

'Indeed.' He took a deep drag and walked to the window, listening to her as he peered down to the street below.

'But I would prefer to minimise that risk while doing my duty and furthering my career, if that were at all possible.' She felt conflicted, wanting to do her bit, of course, but at the same time not willing to give her life freely, simply to be another statistic and to leave her beloved boy without either parent.

'There is another role that does not come under my jurisdiction that you might be suited for. A liaison position,' he said to the window, and she got the distinct impression that, with her response, he had lost interest altogether.

'Liaison?' It sounded vague, but then so had the term 'courier' . . .

Molly walked away from the telephone box and did her best to put Joyce and baby Joe out of her mind. She found this the best, if not the only way to go about her day without the weight of longing for her boy dragging her concentration from each and every task. And she needed to concentrate; today she was starting her new assignment, *liaison* . . . She had a train to catch that would take her within a whisker of where her darling boy was living in the Kent countryside. It was this kind of thought that was derailing and she shook it from her head.

Her new role was indeed different and, while outwardly calm in her neatly pressed blouse, soft cardigan, calf-length skirt and sensible laced shoes, her mind was racing and she sincerely hoped she had the reserves to deal with whatever lay ahead. The man who had briefed her, Mr Allan, had been very specific.

'Not everyone feels inclined to mix with those who are considered to be on the wrong side of this war—'

'And you can hardly blame them!' Her reaction had been raw and unfiltered as she pictured the red and black flag fluttering over the façade of the mairie and heard Mrs Duggan forming the words . . . '*Very unexpected . . . It concerns her brother, Johan*' . . . This was followed immediately by Joyce's happy tone: '*Albert says he's going to love a good gin and tonic when he's older!*' 'Everyone has a story of loss or hardship. Hate is easy to lasso; it becomes a driving force.'

'Absolutely, but this job is about neutrality,' Mr Allan had stressed. 'It's about liaising with the prisoners of war – a welfare check, if you like. We as a nation are proud to uphold the values set by the Red Cross and the Church; it's about treating people humanely and fairly without letting personal prejudice cloud your understanding of the fact that their needs are the same as yours. One human to another. You don't need to like them or approve of them, and you should try not to judge them. This role is administrative, not emotional, and it requires someone with your level of clearance and your level of German language.'

'Yes.' She had nodded in the end.

'Is that a "yes", you understand the requirement – or a "yes", you will take the job?' he had asked.

'Both, Mr Allan,' she had answered coolly. 'Both.'

'Good girl.' He had smiled and then winked; his response gave her the creeps.

It had been no more than a three-hour journey and Molly found herself in the countryside, where the air tasted sweeter, reminding her of a winter jaunt in an open-top MG. The sky was huge and the smell was of the earth and all it grew, rather than the smog of city life and all the anxious people crammed into its streets. She looked to the horizon of the Kentish land in which she stood and pictured Joe in his pram, generously bought by her sister, and thought how lovely it would be to push him in it today in the garden of England, to meander along the lanes and soak up the sun . . .

'Right, Molly, all set. The car's out at the front.'

'Thank you.' She nodded at Telsie, who so far seemed to be the only downside to her new role. Molly had always worked with smart, witty women such as Geer, Marjorie and Violet, but she had never encountered anyone like her new colleague, Telsie, or, more accurately, 'Telsie the third', as the girl had informed her, 'named after my grandmother and mother respectively'. Telsie was petite, pretty and an insufferable giggling chatterbox. In fact, 'chatty' did not even begin to cut it. She liked to stream her interior monologue on all matters, from what she had heard on the wireless, through what she was going to have for her lunch and what she might have for her supper, to the route her bus took on the way to work and details of who was on the bus, along with any other useless snippets that might pop into her head. Telsie shattered Molly's peace and upset her rhythm. Molly was aware that Telsie wanted to be friends, but preferred to keep their relationship professional. Not only was she unwilling to let another Geertruida into her life, knowing the pain of losing that friendship was too high a price, but the thought of spending any more time with the girl than she absolutely had to was not something that appealed. Telsie hummed a popular ditty as they walked to the front of the station and climbed into the waiting car. The driver was a stern and silent young man in RAF uniform, which suited Molly just fine; she was in no mood to chat. Telsie, however, had other ideas. Leaning forward from the back seat as the car pulled away, she tried to engage him in conversation.

'So what's it like working with the Germans?'

'I don't,' he replied, keeping his eyes firmly on the road ahead.

'Have they ever tried to escape?'

'No.'

'But they could, though, right? I mean, they're only on an open farm during the day with other fruit pickers and workers – what's to stop them wandering off and turning up at some remote village and murdering everyone in their beds?'

Molly felt her pulse race as she pictured the boisterous German soldiers from the Café Hubert barging down Joyce and Albert's front door, Joe screaming and her not close enough to make a difference, to save him. A hot flush of unease crept over her skin at this unwelcome thought . . .

'Can you be quiet, Telsie, just for one second?' she asked. 'Let the poor chap drive and let me gather my thoughts!'

Telsie slunk back onto the rear seat.

'Kent is famous for apples and hops. I was trying to think of what you could make with apples and hops . . .' and Telsie was off again, nattering to herself about something inane while Molly and the silent driver kept their peace.

The car slowed as they approached the entrance to the farm, the wheels clattering over the cobbles, and Molly pictured the fore-court of the farmhouse in France, wondering not for the first time what might have happened to Lisette, Jacques, the young girl at the table prepping rhubarb and the others in the wake of events.

The farm manager, Mr Wilkes, was waiting to meet them. He stood with his arms folded across his tank top, shirtsleeves rolled high above the elbow. A tweed cap softened by age sat over his bushy grey eyebrows and darkly tanned face. Spotting his grimy hands, Molly was thankful he didn't offer a handshake.

''Bout time. You're late!' came his bellowed welcome.

'We were at the mercy of the railway timetable, I'm afraid,' she said, smiling sweetly. He ignored her.

'Come on, let's get this over and done with,' he called over his shoulder, as though their very presence was at best an inconvenience and at worst an irritation. She marched behind him, with Telsie following.

'Fruit beer!' the driver called after them – either because the answer had only just occurred to him or because it had taken him this long to feel comfortable enough to speak freely, she wasn't sure which.

Telsie waved at him and laughed loudly. 'Yes, of course – fruit beer!'

The driver beamed before disappearing back into the car. Molly felt the smallest twinge of conscience and reminded herself to be patient with young Telsie.

'So it's carrots they're pulling today?' Molly asked, in an effort to engage Mr Wilkes.

'At the moment it is. We have a nation to feed!'

'Absolutely. And my understanding is that the POWs arrive each morning and are collected at night?'

'That's about the sum of it. The wife cooks all the lunches and includes them at the table. Many of the locals won't sit with them, and I dare say one or two extra ingredients might find their way into that lunch, but what can you do?' He shrugged and gave a small chuckle.

'Do you segregate the POWs from the other workers?' she said, stepping surefootedly over the cobbles and onto the grass verge.

'Nope. If a job needs doing, it needs doing. I don't give a rat's arse who does it! But I don't see much mixing, that's for sure.'

Molly quite liked his lack of formality and undiscerning approach. Acceptance and integration without prejudice were cornerstones of their mandate that she could follow, even if she didn't feel this in her heart.

'Do you have any cows, Mr Wilkes?' Telsie piped up. 'I love them! I'd love six pet cows. I'd name them all and make them wear bonnets on a sunny day!'

'You're addle-pated, you are!' the farmer shouted, and marched off.

Molly and Telsie smiled slightly in response, neither quite sure whether this was an insult or a compliment. Despite Telsie's many irritating habits, it was impossible not to find the girl's sweet, uncensored world view appealing. Making their way down the narrow path alongside a thorny hedgerow, they came to a clearing that opened onto a wide, ploughed field. Dozens of people, men and women, stood bent among the furrows, hands rooting under the lush green fronds for a firm grip to pull the carrots from the earth, then knocking off the soil and tossing them into large panniers as they moved along the furrow.

'They're due a break about now. I'll call them in and you can have your chat,' Mr Wilkes said, stepping forward and placing two fingers under his tongue, ready to make an ear-splitting whistle. The workers stopped what they were doing and stood upright, before stretching their arms over their head or rubbing at the base of their spine and then walking over to a flatbed truck parked in the far corner; from the back of this, they unloaded a churn and some baskets. Molly, Telsie and Mr Wilkes walked across to meet them. Molly lifted her chin to find composure, aware that she was once again about to engage with the enemy. She noted the marked difference between the two groups, locals and POWs. The locals were a mix of men and women, all with dark hair and rosy cheeks, chatting together with obvious lifelong familiarity in their singsong Kentish tones. The other group, sitting on hay bales dotted around for the purpose, were quiet, blond and muscular, without an ounce of spare fat.

'This is your lot.' Mr Wilkes pointed at them, and her face coloured. Being lumped together with the prisoners in any fashion was not a pleasant thing.

'If you could go and chat to the locals, Telsie – find out their take on things, how it's working, et cetera – I'll go and speak to the Germans.'

Telsie nodded and approached the group. Molly ignored Mr Wilkes and walked over to where the men sat. She had been practising German in her head for days now and it came fairly easily.

'Hello, my name is Miss Collway and I am here today representing the Government and agencies who have an interest in your fair treatment. I'm here to . . .' The words abandoned her as a man who had been working on the far side of the field came over to join his countrymen. He walked in long strides, carrying a mug full of milk and what looked to be a bread bun in the other. Her eyes stayed on his face, and many of the other captured Germans followed her line of sight until they too were staring at him, wondering what was such a draw. It was unmistakable – fair hair with a long fringe that flopped over his face, a strong jaw and broad shoulders – he looked terribly similar to Johan, and it threw her completely. Of course, he didn't really, not close up, but when her eyes and heart were continually searching in crowds for one particular face, because her mind refused to believe she would never see that person again – this was her brain clutching at straws. She swallowed, concentrating on her words.

'I'm here to make sure that you're being treated well and to ask if anyone needs medical attention. Are there any other issues you might wish to raise?' She avoided looking at that particular man's face.

'I have a question?' It was the man with whom she was avoiding eye contact who asked this.

'Yes?' She kept her voice curt.

'We were told it would be possible for post to come through from home, but we are yet to receive anything. Is that because the process is taking time or are the letters being withheld from us?' His voice was quiet, intelligent and yet still with the staccato, guttural edge that put her in mind of so much bad propaganda.

'I will certainly find out for you.' She nodded. 'Does anyone have any other issues they would like to discuss – health or welfare problems?'

A slightly older man put up his hand. 'My name is Klaus—'

'Hello, Klaus.' This introduction caused a small ripple of laughter among Klaus's compatriots.

'And I hate fish.'

'I see. All fish or . . .?' This inadvertently caused even greater mirth.

'We have fish at least every other night, and I hate it. I eat it, but I hate it. Is there anything we can do about that?'

'I'm afraid not. I suppose that's one of the perks of being close to the coast.' She held his gaze and the laughter stopped. She knew many a family in the city who would give a lot for fish and all its health benefits right now. 'I will be here tomorrow and there will be a medic here, too, if anyone wants to meet with him. Thank you.' Molly began to walk away, heading towards Telsie and the group of local farm workers, who were seated on similar bales with their milk and buns, the main difference being the lively hum of conversation that hung over them in a cloud. Telsie, she noticed, was among them with a milk moustache and half a bun in her hand.

'Had a nice chat with them, did you?' a big woman called out, her face lopsided by her smirk.

Molly ignored her. 'Ready when you are, Telsie.'

'Don't know how you can bring yourself to stand and talk with them like they're mates in their 'orrible language! Makes my skin crawl, it does.' Again the woman spoke loudly, and one or two in her band nodded their agreement.

Molly more than understood the woman's hatred, but addressed her calmly and directly. 'I think that, no matter how much troubles or divides us, I hope the people we love who are being held against their will or who find themselves in difficult circumstances all over the world right now are being treated with similar care and compassion, because, after all, they are someone's son, someone's brother, someone's husband.'

'I ain't seen my husband for three years! I bet he's not being given double rations and a comfy bed every night with a cushy bloody job!' She threw the last of the milk down her throat and tipped the drips out onto the soil.

'I did tell her you were all right,' Telsie piped up, and Molly felt happy at the girl's endorsement, but also riled by this unnecessary hostility from the woman, wishing she could flop down beside her, take her hand and look her in the eye to tell her, '*I feel the same! I have lost my one true love and my son is away from me! I understand!*'

Instead, she cleared her throat. 'Thank you, Telsie. I think all we can do is make the best of what is often a trying set of circumstances.' She now addressed the group, who had gone a little quiet. 'We will be back again tomorrow if anyone has any issues or questions that we might be able to help with.'

Molly turned to make her way back to the path and saw the man who reminded her of Johan standing only feet away.

196

He raised his hand towards her. 'Thank you for saying that.'

'It's the truth.' She heard the tut and snicker of the woman behind her.

'Here.' He beckoned her closer and held out his hand. She took two steps forward and reached for the photograph he proffered from the pocket of his shirt. It was a little dog-eared around the edges and with a crease running down the middle, but unmistakably a picture of him crouching with one hand resting on the shoulder of a pretty girl and on her lap a bonny baby boy of about two, his other hand cradling the boy's head. They were in rather a grand garden with a bower of yellow roses in full bloom hanging overhead on a sunny summer's day. The couple were smiling, sharing the joy of their little one . . .

'My wife, Liesl, and my son, Otto. It's my name too: Otto. He's named after me.' He beamed at the picture she held in her hands.

'Lovely.' She handed it back to him, stiffly.

'She will always find a way to write to me and I'm expecting a letter from her with news of my son . . .' He swallowed and let this trail.

'As I said, I will do what I can to find out.'

'Thank you!' he called as she marched towards the path.

'Wait for me!' Telsie called after her, catching up only when she had made it to the courtyard and the waiting car. Molly climbed in and slammed the door, rubbing her hand over her face and trying to gain composure.

'If I could just take a minute,' she said to the RAF driver, who discreetly kept his gaze to the front. Telsie jumped in the back and the whole car juddered.

'Well, that went well, and I thought they were quite a nice bunch. I wouldn't worry too much about it.' Telsie looked at Molly and took a sharp breath. 'Molly! What's the matter? Are you feeling poorly – shall I fetch someone? Do you want some tea?'

Molly shook her head.

'Do you feel faint?' Telsie asked, continuing to press her. 'You look very pale. I fainted once. Hated it.'

Another day, another time, and Molly would have pointed out that no one actually liked fainting. But her thoughts were far too preoccupied for that. She took the handkerchief offered by Telsie and wiped her eyes.

'It's okay, Molly. Don't cry.' The girl scooted closer to her side.

'I'm not crying!' Molly sniffed, unwilling to open up and invite further comment.

'In that case, I think your eyes are leaking a bit,' Telsie said with a sweet smile. Molly looked out of the window towards the farmhouse where 'the wife' would no doubt be knocking up lunch, and she thought of Liesl, who was at home somewhere in Germany with her bonny baby boy, wondering as to the fate of her man. The picture had been like holding up a mirror – a reflection of a life that would never be hers . . .

'Don't be sad,' Telsie began.

'I am sad – I am so bloody sad!' The truth escaped after all.

'I am too,' Telsie smiled and nodded.

'No, Telsie, no, you are not,' Molly sniffed. 'You are Miss Perpetual Sunshine! Always smiling, chatting, singing or humming! Jesus Christ – do you ever just let yourself be silent?' She regretted the words the moment they had left her mouth.

Telsie turned to face her as the car pulled out of the driveway to take them to their digs for the night.

'I'm silent when I'm not at work because I have no one to talk to.' She let this permeate. 'I lost everyone, Molly – everyone. My mother, my brothers, my uncles, my aunts, my cousins and my father, all of them, all gone.' Molly felt sick to her stomach with sadness for the girl and no small amount of shame at having kept her at arm's length. Telsie blinked as if it was still too difficult to voice. 'I was silent in the truck that smuggled me out. I could smell the fuel and it made me feel sick, but I kept quiet, like they told me to. So I came here on my own because the captain wouldn't take me, said I was too small and a nuisance, crying and all that. So I was sent on without them. A stranger brought me here and my whole family was in a boat that got hit, torpedoed. Not one of them survived. Not one.'

'Telsie . . .' Molly reached out and took the girl's hand in hers.

'I know.' She smiled, swiping at her own tears now and grabbing the handkerchief back from Molly. 'Fucking war.'

Molly laughed out loud at these words, so incongruous to the girl's sweet nature. 'Yes, fucking war.'

The two sat holding hands as the car trundled along. Telsie's words were a reminder that everyone had lost someone and that some had lost everyone. She was determined to keep this well-paid job and get her boy back as soon as she was able.

THIRTEEN

St Pancras, London
May 1945
Aged 20

Molly lifted her head from her pillow. It was 3 a.m. A good three
hours before her alarm was set in her St Pancras digs, and yet here
she was, wide awake and smiling at the noise outside her window.
It was no surprise to her that people were out celebrating, of course,
especially when those who had been away fighting and posted overseas began to trickle home from the far-flung corners of the earth.
Over the last week or so, she had in the middle of the night listened
to life beyond the window, occasionally popping her head up to
the curtain to watch the beer-drinking, flag-waving antics of the
passers-by. Everyone shrieking their laughter, giddy with joy at the
fact they had come through, but also excited at the many wonderful
things that lay ahead: all the promises they couldn't wait to fulfil,
written in ink to those they loved while not daring to believe they
might come to fruition. Celebrations were highly charged, as the
returning heroes swaggered the streets arm in arm with sweethearts,
family and friends, declaring they would never let them out of
their sight again, never! Blinded by the novelty of being home,
they seemed not to notice the bomb craters in the roads, the gaps

in the streets where houses used to stand or the many families, like Mr and Mrs Davenport, her old neighbours, crying behind their curtains with mixed feelings: delighted for the safe return of their neighbours' sons, while reminded that their own would never come home. And Molly knew what it felt like to be conflicted in this way. She hated the bitter spike of jealousy that lanced her heart whenever she heard of another lucky soul who was now reunited with his loved ones. Even when she heard that her own dear brother, David, was on his way back, a small voice echoed, '*But not Johan, not my love, never him . . .*'

She watched the faded net curtain flutter in and out on the breeze. There was much joy to be taken from waking to the light shining through the glass and to see the moon and stars twinkling overhead, without any need now for the blackout. The lamplight sparkled on the brass button that lived on her bedside cabinet and she sighed with contentment. No longer did she have to wonder whether the bed in which she slept was in the direct path of one of Hitler's bombers or try and calculate how long she would be allowed to sleep before that darned siren sounded and she would have to traipse down to the Anderson shelter at the end of the road, wearing her coat over her nightclothes and with a blanket around her shoulders. And moreover, Joe was safe! He had survived the war and would be coming home. Her heart lifted at the thought. It was a new dawn and a new age, where fearful routine, safety checks, broken nights and anxious days of privation could be consigned to history, along with the names of the departed, etched in remembrance on soft stone walls and memorials throughout the country. There was a new lightness in people's mood, as if everyone finally had the freedom to breathe – freedom to shout and laugh out loud! And it was only with this new chapter upon them that she realised how in wartime the nation had been whispering, holding its breath, afraid of being overheard or of drawing the enemy in their direction. The atmosphere was now something close to euphoric, an outpouring of relief, joy and hope that even she could sense from her bedroom on the upper floors of the dark brick building in St Pancras. It had been a mere three weeks since Hitler had committed suicide, with Germany surrendering soon afterwards.

Molly, like the rest of the British population, certain at last that war really was coming to an end, felt the weight lift from her shoulders and enjoyed the sweet sleep of sheer relief. Her first thought was that it was safe to bring Joe back to the city, and reunion with her boy was all she had dreamed of. She gazed now around her room: it was far from a palace, but she would make it warm and cosy, plus it was only temporary. She had a little nest egg saved that would provide a down payment on a decent rental with a couple of bedrooms. She pictured a pale blue room for her son with aeroplanes hanging from the ceiling and a bookshelf crammed with wonderful stories she would read to him. She was tempted to move out of the city, maybe even somewhere with a little garden, not that Joe would mind St Pancras – at nine months, he was still a little baby really, and as long as he was fed, watered and with his mum, what more could he want? She planned on taking him for long strolls around London, showing him all the sights and maybe even paying a visit to her mother, thinking it would be impossible even for the hardest of hearts to resist such a beautiful boy. A lot of water had flowed under the bridge since she had last seen her mother; the world was a very different place and, having crawled from the shadow of war, she hoped her mother's mood might be less fraught, her temper less frayed. Molly had experienced a great deal over the last few months that had made her realise the importance of family. She decided to do her utmost to heal any rift with her mother, to forgive as far as she was able, even if she might never forget, understanding that, no matter how alien or hurtful it might seem, her mother had a right to her views. People had in fact died for that very freedom.

It still bothered Molly that she had received no reply from Geertruida. She struggled to understand how Mr and Mrs de Fries could have a beautiful grandson but never seek to know him. She decided to write again and, if that failed, resolved to travel to Alresford herself. Molly looked at the latest little black-and-white picture of Joe propped up against her bedside lamp, accompanied by Joyce's most recent letter, and again felt a surge of excitement in her veins at the prospect of holding him in her arms in just a few hours. Not that she would bring him back straight away; they had agreed it was best that she spend time with him in his familiar environment, take things slowly, ease him back into her life. Molly knew it would take all she possessed to be patient; her overriding temptation was to scoop him up, hold him fast, smother him in kisses and never let him go!

She thought of the train chugging through the Kentish countryside and hoped that the fair-haired Otto and the many men like him she had met over the last six months would soon be travelling home to see their own baby Ottos and their Liesls. Her second thought was for her job, the nature of which would be changing slightly. Mr Allan had explained that she and Telsie were to be given a small shared office in Vauxhall in a building they had taken over. It seemed that, for hundreds of thousands of the POWs, life as they knew it would not change that much. Some had requested to stay in the UK, knowing their own country had been decimated and its immediate future looked bleak. For others, repatriation would take time and their living and working situation would continue as it had in the interim. The main difference would be the freedoms they were slowly to be granted to come and go in the local communities, which came with a whole fresh set of challenges.

With Telsie in tow, Molly had visited farms and prisons all over the south-east, talking to German POWs. It had taught her that no matter a person's race, faith or political persuasion they all wanted the same thing: to be in the place they called home with the people they loved and where things were familiar.

With sleep now well and truly dispelled by her meandering thoughts, she reached for the letter and for the umpteenth time read the words her sister had scribbled:

> . . . he's been a proper little scamp today! Whipped off his shoes and socks and flung them from his pram. I only noticed when we got home and it was far too late to go searching for them, the little devil. How we laughed! And he loves tomatoes! Can eat whole slices if I let him and does so most inelegantly, cramming them into his mouth, which I think is part of the joy for him. Albert has grown some in the greenhouse and at the first opportunity Joe will crawl speedily from the house, on a mission and off in search of his favourite feast!

Molly felt a small hiccup of inadequacy mixed with nerves – there were not too many tomatoes within grabbing distance of her single room. It only further stoked her desire to find a little house, deciding almost there and then that to be out of town with a garden was the way ahead. Just the thought of it was enough to make her smile.

The train was punctual and the carriage busy, with an infectious hubbub of laughter. Everyone was smiling, war had ended and they were all in on the joke. Albert was waiting for her at the front of the station; he had left the engine running so the car was warm.

A little too warm, in fact. Molly climbed into the front seat with excitement building in her gut. There was, as ever, a low-level awkwardness between herself and her brother-in-law; they really had very little in common other than both adoring Joyce.

'How are you, Albert?'

'Good, and you?' He kept his eyes on the road.

'Great – happier times for us all, thank goodness.'

'Indeed.' He nodded.

She had forgotten how much her sister was the glue for all conversation and how he was a man of very few words. She considered asking him a question about the stamps of the Commonwealth, beer mats or exotic bird feathers, but really didn't want to hear his response. They continued in silence. Just as they were pulling up to the kerb outside the house, he turned to Molly and hesitated in forming his words.

'I . . .'

'Yes, Albert?'

'He's a smashing little chap,' he managed, before settling his hat back on his head and leaping from the car to open her door. She smiled at his words, but was left with the distinct feeling that he had wanted to say more.

Joyce ran from the front door as the car pulled up. Molly noticed Joe was not with her and her stomach sank in disappointment.

'Molly! Oh my goodness, Molly – it's over, my darling. It's finally over!' her sister called out tearfully as Molly walked into her warm embrace.

'It is,' Molly breathed, and closed her eyes with something close to relief.

'It's been a lot to put up with,' Joyce whispered into her hair.

'It has been an awful lot.' Molly smiled wryly at the understatement. Their hug was long and heartfelt, healing.

On his way inside, Albert pulled a deadhead from the rose growing over the porch, as if the two women were not clutching each other in a state of high emotion out on the pavement. It was what he did: calmly went about his business regardless.

A steady hand on the tiller . . .

'He's asleep!' Joyce said, pre-empting her question. 'I tried to keep him awake, but it was his naptime and he gets a little cranky if his routine is upset, so . . .' She pulled a face. Molly again felt a needle of self-doubt in her veins – she didn't *know* his routine and it made her feel anxious.

'God, it's so good to see you! You look wonderful. I love the short hair!' Joyce held her by the shoulders to take stock of her. Molly declined to give any details regarding her chop.

'I've missed you, Little Moll.'

'I've missed you all,' Molly admitted in return. 'I couldn't sleep last night I was so excited to see him.'

'Come up and have a peep!' Joyce took her by the hand and led her across the square hallway and up the stairs, turning left into a little room in the corner of the house, and there, with his arms and legs thrown out at all angles, looking like a fat little starfish in slumber, was her baby boy.

'Oh! Oh, look at him!' Molly had been dreaming of this moment since she had handed him to her sister on that horrible day in Bloomsbury and had thought about how it might play out every time there was a moment spare in her day, and now here she was and here he was! So close she could touch him. It was . . . wonderful. Her hand flew to her throat, where all her emotion seemed to have gathered, and she knelt by the side of the cot, inhaling the scent of him as she studied her little one. Her stomach folded and her tears fell at the sight of this robust fair-haired boy, whose photographs had not done him justice: a world away from the scrawny baby she had handed over all those months ago.

'He's so big!' Weak at the sight of him, she was lost to a huge and overwhelming tide of love which left her breathless.

'I told you,' Joyce whispered. 'Isn't he beautiful?'

Molly nodded. A knot of feelings stoppered any words that might want to make their way out of her mouth. *Oh, Johan! I wish, I wish you could see him! I wish you were here!*

'I've been longing for and dreading this day.' Joyce's voice cracked as she spoke openly, and Molly was glad of her honesty. 'I want you to be with your boy, I do, but oh my goodness, the thought of not being there when he wakes each morning or to give him his bath and put him to bed.' She paused. 'Looking after him has been the biggest privilege and the greatest joy I have ever known, Molly. It has done something to Albert and me, made us closer, made us feel like a little family. And every time I think of how much I shall miss it, I try to remind myself how much *you* have been missing it up until now, and that's simply not right. Not fair.'

'I don't feel I've taken a proper breath until today, Joyce, not since I last held him. I haven't felt complete, as if a part of me was missing. I've had to shut it away and get on with my day, but it's always been there.' It felt odd to be speaking so freely – all these thoughts she'd kept hidden for the sake of her sanity.

'I can only imagine.'

Both women gazed silently down at this small boy whose little tum rose and fell with each breath and whose rounded cheeks were apple-red. Molly was acutely aware that the remaining days of motherhood were numbered for her sister, who could not conceive, and she felt her pain.

'How about a cup of tea?' Joyce said, breaking the silence. 'I always leave the door open so we'll hear him the moment he wakes up.'

Molly rose to her feet and took one last look at her boy before following her sister down the stairs. To be within touching distance of him was almost too much.

'So have you spoken to Mum?' Joyce asked as she filled the kettle and set it down on the stove.

'I called a few weeks ago, but it's hard to have a conversation with her; she's very angry at me still. So it's all one-word responses, which when you're feeding coins into the phone box feels a bit pointless and is beyond frustrating. I also think she's annoyed that I moved out and abandoned her! But I couldn't stay there, Joyce, not after the things she said.'

'I do understand.' Joyce pulled the glass cloche from the top of a very respectable Victoria sponge cake.

Molly watched as her sister flitted across the linoleum floor from cupboard to shelf and back again in an orchestrated dance, her floral pinny swinging as she gathered dainty teacups, a sugar bowl and the milk jug before setting them down on the pretty oilcloth covering the kitchen table. It was a world away from her digs, which she knew were squalid by comparison.

'I'm going to rent somewhere for Joe and myself, somewhere with two bedrooms and more space than I have right now. I think in my mind I thought it would be how it was when he was newborn and we were in my old room at home, but of course I can see now it won't do at all. He needs more . . .' Her eyes took in the comfortable home in which he was thriving . 'He just needs more.'

'He'll settle anywhere, darling! He just wants to be warm and fed and with his mum,' Joyce offered lightly.

'I did hope so, but seeing how big he's got has spurred me on. I'll start looking right away. I'm thinking of going out of town.'

'Oh really, where?' Joyce opened the lid of the tea caddy and added three heaped spoonfuls of leaves into the teapot she had just warmed with half-boiled water from the kettle, before adding another: 'One for the pot!' She smiled stiffly, as if preparing herself for her sister's response – some location that might be a little out of reach for her.

'Maybe Essex, or Kent even – still commutable to London but a bit greener.'

'I think that'd be perfect. Obviously, I'm hoping you plump for Kent – how I would love to have you on the doorstep when we get back from Canada!'

'Plus it means I can get in to see Mum if that situation ever resolves itself.' Molly tutted.

'It will. It absolutely will. You know what she's like – she always needs to have something to moan about and occupy her thoughts; it's just your turn right now.'

'Well, lucky old me!' Molly pulled a face and the two sisters laughed.

'You know David's on his way home?' Joyce scrunched her shoulders in delight at imparting this good news.

'Yes, he wrote to me. Can't wait to see him – but not I bet as much as Clara.' Molly remembered describing her sister-in-law to Johan: '*Clara is hardly what one would call a coper . . .*'

'He might even be home now, but I expect Clara will keep him in her clutches for a while. So by my reckoning that'll mean a sister for Clementine, and another little cousin for Joe about next February!'

Molly noticed her sister's false brightness and it tore at her heart. 'Good for them, I suppose.'

'Oh yes, good for them.'

The kettle boiled and Joyce poured hot water into the pot. Molly noticed her face fall a little, as if once again reminded of her childless state, unlike Clara and David, who might be adding to their brood.

'Albert!' Joyce called along the hallway. 'Tea, darling!'

Molly, too, felt the flicker of envy in her gut, not that she wasn't pleased for David and Clara to be together again or for how happy Joyce and Albert seemed, but it certainly highlighted her single status and made her ache for Johan, who would never be coming home from the war. Albert lumbered into the kitchen and took a seat at the table. Joyce cut him a slab of Victoria sponge and placed it on a plate with a silver cake fork. He took a large mouthful and then brushed away the crumbs, his tone enthusiastic but his complexion a little pallid:

'Delicious! Did Joyce tell you we have a date to leave for Canada?'

'No?' Molly looked up at this news.

'Yes.' Joyce wiped her hands on the tea towel. 'I was going to tell you later. We go at the end of August, so in about twelve weeks.'

'That's not long. Can you get everything done in that time?' Molly sipped her tea, thinking how she would get their new living accommodation sorted as soon as possible, and then spend as much time as necessary with Joe to ease him back into a life with her and the nanny she would secure to care for him during her working hours. Molly knew she would miss her sister, but there was also a faint stir of relief that Joyce would be far away and Molly would be free to learn Joe's routine and establish her own way of mothering. The thought was wrapped in guilt after how much her wonderful sister had done for her.

'I don't need to take much. I mean, the house is being left pretty much as it is; we'll have an agent keeping an eye on it,' Joyce informed her. 'So it's just a few clothes and bits and bobs, apparently, so Albert says.'

The sharp ringing sound of the telephone came from the hall-way and made her jump. Albert and Joyce were the only people she knew with a telephone at home, and if that was the loud, jarring noise they made, she doubted they would ever catch on – it really was quite a racket and disturbed any hope of peace. It was no hardship, she thought, to find a phone box when the need arose.

'That'll be the telephone.' Albert nodded proudly, pushing his plate away from his stomach.

'I guessed as much.' Molly smiled at Joyce, wondering how Joe could sleep through the din.

Albert wandered to the hallway and answered the call. 'It's David!' he said, to summon his wife and sister-in-law.

'Oh my goodness!' Joyce ran to the phone and Molly followed. By the time they reached Albert, he was nodding gravely into the receiver.

'I see, David. Well, we will of course come as soon as we can. Yes, yes, Molly is here, in actual fact. I'm looking at them both and they're very keen to talk to their brother, as you can imagine, but I'll explain. It's good to hear your voice, old chap. Righto, see you soon. I think it'll be tomorrow. Will do. Bye, David, bye.' Albert put the phone back in its cradle as Molly and Joyce stared at him, wondering why they had been denied the chance to talk to their brother, whom they had sorely missed.

'David's in Bloomsbury,' Albert began.

'Bloomsbury? I thought he'd be home in Dorset?' Joyce was as confused as Molly.

'He was – only been home for forty-eight hours; he sounded frazzled. But he received a call from Mr Mason to say your mother is quite poorly. David said she's in a bad way, but she'd asked Mr Mason not to worry any of you. He took it upon himself to call David, thinking it wise to let him know.' Albert took a deep breath.

'Did he say *how* poorly? What's wrong with her?' Joyce asked the questions that were cued up on Molly's tongue.

'Pneumonia, by all accounts. Dr Venables has been attending her' – Molly disliked even hearing the man's name – 'and it's not looking good, I'm afraid. I think we should head into town tomorrow.'

'You can stay here tonight, Moll.' Joyce met her sister's gaze, and right on cue Joe's cries drifted down the stairs.

Molly felt conflicted, still processing the worrying news that her mother was ill, although her whole being was fired up at the prospect of holding her son!

'Come on.' Joyce pushed Molly in front of her and the two climbed the stairs.

Molly could hardly believe it, knowing she would never forget the sight of her son, no longer a tiny baby, but a sturdy boy now, standing and gripping the wooden bars of his cot with his chubby little fingers. He was wearing a sea-green-coloured fine-knit jumper, his napkin of course, and striped knitted socks, his legs otherwise bare. His hair was quite long now, fair still, and swept to one side with sweet kiss curls at the nape of his neck. And his voice! It was the first time she had heard the sweet rounded burble from his angelic mouth:

'Mmm . . . Mama! Mmm . . . Mama!'

Molly took a step forward, laughing, her heart fit to burst with all it tried to contain, as tears of joy pooled in her eyes, but then Joe frowned and looked around her, craning his neck and flexing his fingers. His feet danced up and down and his little arms reached out to Joyce, and in that second Molly realised he was not calling to her, of course he wasn't, he was calling to her sister. Molly sagged sideways until she was leaning against the wall. Joyce walked over and lifted the boy out of the cot and into her arms, with his own little arms thrown around her neck. Witnessing this act, Molly felt as though she had been punched in the heart. Joyce kissed the sweet top of his head and then noticed Molly, gazing at her aghast and shaking her head.

'He . . . he just started saying it.' Joyce's tone was subdued, apologetic. 'I thought it was sweet and funny, but then I was mortified at the thought of you hearing it, and now you have. I've tried

212

to get him to say "Auntie", but he can't say that yet!' She tried to lighten the mood with a small laugh. 'I don't know what to say to you, Molly.'

'It doesn't—' Molly had been about to say, '*It doesn't matter,*' but the truth was, it did matter. To hear her baby boy call another woman Mama was shattering and something she had not considered, unable over the preceding months to envisage him as this growing boy and not the baby she had handed over. Somehow, while she waited for the war to end and the world to catch up with where it should be, recovering from a life put on hold, she had imagined that Joe's life would have been on hold too, waiting to grow and develop once she came back. But of course it hadn't quite worked like that. She shouldn't have been surprised: these were uncharted waters and they were all going to learn as they went along, but no matter. She reached out to touch his fair hair, the colour of his daddy's, but Joe batted her hand away.

'Are you going to say hello to Molly . . . Mummy?' Joyce coaxed, as she held him tight and he buried his head under her chin. He shook his head and closed his eyes; Molly noticed the glorious length of the lashes that sat on his downy cheek. 'Oh, come on, Joe, say hello to your mum – she'd love to talk to you.'

This time Joe hid his face entirely in the folds of Joyce's blouse and he refused to look up. Molly wanted to shriek her sadness at the whole bloody affair! This was her boy! *Her boy!* And he couldn't even look her in the eye. *This* was what the Nazis had done!

'It's . . . it's okay.' Molly kept her voice steady. She knew it was going to take time and concentrated on each breath, loud in her ears, and not the twisting pain in her heart, which felt like it might dissolve. Getting Joe back and being Joe's mum had been her focus since the moment she had watched the car drive from the house on Old Gloucester Street, and even though she understood he was a little baby who had mostly only known the touch of Joyce and the scent of Joyce, it didn't hurt any the less for that. It was, however, up to her, the grown-up, to keep pace with her son and not rush him. She reached out and placed her fingertips on his leg, touching the skin in the little gap where his sock ended and the crease began at the back of his knee.

Joe kicked against Joyce and made a whining noise.

Molly withdrew her hand, fully understanding in that moment that to this little body she had grown, to this little boy made in love, she was a stranger. The realisation was entirely contrary to her deepest desire that he might retain some small semblance of memory of her – it was clear he did not. It was the hardest blow and yet she dug deep and stood tall and even managed a smile.

'He's not properly awake,' Joyce said, seeing her distress. 'He's bound to be picking up on our nerves. He'll settle.' She gave her little sister wide-eyed reassurance in the way she had been doing for Molly's whole life: '*No, Papa isn't crying, silly billy! He's got something in his eye!*' or '*Of course Papa's not going to die, not for a long, long time. Don't worry about a thing – just go to sleep, little angel, and have the sweetest dreams!*'

'Of course,' Molly echoed. 'He's only a baby, and there I am, a complete stranger in his bedroom. I'd certainly get all hot and bothered if there was someone I didn't know in my room!'

Joyce looked a little flustered, as if uncertain whether she should acknowledge this fact or try to patch things over with more well-meant words of comfort. She reached instead for a misshapen knitted toy from the top of an old pine chest of drawers.

'Why don't you show Mummy your lelephant?' Joyce tried again, holding the grey creature in front of Joe. He grabbed it and held it tightly under his chin. A part of Molly wished her sister would stop trying.

'She loves lelephants, don't you, Molly?' Joyce looked at her with eyes that brimmed, as if she understood how entirely heartbreaking this moment was for her sister.

'I really do, but that's okay, Joe,' Molly said calmly. 'You don't have to show me your lelephant, not today. Maybe another day?'

He peered out from under Joyce's chin and looked at her warily, but the fact he was looking at all was a triumph. She winked at him and wasn't sure, but there might have been the smallest hint of a smile on his face.

FOURTEEN

Bloomsbury, London
May 1945
Aged 20

Albert parked the car outside the house on Old Gloucester Street. Molly wasn't sure if the silence that descended over them was because her sister and brother-in-law were equally aware of the last time they had done the journey in reverse – except that on that occasion she had not been in the back of the car, but leaning desperately from the upstairs window with milk in her breasts and a fierce longing in her heart. Or else it might have been that they were about to walk into their family home, where their mother lay gravely ill, and none of them knew quite what to expect.

Joe had slept for the entire journey in Joyce's arms, and Molly, having been an observer of her boy and his routine for the last twenty-four hours, took the opportunity to cradle his little feet in her hands. A little after one in the morning she had heard his call of 'Mama!', followed immediately by the creak of Joyce's bedsprings, suggesting she slept primed for this very possibility. Molly had sat on the side of the bed in the pretty spare bedroom, her limbs trembling with longing to go to her son. She knew, however, that the sight of her, a stranger in the house, might startle him or make him cry and the hubbub at that ungodly hour would benefit no one. Instead, she hugged herself tight, listening as her sister cooed softly, 'Hello, my precious one!' and 'Sleepy time, my little darling . . .', the repeated squeak of the floorboards suggesting that she was rocking him on the spot. His burble was a conversation of sorts and one Molly was desperate to share with him.

'You are quite remarkable, Little Molly, you know that, don't you?' Joyce broke into her thoughts and, leaning across the backseat, squeezed her sister's hand. 'I can't imagine how hard this is for you, but you're doing brilliantly.'

'It is hard,' Molly acknowledged, 'but it's wonderful too. There have been so many times in the last few months when I would have given absolutely anything just to be in his company, to see him close up, hear him, smell him . . . or to hold his little feet like this' – she smiled – 'and so I'm thankful for even the smallest contact.'

'It was true what I said, dear; he will settle. He'll get used to the situation – children are very adaptable.'

'I know.' Molly smiled at her sister. She might have known it, but it was still very nice to hear.

She climbed from the back of the car and looked up and down this street, which was so familiar, although she found it hard to identify why it seemed different today – brighter than she recalled. Was it the much-missed pots of flowers appearing on doorsteps since the end of the war? Mrs Granton-Smythe's house, she noticed, sported a particularly fine display. Or was it the jewel-coloured curtains and sparkling chandeliers now revealed without blackout measures? Molly could now appreciate the smartness of the street, in comparison to where she was living.

It had been many months since she had last seen her mother and her nerves were palpable as Albert climbed the steps to knock on the front door, with Joyce closely behind and Joe still asleep in her arms.

Mr Mason opened the front door, which surprised and embarrassed her. This man, a mere neighbour no more, had seen her in a state of undress with her darling boy nestling at her chest. He had also kept her on the doorstep in her time of need, made her feel small.

'Good afternoon.' He stood back to allow Albert and Joyce to enter, paying particular attention, she noticed, to her boy.

'Good afternoon, Molly.'

'Good afternoon, Mr Mason. So Mum's not well?'

He nodded. 'Not at all, I'm afraid. She's in a grave condition, in fact. Your brother is with her.'

'Well,' Molly said, taking off her coat and hanging it on the hook in the hallway, as she had done a thousand times before, 'we do appreciate your stopping by to help her. Thank you, Mr Mason, it was very kind of you, but don't let us keep you. I'm sure you have your own family to attend to on a Saturday afternoon and I know Mum would be extremely grateful to you for being here when she needed you. That kind of neighbourly support can mean the world.' Molly looked him in the eye.

'Yes, quite.' The man reached for his coat from the newel post and made for the front door.

Molly looked at the portrait of her father on the wall, paying especial attention to the ink pen in his hand, which was now her own.

'I wanted to say, Molly' – Mr Mason turned hesitantly and held her gaze – 'I wanted to say that I thought—'

'Yes?' she asked, wary of what he wanted to say, hoping it was not about Joe, not with him in her sister's arms in the kitchen, only just out of earshot.

'I thought it suited you very well, being' – he paused – 'being a mother. Yes.' He nodded. 'Being a mother. It suited you very well.'

Molly took the compliment and placed it carefully in her heart, letting the warmth radiate and fill her right up.

'Thank you, Mr Mason. I'm just delighted that now the war is over I'll get a chance to practise that skill.' She smiled at him briefly.

'Indeed.' Mr Mason returned her smile and left quietly.

Joyce appeared without Joe, and Molly looked down the hallway into the kitchen, where Albert was now bouncing him on his knee at the kitchen table, feeding him morsels of shortbread, which Joyce had baked freshly for the journey that morning. It was surprising to see the man so relaxed, letting Joe grab his fingers and bite them, as Albert kissed his soft head and sang some random tune to him. It almost felt like a violation to witness this intimate scene of a man like Albert letting his guard down.

'We'll take it in turns to sit with her, darling; it might be too much for Mum if we all pile in. You go first with David and then we'll go up.'

'Okay.' She had for a second forgotten that her lovely brother was here!

Joyce leaned forward and kissed her on the cheek.

It stirred the silt of unease in Molly, to be treading the familiar stairs in these most unfamiliar of circumstances. It was impossible for her not to think about the night she had collapsed onto her bed on the day she found out Johan had died or the moment she had sat on the bathroom floor with Joe still attached to her. Her mother's words on both occasions had sadly been far from what Molly wanted or needed. She tapped on the bedroom door and walked in slowly. The air smelled stale. The curtains were drawn, turning the room into perpetual night, and there was her mother, no more than a small, grey thing propped up on large pillows, her cheeks sunken and her false teeth abandoned. She was sleeping, her breath a crackly but faltering snore.

'Ah, Molly!' David leapt up from the embroidered nursing chair by the side of the bed and strode across the room to take her in his arms. It was so lovely to feel his solid form, no longer a memory or as the writer of hurried letters posted from far away – he was here and he was safe! One of the lucky ones.

'Oh, David!' She hadn't expected to cry, but she did, great big sobs that left her a little breathless. 'You're home!' She held him tightly. 'You're home!'

'I am, thank God.' He bit his lip and he, too, looked a little overcome. She knew better than to press him for details of his time away.

'And you've walked straight into this!' Molly was reluctant to leave the safety of his hug.

'You know, it's more or less par for the course over the last couple of years, lurching from one crisis to the next, so I suppose I'm well trained.' He coughed. 'And I think it would have been worse if I hadn't had the chance to say goodbye.' He kept his voice soft and low.

'She's that bad, you think?' Molly's limbs twitched at the possibility.

'I do,' he offered matter-of-factly, releasing his sister. 'Is Joyce downstairs?'

Molly nodded. 'Is there no chance she might pull through?' she whispered, aware of her mother's proximity.

David shook his head. 'It's pneumonia, and a bad bout. I think recovery is too much to hope for now.'

Molly stared at her mother, unsure of how she should feel and strangely numb.

'Look at you!' He stared at her as if noting the changes, and she did the same with him. She was shocked at how much he had aged. He carried an unfamiliar scent and sported a tan that were it not for his gaunt face and hollow chest might have indicated the high life.

'David, it is *so* good to see you!' She ran her hand down his bony spine. To her surprise, tears bloomed in his eyes, most unexpected from her serious brother, the man of the house.

'Oh, David!'

'I've wanted to talk to you face to face, Little Moll, for the longest time. I started letters, all inadequate, all clumsy and all abandoned, I'm afraid.'

'Well, we're here now,' she said, leaning towards him.

'Yes.' He held her hands. 'I am so sorry for what you went through, Molly. Truly sorry.'

'You know what happened?' She looked towards their mother in the bed, feeling simultaneously exposed and relieved at his admission. No need for pretence or more secrets or, worse, to have to detail the whole awful ordeal.

David nodded. 'Mum wrote to me, horrified of course, ranting even – the very last thing a chap wanted to receive in already trying circumstances, but there we are. I found it easier to get on with the job if I could believe that everything at home was fine. I know Clara kept a lot of her sadness to herself. I'm only now finding out how tough she's found it all. In fact, it's a topic she's quite fond of.' He gave a wry laugh.

Molly felt a new and warm respect for this woman who was her sister-in-law.

'And what Clara doesn't yet know is that I'm going to be based in London during the week. The hospitals are still fully stretched and I'll be of best use up here, but I'll get digs or stay here and, hopefully, Clara and Clementine can come with me.'

'I hope I can see you more.'

'Me too.' He smiled.

'It doesn't feel real, David . . . what I went through,' she whispered, the first time she had openly expressed such thoughts.

'What doesn't exactly?' he asked gently, and she knew this was the voice of the doctor in him and not her brother.

'If I think about the last couple of years, it all feels like too much. Johan was' – she paused – 'he was marvellous, and we were so very excited about our future, and then to find out I was pregnant and to lose him, and then' – she swallowed – 'it felt like the best option in the world to give Joe a good start and keep him safe with Joyce and Albert, and he really is the dearest little boy!' She beamed. 'But now—'

'But now what?'

'I've been with him this weekend for the first time properly and it's been wonderful! But I'm a stranger to him, and I understand that. I expected it, thought I had prepared myself, but I couldn't have predicted how terrible it would feel.'

'Children are adaptable—'

'Yes, so everyone tells me,' she said, drawing breath. 'But it's really brought home how much I've missed. I thought he'd be fine with me in my rooms in St Pancras for a short while, because I still at some level pictured him as a baby, but I can see that he lives in a beautiful home and to drag him to my place wouldn't be fair. I need to find a decent house sharpish and give him the best life I can. We're starting over, really, and it's a little terrifying to be going it alone.'

'It is, but you can do it.'

'I can and I will.' She nodded, picturing a bedroom painted pale blue with aeroplanes hanging from the ceiling . . .

Their mother stirred. David raced to her side and Molly went quickly to the other side of the bed. Her mother's eyes were milky, her breathing laboured.

'Mary Florence,' she managed, her voice weak. 'God sees all and he forgives all.' She paused. 'Forgiveness.' Again she closed her eyes.

Molly looked at her brother, trying to fathom the nature of her mother's words: an apology, maybe – was she seeking forgiveness? Or had she overheard their conversation?

'Cup of tea?' David whispered.

Molly nodded and they left their mother dozing. David made his way down the stairs and Molly walked to the end of the corridor and slowly opened her old bedroom door. She ran her fingers over the writing bureau and then opened the wardrobe doors, digging underneath the sheets of newspaper placed there to catch the dust. And there it was: a letter, unopened, unsent and addressed to Lieutenant Johan de Fries, marked 'Personal Correspondence'. She brought the envelope to her lips and pictured the words written inside:

I so wish the news could have come from my mouth into your ear and then my lips could have touched yours, but this is the next best thing, a letter.

Molly popped the letter in her pocket and crept back along the hallway. She could hear the sweet tones of Joyce and David, reunited, floating up the stairs as she stepped into her mother's room and slowly took a seat on the mattress by her side.

'I do forgive you, Mum,' she whispered, 'and I hope you forgive me.' Bending forward, she gently kissed her mother on the forehead.

'Two . . .' her mother managed, her voice gravelly, 'two grandchildren . . .'

'Yes. Yes!' Molly smiled, stroking the soft, crêpey skin on the back of her mum's hand. 'You have two – Clementine and Joe.' She felt the smallest pressure from her mother's fingers in return, a hug of sorts and the very best gift her mother could have given her, legitimising and accepting her grandson. It meant everything to Molly and filled her with confidence that she could and would be the very best mother to Joe; she would make him a wonderful little home.

Molly looked up at the sound of Joyce at the door.

'Oh, look at her,' Joyce sniffed, slumping down in the chair David had recently vacated. She took their mother's other hand and held it to her cheek. 'Isn't it wonderful to see David?' Joyce whispered.

'It really is,' Molly could only agree, as she slowly stood and left her mother and sister together.

The kettle, she noticed, was already set to boil on the stove down in the kitchen. David sat at the square table where Molly had eaten more than her fair share of lonely suppers. She thought of the night she had neglected to come home for brawn and pickles: *One drink! And I mean it, one.*

'Albert's taken the little one around the block for a bit of fresh air. He's a dear little thing, Molly.'

She smiled at her brother. 'Thank you.' Her mother's words had given her confidence; only yesterday, she knew, the same phrase from her brother would have left her unsure of the protocol, wondering whether or not it was her compliment to accept. She made the tea, reaching for cups, tea strainer, milk and whatnot with the ease of someone familiar with the kitchen. To herself she gave her great-grandmother's dainty china cup decorated in forget-me-nots.

'Poor old Mum.' She looked around this kitchen, where the poor woman had spent so many hours of her life, her touch on every inch of it.

David nodded. 'I've seen so many young men who would have loved the privilege of dying at an old age, safe and warm in their family home' – he paused, pinching the bridge of his nose – 'so I know how fortunate she is, even though it's sad for us.'

'Of course.' She thought, as she often did, of Violet.

David shook a cigarette from a packet and lit it, inhaling deeply. He offered her one.

'No, thanks, I don't. Someone put me off at a very young age.'

David laughed. 'How old *were* you?'

'About nine!' she tutted. 'I was fascinated, watching you smoke out of the attic window. I thought it looked very cool and so when you passed it to me . . .' She pulled a face.

'I remember you coughing like billy-o and retching until you were sick. I felt very bad.'

'You did *not* feel very bad, David! You laughed until you had tears running down your face and all at my misfortune, you rotten thing! Can you imagine me giving a cigarette to Clementine?'

'No.' He grimaced. 'What an awful thought. Do you forgive me?'

'I do.'

They both laughed. His next words, however, were more sobering.

'You know, Moll, what you said about everything being a little terrifying . . . You don't need to live by anyone else's standards, you just have to do what's right for you and Joe.'

'I know that.' She splashed milk into the teacups.

David nodded. 'Are you happy?'

'Happy?' she repeated, as the kettle boiled. 'I think happy would be a stretch, but I'm perfectly *fine* and I'm optimistic that happy is achievable.' She doused the tea leaves with hot water and popped the lid on the teapot. 'I think, like all of us, I'm still processing what I've seen and what I've lost.' She gazed into her brother's eyes, knowing he would understand. 'I've been in some terrible, terrible situations . . .' Again the soundtrack and pictures played in her head, the way Violet had looked at her and that gurgle . . . that appalling gurgle . . .

'Okay, but promise me, Molly' – David's tone was deadly serious – 'that if you are ever *not* fine and the world feels like too much, then please, please promise that you will tell me so I can help you.'

'Okay, David, bossy boots!' She rolled her eyes.

He stood and caught her wrist. 'No, Moll, I am not joking. There's something about you that I've seen before.' He drew breath. 'I think you're trying to contain everything, but sometimes when we try to keep everything bottled up, when we tightly pack our emotions, we crack and it all comes leaking out.'

She stared at him but did not disagree.

'You've been through a lot and, if ever you feel that you're on the edge or things are unravelling, call me or get someone else to call me and I'll help you. Promise me!' He spoke with an urgency that told her he was not prepared to lose anyone else, while his reaction suggested that he considered her unravelling to be a distinct possibility. It scared her more than she could say.

'I promise.' She tilted her head and their eyes met. 'I promise.'

Molly opened the French windows and looked out over the cottage garden. It was a space full of possibilities; bowers heavy with blossom that promised a good crop of apples in late summer, a glorious climbing lilac against the back wall and overgrown winding paths that, when cut back, she could picture a little boy with a strong sense of curiosity hopscotching along to build secret dens in the wide hedging.

'And it's not too far from the local school?'

'No, a ten-minute walk at most. How old is your child?' the man asked.

'He's only a baby, but they grow up fast. I blinked and nine months passed!' She laughed at the truth of this statement.

'Absolutely. Well, this is a lovely family area, quiet. Chelmsford is a good place to live.'

Molly nodded; she could certainly see herself in a lovely little cottage like this.

'I'm assuming that you will need to return with Mr Collway?'

'Oh, that's very sweet of you, but my father died, and I really see no need to bring my brother over; after all, he won't be living here. It would be me and my son, just the two of us.' She held the man's gaze and kept her voice steady, knowing she was going to have to get used to the conversation and face it head on.

'Of course.' The man inclined his head, indicating she had made her point.

'I had intended to rent, but a mortgage does seem to make sense,' she thought aloud.

'Absolutely.' This, she learned, was his habitual word. 'I know a lot of people are wary of mortgages – they think it's debt, but it's more of a very favourable loan from the bank and at the end of the term, you will own the house outright, something you never get with a rental. A home is for life.'

'Yes.' She thought of the house in Old Gloucester Street that her parents had bought when they were first married and which now, after her mother's funeral in three days' time, would become part of the estate, to be divided up between herself and her two siblings. 'What's the price again?'

'It's on the market for eight hundred pounds.'

'That's an awful lot of money.'

'It is a lot of money, but it's also security for the future and a jolly nice place to live.'

'Absolutely,' Molly agreed, feeling her cheeks redden as the word popped out. 'Can I go and have another look at the bedrooms? I forgot to look at the view.'

'Yes, of course, but please do mind the stairs; this is a very old cottage and they're a little steep.'

Telsie jumped up the moment Molly walked into their shared office the following morning.

'So what was the house like?'

Molly was touched the girl had remembered. Telsie's enthusiasm, however, for this and all things, no matter how mundane, was standard.

'Quite lovely, actually. Quaint, with the most glorious garden. I told the bank I'd take it!' She shrugged her shoulders, smiling at her colleague.

'Goodness, that's huge – you've bought a house!' Telsie clapped her hands in joy.

'I did or, more accurately, I am buying a house.'

'A house, Molly! Your own front door, your own garden, your own kitchen – how very exciting.'

'It really is. And a bedroom for Joe and even a spare.'

'Joe, your son,' Telsie confirmed.

'Yes.' Molly hadn't mentioned him often, preferring not to mix her personal life with her job. 'I can see us living there.'

'Family is everything,' Telsie whispered. Molly was again reminded that this girl had none, and it was jarring. She couldn't imagine a life without the support of Joyce and David.

'Well, once I've got the keys and have got settled, you should come and have tea. I can't promise any great patisseries, but I might be able to rustle up a biscuit.'

She felt embarrassed at how the girl's face lit up, as if she had offered her something precious.

'Oh, Molly – yes! That would be absolutely wonderful.'

'Well, that's all settled then.' It felt good to know how much joy a simple invitation had brought the girl.

This conversation came at the end of the day, as Molly wrote the last of her notes on one of three men they had visited the previous week in Sussex, who was in a relationship with a local girl called Millicent. The girl had slipped her hand inside his as they spoke to her directly.

'What can I say, Miss Collway? I've had a lot of stick, what with people spitting at me in the street, calling me the worst names imaginable. My own mother won't have him at her table, but Ralph is a good man and you can't help who you fall in love with, can you?'

'No, you can't, Millicent,' she had agreed. 'No, you can't.'

'I didn't know whether to mention it earlier because I didn't want to upset your day, but I was very sorry to hear about your mother,' Telsie offered quietly, as Molly closed the file.

'Thank you, Telsie. It was a pleasant death, really. My brother and sister and I were with her and she just went to sleep.' Molly pictured the rather anticlimactic moment, as she and David sat on either side of their mother, cups of tea in hand, while Joyce leaned on the windowsill. They watched her slow, stuttering breaths, and then suddenly she wasn't breathing and that was that. 'It's strange because we weren't close, not for a couple of years now, and I think I should be feeling more, but somehow I don't.'

Telsie nattered so much it felt easy to be this candid. The girl seemed to consider this. 'That's strange for *me* because I lost everyone all at once and so no one had the individual grief they deserved; instead it was all lumped together in one big bundle of sadness and it's hard for me to think about any one of them – they're all entwined in my head. I don't know how they died, not exactly, which is probably a good thing. I picture them in the water and dream they call to me with their arms stretched up and their eyes pleading, but I can't get to them.' She tapped her forehead. 'I can't let myself think about it or I go cuckoo.'

Molly understood this, remembering not so long ago, when the image of Johan leaning on a postbox was enough to see her crumple with grief. 'I'm so sorry, Telsie. I should think more and speak less.'

'Now I'm sorry for making *you* feel bad.' Telsie sighed. 'Can we just call it quits, because there's one hell of a lot of feeling sorry going on here and I have a bus to catch.'

Molly laughed. She might not have intended to make a friend in Telsie, but it seemed to be happening anyway.

'I hope everything goes okay with the funeral.' Telsie smiled. 'See you the day after tomorrow.'

'Yes, see you the day after tomorrow.'

Telsie grabbed her handbag, swinging it as she waved cheerily and practically skipped from the building.

Molly got back to her digs and couldn't help but compare them to the sweet cottage she had found in Chelmsford. One look at the grubby hallway and Molly knew she had done the right thing in buying the cottage. She pictured Joe in his little pyjamas while she read him a bedtime story and kissed him goodnight . . . How she longed to feel his arms around her neck when he held on to her like he did Joyce. With her old peach-coloured housecoat pulled up to her chin, she tried to identify a lingering scent from her baby Joe on the fabric, once or twice catching a gentle whiff, breathing so deep and fast that it left her quite light-headed. Her desperate need to smell his baby odour left her spent, but it was worth it just to inhale one tiny molecule of her boy, of her milk and of their too brief time together. The thought alone was enough to make her smile, even as she sat on the saggy bed in the small room where old layers of wallpaper hung in flaps from the walls, revealing tea-coloured stains of damp plaster. She picked up her precious brass button and ran it over her cheek for comfort, missing her love and their precious boy.

Molly barely slept, which was not unusual, but lay silently mourning her mother, her sadness somewhat eased, however, by their final exchange. She rose early and washed herself in the little plastic basin with water warmed on the hot plate in a saucepan, once more picturing how she and Joe would take their baths in a tin tub by the fire in the cottage in Chelmsford. She brushed her hair and swept it up at the side before fastening it with a tortoiseshell comb, and pulled her one good dress from the wooden hanger: mustard-coloured wool with a pussy-bow tie-neck and a high-waisted skirt. It was important that she looked her best, wanting not only to pay her respects to her mother in the right way, but also to send a very clear message to the likes of Mrs Granton-Smythe that she was a single woman in control, a single woman with a son.

David and Clara had spent the night with her mother in the house; Clementine was with her maternal grandparents in Dorset, deemed too young to be present. And Joe was apparently being dropped with Mrs Mason until after the funeral, their neighbour having positively leapt, according to Joyce, at the chance of babysitting the little one. The plan was still for Joyce, Albert, Molly and Joe all to spend time together to enable a smooth transition and, with things in train to secure the cottage in Chelmsford, they had decided that Joe would come to her when she had the keys and just before Joyce and Albert left for Canada.

Molly rapped now on the front door, and Clara answered, her eyes puffed from crying and her nose running.

'Oh, Molly! Hello, dear. I do hate death.'

Her sister-in-law's comments put her in mind of sweet Telsie, who also had a knack for stating the obvious. Nothing but glib responses sprang to mind, and so instead she stepped over the threshold and held her in a brief hug. 'We shall all get through it together.'

Clara sniffed and closed the front door. 'I told David you'd want to go and sit with Mother before the funeral home come to collect her. She's in the parlour.'

'Righty-ho.'

With some reticence, Molly slowly opened the door to the parlour before entering. The dark wood coffin with its brass adornments lay on the dining table in the centre of the room. The air was tinged with the camphor oil her mother favoured for all skin creams and potions. Molly had seen a lot of death and yet this was different, a welcome reminder that not all death was violent or bloody but could be calm, timely, natural and even beautiful.

Her mother's skin looked pale and waxy, her eyes were closed and her face was free of many of the lines etched by grief and worry that had made their home in tributaries along her forehead and around her eyes and mouth. She looked younger than Molly remembered. She had been dressed in smart navy with a lace shawl collar and lay with the faded Bible she had received at her christening clasped to her chest, a sprig of lavender in her fingers. She looked quite lovely and Molly wondered if this had been Clara's idea. Molly sat on a carved mahogany dining chair by the side of the table and took a deep breath.

'I don't know what to say, Mum. I think about all the times I was sharp with you, angry, and it felt justified, but now?' She swallowed to clear her throat. 'We all end the same way, don't we? We are all but dust, and I am going to remember that because it puts the futility of all our heartache and all our desires into perspective. We are all but dust.' She paused. 'I would like to thank you for your final words to me; they are and will always be a great comfort and I shall tell Joe all about you. I will tell him of the time when I was small and you sat right here by the fire at Christmas, when stray wrapping paper landed on your head and you laughed and . . . it was magical. And the tree was so beautifully decorated, and David told me that when one of the baubles broke, magic would . . .'

The door of the parlour opened and Molly fell quiet.

'Oh!' Joyce welled up at the sight of their mother in repose. 'Molly!' Joyce reached for her and she went to comfort her sister. The two stood holding hands, staring down at the coffin. 'We're orphans now.' Joyce sniffed and, for some reason, maybe from nerves or with the intoxicating headiness of grief, Molly started to laugh. Joyce joined her and the two folded double, laughing until they cried, wiping the tears from their cheeks and covering their mouths at the inappropriateness of their actions, while wheezing the word 'Orphans!', which would set them off all over again. The door opened and Albert poked his head in. He took one look at the two sisters and slowly closed the door again. And all the while their mother lay in the middle of the room, the quietest she had ever been in such a crisis. And still Molly sensed her utter disapproval at how her giddy daughters were hijacking her funeral with their daftness.

'It simply won't do, Mary Florence! It won't do at all!'

Molly found the service perfunctory at best, suspecting in part that this was down to her faith having been sorely tested in recent years, to the extent that she now felt ready to declare herself a non-believer. Heaven was a nice idea and reconciliation a lovely dream, but she feared the reality was nothing of the sort. The slightly hurried feel was also in part down to the Reverend Monroe, who seemed more than a little jaded with the whole funeral business, so that his sermon was a tad rushed, the prayers too fast and his manner twitchy, as if he had a cup of tea cooling somewhere or some other place he would rather be. And this Molly more than understood. It was the price they all paid for the long years of the war: their general fatigue with death and an acceptance of horrors that would otherwise appear sickening or dreadful if they had occurred in isolation.

With earth thrown in damp clods onto a coffin that now lay next to that of their father, the Collway siblings walked arm in arm from the church and back to their family home.

'I thought it went well,' David said.

'I did too.' Molly could only agree.

'Do you think she's with Papa?' Joyce smiled at the thought.

Molly exhaled slowly. 'I hope so.' And that was the truth. They fell silent until reaching Old Gloucester Street.

'Do you want to go and fetch Joe?' Joyce asked casually, but Molly was more than aware that it was the first time her sister had relinquished her lead role. She was trusting her, and this was an opportunity.

'Yes, I'd like to, very much.' She nodded, ripples of joy dancing through her veins, knowing this was how it would feel when she collected him from school . . . from the library . . . from a friend's. *Hello, I'm Joe's mother . . .*

David peeled off and rummaged in his pocket for the key to their old home.

Molly looked back at Joyce, who looked a little lost standing there on the pavement, her smile a little too fixed.

'Do you . . . do you want to come with me? But maybe stand back – be there just in case?' She bit her bottom lip, this clearly being such an extraordinary event for them all, without any precedent.

Joyce nodded and continued along the road behind her. It was only a few feet to the Masons' front door, thirty at most, and yet it seemed like the longest journey, covering miles and miles and months and months, and Molly felt her legs tremble with each step.

Her tongue stuck to the dry roof of her mouth and her palms were clammy. This, she knew, was their beginning and, if it was excitement that bubbled to the top, it rose from a soup of self-doubt and concern. She increased her pace, turning to look at her sister, who smiled her encouragement. 'Go and get your boy!' Joyce managed, with a crack to her voice.

Molly walked up to the front door and knocked lightly, thinking back to the day she had done so with Joe wrapped in a blanket, when she had needed help that was not forthcoming. She was determined to reset the narrative. Before she had the chance for any further thoughts on that day, the door opened and Mrs Mason stood there in her double string of pearls over a fuchsia twinset. Molly heard a small voice call out, 'Mama! Mama!'

She bent down to greet her little one, crawling with speed towards the front door. Joe sat on the step and stared at her with his lelephant in his mitts. Judging by his expression, she was most definitely not who he had been expecting.

'He's been a darling.' Mrs Mason smiled fondly at the boy. 'I hope the service went well,' she offered, her tone a little clipped.

'It did, thank you.' Molly couldn't take her eyes off her son. 'And thank you for looking after Joe.' Even having the conversation seemed to give her status, placing her firmly in the mind of this woman as his mother – and it felt wonderful! She bent down to pick Joe up, her manner a little awkward as she was unsure of the best way to gather him up. She had seen Joyce do it several times but was hesitant: should she grab him under the arms or hoick his bottom under her arm? She faltered, fraught with nerves, and Joe seemed to sense her lack of confidence and began to cry. He was heavier than she had thought, and Molly grappled with him, pulling his arm and trying not to topple over as she lifted him an inch or two before watching as he wriggled out of her grip and plopped back down onto the parquet flooring, where he tumbled backwards and banged his head. Molly's heart raced, and she glanced back at Joyce, whose hands had shot out as if she could intervene from that distance. Molly bent down again and pulled her baby to her, but by this stage Joe was crying hard, verging on the hysterical.

'It's okay, Joe! Don't cry, darling, it's okay!' she tried, but her words were shot with nerves, making them spiky and hard to handle. Even Joe, no more than a baby, could sense it.

'Ma-ma!' he screamed through his tears. 'Ma-ma!'

Molly looked imploringly back at her sister. Joyce ran up the path and, in one swift and practised move, scooped the boy from the floor and up into her arms, where he clung on for dear life, crying until his sobs turned into hiccups. Mrs Mason watched the whole thing unfold.

'Poor little mite.' She looked directly at Molly, who was torn between wanting to scream at the woman or make a run for it. Mrs Mason robbed her of the choice and shut the front door firmly in her face.

'What a cow!' Joyce said, while shushing and coddling Joe into a state of calm. 'And to think that we're newly orphaned as well!'

They smiled, but the bountiful laughter of earlier was missing.

'I can't believe I dropped him,' Molly said, feeling a little sick and placing her hand on her stomach.

'You hardly dropped him! Dropping is when they fall from a great height or are lobbed somewhere carelessly. Don't be so hard on yourself – you merely watched him topple an inch. That's really very different, darling, and he *is* a little awkward to get hold of.' Joyce's tone was appeasing, but her manner was flustered.

The two women walked slowly back to their childhood home, where visitors were starting to turn up for the wake. Molly stole glimpses to see how Joyce was managing so casually to perch her son on her arm. She made it look so easy.

'I know how you're feeling, Molly, and you mustn't. We knew this transition was going to be tough for us all, and it is, but every day we make little advances, and there are still ten or so weeks to figure it all out before we go off to Canada. That's plenty of time,' Joyce said brightly, but with tears blooming in her eyes.

Molly was reassured at her sister's words and torn by the distress she was trying to hide.

'I just want to do a good job and I want him to love me,' she admitted.

'You will, and he does! Of course he does – don't you?' Joyce kissed his little face.

'Do you know, Joyce, I marvel at how you are always calm, always kind and always know the right thing to say. And you never have a hair out of place and your lipstick is never smudged.'

'I don't know if that's true—'

'No, it is,' Molly said, cutting her off. 'I can joke, but we're lucky to have you, Joe and I – all of us.'

'We're all lucky, darling. You don't know it yet, Molly, but you are a sunflower and I am a mere dandelion!'

'You are hardly a dandelion!' Molly laughed off the compliment.

'And I can't wait to see your new house! It'll be the making of you – a place to start over, your first proper home.'

A home for life . . .

'And it should be yours before we go?'

'Fingers crossed – that's what everyone is working towards. His bedroom is already painted blue and I thought I might hang Papa's aeroplanes from the ceiling.'

'Oh, I think he'd love that!' Joyce offered with false brightness, as her face fell.

'And I've been thinking that if the cottage isn't ready, we could always come and stay here until it is.'

'That's a great idea. I bet you can't wait.' Joyce gave Joe an extra little squeeze.

'I really can't. I've made enquiries for a nanny in Chelmsford and will start interviewing next week. It's something I can afford now, with my inheritance, and it feels like a sort of gift from Mum. But if everything is delayed, I'll take time off work and we'll stay in Bloomsbury. Telsie can manage without me for a bit and there are lots of other liaison teams.'

The sisters stopped to stare up at the house, where people were now arriving in a steady stream for the wake.

'Why don't we take him for a lovely long walk next weekend, and I can hold back a bit and the two of you can play and get used to each other. How does that sound?' Joyce offered.

'That sounds good,' Molly said, and then sighed. 'Right, are we ready for this?' She nodded towards the house.

'No, but I don't think we have much choice, do we?'

'After you.' Molly ushered her sister up the steps, holding Joe's lelephant-free hand and, to her great surprise, he didn't pull it away.

FIFTEEN

Molly put the key in the front door and pushed it open. She looked around as if expecting a bit of a fanfare, but there were no shouts of congratulation or whoops of joy. She had just a single suitcase, a bucket and a scrubbing brush, and a brown paper bag full of golden plums. The soft, sweet fruit felt like the perfect way to toast her new home. Slowly, she walked from room to room, throwing open windows and running her fingers over the wonky walls – *her* wonky walls! The kitchen was small but perfect, and compared to the single hot plate she had got used to in St Pancras, it was pure luxury. Her bedroom was large and square with a glorious view over the back garden.

'I wish you were by my side . . .' she said to Johan, as she sometimes did.

She devoured a plum before setting to work, greedily swallowing the divine sweet mush of fruit, which was like no other. It was certainly one of the best things she had ever tasted and her mouth watered for another. She decided her second plum would be her reward when she had finished her chores. Without further ado, she tied a scarf around her head, grabbed the scrubbing brush and the bucket and trod the steep stairs, making her way up to Joe's room, which she had one week to get ready. It was a good size, rectangular with a pretty cast-iron fireplace in the middle of the long wall. She liked the wooden floorboards and decided to make his bedroom cosy with a cheerful rug to cover the floor and to stop the draughts coming up through the gaps. The walls were painted a glorious shade of sky-blue. She set to, washing the paintwork down and scrubbing the floor. It was exciting to see it come to life, transforming into the room she had held in her mind's eye, making her mark on her new home. Her nagging fatigue was offset by the giddy realisation that in just one week Joe would be in her arms for good! With an aching wrist she worked until dusk bit, stopping only when thirsty and remembering she had left all the doors and windows open downstairs. Standing back in the narrow hallway, she admired her handiwork. It was certainly clean!

Having rinsed out her bucket and brush, Molly stepped out into the garden and closed her eyes, feeling the last of the sun's warmth on her skin and listening to the sweet sound of birdsong. The lilac on the back wall was still in bloom and the scent filled the air. She felt a sense of peace that had been missing since the start of the war, mixed with pure joy at the thought of collecting Joe at the weekend. That gave her a whole week to get the room finished and put a few sticks of furniture in place.

'Slow down, Molly!' Telsie had called when Molly almost ran to the waiting train with her colleague traipsing along behind. 'Time can't run any faster, you know!'

Molly laughed – that was exactly what she was longing for, desperate for the weekend and Joe's presence in their new home.

With the house in Tonbridge almost closed up and moth-balled, ready for her sister's departure to Canada, Molly thought it best that Joe be brought to the cottage. Not only did it give him a chance to settle with everyone he loved within reach, but also an opportunity for Joyce and Albert to see his new home. She was ridiculously excited to show them the place she had worked so hard on for every spare second in the last week. His room was fresh and clean. A wooden single bed was pushed to one end of the room, with a bookshelf on one side and a small cupboard on the other where little wooden hangers clanged together ready to receive his clothes. The pièce de résistance was the six hand-painted balsa-wood planes she had strung from the ceiling at different heights. They had belonged to her Papa and been long ago discarded, boxed away in the attic. Molly had always liked them and, with the house in Old Gloucester Street being sold, had known exactly where to put them.

Sitting on the floor of Joe's bedroom, she looked up at the planes and, without warning, felt the rug judder beneath her, as if she were still seated in the bumping Lysander aircraft that had spirited her in and out of France. A small scream left her throat. She couldn't tell how long it lasted, but it was frightening enough for her to place her palms flat on the floor and fight for breath. Molly crawled on all fours across the rug and sat back against the bed, waiting for her heart rate to level and her breathing to ease as she wiped the sweat from her top lip. The experience had been unnerving and left her more than a little shaken.

The knock on the door came at a little after eleven in the morning. Molly opened it with a flourish and was a little taken aback to see the trio standing on her pathway. Joe looked adorable in his little shorts, white shirt and Fair Isle jersey, smart socks and polished T-bar sandals. The same could not be said for Albert, who was usually so clean and chipper, if a little contained, but today looked slightly dishevelled, as though he hadn't shaved properly and was in need of sleep. Joyce, immaculate as ever, had the curve of a smile on her face and baby Joe in her arms, but beneath her eyes sat the indigo smudges of a woman who was exhausted. And Molly understood, knowing exactly how her sister was feeling, as she had felt the same ever since the day she had handed him over. Even Joe seemed a little subdued. He had crammed one leg of his lelephant in his mouth and lay resting his head quietly on Joyce's chest.

'Hello!' Molly bent down low and spoke into the face of her son, who knew her well enough now not to howl. His eyes smiled and it was as glorious to see as it had been the very first time. 'How was your journey?' she asked.

'Good.' Albert coughed. 'Not bad at all.'

'Well,' Joyce said, stepping over the threshold, 'this is a lovely place, Molly.' Molly noticed the croak to her sister's voice; it was as if she might be coming down with something. 'I love the cosiness of it, and the front garden is so pretty. It's perfect. I think you'll be very happy here.'

Her words were kind and yet there was a reticence to her tone and a formality that made the atmosphere a little awkward. Molly was more than aware of how her sister's heart was breaking.

'Thank you, Joycey. I'm already happy here, especially today,' Molly said, hugging her sister and her son at the same time. It felt odd to be filled with such joy at the return of her boy and yet know it was shaded by Joyce's sadness. Her beloved sister had shown the most selfless kindness towards her and Joe, yet her reward was to hand back the very thing that had brought her such happiness. It was a cruel and impossible puzzle.

242

'Would you like to see the garden, Joe?' Molly said, clapping her hands and holding out her arms. Joe slipped into them without any fuss and laid his head on her shoulder. She relished the weight of him and carried him on her arm, in the way that she had learned. They walked through the French doors and out into the back garden. 'Look!' she said, pointing to the lilac. 'Can you see all the little buzzy bees collecting the nectar they need to make our honey? And look here, Joe.' She crouched down and showed him a large iron bird bath she had found in the undergrowth. 'This is where the birdies come every morning to have a bath and a little drink – can you imagine?' To finally have him in her arms and be showing him their home was thrilling, a dream. Joe, however, seemed only vaguely interested and looked back constantly over her shoulder to locate Joyce. She reminded herself not to overwhelm him with a trip upstairs to see his grandpa's aeroplanes. This was a big day for him too. She blinked, erasing the memory of what had happened earlier, an unnerving and unwelcome flashback that had left her unsettled.

Spying Joyce and Albert in the kitchen through the window, she saw them locked in a tight embrace; they sprang apart like teens caught out at the sight of her, Joyce wiping her eyes. Molly took Joe inside with a low hum of dread in her mind, knowing what her sister was going through. There was nothing good about making this person she loved so much feel this way.

'I made some shortbread!' Joyce enthused, blowing her nose before pulling a tin from her shopping bag. 'I didn't want you to go to any trouble and I know you love it.'

'Oh, I do! Thank you, Joyce.' Molly put Joe on the floor to crawl and filled the kettle with water. Without the chatter of conversation as a dampener, the sound of the water hitting the metal base seemed offensively loud. 'Do sit down.' She pointed to the chairs at the kitchen table, hating the formality of her tone. Joyce and Albert stiffly took their seats.

'The weather's been nice.' Joyce coughed again. Albert, Molly noticed, had reached for her hand under the table and cupped it within his.

'Yes, it has.' Molly turned away, closing her eyes briefly as she reached up to the shelf for the cups and saucers. The atmosphere in the small kitchen was oppressive and awkward, each one of them wrestling with the heart-rending enormity of having to give up Joe. The stilted conversation and polite small talk seemed to crush them all with a physical weight. Molly poured tea for everyone, standing so that she could keep an eye on Joe, who was currently trying to push lelephant up the wall.

Joyce took a sip from her cup. 'His . . . his clothes are in the boot of the car, along with a basket of bits and bobs: his bottles and formula, a couple of little teds, his . . . his rattle, which he doesn't really like any more, but . . .' Her voice fell away.

Molly didn't know whether to rush forward and take her sister in her arms or let her be. 'Thank you. His room is all ready. I'll sleep on his floor tonight, I think, so I can watch him, partly because I don't think I will ever get used to him being asleep under my roof but also, if he wakes, I want to reassure him instantly.'

Joyce nodded. 'He usually settles quite quickly once you hold him and rock him a little. Keep the lights low and, erm, don't . . . don't get overly chatty or it wakes him fully. I learned that the hard way.' Her eyes brimmed with tears and she fidgeted with her hands.

Molly took a deep breath and locked eyes with her sister. It felt like the cruellest blow of fate that in order for her to find happiness it had to come at the expense of her sister's. 'I know this is hard, Joyce,' she said tenderly. 'I've been right where you are and I understand how difficult it is. I promise you, just as you did to me, that I will look after him well. He is safe and he is loved!'

Joyce again tried a brief forced smile that was heartbreaking to see. 'I know,' she whispered. 'I know that, darling, and we shall see you both when we get back from Canada, and it will pass very quickly, I'm sure.' She stood suddenly and brushed imaginary crumbs from her lap. 'I think we should go, Albert.' Her smile again was broad and fleeting, but her eyes told a very different story. 'You know, Little Moll, I can feel I'm going to get upset and I really don't want to do that in front of Joe, or you. It's not fair.'

'Oh, Joycey!' Molly walked over and held her sister in a gentle hug; she could feel the shake of her sister's body in her arms as she cried. And even in the midst of this most joyful day, the thought of which had got her through the toughest challenges of the last few months, Molly's heart broke for her sister, knowing all too well the cutting pain of separation.

'I'm sorry! I promised myself I'd not fall apart.' Joyce wiped her face with the sleeve of her blouse. 'Come on, Albert, let's fetch Joe's things from the car and leave him to get settled,' she said, sounding as bright as she was able.

Joe began to cry, a soft murmur. Molly picked him up and rocked him on the spot. But instead of settling, his tears and volume increased, building to a deafening crescendo until, finally, he flung his body over her arm with his little hands reaching out to Joyce. 'Mama!' he yelled. 'Mama!'

Joyce stepped into the hallway with her hand over her mouth and Joe screamed louder, calling and twisting his body, his face contorted, unable to comprehend why she wasn't reaching for him. His little feet kicked at Molly's stomach in an effort to get to Joyce.

'There, there, little one; there, there, darling! Don't cry, Joe; don't cry!' Molly tried to soothe him, running her palm over the soft hairs on his warm head as she cooed with anxiety and the fear rose in her gut. The thought that she didn't know how to make it better was almost overwhelming. Albert, as if unable to stand it any

245

longer, went through into the hallway to stand with his wife. Joe went quiet and Molly felt a warm wave of relief, until she realised that his body was rigid and, even though he was quiet, his distress was mounting. Her baby boy might not have been yelling, but was so utterly consumed with distress that his mouth hung open in a silent scream as if the breath wouldn't come. A line of dribble ran from his mouth and snot from his nose, while tears sprang from his eyes. His face had gone quite red . . . And then it came, the sound that had been building: the closest thing to hysteria Molly had ever heard. Joe let out a high-pitched, ear-splitting wail of sadness that hit her in the chest and bounced from the walls. It killed her to hear this level of pure sorrow from someone so little. It was a terrible noise and one that plunged Molly straight back into the scene at the Café Hubert, with the screams and yells above the chaos, the sounds Violet had made and then the sight of her body slumped over Pascal's corpse, causing the same level of panic to rise again in her chest. She thought she might be sick as her body froze.

Joe drew breath for another scream and Molly's every muscle coiled painfully in preparation. She looked towards Joyce, aghast at how desperately she wanted to hand him over, quite unable to cope.

'Mama!' he screamed, and then, drawing another breath, he called again to the woman he loved, the woman who had fed him his bottles, settled him and rocked him to sleep every night. 'Ma-maaaa!' He once more hurled himself forward, and Molly stared, grappling with his legs, powerless and unsure of what to do next with his wriggling form, struggling not to drop him, pinching his skin in her tight grip, which of course only made him scream all the louder. Her heart racing and her mouth dry, she watched as Joyce seemed to wobble, as though her legs had given way, slumping against Albert, who wrapped his arm around her, holding her upright. And there they both stood, bowed and entwined, unified by their own all-consuming heartbreak. Molly watched them with a rumble of doubt in her gut, not that she could admit it, not even to herself, but wanting nothing more in that split second than to put her beloved baby down, open the front door and run run run!

Molly stared down now at Joe, who was crying so hard that little purple dots had appeared around his eyes, and on his temple, where the tiny blood vessels had burst in his desperation. A new spike of panic hit her – what was happening to this little baby boy who, without words, was expressing his need and his fright in the only way he knew how? And now a new thought struck, that while she had considered how to minimise the hurt for Joyce and Albert, searching for the words that might offer some balm for their aching hearts, how might she do the same for Joe? The next sound was a low moan, a throaty cry. Molly looked towards her sister, but to her surprise found it was Albert who was now sobbing.

'He's my boy, Molly! He's my son and I love him. Please don't take him away from us. We're a family – a family!'

'No, no, Albert, don't! Don't you dare!' Joyce rallied a little and placed a finger on her husband's lips, shaking her head at him, her voice panicked, her face close to his. 'Don't say another word! We talked about this. You can't do that to Molly, you can't! It was always the arrangement – always. It was temporary. *Temporary!*' Joyce rubbed her eyes and her face, smearing mascara through her eyebrow and across her forehead, then she wiped her lips on the back of her hand, and her lipstick sat in a slick over one cheek. Her hair had fallen forward and with her runny nose and red eyes she looked quite undone, as she pleaded with her husband, doing her best to keep her side of the bargain and do the right thing for her sister as well as the man she loved.

Paralysed with indecision and a wrench in her gut that her dream of motherhood might fast be slipping from her, Molly stared at the two of them: a partnership. She could see they were as utterly, utterly broken as Joe himself sounded. Walking slowly forward, she knew there was only one thing that would calm her baby. She held him out and Albert stepped forward, gathering his boy to his chest, little caring that his tears continued to fall. His large hand sat squarely in the middle of Joe's back, Albert breathing into his soft hair.

'It's all right, son, you close your eyes. It's all okay. Don't cry, my boy, don't cry. I've got you. I've got you now . . .' Albert didn't bother wiping the tears that dripped from his face.

It was almost instant. In the safety of Albert's arms, Joe stopped crying. His breath stuttered and he took deep, deep breaths, as if exhausted by all the exertion, until finally he closed his eyes and drifted to sleep with his face pressed against the front of Albert's shirt, his little fingers hooked around the buttons. His whole body slumped trustingly, abandoned to the care of this man. The sight of his little fingers gripping on to Albert was like a punch in the throat for poor Molly. Weak and disappointed, but relieved that her boy was quiet now, the troubling thoughts and images of the Café Hubert could drift from her mind. It scared her how quickly her fear had flared with its powerful and threatening memories.

The weary troupe who had lived through war now stood in the narrow hallway in silence, as if this new battle was one they had not fully expected and the shock of it had left them spent and exhausted, leaning on walls and banisters with hair loose, throats and noses clogged with tears, feelings stripped bare, hearts and wishes raw and exposed. They were done now with polite conversation about the weather, with no desire to distribute shortbread from the tin or to discuss the garden. This was a time for honesty and directness, for fears and desires to be openly expressed because what now lay at stake was not only the shape of their family, the roles of two sisters so close they were friends but, more fundamentally, the happiness and security of the little person they all held most dear: baby Joe.

'I don't know . . . I don't know if I can do it,' Molly said, shaking her head. 'I thought I could, but the truth is, Joyce, I don't know if I'm ready, and Joe certainly isn't.' She paused to wipe her face. 'How is this going to work?' Her voice was shot through with desperation, hoping someone had the answer.

'It's okay, darling,' Joyce soothed her, as she always did. 'We'll find a way – we will.' Joyce took a deep breath, rubbing her eyes, which were looking sore.

'No,' Molly interrupted, 'it's not okay. Albert is right – you *are* a family and Joe feels safe with you both.' The irony was not lost on Molly that this had been her greatest wish. She sat down hard on the bottom stair with her head in her hands, at the realisation of what shattering those bonds might mean for Joe, along with the risk that she might not be able to cope at all because she was, as someone had reminded her, nearly broken. She looked at her little boy, sleeping so peacefully now on Albert's broad chest, still holding on. Someone seemed to have pulled the plug from her stomach so that all her hope and confidence had drained away, leaving her utterly hollow. Joyce came and sat next to her, budging her up against the wall, breathing a sigh with something akin to relief.

'We'll get there, Little Moll. We'll get there.' Joyce turned her head to kiss Molly gently on the hair. 'It's a tangle, Molly, it is, but we can unmuddle it, we can—'

'How, Joyce? How do we unmuddle it? What's the plan? I *had* a plan, but I was thinking of what was best for me, how to get Joe back, and not necessarily what was best for him. And I never even questioned whether I was ready or even capable of looking after him. I see that now. So bloody naive.'

'You're both ready and capable. He's your baby, Molly, and—'

'I *know* he's my baby, Joyce, but what do we do? Hand him back when he's two? Twelve? Twenty? *Now* is the time, when he's too little to fully understand, but just look at him!' She pointed to where Joe slept soundly in Albert's arms. 'I love him,' she whispered, breaking off as her tears threatened, 'God knows I love him more than I knew was ever possible.' She composed herself. 'And the fact is, I love him too much to see him so distressed. He wants to be with you; he wants to be with his mum. And I think I want that for him too, just for a little bit longer. I need to sort my head out, Joyce. I'm scared.' The words slid down her throat like glass.

Joyce squeezed her sister's hand. 'It's been one hell of a day. Why don't we take him home to Tonbridge, let him settle and try again at the weekend? I think we all need to calm down a bit. He's no doubt picking up on our high emotions, and that won't help at all. We're all exhausted. The build-up to today has been a lot—'

'It has been a lot.' Molly thought of her frantic decorating and lack of sleep. 'You think that's it – maybe we all just need a few good nights' sleep?' She felt a glimmer of hope that all was not lost: this was not a disaster, merely a delay.

'I do. And I need to talk to Albert, properly talk to him. He had no right to protest the way he did, not that I don't understand it.' She looked with love over to where her husband stood with the baby. 'And we'll come back on Saturday and try again. What do you think?'

Molly nodded. 'I think that sounds like our Plan B.'

An hour later, Albert handed Molly the sleeping child. She rocked him in her arms and kissed his face. Holding him close, she whispered words of love and promise before giving him to her sister.

'See you in a week,' Joyce whispered, a reminder that it was not far away.

Molly climbed the stairs and lay curled on the single bed in Joe's blue room with the balsa-wood planes circling and swinging overhead in the breeze. She heard the sound of Albert's car starting, no doubt warming the engine before their long journey, when he would drive their little family home. Self-doubt sat in her gut like a boulder, along with a fear so pervading it sent her thoughts into turmoil. A ferocious roar of tears followed as she expressed her desperation in the only way she knew how. She had wanted this day which had lived in her imagination for so long to end differently, and her disappointment was acute.

After a restless night punctuated by a jumble of disturbing thoughts and where sleep had been in short supply, Molly rose and dressed for work, but other than smoothing her skirt and tucking in her blouse, today she paid very little attention to her appearance. Her hair went unbrushed and her face unwashed. What on earth did it matter anyway? With no inclination for breakfast and still full to the brim with all that had happened the day before, she left the house. She had the time booked off as leave but knew there was little point in sitting at home, not when there was work to be done, and the disappointment of being in the house without Joe for another whole week was more than she could cope with. She would contact the girl she had hired as a nanny and delay her start. The image of Joe in his little shorts and jersey, the sound of his scream as he reached for her sister and the way she had felt the ground shake beneath her, all played in a continuous loop in her head. The swell of longing for him, every bit as strong as in that moment when she had handed him to Joyce on that first terrible day, was now laced with doubt over her own ability to comfort him.

She yearned for Johan with fresh sadness, as if the news of his passing had come recently. Not that she had ever forgotten him, but the panic she had once felt at her loss had waned to the point where she was able to contain it. Yet today, that same original panic and heart-wrenching despair was somehow as strong as it had ever been. Molly felt fragile and very alone, thinking how much easier life

251

would be if, like Clara, she had a David and, like Joyce, her Albert. The irony being, of course, that if she had a David or an Albert she would also have Joe. Not that she was remotely interested in a relationship; it was about the furthest thing from her mind. Even the thought of it set up a churn of disloyalty in her gut. She picked up her pace along the street, looking forward to finding rhythm and order in the execution of her professional role. She was even looking forward to Telsie's tittle-tattle; her chatter was the perfect background noise, a distraction to her inner distress.

'*Ma-maaa!*' She heard again her boy's desperate yell and Albert pleading, '*He's my son! We're a family! Please!*'

The door of their shared office in Vauxhall was closed. Molly walked in and with a trembling hand raised the venetian blind and opened the window to let air into the fusty space. She hung her jacket on the coat stand in the corner and switched on the lamp on her desk, ready to check the files allocated for the day. Looking up at the sound of a knock on the door, she was expecting to see one of the junior admin clerks with the case notes for the day, but instead it was a woman she had not seen before, a smart woman in a suit carrying a stunning bouquet of wildflowers. As if freshly plucked, these bore the scent of fresh dew, while sprigs of grass wound through the stems added to their charm and simplicity.

'How beautiful,' Molly said, with a smile. 'Hello, I'm Molly.' It had been a long time since she had felt part of a wider community in the workplace, not since she and Geer, along with Marjorie to some extent, had been friends in the office. She wondered why someone would bring her flowers – out of respect for her mother's death, perhaps? Surely not after all these weeks.

'Oh yes, good morning.' The woman took a step forward, running her fingers over the blowsy-headed blooms. 'We thought' – she swallowed – 'we thought some flowers might brighten your office today.'

'Well, that's terribly kind of you.' Molly stepped forward to take the flowers. 'They're just the ticket, thank you.' She held her voice neutral and her emotions in check. 'May I ask the reason for bringing me flowers? Not that I'm complaining.'

'Oh.' The woman seemed at a loss. 'Well, they're because we were all so dreadfully sorry to hear about Telsie. She was always such a ray of sunshine, so happy and sweet . . .' She shook her head.

'Telsie?' Molly stared at her, feeling more than a little foolish. 'What are you talking about?'

The woman looked up sharply and took a breath. 'I'm so sorry . . . I thought you knew.'

'Knew what?' Molly whispered.

'Telsie left here on Tuesday evening. She . . . she went to Vauxhall Park, and they found her hanged.'

'Oh no!' Molly cried out. 'No!'

Molly was aware of falling or, more accurately, of the ground rushing up to meet her. Clinging to the floor, fearful of falling further as the floor beneath her shook, the smell of aeroplane fuel was strong in her nose. Only vaguely aware of the woman coming to her aid, picking her way through the flowers that now lay strewn about the floor, it was hard for her to catch her breath. 'Get David . . .' she managed. 'Get David – please, please get my brother, my brother David . . . I can't . . .' Molly rolled onto her front and closed her eyes, her forehead laid on her arm, as if she somehow believed that if she kept her eyes closed and lay very, very still it all might just go away . . .

Sometime later Molly was aware of a kerfuffle in the doorway of her office and felt David's hand on her wrist.

'That's it, Moll, deep breaths. Stay as you are, but take deep, slow breaths.' He breathed in deeply and exhaled slowly, as if she might need a guide. Molly gripped his arm and looked up. 'David . . .'

'Don't try and talk right now, just keep breathing. Deep breaths . . .'

Molly started to cry. 'I don't know how it ends, David – I don't know how it all ends!'

Crouching down in front of her on the floor, he pulled her to him and held her tightly. 'You don't need to worry how it all ends, Moll, you just need to make peace with your choices and let life unfold.

'You know, you don't look like you, Little Moll, and you don't seem like you,' David suddenly said, with barely disguised emotion. 'You're so tightly coiled.' He rubbed her hands in his own, trying to warm her fingers.

'I don't feel like me,' she whispered.

'You had a bad war, a very bad war.' He nodded, his expression kindly. 'Lots of us did, but this can't define you, it can't become everything.'

'It already is everything.' She closed her eyes. 'I've lost Johan and now I feel I'm losing Joe.'

He shook his head. 'You're not losing Joe, and you won't always feel this way, I promise you.'

'I feel right now that I don't want to go on, David.' For the first time ever, she was able to say this out loud.

David stood up and gazed out of the window. 'I've spent the last couple of years in a field hospital, trying to piece together the injured, the damaged – sometimes the very badly damaged – and it has never failed to amaze me how men cling to life, even when it might seem kindest that they did not.' He shook his head, as if to erase a memory. 'And yet here you are, my dear, dear Molly, safe and sound, one of the survivors, and you are telling me you would rather not be here?'

She nodded.

'Well, it's quite simple,' David said, clearing his throat. He stood up very straight, his stance determined and his voice the no-nonsense tone that reminded her of their mother. 'I will not let you give up on life, I will not, because that would be a bloody waste. You have so many wonderful things ahead of you. The war is done and now we all need to live for every one of those who lie in scrappy graves and would give anything to be in our shoes.'

Molly felt a pulse of gratitude, not for his words but for the sentiment behind them.

'Some people are able to bounce back from exceptional causes of stress and some people are not. It's nothing to be ashamed of.'

'I suppose not, although I'm not ashamed. And I've been coping well: I hold down my job, I keep myself presentable, I have my new home, and all of it was possible because I did it for Joe. All of it was to have Joe come back to me, but now—' She swallowed, picturing again the way he had swung away from her, kicking his little feet and screaming with his lungs fit to burst.

David held her gaze. 'You have *always* done what is best for Joe. You put him out of harm's way.'

'Yes, but what about me, David? What was best for me? I'm now paying the price, living the consequences.'

'What can I do to help you, Molly? What do you need to get better?'

'I need help.' She sat up straight herself now and wiped her nose, looking her brother in the eye, and suddenly the whole of the last couple of years seemed to catch up with her. Molly knew she was on the edge of the abyss. 'I need help so I'm able to care for him properly without wobbling, without wanting to run.'

'And you will, Little Moll, you will.'

David glanced across to his sister in the passenger seat of his car. She gripped the wide leather seat with one hand, clutching the thick wool blanket tight at her neck with the other, yet still she shivered.

'Nearly there, Moll.'

She nodded, knowing that to remain calm would give her the best chance of keeping the sadness that threatened at bay. It was hard enough trying to breathe through her tears.

'It's all going to be all right, old girl,' David said to comfort her. 'We've had good advice from Dr Venables.' He paused. 'You're not well, Molly, and it's painful for me to see you like this, but you are not the first and, sadly, you won't be the last. To ask for help is brave – vital, in fact. The casualties of war are many in number and the wounds far more varied than mortar and bullet damage.'

I might have preferred that . . . She kept the thought to herself.

'I feel as if I've been going at a million miles an hour without looking up, but now I'm scared, David,' she whispered.

'Because it is daunting, that's why. But Winterhill Lodge is a terrific place – on the coast, with wide, sandy beaches. It all sounds rather nice. And after resting up, you'll come back as good as new.' He tried to jolly her along, as if this were any old jaunt and they were not heading to the hospital in Lowestoft and a facility for those with mental challenges: an asylum.

'I've made some calls, Molly, and have been assured that this place has a first-class record for treatment. It will do you good to get away from it all for a bit, to take a breather from life, and then you can come out feeling brand new!'

'I don't want to feel brand new, David. Right now I want to go to sleep and not wake up, not ever.' She braced herself for the next rolling sob that engulfed her. It was as if now that she had acknowledged the crack in her armour, her sadness spilled from her like smoke.

'And that, Molly, is the issue. You have to trust me on this.'

'Do I have any choice?'

'Yes, you do, darling. You have all the choices. You are choosing to admit yourself and can leave whenever you decide, but I fear that if you don't go to a place where professional help is on hand, somewhere you can take your time and get well . . . I'm worried you might do something stupid. And I simply can't let that happen.' David gripped the steering wheel.

'My friend did something stupid – Telsie. She wasn't really a friend, but . . .' She closed her eyes and saw the girl's smiling face. 'She was always so jolly, and yet she did that.' Her tears rolled down her cheeks. 'Violet, too. And the truth is, I envy them their bravery, I do. I don't want to live without Joe and without Johan, not really. I've told Joyce to take my boy with her and to keep loving him, keep him safe, and it hurts so badly that I wonder if it would be less painful not to be here at all . . .'

'You can't think like that, Molly, you can't.'

'I can't help it, David. I was supposed to be welcoming Joe home this weekend' – and just like that her tears came again, her voice raw – 'but instead he's going to Canada, bloody Canada, David! Thousands and thousands of miles away from me!' she sobbed.

The phone call with her sister, while David made the arrangements to take her to Winterhill, had been painful but necessary.

With her throat almost too tight for words, and her heart too shredded for anything other than tears, she had held the phone close.

'It *will* be easier when he's a little older,' Joyce had reassured her, sniffing too, 'and if you really think it best, we will take him to Canada with us, just while you get better, and I'll explain it all to him. And then when he comes home to you, it will be less traumatic because he'll understand more and will be old enough to ask questions . . .'

Molly listened to her sister's words, hoping she was speaking the truth and knowing she was pure in her intentions.

'I think it's what needs to happen, Joyce.' Her words coasted on her tears. 'I think it's what needs to be done. I feel a bit like everything is disintegrating and I need things to be more stable.'

'My poor darling. You won't always feel this way' – Joyce had echoed their brother's sentiments – 'and it won't be for ever, Molly darling. It won't be.'

'Joyce, please tell him every day that I love him,' she squeaked, quite unable to picture her baby Joe boarding a plane bound for Canada.

'I will, I will. And I want you to know how much I love this little boy! I truly do. I want him to feel safe and not need to worry about ghastly grown-up things.' Joyce had drawn breath. 'But equally as importantly, I do so want to do the right thing for you, too, for all of us. We'll work hard to find the balance, I promise.'

Molly had nodded down the line. 'I just want him to feel safe and I don't want him to be confused.' She had paused then, digging deep to find the strength. 'I want to feel better and I know when he comes home that will be the final part of the jigsaw for me.' She had sobbed silently, knowing this was for the best, despite how much it hurt.

'Oh' – Joyce had taken a sharp breath – 'it will! And he will always be your child, Molly. He will *always* be yours, but if you ever think about losing a moment of rest out of concern that he does not have the very, very best life, then please don't, because he will have the whole world and he is loved! He was – he *is* – the greatest gift for however long I am responsible for him!'

'I shall always love him and you.'

'I know. We are one family, Molly, all of us. He might call me Mama right now, but never forget I am your sister who loves you very much and we are raising him in the same family. We are all *one* family.' Again the tears came, robbing her briefly of composure. 'He loves you, Molly. Joe loves you. We can get through this – we can and we will.'

Even now as the car trundled along, a small smile formed involuntarily on Molly's face. It was a lovely thought that Joe might love her in some way, despite the pain of the knowledge that she would for the time being play a secondary role in his life. She recognised that it was far, far better than no role at all at a time when she had to concentrate on getting better.

'Everything is such a mess, David. I feel as if Johan and Joe were my one chance and it has all been taken away from me.'

'There will be other chances when you're feeling better. Joe will come back.'

Molly gripped the blanket more tightly at her neck. 'But I'm broken, David, more than I want to admit. I'm broken.' She turned away from her brother and stared out of the window, barely aware of the fields rushing by as they headed towards Winterhill Lodge.

'You will mend, you will,' he said resolutely.

'I'm so tired. I don't want to think any more.' It seemed as if the exhaustion that she had kept at bay for the longest time now washed over her in waves. Her mind was empty, numb and yet, conversely, also racing. It was hard to know whom she cried for the most: her beloved Johan, with whom, for the want of a bit of luck, she would be strolling along the Embankment right now; Joe, her baby boy, for whom she cried a river; Telsie, the sweet girl who had felt her only option was to swing from a tree; Violet; Pascal . . .

'Why didn't I spend time with her, David? Why wasn't I her friend?' she asked in breaks from her tears.

'Because we are all busy with life and survival, my dear. We have *all* in recent times been so very busy with life . . .'

◆ ◆ ◆

Winterhill Lodge, she would come to realise, was aptly named. It was a Gothic structure of meandering proportions with areas under canopies or behind turrets which remained untouched by the sun. The windows had bars and the doors were thick and imposing. David booked her in, the paperwork no more than the jotting of basic details and a couple of signatures, all quite straightforward, as she was admitting herself of her own volition. A stocky orderly took her handbag and her watch; she rubbed the space on her wrist where it had always lived. He handed them to David.

'Clara and I will keep safe everything you own, I promise you. We will go to the cottage if you like and lock away anything precious. It will all be waiting for you when you come home.'

'I have . . . I have a button. It's . . . it's my most precious thing – in the little walnut box in the sitting room. Please, please don't let anything happen to it. I don't care about anything else. It's brass and it has, erm . . . it has a naval crest and a knot of rope on it.'

'A button. Right . . .' She saw him look up and catch the eye of the orderly. 'I'll find it and make sure no harm comes to it.'

'I feel as if I'm falling.'

'It will all be okay, Molly, I promise. I'll see you soon. Take your time and let them help you get better.' He kissed her then, a gentle, lingering kiss on the forehead, and she watched him turn and leave her in this strange place, all alone.

She watched as his shadow disappeared around a corner and out of sight.

As an emergency admission, Molly was seen by a certain Dr Fanthorpe, who wore thick glasses and hummed as he stared at the form on the front of his clipboard, seeming most unmoved by her sobbing, which she quickly learned was standard behaviour at Winterhill. Tears of distress were ignored, along with wailing, screaming and the banging of various objects or the flat of palms against the metal doors or window bars at all hours of day or night. Despite the mayhem, the place was at first a refuge where she welcomed the oblivion brought on by the drugs. She barely noticed the shiny painted walls and squeaky linoleum floors; the bare rooms devoid of art, beauty and comfort; the sharp stick of cold metal needles into her skin; and the scowls of those working in an environment that must have made them, too, feel like prisoners. Molly understood, because Winterhill Lodge became *her* prison. She was free to leave at any time, but in the first couple of months just one look at the frost-covered grass, grey winter sky and the whole wide world that lay beyond its walls and courage failed her. The pull of the cot bed in her room and the cool slip of a needle under her skin to help her escape was irresistible and easy.

After three weeks, Molly had visitors. David and Clara came and sat in front of her and she was embarrassed at her unkempt locks and lack of conversation, picking at her cuticles as they talked about the weather and Clementine's many achievements at school and the new baby they were expecting.

'Hetty for a girl and Maynard for a boy,' Clara explained.

'God, I do hope it's a girl,' Molly joked, and David and Clara laughed raucously, as if delighted that she was still in there somewhere . . .

It was, Molly knew, kind of them to visit, but she would actually rather they hadn't.

Molly did indeed feel she had disappeared somewhere inside herself, able to view the life before she had come here only in small snippets. The way she would come to think of it was that inside Winterhill she didn't exist and was no more than a shadow, sliding quietly from bed to chair to psychiatrist's couch and back again, going through the motions of life without actually living. In truth, she didn't dislike the drug-induced haze in which she spent time. Not only did it stop her worrying about all the things she couldn't fix, but also it dulled her sadness to the point where thoughts of Johan, Joe, Geer, Violet and even Telsie were fleeting and less spiky, bouncing on a cushion of medication that took away much of her pain.

And then slowly, nearly three months after she had arrived and following numerous sessions to deal with her emotional post-war pain, things began to subtly change until she began to notice a different kind of feeling and a different kind of thought. It was as if a light had been switched on in a previously darkened place, a window opened to let in the air. Suddenly the smell of her surroundings seemed unpleasant to her and the noises almost unbearable. It was a sensation not dissimilar to waking up. This period of new-found awareness was followed by the slow realisation that a different life awaited her. A life where she was free to come and go as she pleased, take a bath if she so desired, tend the lilac on the back wall of her garden, style her hair and read a book late into the night, free to eat what she wanted and when she wanted.

I would like a jacket potato with butter that drips down my chin and the skin blackened.

She smiled to herself, able to think now about Violet without quaking in her limbs.

'Well, look at you, all cheery today! What are you thinking, my love?' one of the kindly nurses asked, as she ran a bath for Molly, in which she would wash under supervision.

'I'm thinking that I would like to go home,' she said, smiling at the woman. Her smile in itself was a new thing. 'I want to go home.'

Dr Fanthorpe was duly summoned.

262

'You're ready to leave Winterhill, you think?' His tone, as ever, was neutral, businesslike. He circled his chin with his thumb and forefinger as he spoke.

'Yes, I am.' She nodded from the other side of the table, her voice clear and steady. 'I don't feel so anxious, my thoughts are a lot calmer and I no longer wish to be medicated. I don't need to be here any more.'

'Can I ask what has brought you to this conclusion?' He sat now with his pen poised over her open file.

Molly took her time. 'Big Betty had a visitor yesterday,' she said, mentioning a large, boisterous inmate who enjoyed a certain notoriety. 'A woman, and she was wearing a red coat. It was the first time I could recall seeing such colour inside this grey, grey world. I had almost forgotten that such a shade existed. She walked past me, and she smelled so wonderful! A rich, lemony scent. I've not smelled anything like it in the longest time, and after having that in my nostrils, I became overly aware of the odour of this place.' She wrinkled her nose, as if still filtering carbolic soap, bleach, shit and the unique odour of human misery. 'It made me yearn for my garden, for the scent of flowers, fresh-baked bread, eau de parfum, bananas . . . all the good things, Dr Fanthorpe. And I realised that if I'm aware of these things, *longing* for these things, then the cloak of sadness that has obscured my vision and wrapped me tight for so long has been lifted, and that's it.' She shrugged her shoulders. 'I am ready to go home, to tend my garden and eat well.'

Dr Fanthorpe did not write a single word, but instead replaced the lid of his pen and stowed it in the inside pocket of his jacket. He nodded and smiled broadly at her. 'I think, Miss Collway, that sounds like a lovely way to live. Let's make the necessary arrangements to get you out of here when you're ready.'

'I'm ready now.' She nodded, holding his gaze. 'I'm ready now.'

SIXTEEN

Tonbridge, Kent
1952
Aged 27

Molly took one last long look at the view out over Vauxhall Bridge and began to clear her desk, packing up her personal belongings and placing them carefully in her handbag. She wanted to take the few small items left to show for a role she had been in for eight years: a powder compact with a mirror and a photograph of herself and a young blonde woman on a farm, circa 1944. The young woman standing behind Molly was beaming over her shoulder into the camera and her hands were raised, palms out, as if she were mid-dance. In the background, a line of men in farming overalls were bent over, picking potatoes, if she remembered rightly. Molly ran her finger over the girl's happy face and shook her head, still finding it hard to accept that to take her own life had felt like the best option.

Sweet Telsie . . .

A couple of francs and a handful of centimes had somehow also found their way into her drawer; they clinked in her palm as she remembered that the only thing she had bought on that trip had been a foul cup of chicory and sawdust masquerading as coffee.

She swallowed, picturing the waitress who had served her, coiled into a ball with her hands over her ears, knees up to her chest and her eyes screwed tight shut . . . *I hope she made it.* It was a thorn in Molly's mind that she didn't know the fate of half of the people who had been present in her life, some only briefly and others who had mattered, people she had loved like Geer – where was she now? she wondered. She supposed that was the nature of war, with families dispersed, bonds of friendship broken, community links smashed and everyone having to start over in a changed new world.

Molly had been as good as her word and made the trip to Alresford in the spring after leaving Winterhill Lodge. She had walked around the little market town just emerging from war, where hanging baskets were already abundant, flowers peppered the verges, lawns were neat, net curtains sparkling white, kerbs swept, front steps polished and where people walked slowly and chatted readily. Seven years on, not much had come off the ration since the war, but that still couldn't take the shine off the joy of simply being alive. The butcher stood proudly outside his shop with a clean apron and with some chunks of meat, offal, the odd string of sausages and a few precious hen's eggs in his window, his lady customers leaving with a few slices of bacon perhaps, wrapped up in waxed paper and string, or an egg or two nestling in their baskets, all of them sporting the quiet, hesitant smiles of survivors. Likewise the baker, ironmonger and cobbler were all jolly men, happy to be home and to have life and business somewhat restored. It was a genteel place and one Molly could see the appeal of, the kind of place she might have chosen to raise a child, rural and calm. This she considered as she walked the lanes, that if fate had been a little kinder she would have been here with Johan, sharing the insight of a local. Her heart still twisted at the thought, her stomach folding with longing for the man.

The postmistress behind the counter of the local post office seemed like a good person to ask when it came to knowing who might live where. Molly waited until all the customers had been served and took advantage of the momentary lull in trade.

'I'm sorry to bother you, but I'm looking for a family I know who live around here, or at least they used to. He is a doctor and his wife a nurse; their name is de Fries.'

'Oh yes, yes!' The woman nodded in instant recognition and Molly felt her spirit soar with anticipation. Was she really this close to locating not only Geer but also the people who would have been her in-laws, Joe's grandparents? The woman scratched her whiskery chin and thought hard. 'They had a daughter who was quite lively, I seem to remember.'

Molly laughed. *Yes, she is!*

'And a son, who I believe was killed in the war.' This phrase was quite standard and could be applied to at least one family in every street in every city, town, hamlet and village in the country. Not that it made it any easier to hear.

Molly nodded. *Yes, he was.* And suddenly there was no place for laughter.

The postmistress continued, her voice quiet now. 'I think it was that tragedy that spurred the move. I know they left soon after the war ended, if not just before. I don't know where they went, I'm afraid. The big old house was empty for a while, and now the Wentworths live there – city types.' She pulled a disapproving face and went back to her business.

Molly's hopes had been dashed as quickly as they were raised, and she slowly walked back to the bus stop, great rocks of disappointment lining her gut and weighing her down.

'Miss Collway! Glad I caught you – sad day, happy day? Which is it?' Mr Allan dragged her back from the memory as she gathered the last of her belongings. He rested on the edge of her desk with his legs splayed and his narrow black shoes tapping the table leg as he exhaled his foul cigarette smoke.

'A bit of both, I think. It's a natural end for me.'

The role of POW liaison was quiet now, with most either repatriated to their homeland or else living fully integrated in their adopted communities. She had been asked to consider a new role in helping to coordinate migrant welfare services, but had politely declined. Since the end of the war, there had been an influx of brave immigrants from all corners of the Commonwealth to this strange country, saying goodbye to everything familiar and often turning up with little more than a suitcase, valiantly answering the call to help rebuild Great Britain. But in truth, Molly wanted something quieter, a job with a predictable routine, less travel and something that would give her time to tend her garden and live at a pace that suited her. It wasn't that the job seemed beyond her capabilities, far from it, but she knew from painful experience that if her mind became overloaded, the pressure too much, there was a danger she might break down altogether. She had learned to manage her mental health, by taking things slowly and seeking refuge in her garden. She knew also that maintaining a calm life on an even keel was how she kept her mind intact.

'It'll be a shame not to be working with you any more,' Mr Allan said suddenly.

'Well, that's a very nice thing to say. Thank you.' Molly smiled in gratitude as she gathered her navy half-sleeved cardigan from the back of her chair. 'I've certainly had some experiences during my time here.'

Mr Allan rose from the desk and drew closer. Placing a hand on her waist, he breathed, 'I hoped I'd catch you before you left. I wanted to say that I've always found you terribly attractive.'

'Oh, for goodness' sake!' Molly shucked off his hand, her heart racing. His attentions were most unwelcome, the way he pawed her flashing her right back to the Café Hubert and the feel of the officer's hand sliding up the back of her leg. She shuddered – this was the kind of thing that set her back, unnerved her and stirred up an unwelcome silt of terrible, terrible times.

'I mean it, Molly. I would like to buy you dinner. Any time, you just give the word and—'

'Dinner? I see, and would Mrs Allan be joining us?' she interrupted as casually as she could manage, while grabbing her handbag and white cotton gloves from the desk, eager to leave. She felt a spike of anger, knowing that after eight years of service here, this vile encounter would be her last memory of the place.

He smirked at her and then again stood uncomfortably close. 'Come on, Molly, don't be spiky,' he insisted. This time he reached out to take her hand, and she pulled it away with force.

'Spiky? Why don't you fuck off, Mr Allan!' she yelled as she marched towards the door.

'Ah, I get it,' he called after her. 'Are you one of those girls who prefers the company of women? I mean, I've often wondered, what with no husband, and so on.' He wiped his mouth with the back of his hand, then slicked his Brylcreemed hair back over his forehead.

Molly paused at the edge of the door and looked back at the office that had been her little domain for nearly a decade. 'Do you know, Mr Allan, I have absolutely never considered that, but if I were forced to choose between having sex with a woman or with you, I would jump at the chance – *any* woman, in fact, would be infinitely less repulsive to me.' And with that she swept from the room and ran along the corridor to the lift as fast as her kitten heels and shaking legs would carry her, jabbing her finger on the call button, keen for the doors to open and give her sanctuary, lest he should reappear. Thankfully, he did not.

Molly put the incident with Mr Allan out of her mind. Not even he could dampen her mood, the pig. She left the railway station with a slight sway to the full skirts of her wide-waisted frock, happy for two reasons: first, that a new chapter in her life was about to begin and for the first time ever, not in fact since she had started school, she had no definite plan. It felt a little liberating, a little intimidating and a whole lot exciting. Second, and the main reason for the smile fixed on her face, was that Joyce, Albert and Joe were coming home! Home for good. Just the thought of being able to visit them whenever the fancy took her filled her stomach with butterflies and joy. They were arriving any day now and she could barely sleep for the excitement pinging in her gut.

Albert's posting had at first been for a year at most. This was then extended and extended again until earlier this year, when they decided to come home. Joyce had at each turn consulted Molly, and if she had not asked outright for permission to stay abroad with Joe, then it was certainly implied. Phone calls were rare. The first from Joyce had been tentative, quiet.

'How are you?' she had asked gently.

'Good, okay, working and busy with the garden . . .'

The calls had continued twice yearly, as did improvements in Molly's well-being, and then came a sea change. With Joe firmly established and living his life in Canada, she was the one who led the questioning, and always with the same simple barometer.

'Is Joe happy?'

This was all she needed to know. She had made the ultimate sacrifice and the point of it was not only to stop her boy suffering through separation from the woman he had come to know as his mother, but also that the stable life Joyce and Albert could offer him was all she wished for, unmarred by an unmarried mother who could not wholly rely on her own mental stability.

Over the last seven years, she and Joyce had exchanged letters and photographs with increasing regularity. The first, like their short telephone calls, were awkward, ridiculously formal, stilted and dull. They made no mention of Winterhill Lodge, bar the cursory addition of 'Hope you are well' dotted at the end, almost as an embarrassed afterthought. Molly understood. It was a difficult subject to broach in writing; she herself found it pointless to detail an unchanging routine set within four shiny, magnolia-painted walls and knew it would be hard for Joyce to ask someone who was in a facility for the mentally ill how they were feeling. Not only had it been an uncomfortable topic back then, but any enquiry had felt like pressure when the reply could only be negative or confused. Once she had left the place, gone home to her cottage in Chelmsford and back to her job in town, the tone of their communications changed. Molly liked to sit in her armchair with her French doors open, no matter the weather, and with a heavy book resting on her knees, she would write to Joyce, using her trusty fountain pen.

It took a good few months of back and forth in this way until it became their predominant form of communication. It was like learning a foreign language at which they grew more fluent with practice, but it was also a matter of trust. It was one thing to speak freely with someone you loved, letting the words tumble out face to face, but quite another to put those same words on paper: immortalising them, unable to take a breath, a beat and reframe the meaning. Each took tentative steps, testing the written word, adding a small mention or word that exposed vulnerability or hurt, until they reached the point when their innermost thoughts, sentiments and secrets flowed. The trust implicit in and the comfort gained from these communiqués was immeasurable.

'Sometimes I cry, Molly. I cry because we lost Mum, I cry because I miss you and I cry because I'm a long, long way from home . . .'

'I miss him, Joyce. My heart and arms ache for him. I suspect they always will . . .'

'I have a deep worry, Molly, that I have put myself forward to be Joe's mum – but supposing I'm not doing it right? Supposing I fail . . .'

'You know, Joyce, on a low day, I wonder if losing Johan and in a sense Joe is punishment for some misdemeanour, meted out by a God I don't believe in . . .'

'Albert and Joe go on boys-only trips fishing and camping, or they play cricket, and I feel a surge of jealousy in my veins to be excluded. Is that what it's like for you, my darling? Because it hurts . . . I know how it hurts . . .'

'I think one of the hardest things for me, Joyce, is how Joe fills so many of my thoughts and yet I know I will not enter his . . .'

Many letters from her sister contained photographs, finger paintings and other small gifts that helped to connect their lives: a wide russet maple leaf, a snippet cut from the local newspaper detailing Joe's win in the hockey team and a gold-painted Christmas star baked from salt dough, rather lopsided and lumpy, but still the most beautiful thing ever to grace Molly's Christmas tree. These letters and the odd telephone call at Christmas helped fill a pocket of loneliness left by her family's absence, but it was nothing compared to being able to hold her boy, read to him, see him face to face, hear his voice, judge his expression – and she couldn't wait.

It had been nearly three years since 'the' phone call. The one they had both known was looming from the outset, and the one Molly had dreaded deep down in her bones. It felt different to the others, more formal. Joyce's breathing had been hesitant and Molly's tone calm, resolute, yet underpinned with a deep-seated sadness. The words and their consequences were, both knew, unavoidable, not that it made saying them out loud any easier.

'We're at a crossroads, Molly.'

'I know.'

271

'He's getting older and takes for granted that we're his parents. He's settled and I'm not sure how to go forward. It feels as if we're all lurching from one year to the next, waiting for the decision on . . .' Joyce ran out of words.

'On what happens next,' Molly interjected, picking up the baton. 'On whether we start to plan how I take Joe back, or—'

'Orwhetherhestayswithus.' Almost choking, Joyce rushed through this phrase as if she needed to spit it out as fast as possible.

Her words had been long expected, but their effect was shocking, sharp and painful, like the jab of a metal needle beneath her skin.

'I think . . .' Molly took her time, having rehearsed the phrase in her mind many, many times. 'I think it's done, Joyce. I think it's gone too far for me to swoop in and try and pick up where we left off. I think . . . I think you're his mum now.' She didn't cry. Didn't fall. Didn't break. There was no crescendo of distress, as there might have been years ago before everything settled, before things calmed and practicality elbowed sentiment off the top spot. The exchange was instead a calm recognition of the inevitable. The idea had at first been like a knife in her throat, the concept monstrous! But over time she had swallowed the knife and it had dissolved inside her. And an idea, something utterly unimaginable, like grief, like loss, like war . . . had slowly become normal because she had lived through it and lived with it. What indeed was the alternative? Not that she didn't on occasion fall to the floor in deep sorrow at the fact that Joyce had her son – *her son*! But certainly she had grown used to it, as humans will do with any situation, no matter how impossible it might seem in the beginning. At first she had worried that history might damn her for giving up too easily on her boy, but after a while, she began to hope that history would mark her as a woman who did the very best for him and had made the ultimate sacrifice for his well-being.

Upon hearing her words, Joyce had wept with what sounded like relief.

'Oh, oh, Molly! I don't know what to say, I don't know how to—' She had stopped abruptly, choked by emotion. There was then a beat or two while Joyce cried and Molly gripped the phone.

'I guess I will be his aunt.' She had closed her eyes and her chin had dropped to her chest.

'The best aunt! The very best!'

Aunt. It was this word that caused the biggest flash of hurt – it relegated her in the worst way possible. She felt the loss deep in the centre of her being, where the pain was most intense. But then Molly had gathered herself and, leaving a trail of regret in her wake, she had kept calm and carried on.

Molly put her key in the front door and kicked off her shoes. She raced to the kitchen and popped the kettle on before making toast, which was all the supper she fancied. Her plan for the evening was simple: she wanted to prune the lilac and deadhead her roses before watering the lawn, and then tomorrow – well, who knew? She might, as a woman without gainful employment, even sleep in! At a little before 9 p.m., she was starting to think about turning in her toes for the night when the telephone rang in her hallway. Joyce and David had insisted on her installing it when Joyce and Albert went to Canada.

'Chelmsford 286?'

'Molly! Guess where I'm calling from. I'll give you a clue: Tonbridge!' Joyce sounded excited.

'That's not a clue, you dolt, that's the answer!' Molly laughed as her throat tightened with emotion. 'You're home!' *Joe's home . . .*

'I am, my darling. So I suggest you cancel your plans for the weekend and get over here. I can't wait to see you!'

'Can't wait to see you either.'

'I'm a bit nervous, Moll.'

'Me too.' Molly nodded. 'But it'll be okay, won't it?'

'Of course it will. We'll make it okay . . .'

It had been seven years since she had last made the journey. Tonbridge had in that time grown. It felt lively, busy with the building of houses to accommodate all the newly arrived families who had moved out of the city. She turned into the road, where memories lurked, remembering the weekend she had finally got to hold her boy and they had learned that her mother was ill. She pushed the memory back down in her gut; it was too much to consider on top of everything else today. Slowly, she walked up to the front door. And there it was, coming from an open window upstairs: the sound of a child's laughter, the sound of a little boy who was happy. Her heart thumped in her chest as she rapped on the door.

'She's here!' Joyce yelled over her shoulder as she opened the front door, and the two sisters stared at each other, taking a second to note any obvious changes. Joyce looked neat and well, her skin clear and her hair shiny, despite the inevitable shadows of fatigue under her eyes after the lengthy journey from overseas. She looked to Molly like a woman who lived a good and healthy life, and Molly was glad for her, knowing that her boy, too, had shared that environment. There was a sliver of nervous tension in the air as the two navigated their way through this moment they had both been looking forward to but simultaneously dreading.

'I worry, Molly, that you might change your mind and take my son! I can't write any more plainly than that. It's the one thing that jolts me from my sleep in the early hours. Selfishly, I can't even bear to consider it: it's far too terrifying . . .'

'I worry that when I see him I won't be able to contain myself. I'm scared of falling apart, of embarrassing myself or upsetting him . . .'

And now here they were.

'Oh, Joyce!' Molly's first words. 'You're here! You are actually here.'

Her sister stepped forward to trace her fingers across Molly's cheek, exclaiming, 'How wonderful it is to see you! I've missed you so much.'

'Same.' Molly nodded, feeling a surge of love for her big sister, this woman she had entrusted with her own most precious flesh and blood.

Joyce cried. 'We've been such a long way distant.'

'It *has* been a long way.'

'Come in! Goodness, come in!' Joyce stood back and beckoned her inside. 'I have to warn you that the house does smell a little strange.'

'What is it?' Molly asked, sniffing at the less than fragrant atmosphere.

'Mustiness, damp, mothballs and I think I detect a base note of rotting mouse.'

'How lovely!' Molly smiled.

'Yes, quite lovely,' Joyce said with a grin.

Molly stepped over the threshold and Joyce enveloped her in a fierce hug. Releasing each other, they then stood side by side and gazed at their reflection in the looking glass in the hallway. Joyce seemed to look at her for the first time, drinking in every detail of her face, which Molly knew had aged twenty years in the last eight.

'We're starting to look like Mum,' Joyce said, pulling a face.

'Speak for yourself.' Molly smiled, knowing it was true and also that the older they got, the less apparent was their age difference. Before they had time to plan things further, the sound of feet thundering on the stairs caused them both to look up, and there he was: standing on the stairs in a smart checked shirt and cardigan, her beautiful, beautiful blond boy! He looked so much like Johan it was almost painful to stare at him. Her temptation was to cry, to wail aloud at the very sight of him, to run to him and hold him. Instead, she bit the inside of her cheek and stood still, trying to readjust the picture in her mind of her baby boy.

'Hello, Joe.' She managed to keep her composure and could sense the quake of nerves in her sister, standing so close by her side. The words felt like sugar on her tongue, being able to address him in person like this.

'Hi!' He smiled, a gap-toothed smile that melted her heart. He was so handsome, his expression so self-assured! He gripped the banister and Molly tucked her hair behind her ears and took a step forward, keeping her voice steady and her manner calm, in contrast to her heart which stuttered with longing and the pang in her gut as she yearned to hold him. It was wonderful to be this close to him, to Johan's boy!

'Now, I don't suppose you remember me, but I'm . . . I'm your Auntie Molly.' There. She had done it. Said it. Set the tone. Placed the framework and carved out the future. It was a simple enough word and yet one from which there was no going back. This was a huge moment and yet, to his ears, almost casual, just the way it had to be.

'Oh sure!' he said, and she heard the faint twang of a Canadian accent. 'She talks about you a lot!' He rolled his eyes as if 'a lot' might just be 'too much'. The two women laughed.

'I do.' Joyce, too, stepped forward now, her voice thin. 'I tell him all about our childhood and how you were always brave and fearless and such fun! And how I envied your and David's closeness.' She winked at Molly.

'Thank you for your presents, Joe – you're a very good artist. I've put some of your pictures on my wall and they look wonderful.' She spoke casually of these items, which, over the years, had arrived in the post and knocked her sideways. The things she held to her chest and touched to her lips: paper he had drawn on, dough he had shaped and photographs he had posed for. All of it meant more to her than this little boy could ever possibly know.

'No problem.' He looked to Joyce. 'Mom, can I go and explore out the back?'

And there it was, another small word – 'Mom' – and one that spilled so easily from his sweet mouth while at the same time it pierced her breast. This was, she knew, something she would need to get used to if they stood any chance of making this thing work.

'You can, but don't get dirty.'

The two women watched as he raced down the stairs and out of the hallway.

'Oh, Molly!' Joyce turned to her sister and took her in her arms, holding her tightly as Molly screwed her eyes shut and just for a second imagined this was herself welcoming Joyce into her home to see Joe, her boy . . . It was sad but wonderful to picture.

'He's tall,' Molly noted.

Joyce nodded at her sister. 'Cup of tea?'

Molly followed her into the kitchen, which was littered with half-unpacked boxes. The kettle and cups, however, were on the countertop, essential. Joyce filled the kettle and set it to boil.

'He looks like you. Can you see it?' Joyce asked with her back to her. 'And because of that, people say he looks like me and I love to hear it. It makes me feel more connected to him.'

'I can only see his dad when I look at him, but then maybe that's because I want to.'

Her sister turned to face her now, her eyes brimming, as if this misfortune was something she could not bear to imagine. 'You must miss him so much.'

'I really do.' *I miss them both* . . . Molly paused to wonder what Johan might have made of the whole business. 'I keep waiting for the hurt to properly fade, and it has a lot, but not entirely. He once said that children need to feel safe, need to know there's a steady hand on the tiller or else it's not fair on them, and I cling to that – it justifies where we are, really. I wish . . . I wish you could have met Johan. He was special.'

'Well, if he was good enough for you, I don't doubt it. You're making a good life, Molly. You still love the cottage?'

'I do, the garden particularly. It's the place where I'm most happy. I can't wait to show it to you.' She remembered the first time she had seen it, picturing her baby boy hopscotching over to find secret dens built in the wide hedging – and now he was an eight-year-old boy out exploring in a different back garden and it had all happened in a blink. She knew that in another blink she would be almost a decade older again, and then another blink . . . and all with Joe at arm's length. Her sister's boy. She tried not to think too far ahead, unable to imagine how it all might pan out.

'David still has some of the bigger antiques and bits and bobs in storage for you – pictures, ornaments and whatnot from Mum's house.' Joyce changed the topic and with it the atmosphere.

'Yes. I've never got round to collecting them, but I suppose I should.' Molly thought of the house and of her mother without the gut-folding anger that had been present for so long and with something much closer to love, because life was too short.

'Hello, Molly!'

She turned to see Albert, who had gained weight and lost hair, but still retained that stoic half-smile that got him through life. There was a beat of unease that the intervening years had failed to dilute. She wondered if he, like her, still thought back to the day he had broken down in her hallway and cradled baby Joe in his arms.

'Albert.' She smiled, pleased to see him. To her surprise and with a measure of unease, she watched him walk forward and wrap her in a cautious hug and then, to her mortification, he started to cry. 'I don't know how we can ever thank you, Molly, I just don't . . .'

She pulled away from the big man's grip and put her hands on her hips, moved by his words and grateful for his actions. 'Well, here's the thing, Albert. The last time I saw you, you cried, and I've not seen you for an age and, apparently, you're still crying. This really won't do! We need to find a way to stop those tears or else the next fifty or so years are going to be a little awkward.' She seated herself at the table.

Joyce, she noted, mopped her own face with a tea towel before speaking from the heart.

'We are lucky, you know, we all are. Just to have a part in his life, just to spend time with him, which you can, too, Molly, whenever you want. Yes, you're his aunt, but you are also a spare mum to him, as well as my sister and my greatest friend. He will always be in your life and you will always be in his.'

'That's all I've ever really wanted.' Molly swallowed the tears gathering at the back of her throat.

'Our boy will be so loved.' Joyce beamed.

'Our boy . . .' Molly liked the sound of that.

'What's going on?' Joe asked from the back door, where he had appeared with a leather football under his arm.

'Nothing!' Joyce sniffed. 'It's just very emotional for Molly and me as we haven't seen each other for a long time and we love each other very much.'

He pulled a face and dismissed her words with a slight shake of his head. 'Do you want to come outside and stand in goal, Auntie Molly?' he asked, bouncing the ball on the floor.

'In goal?' she asked, as she rose from the table.

'Yes.' He nodded. 'You have to try and save my goals while I kick the ball at you.'

'Why, I'd love nothing more!' She walked towards the boy, who, without further ado, took her hand. An act so simple, so small and yet she knew she would never be able to describe the feeling of his little fingers wound around her palm, but knew also that she would never forget it. She looked back over her shoulder to see Albert with his head on Joyce's shoulder, both clearly overcome with emotion, and she quite understood, walking into the garden with her son by her side, her hand inside his, as if it were not the most magical moment of her life.

David and Clara arrived in Tonbridge a little before teatime with the teenage Clementine in tow and Hetty, who was seven. Her brother was as pleased to see her as ever, while looking at her carefully with his professional hat on. It was only when he gave her a subtle nod and a wink that she felt she had passed the test. The adults congregated around the kitchen table.

'Why don't you go and play in the garden with the little ones?' Clara suggested to Clementine, who these days preferred to sit among the grown-ups, thereby stifling their conversation.

'I'd rather stay in here, thanks,' she huffed.

'You might like to spend time with Joe? You haven't seen him for an age?' her dad said, in an effort to coax her.

'I don't *want* to play with the children. I hate children! Hetty drives me mad and Joe is just another child, like Hetty!' She folded her arms across her pale pink cardigan.

'You won't always hate children, darling. You'll most likely have some of your own one day!' Clara said to placate the thirteen-year-old, as Joyce and Molly exchanged a knowing look.

'I am *never* going to have children because I am never going to get married!' Clementine asserted. This time, Joyce pulled a face at Molly and she knew that, like her, her sister was thinking that the two were not mutually exclusive. It was a nice moment of shared humour that reminded her of why they were close.

'Clementine, would you mind keeping an eye on the little ones for us?' Albert fished in his pocket. 'I would fully expect to pay for your babysitting services.' He pulled out a few shillings and handed them to his niece.

'Wow!' Clementine grabbed them, her mouth open, eyes wide. 'Thank you, Uncle Albert!' she said, beaming, and strode out to the garden to get on with the job in hand.

'Takes after her mother,' David chuckled. 'Easily swayed with a bribe.' Clara slapped her husband with her gloves and laid them back on the table. It felt good to have the family reunited, as if peace of mind was now restored, the jigsaw complete. And Molly felt surrounded by people who loved her and whom she loved back. Despite everything, she really did feel like one of the lucky ones.

'So what's it like to be back?' Clara asked as she sipped her tea.

'It's wonderful, of course, apart from the house,' Joyce said, wincing.

'What's wrong with the house?' Molly asked.

'I don't want to sound spoilt, but where we stayed in Canada was spacious and open-plan. This now feels a little claustrophobic.

I'd like to smash down the wall between the kitchen and the dining room and make one, bigger room.'

'But everyone would see the kitchen and you'd be able to see everyone eating!' Clara added, a wrinkle appearing at the top of her nose, as if the very thought was preposterous.

'Well, that would rather be the point, Clara.' Joyce smiled. Molly hid her laughter in her teacup.

David intervened to change the topic. 'I see there's a new Agatha Christie play opening later in the year – *The Mousetrap*. A friend of mine is involved in the score. He can get us good tickets if anyone's interested. I thought we should go when it opens in case it only has a short run.'

'Think I'll pass!' Albert grimaced. 'I am not a theatre person. Bloody chairs are always too small to be comfortable.'

'What about you, Molly? You like the theatre.' David smiled at her, her lovely big brother.

'Yes, I'll come. I mean, why not? I like being in town, and now I'm footloose and fancy-free, for a while at least . . .'

'You should come in for lunch next week! The Barts canteen isn't up to much but the lunch steward is not averse to serving the odd sherry to toast the King.'

'Queen!'

'We have a queen!'

'There's a queen now!'

Molly, Clara and Joyce all chorused together to remind him that they had a new monarch on the throne.

David hit his forehead with his palm. 'I still can't get used to it. Not that I don't think she'll do a marvellous job, but a king is all I've ever known! Anyway, Little Moll, we can have a proper catch-up.' He looked her in the eye and she knew this meant a heart-to-heart about her mental health. She was grateful for his love and concern.

'I'd like that.'

'Mom!' Joe called loudly from the garden and it was almost automatic the way David and Clara looked at Molly.

'Coming!' Joyce called, and went outside.

There was a moment of quiet hesitation as the family navigated these new and uncharted waters. It was Clara who spoke first.

'You know, Molly' – she paused – 'you really are quite a remarkable woman.'

'She is,' Albert concurred, and they continued to drink their tea in silence.

Molly felt a lump rise in her throat and gave Albert a wide-eyed stare, warning him not to cry again, and they both laughed.

SEVENTEEN

London
1968
Aged 43

Molly sat alone on the train, smiling broadly, despite the man in the seat opposite blowing cigarette smoke that hit her full in the face and which she knew would cling to her hair. This happened on occasion, this secret burst of inner happiness, when a thought or memory from the weekend just spent filled her with such joy that she was able to live off it for days to come. Yesterday, the family had celebrated Joe's twenty-fourth birthday. It was an odd thought that he was now older than she was when she had given birth to him and yet, when she looked at him, fresh out of university with the ink on his civil engineering degree still wet, he still seemed to her like a child in many ways. She had arrived at the house in Tonbridge, admired the new addition of a kitchen-cum-dining room, very American and open-plan and with all mod cons: a recessed stainless-steel sink with a drainer and Formica worktops in a faux-marble pattern. Joyce was terribly happy with it and Albert, as ever, stood quietly in the background, enjoying his wife's delight at the fruits of his labours. A cupboard with a sliding glass door was suspended from the ceiling on chrome rods, holding all of Joyce's fancy crystal, to which Molly had to pay especial attention as her sister demonstrated the sliding mechanism.

'Isn't it clever?'

'Very,' Molly offered in her subdued manner, and would never have confessed to preferring the soft lines of her own cottage kitchen, the pale wood and mismatched shelves that housed her equally mismatched cups and saucers. 'What on earth is all this?' She laughed at the strips of blue crêpe paper fashioned into streamers and strung around the room as though Joe was still a child. Joyce had suddenly grabbed her wrist and pulled her into the downstairs cloakroom. Molly was a little taken by the urgency of it.

'Right, just quickly, I've sent David, Clara, Clementine, Hetty and the gang up to the top of the garden . . . Oh goodness, I'm all of a dither!'

'Calm down, Joyce, what's wrong? It's only a birthday party!' she reminded, her words belying the whoosh of excitement in her gut at the prospect of seeing her boy.

'You're right, of course, but here's the thing . . . Joe will be here any minute with his new girlfriend, Estelle – he seems quite keen.' She fanned her face, still pretty despite the lines that criss-crossed around her eyes and puckered her top lip.

'Yes, so you said on the phone.'

'Please promise me you won't laugh, Moll.'

'At Estelle?' She wrinkled her nose, trying to figure out why Joyce might think she would laugh at the poor girl on their first meeting. 'Why would I?'

'No! Good heavens, not at Estelle – at the birthday cake! Clara insisted on doing the honours, and you know I can't say no to her because she can be so terribly sensitive.'

Molly rolled her eyes at the complete ridiculousness of it all, especially as Joyce could be very persuasive but didn't seem to recognise the fact.

Joyce continued to witter. 'Anyhow, it's a disaster – a complete disaster – and everyone's being polite, and because David is so wary of upsetting his wife, we all have to smile and pretend it's a work of art, but it's hopeless! It's supposed to be a chocolate sponge, but heaven only knows . . . Just don't laugh!'

'I won't laugh.' Molly drew a cross over her heart.

'Well, that makes me feel a bit better. Do you think I should brief Joe?'

'No, for goodness' sake! You'll make it a much bigger deal than it needs to be. It can't be that bad.'

'You haven't seen it—' Joyce whispered in horror.

The doorbell rang and both women smiled.

'That'll be our boy.' Joyce kissed her sister warmly on the cheek. 'You doing okay?'

'I *am*! Stop fussing and open that door!'

Joyce hurried from the cloakroom and Molly took a minute to compose herself. She gazed at herself in the looking glass over the basin and tucked her straight hair behind her ears, then ran a finger over the edges of her mouth to neaten her pale lipstick. She thought for the first time in an age of Geertruida, who had always favoured the reddest lips. Even after all these years she still felt the pang of lost friendship in her belly.

'Mom!' And there it was. The word that drew her from her memories, sending a jolt of current through her bones, still with the power to make her gut knot.

'Come in, come in! Happy birthday!' Joyce called.

Molly came out of the cloakroom and raised her hand in a wave.

'Auntie M!' Joe, her sweet, sweet boy, walked towards her, with a gait and expression so much like his father's it almost took her breath away.

'Happy birthday, darling.' She let him envelop her in a hug, feeling the delicious warmth of his skin against hers and breathing in his scent. Molly closed her eyes briefly within his arms and remembered the moment twenty-four years ago when she had felt him slip from her and held him close on the bathroom floor: all arms and legs and surely the most beautiful thing she had ever seen.

'So what do you think, Auntie M – do you like the beard?' He called her M, she didn't know why. He always had and it meant more than she could ever possibly explain.

'. . . I shall call you M – and everyone will think it's short for Molly, but you and I will know differently. M for "marvellous" . . .'

'Hmmm . . .' She reached out and used the excuse to touch his chin softly. 'I can't say I'm that enamoured, but what do I know?' she said with a shrug. 'And your hair is very long!'

'Thanks!' He took it as a compliment she had not intended. She and Joyce chuckled.

'So where's the girlfriend?' Joyce asked, closing the front door.

'Ah, change of plan. She's travelling from Oxford so I said I'd meet her here.'

'Ah, lovely,' Joyce said, clapping her hands in delight.

'Joe!' Clementine and Hetty came through the back door and were keen to greet their cousin. Their own children, three in all now, plodded along behind. Clementine's twin boys – Arthur and Lindsey, named after their great-grandfather – were both fretful. They garbled at the same time some convoluted tale of how their cousin, Hetty's daughter, Frances, had been mean to them, and somehow involving stolen sweets.

'I'm sure she didn't mean it.' Clementine's husband, Giles, removed his pipe and tried to console his boys. Molly saw him exchange an understanding look with David, his father-in-law, suggesting that actually Frances might well have meant it, whatever it was she had done *this* time. Not that Clementine would hear a word against her sons, the apples of her eye and suitably spoiled.

David came over and put his arm over her shoulder. 'Hello, Moll – twenty-four, eh?' She knew this was her brother's subtle way of acknowledging the significance of this day for her and quietly thanked him for it.

'I know, all grown-up and beardy.'

'Yes.' David clicked his tongue. 'Very beardy. Wouldn't have lasted five minutes in my regiment looking like that!' He chuckled and Molly once more silently gave thanks – the very reason she had stepped forward to help make the world a better place, free of war, so that her beloved child would never have to.

'Okay, everyone! Here we go! Ta-dah!' Clara could be heard from the kitchen, and suddenly there she was in the hallway, dressed in an ornate beaded kaftan and holding a wooden breadboard on top of which sat a monstrosity of a cake.

'Good Lord!' Joe gasped at the brown, misshapen boulder, which had five candles stuck in at odd angles on the top. 'Did the kids make it?' he laughed, as if wanting in on the joke.

'No! No, they did not! *I* made it!' Clara tutted loudly. Molly and Joyce stared at each other and Molly bit the inside of her mouth to keep her promise.

'It looks like poo-poo!' Frances announced, and the boys forgot their beef with their cousin and laughed loudly.

'Frances!' Hetty called out. 'It does not look like poo-poo!'

'It does!' the twins giggled, jumping up and down. 'It looks like poo-poo!'

'It's chocolate!' Clara shouted loudly, as if this might calm things.

Molly wasn't sure who laughed first, but would have said Joyce, until they were all howling, all, that was, except Clara, who stormed off to the kitchen with the offending article.

'Well, that's my evening ruined – you think she'll let this go?' David laughed, in spite of his dire prediction.

Molly looked around with a feeling of warmth at the family – her family – and remembered what her sister had said all those years ago . . . '*We are one family, Molly, all of us. He might call me Mama right now, but never forget I am your sister who loves you very much and we are raising him in that family. We are all one family . . .*'

In the midst of the mayhem the front doorbell rang. Joyce wiped the tears of laughter from her lashes with the edge of her tea towel and opened the front door. In walked a pale girl with very long hair. Molly, however, was not looking at her but at Joe, who was staring at the girl, his eyes wide and an enormous smile on his face, as if seeing her felt like coming home. Molly might have been forty-three, but just like that she was nineteen again and her stomach folded with longing for the man she had loved and lost, yearning to dance in his arms one more time.

Estelle. Molly had liked the girl, with her confident, easy manner and intelligent conversation. She thought about her now, still smiling as the train pulled into Liverpool Street Station.

It was undoubtedly her favourite time of the working day, that twenty-five minutes before the department opened to the rest of the hospital for what was always a busy day. She drew in the scent of the room, not dissimilar to that of a library, a mixture of dust, thumbed pages and the energy recognisable to anyone who has searched for or read the written word while standing. These precious minutes felt like her thinking time as she prepared for what lay ahead, organising and checking the files for St Bartholomew's Hospital, or Barts, as it was affectionately known, where she had been working in the records department for nearly sixteen years now, first as a clerk, but now running the department with an assistant. Going to meet her brother there for lunch all those years ago, she had spotted an advertisement looking for administrative staff and had wandered in. She had been neat, smart and had assured them of the very best references from the Ministry of Defence, thinking she would circumnavigate the vile Mr Allan. David had teased her afterwards that a quick mention of her brother working on-site as a senior consultant would have done her chances no harm.

Molly recalled a time when she had flirted with the idea of a career in diplomacy or the Foreign Office, but that was before her life had changed in ways she could not have imagined. And now, with one foot in middle age, she found the sorting of paper and cardboard folders for patients entering the wards or leaving their care to be absolutely reward enough. There was something comforting about the organising and bundling of stacks of paper, the placing of files into alphabetical order and the auditing of the large metal filing cabinets that stood in proud banks along the rear wall of the large office. It was a job with rhythm, routine and order, and it helped calm her sometimes less than ordered thoughts. At the end of the day she found it most satisfying to know that patients A–C had been neatly filed or handed over to the relevant departments and drew motivation from doing the same thing the next day and the day after that . . . It was a role that helped oil the machinery of the glorious National Health Service now providing health care to all those in need, regardless of their ability to pay: a truly wondrous thing.

'Good morning, Miss Collway!'

Mr Kendall, who also worked in the administration department, offered his customary greeting across the large foyer. He had been one of the first staff members to welcome her when she took up the role all those years ago.

'But there must be some mistake!' he had shouted on her first day, so loudly it had caused everyone to look in their direction and a blush to spread over her cheeks. 'The records office is traditionally the spinster department – it's where the women in tweed hide!' She had pictured her very own tweed skirt and vowed never to wear it to work. 'Surely to goodness, dear, you need to be somewhere where the pretty girls go, such as the maternity reception or podiatry!'

At the time it had felt like a lovely compliment and Molly smiled to think of it now.

'Good morning, Mr Kendall.'

She also now hated the word 'spinster' – detested it like no other. It irked her that the word 'bachelor' implied naughtiness, a cad, someone who maybe liked to play the field, refusing to be shackled for life! And yet 'spinster' was in her experience a state to be pitied. She had remarked as much to Mr Kendall some years back, who had simply clasped her hand and told her, 'You worry too much, Miss Collway, and fret not – for the times they are a-changin'!'

Molly had removed her hand quickly. 'Not for me, Mr Kendall. I am quite happy with my lot, thank you very much. And why does everyone assume I need a man?'

And this was her truth. Her cottage in Chelmsford was her haven, her work satisfying and her garden a joy, while the love of her family sustained her and she saw her son with a regularity that gave a warm dimension to her single life. And as for the lack of romance, well, as someone had once remarked to her, no one gets all the gifts!

'Well, aren't we a bundle of sparkle-dipped sunbeams today!' he had teased, and she had laughed.

Janice, Molly's young assistant, spent the few minutes before the office officially opened scratching her peroxide roots and studying her face in a compact mirror, trying to ascertain whether the black butterfly flicks of eyeliner that ran along her lids and up at the corners of her eyes towards her temples were as even as she hoped. Fascinated by the girl's make-up, Molly stared at the clogged and tarry eyelashes overwhelming her pretty eyes and the panstick foundation which stopped abruptly in an unfortunate line below her chin and left orange-toned licks on every scarf or collar. Her choice of clothing was equally intriguing. Aware it was now the height of fashion, it was still quite shocking for the demurely dressed Molly that Janice and many of her peers wore skirts, often in various shades of suede, that barely covered their modesty. Estelle, she had been pleased to notice, had been wearing some rather attractively patterned trousers. Once or twice Janice had bent over to retrieve something from a lower drawer of a filing cabinet and Molly and any nursing staff who happened to be browsing were given a full flash of Janice's own lower drawers. Molly hadn't known where to look and ridiculously took the embarrassment Janice herself lacked and made it her own. It took all her restraint not to whip off her cardigan and rush forward to shield all and sundry from the sight. She knew the action alone would have been worth performing just to make Joyce laugh in the retelling.

Janice inhabited an unfamiliar world where sex, multiple boyfriends, wardrobes stuffed with clothes and even drugs were discussed freely and enjoyed openly. It wasn't that Molly liked the life Janice lived per se – heck, she could barely comprehend it – but envy her she did. Not necessarily her choices, but that she had a choice at all. Joe, she knew, enjoyed similar freedoms; he had travelled a little, often visiting countries once considered as the enemy. Hearing him talk fondly about a visit to Germany was hard for her to comprehend – even in his own lifetime she had been forced to black out the windows and hide in a flimsy shelter, while bombs from low-flying aircraft sent by that very country did their best to destroy the city she loved. His view was soberingly balanced: 'You should see the pictures of Dresden just after the war, Auntie M. It really makes you think . . .'

It played on her mind sometimes, the fact that for the want of a couple of measly decades and the societal change that came with 'the pill' and the rising awareness of women's liberation, Molly might have been free to keep her baby boy and work for her own keep. She knew her mother's harsh views had been largely dictated by what the neighbours might think, tragic as that was. While it still wasn't common, she knew that in this day and age to have a baby out of wedlock was not the dark stain of shame it once had been.

It seemed that Molly's fascination for a life lived differently was mutual. She thought back to the day when Janice was lifting the ordered bundle of files for day surgery, ready for collection by the junior nurses, and had asked her outright, 'Where were you before this?'

'Where was I before what?' Molly was only half listening.

'Where did you work before you came here?'

'Well, I worked for various ministries before and after the war and I was ill for a spell and then I came here.' She gave the potted version.

'Various ministries? God, that sounds boring!' The corners of Janice's mouth drooped in distaste.

'It was. Very. It was boring and I was boringly safe.'

Run run run!

'Why were you ill?'

'Hmmm?' Molly gave by way of response, thinking of that morning over twenty years ago now when she had clung to the floor as she unravelled. *Sweet Telsie.* She could still see her pretty face smiling as she waved goodbye and sense the pain of losing Joe like a fresh and painful wound.

'I asked why you were ill?' repeated this girl with the social grace of a rhino.

'I had a mental breakdown, Janice. I lost my mind for a bit. Quite literally. So I went to a facility dealing with mental illness and I stayed for a few months until I felt better.' She looked the girl in the eye, giving the facts pure and simple, without shrouding them in a blanket of shame.

'So why did you have a mental breakdown, do you think?'

'Well, that's a good question.' Molly liked the girl's candour and paused from her task, tapping her pencil on her teeth. 'I think it's because too many sad things happened to me in a short space of time. It was as if I didn't have a chance to process any of it and then it all hit me at once, like a conveyor belt going slowly and then suddenly speeding up so fast that everything falls in a heap on the floor. That's what happened to me. I fell on the floor.'

'Oh my God! Did you get bombed? Was that one of the bad things?' the girl asked, wide-eyed. 'My nan's road did. One whole family gone in a minute, she said! They were in bed when it hit and my nan said that bits of bed and all the blankets were hanging on to the planks of the floor still left and you could see the wallpaper on the walls and the pictures and the wardrobes with clothes in, even the bath, but all the people had tumbled to the basement and were dead, like toys in a smashed doll's house. Can you imagine?'

Yes. Yes, I can . . .

'And you don't have a husband, Miss Collway?'

'No. No, I don't.'

'Are you . . . I mean, do you like . . .?'

Molly swallowed the embarrassment rising up from her chest and over her neck; this was a subject that left her feeling uncomfortable, no matter how modern. She thought of the ghastly Mr Allan making a pass at her.

'I do like men, Janice,' she offered, 'or rather I liked one particular man.' *And no one, no one has ever ignited the flame for me that
burned so brightly for a short time . . .* 'Let's just leave it at that, shall
we? I really don't know what it all has to do with sorting patient
records, which is precisely what we are here to do.'

'I can't wait for today to be over!' Janice said, spitting on her
fingertip to remove some flecks of mascara from beneath her left
eye. The words pulled Molly back to the present.

'Janice, we haven't started work yet and you're already wanting to be gone,' Molly commented in her firm but friendly way,
reminding herself daily that Telsie had needed more kindness than
perhaps she had offered and not willing to make the same mistake
with Janice. She knew from her own experience that you never
really knew anyone's story.

'I know, but I'm going to see The Doors at the Roundhouse
tonight and I am so excited!' The girl jumped up and down on
the spot, the vinyl of her white go-go boots creaking, and Molly
nodded, quite unaware that the girl had any interest in buildings
or their architectural features. It gave her hope for Janice – maybe
there was more to her than at first appeared.

Mr Kendall waltzed over and rested his beringed hand on the
wooden counter of the half-door where files were handed in and
collected, his jewels entirely in keeping with his role as Barts roy-
alty, having worked in the hospital since before the war and being
popular with all and sundry.

'So here we are, ladies – another glorious day awaits!'

'Indeed.' She smiled at the man. 'You look very smart today.'

'What do you mean *today*?' he said, placing a hand at his
throat. 'Darling, I look extremely smart every day!' he called as he
sauntered up the corridor.

She laughed at this truth. The man was always as neat as a pin. Molly admired his natty, brightly coloured silk bow ties, which added a splash of joy in all weathers.

Mr Kendall fascinated her: the first man she had ever known to be openly homosexual. Although, of course, there would have been others in her life who sadly would have had to keep their life and their loves secret up until the previous year, when private acts of homosexuality had been decriminalised between men over the age of twenty-one. Molly knew full well what it felt like to live a life tethered by convention and disapproval, at least for a while. It was as stifling as it was cruel.

'Ten minutes, Janice!' She liked to give the warning so that make-up was put away and smiles fixed in place by the time the medics were forming an orderly queue at the counter.

'I need to visit the ladies,' Janice announced, pulling a face.

'Janice, you have had all morning to visit the lavatory!'

'I didn't want to go then, but I want to go now,' she said with some urgency.

'Oh, for goodness' sake!' It bothered Molly that the girl could not judge her own bladder. 'Surely you can wait until your break.'

'Well, you'd better hope I *can* wait until my break or else you might want to call Fred the caretaker to come over with his mop and bucket.'

Molly ignored the girl's vulgarity but made a mental note to recount this scene to Joyce.

'Aye aye,' Janice said softly, scooting over to Molly. 'He's here again.'

'Who's here again?' Molly asked, confused, having totally lost the thread.

'Dr Jones,' Janice hissed from the side of her mouth.

Molly looked up and saw the man approach. 'That's not Dr Jones, it's Dr Bradford,' she whispered back, recognising the man.

'Yes, but that's what I call him because I think he looks like Tom Jones.'

Molly tutted.

'I think he fancies you, Miss Collway,' Janice whispered, pulling another face.

'Oh, don't be so ridiculous!'

'Well, how else should I say it?' Janice looked genuinely perplexed.

'I don't want you to say it in any way at all because it's complete poppycock!' In her embarrassment, Molly's reply was perhaps a little snappish. She was unnerved and surprised at her small frisson of excitement at the possibility that Janice might just be right. It was true that Dr Bradford and she had in the past shared a small smile and maintained eye contact a fraction longer than was strictly necessary as he collected his patient files. The girl's words were, however, as ridiculous as they were flattering.

Janice fiddled with her hair. 'How many senior doctors come down to collect or drop off their own patient files?'

'I really have no idea. Where exactly is this heading, Janice?'

'That doctor comes down at least once a month, if not more—'

Molly rolled her eyes.

'And I've noticed that if I'm at the hatch, he makes out to look at a file and then stands in the corridor until I disappear inside and then he pops up and you help him with his query – suspicious, don't you think?' Janice was now chewing the ends of her hair, a habit Molly found quite revolting.

'Well . . .' Molly thought about it and was surprised to find that her memory where the doctor was concerned was surprisingly sharp. He did indeed come down to the records department with more regularity than any other doctor . . . and he did always wait for her to assist him . . . Molly stopped talking and looked at Janice as the penny dropped . . . Could it be . . . could it be, as the girl was suggesting, that he did in fact just want to talk to her? Her heart beat a little faster at the prospect. There certainly did seem to be some kind of connection between them. 'Maybe he's simply passing by and it's easier than waiting for the files to be collected.'

Janice laughed more loudly than was appropriate in a hospital setting.

'Yes, that's right! Silly me!' Janice sighed and rolled her eyes. 'I have noticed how the doctors tend to do the nursing chores just to save the poor ladies some work!'

'I think you're making something out of nothing – don't you have work to do? Why not dust the shelves?' Molly suggested, grabbing the yellow duster from the drawer and flinging it playfully at her junior colleague.

'Well, maybe I am making something out of nothing, but here he is – again.' Janice laughed. 'Just nipping to the ladies.'

Molly wanted to call her back, but under what pretext? The fact that she did not want to be left alone with the doctor who was heading straight for the counter because of teenage nerves swirling in her stomach? It really was all as farcical as it sounded.

He walked over with a somewhat cautious air.

'Good morning,' he said, running his fingers through his thick, dark hair.

'Good morning.' She smiled, as if she had only just noticed him. 'How are you today?'

'Yes, I'm fine, and thank you for asking.' He coughed. 'I need the files for follow-up appointments under my name, please.'

'Yes, of course.'

'It's Bradford, Dr Rex Bradford.'

'Yes, I remember. But I didn't know the R stood for Rex. That sounds like the name of a movie star.' She spoke without any apparent shyness and, much to her relief, he laughed loudly and without reservation. It was flattering, being able to elicit a response like that from a man as handsome as him.

'A movie star, eh? Well, that might be nice, but no, I am nothing of the sort. Although I did a long time ago take part in a couple of army revues to lift morale. The critics loved me.'

She could tell by the crease at the sides of his temples and the downward tilt to his gaze as he said the words that he meant during the war, and also that he wanted to say no more. This was quite common – the 'least said, soonest mended' approach to the horrors of war that could keep a chap awake. She thought for the first time in a while of her own dad and his night-time shouts of terror.

'And now I work on the top floor.'

'Cardiology,' she added politely.

'That's right. And I believe you have a connection to David Collway?'

'That's my brother – my much, much older brother.' She gave him a warm smile.

'I've heard he's a good chap. I don't know him other than on nodding terms.'

'Well, *I* think he's a good chap, but then I am a little biased,' she said.

'My office is on the floor above his,' he said, pointing to the ceiling.

'Gosh, that's really quite a trek to come and collect your own patient files.' She liked the fact that he actually blushed.

'Yes, I do visit rather a lot.' He smiled at her.

Molly felt emboldened by the tone of their exchange. 'Do you like the exercise it gives you, Dr Bradford? Is that why you make the journey?'

'Please call me Rex. And in the spirit of openness, no, I do not particularly like the exercise or the trek, but I do like talking to you.' He held her gaze and she felt the stir of something in her gut, a bit like excitement, a bit like happiness.

'I see.' She looked him in the eye, feeling confident, sassy and with a rare pull of sexual attraction for this man.

Rex leaned forward. 'Is that "I see", as in now I've come clean you would rather I did not darken your counter again, or is it "I see" as in I would love to accompany you for a cup of tea on Sunday, somewhere yet to be decided as my mind has gone completely blank!' He laughed again.

Molly was unused to this kind of interaction. It felt risky and exciting. She took her time, making a judgement call.

'I think . . . I think the latter. I would like to come for a cup of tea with you, Dr Bradford—'

'Rex.' He cut in.

'Yes, Rex. And I'm Molly.'

'I know.' He held her eyeline. 'I made it my business to find out – Molly.' It was as if he was trying the name out on his lips, and she liked the way it sounded.

Janice came trotting across the floor and took up her position behind the counter. Molly avoided making eye contact with her. Rex gave Janice a cursory nod.

'Let's say Claridge's, three o'clock?'

'Yes. Splendid. Lovely.' She wanted him to leave or, more specifically, wanted him out of Janice's earshot.

He glanced at his watch and set off towards the stairs.

'You forgot the files!' she called out.

'I'll send someone down for them,' he replied, smiling.

'So? What did he want?' Janice asked with a slight smirk.

'He wanted to take me out for a cup of tea.' Molly decided to come clean, knowing the girl would only badger her for ever after if she did not.

'Aha!' Janice leapt forward and wrapped Molly in a crushing hug. 'I bloody knew it!'

'Janice, please, for goodness' sake – we're at work!' Molly disengaged herself and smoothed the front of her blouse, but in truth she was delighted at the whole carry-on, Janice's reaction included. Excitement stirred in the pit of her stomach for the first time in as long as she could remember.

Rex . . . She sounded the name in her head – the name of a movie star . . . *Dr Rex Bradford* . . .

EIGHTEEN

Mayfair, London
1968
Aged 43

Molly paced the Brook Street pavement with anticipation in her gut. It was 3 p.m. on the dot and, while she didn't want to be late, she was also overly concerned with arriving first, which would not be the done thing. Her nerves fluttered and she hoped she had chosen the right outfit. She remembered what Mr Kendall had said:

'*Breathe and remember it's supposed to be fun, not an ordeal. Don't wear the coral lipstick; it will drain your complexion in this winter light. Go for a bolder shade, a rust or a red, and smile, Miss Collway – remember to smile!*' He had pinched his cheeks to draw up the corners of his own mouth to demonstrate for her. The memory alone was enough to make her laugh and there it was, her smile.

Well done, Mr Kendall!

Molly checked that the chunky faux-malachite necklace was sitting straight under the collar of her navy blouse and then strode confidently through the door. She was, after all, the same woman who had flown into France in the dead of night and boarded a train in the dark with a toxic cargo sewn into her handbag . . . The place was glossy and glamorous in the way that big hotels did so well, and something she had quite forgotten. Vast plants sat proudly in brass planters atop marble tables. Art deco wall lights gave off a uniform glow. It put her in mind of the Ritz, where she and Geer had on occasion gone for a tipple in the bar. Her smile was wistful now, knowing how her friend back in the day would have danced into these shiny surroundings, arms flung wide with devilment coming off her in waves that proved alluring to all who surrounded her.

Dear, dear Geertruida . . . where are you now?

Molly spied Dr Brad— Rex, sitting at a table and was delighted to see he looked a little anxious, smoothing his hair as if a stray lock might seem important to him. It helped to see that he was not overly suave or cocky. Noticing his shirt and tie, she was glad that he found her worthy of making an effort with his dress. He looked up and waved her over. She was thrilled that someone was waiting for her, waiting to spend time with her.

'Hello, Rex. Well, isn't this lovely?'

'Molly.' He smiled and pulled out the chair for her. 'Yes, it is.'

'Thank you.' She sat and popped her handbag on the floor by the chair.

'I've taken the liberty of ordering afternoon tea. I hope that's all right?' There was the slightest quaver of nerves to his voice.

Molly noted the waiter in white gloves who was standing to attention mid-restaurant. She gazed at the white china teapot and the dainty milk jug next to the cups and saucers set just so. Rex poured. For the time being, they both ignored the silver three-tiered cake stand with its delicate array of dainty finger sandwiches and beautiful patisseries.

'This is such a treat. I can't remember the last time I had afternoon tea, unless you count a cup in front of the fire with a biscuit,' she said with a laugh.

'So where is home for you?' he enquired, briefly meeting her eyes.

'I have a little cottage in Chelmsford. It's a lovely spot in a quiet street, but the town is growing.'

'Everywhere is growing – a good thing, I think. People need housing and, if there are jobs, it has to be good for the country.'

'Yes, I agree. I think going through war can make you fearful of change. All we wanted was stability, wasn't it? We tried so very hard to keep our world from changing back then, and so now, when it happens by default, it can feel quite alarming, even when it's change for the better.'

'I've never thought of it like that, but yes, I think you're right . . .'

'And where do you live, Rex?'

'Richmond – been there for nearly ten years—'

'Richmond's nice, not that I've been for yonks. I tend to spend my spare weekends with my sister, her husband and my nephew.' After all these years, she was finally comfortable with the shape of the word in her mouth. 'They're down in Tonbridge, Kent.'

'I like to be near the river – a place to walk and clear my head.' He rubbed his forehead.

'For me that place is my garden. I've become a bit obsessed with it – you know those green-fingered people who go out in all weathers with a pair of secateurs in a sou'wester? Well, I'm one of them.'

Rex gave a short laugh. 'My wife was the gardener. She passed away three years ago now.' He blinked.

'Oh, I am sorry.' She held his stare and he nodded, as if acknowledging the hurt and Molly's acceptance of it.

'Well, that's life, isn't it? We all go through it.' Rex reached for his teacup. 'We all think we're immune from the bad things, but none of us are.' His words felt like another connection of sorts – she herself had not been immune and hoped he might understand a quiet, complex character such as hers.

Molly sipped her own tea. 'That's true, and yet sometimes it can feel as though we're the only ones who have ever been hurt.'

'Yes.' He nodded, and the two locked eyes.

And just like that the conversation was suddenly easy and Molly felt the residue of any nerves leave her stomach. She smiled at the man sitting opposite her, who, she had to agree, in a certain light did have a bit of the Tom Jones about him . . .

'Would you like to walk after this, Molly? I do like a stroll on a Sunday afternoon.'

'I'd like that very much,' she said, sipping her tea. 'Hyde Park would be nice.' She mentioned the closest spot, anything other than risk him suggesting the Embankment.

'Yes, Hyde Park would be nice,' Rex agreed, taking her plate to offer her a delicious sandwich.

'Well?' Mr Kendall grabbed her arm almost the second she stepped inside her office. 'I want to hear all about it – all the juicy details!' he demanded, waving his hand in the air.

'It was nice,' she said with a coy smile, shaking off her coat and pushing her silk scarf down into the empty sleeve before placing it on her personal hanger on the hooks outside in the corridor leading to the X-ray department.

'Nice?' He grimaced. 'Oh please, Miss Collway! "Nice" is for a decent macaroon or good weather. Nice is not passion! It's not lust!' he declared. 'Nice is a day out with your grandmother!'

'Well.' She swallowed, wishing he would keep his voice down and wary of Janice arriving any moment and joining in the badgering. 'There was certainly no passion or lust, not in the middle of Claridge's.'

'More's the pity!' he cut in.

'But,' she giggled, 'I am going to see him again next Sunday and we're going to Kew to look at the plants and walk in the gardens.' She had informed Joyce of their plans down the telephone yesterday.

'Oh my goodness! Richmond is only a hop, skip and a jump from Kew – I bet he's planning on taking you back to his place after for a bit of rumpy pumpy!'

'Joyce, first of all, he is not like that—'

'All men are like that!' her sister had interjected.

'And secondly,' Molly had said, ignoring her sister, 'I don't think anyone actually uses the words "rumpy pumpy"!' She had laughed.

'Apart from me.'

'Apart from you.'

'A second date!' Mr Kendall clapped his hands, pulling her back into the present. 'Well, this is progress indeed. Right, what are you going to wear?'

'Good Lord, I haven't given it a moment's thought!' she lied, knowing she was going to wear her wine-coloured jersey shirt dress, pair it with some knee-high boots and had already decided to get her hair set on her day off. Not that she was about to share that level of detail with Mr Kendall.

'Well?' Both turned to see Janice racing across the floor towards them, her heels clicking on the parquet floor in her haste. 'How did it go?'

'They're going out again!' Mr Kendall stole the punchline.

'A second date!' Janice looked just as delighted as Mr Kendall and Molly had to admit that their level of interest in her well-being was quite lovely.

'Well, we haven't used the word "date" exactly,' Molly said in an effort to quell their excitement, 'but it will certainly be nice to see him again.' It was as much as she was prepared to give away.

'Anyway, I can't stand here gossiping with the two of you all day – I have a department to run. Come along, Janice!'

'I would say she has a definite spring in her step and a smile on her face, wouldn't you, Janice dear?' Mr Kendall made out to whisper, but loud enough for Molly to hear.

'I would, Mr Kendall, I really would!'

And despite herself Molly laughed, really quite taken by the whole turn of events.

Sunday came around quickly. Molly stood in front of the iconic Palm House, where they had agreed to meet. It was a cold day, but the sun was shining and the world looked beautiful.

'Molly!' She heard him call out and it was her turn to wave as he trotted along the path in his navy mackintosh.

'Am I late?' he asked, breathing heavily.

'No, I'm early – always am. Force of habit.'

The Église Saint-Martin.

Right on cue the church bells rang out.

One . . . two . . . three . . . four . . . She was in place and on time. Four o'clock . . .

'It's so nice to see you. I've been thinking about it all week.' His openness was as surprising as it was welcome.

'Well, that's such a nice thing to say to me.' She meant it, and when he took her hand and linked it through his crooked arm, she nuzzled in.

'This makes it two Sundays in a row; people will start to talk,' he joked.

She laughed and thought of her two nosey colleagues and her sister, who were already talking.

'So, Rex, you know all about my job; I want to know about life as a cardiologist!'

'Oh, you really don't!' he laughed. 'It's not as interesting as it might sound.'

'Try me.' She liked walking along by his side, liked the height of him, the solidity of him and his scent, which was woody and clean.

'I became quite fascinated with hearts during my time in theatre, how they functioned, how they went wrong and how I could fix them. I knew I wanted to specialise in it if I ever' – he swallowed – 'if I ever got home again.'

'Did you have a terrible war?' She hardly dared ask.

'Didn't everyone?' he jested, but she caught the flash of naked fear in his eyes.

'I don't talk about it much,' she admitted.

'Nor me. It feels as though everyone who was there has their own story, and mine is no different. And those who were lucky enough *not* to be there don't want to be reminded or simply can't imagine what it was like.'

'Yes, and that's why we fought, of course, so those who came after would *not* know what it's like to see their blood or that of their friends running into the earth of which they will forever be a part.' She knew Johan's words by rote and the two stopped walking.

'That is beautiful. Is it a poem?' he asked sincerely.

'In a way.' She squeezed his arm.

'I like it very much.' He looked into the middle distance, took his time. 'I was a prisoner of war.'

'Oh, Rex!'

'Yes.'

'I don't know what to say,' she said truthfully, 'apart from how truly appalled I am to hear that.'

'You ask if I had a terrible war and I suppose it's fair to say I saw terrible things and I did terrible things. Sometimes you have to, just to survive.' He blinked.

'Yes, you do.' Molly knew that the experiences she had heard from the men she had worked with and the pictures she had seen herself would stay with her always. She believed everyone should see and hear them – a way to make sure that nothing like it would ever be allowed to happen again. 'Where were you?'

'I was initially in Stalag Luft I, Western Pomerania, Germany. Made myself a bit of a nuisance escaping, and then from a few other places, and finally ended up in Colditz.' He took a deep breath. 'I don't tell people usually. I don't know why I've told you. I suppose I wanted to.'

'Well, I'm glad you felt able to.' Molly felt the conversation bring them closer together, in the way that an exchange of secrets often did, and was thrilled at the deeper connection this shared experience had forged between them.

The two walked on in silence for a moment until Rex turned to her. 'Would you like to come to my house? It's only a hop, skip and a jump from here.'

Molly bit her lip to stifle a laugh and nodded vigorously.

'We can grab a taxi,' he smiled, pulling her towards him. She felt a bit dizzy and really rather excited.

He lived in a neat and sturdy red-brick house, very similar to Joyce and Albert's place, but without the homely atmosphere and smart decor. If anything, it felt a little cold, sad even. It felt like somewhere in which Rex ate and slept, rather than lived. Molly was reminded for the first time in years of her digs in St Pancras, which had merely been somewhere to lay her head, functional and quite brutal, which, with her head and heart broken, was the very last thing she had on her mind. It felt odd for Molly to be here among all the personal things treasured by Rex's dead wife: another woman's choice of crockery, a set of what looked like 'best' china in a glass-fronted display cabinet and framed tapestries on the walls. She stood a little awkwardly in the rather sparse kitchen.

He laughed a touch nervously as he shook off his mackintosh. 'Would you like a cup of tea, Molly?' he offered. 'Can't promise the level of service we had last week, though.'

Molly liked the way he moved and studied the definition of his muscled back beneath his shirt. There was an intense burn of desire in the pit of her stomach. 'I don't want tea, Rex.'

'Well, what do you want?'

She took a step closer, let her handbag fall to the floor and reached up to kiss him hard on the mouth.

The two lay on the rug in front of the coal fire with a floral counterpane pulled over their naked forms. She ran her toes along his shin and tried not to think of Johan, tried not to dilute thoughts of Rex with those of the only other man she had slept with.

'What do you think of the phrase "rumpy pumpy", Rex? Are those words you would ever use?' She hid her laughter.

'I don't think so!' He kissed her head. 'But if you want me to . . .' He let this hang.

'No, that's fine. Aren't we the daring young things?' She leaned on her elbow and gazed at his handsome outline. 'Sex on a Sunday afternoon! Although I suppose it is the sixties.'

'I want you to know that I don't make a habit of this, Molly.'

'I didn't think you did.' She liked his honesty, his slight hesitance and shy diffidence, when he had every reason to be bold and self-assured. 'I feel honoured that you shared your war story with me today, Rex, I really do. It means a lot.'

He kissed her again.

She took a deep breath. 'My war was an adventure.' She laughed drily at the understatement. 'Wonderful in some ways,' she said, as she remembered dancing with Johan to the sound of Billie Holiday . . . 'But it was what came after that was very . . .' She stopped talking.

'Very what?' He leaned up to face her and asked with such intensity that it felt like the most natural thing in the world to confide in this man.

'Very difficult.' She gulped nervously.

Rex ran his fingers over the side of her neck and it sent a glorious shiver down her spine.

'I lost the man I loved – he was killed – and I then spent some time working in France, all terribly hush-hush.' She shook her head, hearing the sounds Violet had made. 'And afterwards, things certainly overwhelmed me and I lost my mind for a while. I had a breakdown.' She looked up briefly and his expression was listening and intense. 'So I went into hospital, a place in Lowestoft for the mentally ill. I had given up entirely and I was very fragile. I hoped it would be a quick thing – you know, a spot of sea air, clear my head – and I'd be brand new, but it wasn't quite like that.' She paused for a beat to order her words. 'I spent a few months dosed up on a cocktail of sedatives and tranquillisers. Much of it is a blur, as you can imagine, but certain days and certain events are still sharp.'

'Oh, Molly, you poor thing.' He took her hand in his and it helped.

'I've told no one about this either, not outside my family, but it feels good to tell someone.'

'I know what you mean.' He gripped her hand and the two settled back on the rug, her head on his chest, looking up at the swirly pattern on the ceiling. Rex was quiet and she took this as her cue to continue. It felt cathartic, just talking about it.

'It was like sleeping among the damned.' Molly swallowed. She looked up at Rex, expecting comment, but instead he held her tightly. She thought of the day David had driven her to Winterhill Lodge.

'*It has wide sandy beaches. It all sounds rather nice . . .*'

But it hadn't been rather nice.

'The other residents were poor souls, all suffering from mental breakdowns, the effects of war, people reliving their own personal horrors, crying out in the night.' She swallowed. 'Along with some elderly people who were just senile. They tended to wail during the day, so it was always noisy. I got attacked a couple of times. Violence was common. I remember cowering from the blows of one particular patient called Big Betty – a huge woman.' She shuddered at the memory. 'They removed all her teeth to stop her biting staff and patients, but Betty found another sport: she liked to thump unsuspecting targets on the back of the head, creeping up quietly behind them and watching them fall like coconuts at a shy. And then the odd staff member was just quite disinterested – as though they didn't think we were people. I thought I might stay there for ever at first, and actually, in the grip of my illness, the prospect didn't bother me too much. It was a truly dismal place: no birds to be seen on the grass outside or in the air and with bars on the windows.'

'How did you leave?' he asked quietly.

'I got better is the simple answer.' She smiled at him. 'I woke one day and felt more present, more aware and knew I was emerging from something. I didn't know what, but I knew that I wanted to leave and that was the start of my recovery.'

Molly looked up at Rex. The memory was hard for her, but she took a deep breath and carried on with an edited version. 'So yes, I spent time at Winterhill and then returned to my little cottage in the Chelmsford suburbs, and then bit by bit I began gardening and going outside a little more, and slowly, gradually, I felt able to see people, talk to people, and I went back to work, and pretty much put it behind me, as far as you're ever able. But that's not what defines me, because I don't let it.'

'I think you're incredibly strong,' he said reassuringly.

And Molly smiled, wondering what he might think when she told him her full story, which could wait for now . . . She felt unburdened by the sharing of part of her history and the fact that he had not run for the hills.

Rex drew his arm from her shoulders and rose to his feet, reaching for his shirt and underwear. 'I think we both deserve that cup of tea now, Molly, don't you?'

'I do. A cup of tea would be lovely.' She pulled the cover up to her chin and lay back in this unfamiliar room, enjoying the sense of peace.

With their clothes restored and tea drunk, they sat together at the kitchen table. The atmosphere was oddly formal, considering how intimate they had been, in every sense.

'It's been quite a day. I think the next time we meet we should only do and talk about fun things!' Rex asserted.

'That's a deal.' She smiled, already very much looking forward to the next time.

Rex waved her off at the railway station. It was late when she got home, but still she kept her word and phoned her sister.

'Right, I want all the details!'

'What is it with people and details?' She giggled, still feeling gloriously languid, her muscles soft, her guard down.

'This is so thrilling, Moll! I've been beside myself all afternoon! Tell me everything.'

'Well, his name is Rex and he's quite fancy – got a bit of the Tom Jones about him.'

'How absolutely glorious!' Joyce squeaked. 'And did you go back to his?'

'Joyce, I am not that kind of woman.' Molly laughed.

'Oh crikey! You did – I can tell by your voice! You dark horse, Molly! How wonderful! And do you want to see him again?' Joyce pushed, her tone as eager as that of a child.

Molly smiled down the line. 'Yes, I rather think I do.' The two women squealed like girls who were still very excited about boys.

'So should I be looking at hats? And the big question is, are you going to beat Joe and Estelle up the aisle?'

'Oh, don't be so ridiculous!' Molly laughed, but didn't say no . . .

On Monday morning, as was now the pattern, Mr Kendall was waiting for her, keen to hear all about her time with the rather handsome Dr Rex.

'So come on, Miss Collway, tell me all about Kew! It's been an age since I was there.'

'Well, it was lovely, of course.'

'Of course. And how is Dr Bradford?' he asked with a wink.

'He's quite lovely too.' She looked around and, confident the coast was clear, whispered to her friend, 'I must admit, I like him, Mr Kendall, I do. "Like" is a good word for it. We had a smashing day and a very good chat.'

'Well, this is marvellous!' he said, clapping his hands in delight. 'Should I be looking at new hats?' He patted his coiffed hair.

'Oh dear God, no!' Molly scoffed. 'That's exactly what my sister said! But we *were* very open with each other about our past, which was surprising for me. I told him things I usually keep to myself. All a bit unnerving in hindsight, like . . .'

'Like letting someone in? Like giving permission for someone to get close? And yes, Miss Collway, that is a fearsomely brave thing.'

'Well, I don't know about brave.' Molly thought again of Violet. 'Although I suppose making the leap does feel risky,' she confided.

'I think, sweet lady, that if you're not ready now, then you never will be and that would be fine too. But you know—'

'Miss Collway!' Janice came running up the corridor, cutting Mr Kendall short and with what looked like post in her hand. 'This was in the pigeonhole for our department – a letter!' She waved it in the air before setting it in Molly's palm.

'Well, yes, Janice, I think even I could have deduced that!'

'It's a love letter!' Janice squealed. 'I can tell.'

'Oh, don't be ridiculous! Who would send me a love letter?' Molly tutted, as Mr Kendall and Janice exchanged a knowing look.

'I cannot think for the life of me!' Mr Kendall drummed his fingers on his chin as if in deep thought. The three of them laughed out loud in a rare giddy moment in the corridor. It was unusual, to say the least, receiving a letter at work, and Molly felt her heart race in anticipation as she opened the envelope and scanned the contents.

Molly,

I do not have your home address and so please forgive me sending this to your department. You are more than I hoped for – a warm, kind and intelligent soul.

She looked at her colleagues and giggled – was this actually a love letter? And why was she even giggling in this coquettish manner? She was a woman of forty-three, for heaven's sake, not some impressionable teen!

'Oh come on!' Mr Kendall said with a nudge. 'Don't leave us guessing – what does he say?'

'Please, Mr Kendall, a lady never tells!' she said, fanning her face with the paper and then returning her gaze to its contents.

> *But after our frank conversation, which I treasured, I have decided to reply with equal candour. The simple fact is that you are a wonderful person, truly wonderful, but I fear that your experience is too much for me. Your burden, which you carry so stoically and with such calm, is too much for me to contemplate. I barely cope with my own thoughts and memories and simply cannot imagine having to cope with yours too. I do hope you understand. It's not a personal thing to you, but is much more about my own state of mind. I'm like a man with a small float who just about manages to keep my head above water and to let someone else hang on would sink me and possibly sink us both. I shall miss . . .*

Molly stopped reading and cleared her throat. She popped the single sheet of paper back inside the envelope and tore it once, then twice, before throwing the pieces in the wastepaper bin by the door. Janice's hands fell to her sides and her smile faded. Molly gave her junior assistant a withering look, then glanced up at her other colleague.

'I think it's fair to say, Mr Kendall, that you will not be requiring a new hat any time soon.'

She never mentioned Dr Rex Bradford again. And from that day on, a junior nurse always made the journey to collect and drop off files for cardiology.

For Molly, the rest of that first day when she received the letter could not go quickly enough. Her manner was short, born out of discomfiture. She felt angry and naive to have been so open with the man. She went home that night, taking her usual train and walking from the station to her home, counting the streetlamps, as was her habit. She put her key in the door as she always did, but did not, as was usual, switch on the light in the hallway. Neither did she ease off her shoes one by one and place them side by side in the cupboard under the stairs, ready for the morning. Nor did she hang her coat on the hook inside the door of the cupboard with her scarf pushed down the arm for ease of discovery. No, instead of following her normal routine, which would otherwise include the popping on of the kettle and removing her supper from the fridge, she walked straight into the sitting room and, in the half-light, reached for the little walnut box. Taking it in both hands, Molly settled back into her armchair, the task trickier than usual with the bulk of her coat padding her seat. Gently she lifted the lid and carefully took out the little brass button nestled in the corner, first running it over her cheek and then clasping it snugly in her palm.

'You . . . you're probably right, Dr Rex,' she whispered. 'It is all too much . . . All too much.'

Molly regretted giving so much of herself away quite so freely, and this was nothing to do with sex, but rather that tiny inner kernel of hurt, tightly packed with secrets, that she carried always. The things she sometimes thought about when alone . . . that was what she had shared and was now angry at herself for having done so. She would have hoped that at her age she was a little less easily impressed by a man who was handsome, with his back strong and his arms comforting, to give away that little stone on no more than a whim, and yet she had done just that. She had cast it out like a hot thing to be passed palm to palm: its contents incendiary. And now here she sat. A little let down, having got quite caught up in the whirl of it all.

The telephone rang in the darkness and gave her a start. Molly put the little box on the table and lumbered from the chair to answer it.

'Chelmsford 286.' Molly gave her customary greeting when answering the phone.

'Hey, Auntie M.'

'Joe! Well, how lovely to hear your voice. How are you, darling?' She closed her eyes and let her love for him flow down the curly wire.

'I'm good – great, in fact. Have you got a minute?'

'Of course!' *For you I have every minute of every day . . . I could listen to your voice for hours and hours . . . and then I would replay every word in the quiet hours in my head . . .*

'I just wanted to ask you, what did you think of Estelle?' he breathed.

'Well, I thought she was just lovely. She seems smart and confident. I said to Joyce it was great how she just waltzed in and chatted and sat down, drank tea. Played with the little ones. There was no awkwardness or formality. It was as if we had known her for years, and that must have been quite an ordeal for her, coming to meet your mob.'

'*My mother waited for him on that Sunday, waited all afternoon. She . . . she had baked a cake and he never arrived. You took that last day from her. You took it from us! And I will never, ever forgive you for that . . .*' Molly cursed the thickening of her throat and ran the edge of the brass button over her cheek.

Joe laughed. 'That's kind of the thing – it's like I've known her for ever and nothing seems to faze her; it's just easy. I really . . . I like . . . It's like . . .'

'Do you love her, Joe?'

'I do.' She could tell he was smiling. 'That's exactly it, Auntie M – I love her.'

'How exciting, darling!' There was a flutter of joy in her gut. Her boy was in love!

'It is.' Joe took a deep breath. He sounded content. 'It really is. I can't stop thinking about her. All I want to do is be with her! It's nuts! Have you ever felt like that about someone?'

She took her time, wanting more badly than ever to tell him about the beautiful soul who had been his father. 'I have.'

'But you didn't . . . It didn't . . .'

'He was killed in the war.'

'Oh, that's horrible. How sad.' Joe's mournful tone for his father quite took her breath away. Molly sat up straight and did her very best to stay composed. Just speaking to Joe diluted her hurt over Rex, a warm reminder that she was loved.

'It was. It is. But you know, Joe, I wouldn't change a thing, not for a second, because we shared something incredible and true and life-changing, and I think if you're lucky enough for that to come along, you have to grab it with both hands and never let it go.' Her voice cracked. *You, Joe! You are the incredible life-changing thing and I give thanks for you every day!*

'I intend to, Auntie M.'

'Good for you, darling' – *our precious, precious boy* – 'good for you.'

NINETEEN

Molly scanned the shelves of the toyshop, pondering what to buy an eight-year-old boy for his birthday. Estelle had said to get a book token, but that felt a bit of a cop-out. Joe had given no indication that his son, Adam, was a reader. *Adam* . . . her grandson, who also called her Auntie M and was sweet and curious, very much like his dad, but with his mum's placid nature. Molly wanted to spoil the boy rotten but knew her role well enough to hold back a little and let Joyce and Albert buy his first set of football boots, pet rabbit and bike. The first time she had met the little fellow had been a glorious and difficult day. It was eight years ago now that Joe had proudly plonked his first child into her arms and placed a smacker on her cheek.

'How about that then, Auntie M? Isn't he brilliant?'

Molly had stared at the little boy in her arms, all arms and legs, and had felt quite overcome, only able to nod because yes, he was absolutely brilliant! She might have been in her fifties, but in that moment she was taken back to that day in the bathroom of Old Gloucester Street, recalling the feel of her back against the bathtub and the smell of her blood on her hands and on her baby. The way he had cried, the umbilicus still connected, as she swaddled him in a towel and held him close . . .

'Oh, Auntie M! Don't cry, you sentimental old thing!' Joe had put his arm over her shoulder.

'I am, Joe – a sentimental old thing!' she had managed through her tears, unaware that she had been crying. Joyce had walked in and stared at the three of them – Molly in the armchair holding baby Adam, and Joe, perched on the arm of the chair with his arm about Molly's back – and her expression was one that was hard for Molly to fathom, but looked awfully like guilt. It was one of the few moments when all Molly had given up and all she herself had experienced once again reared its head and threatened to derail her. A reminder that the fragility she had succumbed to so long ago was not gone entirely.

'Can I help you, madam?'

Back in the toyshop, Molly turned now to face a young man with a name badge pinned to the lapel of his brown pinstriped suit: 'Barry'.

'Yes, please, I'm struggling to know what to get an eight-year-old boy for his birthday.'

'Ah, follow me.'

Molly did just that until they stood in an aisle with small plastic figures on display that were the oddest things she had ever seen.

'What are they? I was thinking maybe a board game or something like Uno.'

'Trust me, madam. These are all the rage. They're from a new film, *Star Wars*, and kids can't get enough of them.' He handed her three. 'These are Han Solo, Luke Skywalker and Princess Leia. Any eight-year-old boy would be chuffed with these.'

'Well, if you say so!' She took them to the counter to pay. Barry followed her.

'Mind you, if you ask me, I suspect the whole *Star Wars* thing will be a bit of a flash in the pan, but as long as he likes playing with them, right?'

'Mmm.' She nodded and paid for the figurines and left the toyshop, heading for the supermarket next door to pick up a few bits and bobs.

Molly tuned out the irritating music piped into the supermarket via a slightly crackly sound system. She couldn't identify the tune but would have guessed at Bobby Crush, who she'd heard on the wireless, with a lively piano piece that she found quite unsuitable to aid browsing. Standing in the aisle, she stared at the array of teabags, narrowing her eyes to try and atone for her eyesight, which, since she had hit her fifties, was less than perfect. She scrutinised the display, trying and failing to see the difference in two alternative packets of her usual brand. One bore a picture of Her Majesty the Queen on the front and the other the regular logo. She reached up for one of each and studied them in her hands.

'What is the difference?' she wondered aloud, as had become her habit.

'Nothing. There is no difference, except that the box with the picture feeds the nostalgia.'

Molly felt her heart give a little skip and took a sharp breath. The voice spoke again.

'I don't think there's a single thing available in this whole supermarket that isn't telling us it's Jubilee year, as if we need reminding.'

She turned at the voice she recognised so well, the cockney accent as strong as it had always been despite the croak of age that subtly lowered the register.

'Oh my goodness – oh, Marjorie!' To say the name out loud felt odd and Molly wondered if she were real.

'Hello, Molly. I saw you through the window and did a double take myself. I can't believe it – fancy seeing you here! I was hardly going to walk past without stopping to say hello, was I?'

'Goodness me!' Molly repeated, one hand at the base of her throat as she tried to catch her breath, studying the face of her former colleague who had kindly stood outside the office while she made an illicit phone call. Her last phone call with Johan.

'*I can barely . . . It's . . .*' His beautiful voice had fractured and stuttered between the silences but was as clear to her now as if she had heard it yesterday. '*I'm going . . . for a while . . . Nothing to . . .*'

Nothing to worry about . . . Is that what you were going to say to me, Johan?

It was almost instinctive, the way Marjorie stepped forward and wrapped her in a hug, crushing the boxes of teabags between them. Marjorie, the agent who had put her in touch with Mr Greene and Mr Malcolm . . .

'Been a long time, Molly.'

'Yes . . .' Words failed her as her mouth struggled to catch up with the thoughts that hurtled and spun in her head. 'There's so much I want to say, I don't know where to start! How long is it since we've seen each other?'

'Thirty-odd years,' Marjorie confirmed.

Molly stared at this woman, whose skin was a little sallow now; her hair was styled into a Purdey cut, but flecked through with the beginnings of grey. Her once full lips were now a little thinner and sported the tiny carved lines snaking their way up to her nose typical of a smoker.

'We've both grown older.' Marjorie ran her fingers over her own less than taut neck, seemingly aware of the scrutiny.

'Lucky us.' The words came out without too much thought, but Marjorie nodded.

'Yes, lucky us. How's your family?' It felt like the most mundane of questions, but it didn't occur to Molly that she might mean a husband, children . . .

'My brother David passed away only last year, very suddenly – his heart.' To say it out loud still caused a lump of emotion to rise in her throat. 'I think we all thought he'd go on for ever.' She pictured Clara at David's wake, unnervingly quiet, subdued, and was reminded that, without him by her side, Clara was not a coper.

'It's hard, isn't it.' It was more of a statement than a question, suggesting, unsurprisingly, that in the intervening years Marjorie had experienced similar losses.

'So there's just my sister and me left now: Joyce and her husband and my nephew . . .' She let this trail.

'Your nephew?' Marjorie asked, her eyebrows raised briefly.

'Yes.' Molly held her stare.

'I see.' Marjorie gave a small nod of understanding and smiled at Molly, as if she recognised the sacrifice and respected her for it.

'Yes. In fact, I've just been shopping for his little boy who's eight – *Star Wars* figures.'

'What's *Star Wars*?' Marjorie asked.

'Oh, some new film, apparently.'

A girl walked past with rings through her nose and a collection of graduated studs snaking up the outside of her ear. Her make-up was heavy, dark-ringed eyes and black lips. Her hair was green and backcombed into a knotty mess. Her trousers and jacket were tartan with leather strips and zips sewn randomly that appeared to serve no purpose.

'Sorry, excuse me, could I possibly just . . .' the girl asked sweetly, reaching past Molly to select a box of Earl Grey from the shelf. 'Thank you.' She smiled and continued down the aisle. The women watched her walk away, taking in her attire.

'To think old Mrs Templar used to keep an eye on our hemline and tut if we wore too much lipstick!' Marjorie laughed.

'Garish!' Molly had quite forgotten the comment and the woman until that moment when it left her mouth.

'Yes, garish!' Marjorie laughed again.

'Oh my word, she was such a character, that Mrs Templar, tapping her watch and walking around with her clipboard as though it was surgically attached.' Inevitably, her thoughts turned to Geer, as, apparently, did Marjorie's.

'Did you and Geertruida ever—'

'No,' Molly said, cutting her short. 'I never saw her again. I've tried to track her down, but without any luck.' It amazed her that to say these words out loud brought a tightness to her chest and caused sadness to slip down her throat, even after all this time. It was a surreal experience, being confronted by this woman who was the only link to the people she had lost and a life she had tried to bury.

Marjorie nodded and took her cue no doubt from Molly's tone and the straightening of her shoulders, as she said no more about the girl with whom Molly had once been so close.

'Has life been . . .?' Molly let this trail, unsure of the right way to ask how Marjorie herself had fared, and indeed what did she expect – a run-down on the last three decades while she chose teabags?

'Yes.' Marjorie smiled. 'Life's been good, or more accurately, life *became* good.'

'Yes.' Molly knew what she meant, thinking of how far she herself had come from her time at Winterhill to the pleasant life she now led. It was, she realised, impossible to have lived through the war and not come away with a unique set of mental cuts and bruises. She wished that sweet Telsie had had the same realisation and not given up on life. 'As someone once said to me, we all walk the same path. We all trip, but more often than not we are so focused on looking ahead that we don't notice the stumbles of those around us. And we all keep plodding on, because what's the alternative?'

'It's the truth.' Marjorie smiled. 'I've got two girls,' she elaborated. 'Well, hardly girls now, both grown-up, one teaching music – her dad's a musician, or was; he doesn't play much now, prefers crosswords. Age, eh? It happens to us all.'

Not all . . . Molly swallowed the thought.

'My other daughter is about to have her third child, if you can believe that.' Marjorie shook her head, as if she could not.

'A grandma!' Molly clutched the bag with the plastic figures in it to her chest – for her grandson . . . *Adam* . . . 'How wonderful.'

'It is. They keep me on the go, mind, Nana this and Nana that – I love it. Can't pretend I don't.'

There was a beat of silence while Molly gathered her thoughts. This chance meeting was, she knew, too important for her not in some way to reminisce, not to stoke the painful memories of the very worst time in her life. It was like jabbing her tongue on a rotten tooth, almost impossible to resist, with some small amount of pleasure to be taken from the hurt.

'You were always very' – she swallowed, her mouth dry – 'you were always very kind to me, Marjorie, and it made such a difference. Thank you for that.'

Marjorie held her gaze and took a slow, deep breath. 'You know where he died?'

Molly had not expected the question nor the sudden reference to her love and was surprised at how much it threw and delighted her. It was, of course, horrific to remember the details, but this was underlined with a note of pure joy that rang out in her mind. How wonderful it was to talk about him at all! To be in the company of someone with a link to her beloved Johan, no matter how tenuous.

'Yes, Slapton Sands, Devon.' The incident during which Johan had died had only recently come into the public domain. 'An exercise rehearsing for the D-Day landings.'

'Yes.' Marjorie nodded, as if already aware.

'I think it was mainly American allies that were killed, but a few Brits too. Johan was one of them. The last time I saw him, he told me he was one of the lucky ones, and I believed him. He said he would be safe and sound in Devon.'

'He had every reason to believe he would be; it was the most tragic set of events. I heard it might have been as many as a thousand that died over two days, maybe more.'

'That's terrible.' Molly tried and failed to picture a thousand people like her, all mourning the men they loved.

'Yes, Molly, terrible. For you especially. I remember your face at the time and that you were' – she paused – 'quite unwell.'

'I was. Did you . . . did you ever get the letter I sent to you at the Ministry? During the time I was absent?' She bit her lip.

'No,' Marjorie answered, a little too quickly and with a practised gaze.

Molly wasn't sure she believed her. She put the boxes of tea back on the shelf and reached into her pocket for her handkerchief. She blew her nose and wiped her eyes. 'You know, I have a wonderful family and I'm happy, but I never met anyone else like him.'

'You didn't marry?'

Molly shook her head, thinking briefly of Rex and refusing to feel shame about her battles with her mental health. It was his loss and for her a lucky escape.

'I was quite, erm . . . I was unwell after the war and then it felt easier to stay quiet, stay alone and forge my own way. For a while I was so very disappointed by the way things turned out. That's the truth. I loved him and yet I barely knew him. But as I say, I now have a lot to feel thankful for. I think, when you're young, you

327

reckon you're owed the fairy tale, but of course you're not, and it doesn't work out for everyone, does it? And yet I still have a good life, an ordinary one.'

'I'm glad, Molly. You deserve a good life. War intensifies everything, doesn't it? The normal rules don't apply.'

Molly smiled at hearing the very phrase Johan had used. 'He said once that time was compressed, stolen. And I thought I understood what he meant when he said it, but I certainly do now I'm able to look back. It was so intense, so all-consuming, and yet was no more than a blink in time.'

'I think,' Marjorie began, 'that we all choose how we remember and how we celebrate the lives of those we lost. There's no hard and fast rule, is there? But I do think sometimes a bit of nostalgia can be good, comforting.' Marjorie reached up to the shelf and gathered the box of tea with the picture of the Queen from the shelf, placing it in Molly's basket.

'It's been so very lovely to see you, Marjorie. I shall think about it long after we've said goodbye. You are the first person' – Molly coughed to clear her thickening throat – 'you're the first person I've had to talk to about him in as long as I can remember, and I'm very grateful for that. It may seem like a small thing, but it's actually of such great significance to me. Small things can mean so much. I have a brass button from his tunic that fell off the first time we met, the first time we danced; it's terribly precious to me. Just an ordinary button.'

'I can imagine, my love.' Marjorie placed her hand on her forearm and took a step forward, her voice low. 'You did a wonderful thing, Molly. A very brave thing. You were in the gravest danger, transporting those keys . . . If they'd *found* you, found them . . . they'd have tortured and killed you, without a doubt.'

Molly felt the blood rush from her head and she felt icy all over, her breath stuttering. 'It was wartime . . . We all did what we had to, didn't we?'

'And your cousin, she was a remarkable woman, too,' Marjorie said, as their eyes locked. 'Violet.'

'Violet. Oh my God, Marjorie! I still see her face!' Molly swallowed. It was the first time she had said Violet's name out loud since that night. Her eyes brimmed.

'Yes, she did wonderful things – brave things that made all the difference to an awful lot of people, who have no idea that it's her they need to thank and remember in their prayers, such was the nature of her work.'

Molly nodded. It seemed incredible, but it was true.

'I . . . I don't know whether to thank you for asking me or curse you.'

Marjorie fixed her with a stare. 'I can imagine, but you did it anyway.'

'But it went wrong – Violet and Pascal, they . . .'

'Yes.' Marjorie kept her voice level. 'But that was not their first time at the rodeo: they knew the risks and it was a chance we were all willing to take because the reward was so great. You have to know that nothing was ever undertaken without the utmost thought or planning.'

'But it was a trap, Marjorie! There was a mole: Jean-Luc – I saw him as a prisoner in the ranks walking towards the station, but he wasn't a prisoner . . . He was supposed to be one of the motorcycle riders that night – he betrayed Pascal, told the Germans . . .' Molly glanced over her shoulder and felt the old sickness rise in her gut. To talk about it so freely felt strange and oddly wonderful, like letting something trapped out of a bottle.

'I know.' Marjorie paused. 'He didn't survive the war: that's all you need to know. And you did your bit, called out to the General, caused a distraction – you tried! And then you went back, informed on Jean-Luc, identified the mole. That was *huge*, bigger than you know . . . Trust me, if you hadn't, we'd have lost a lot more than those two that night . . .' Marjorie shook her head. 'You were the courier, Molly, but also an extra pair of hands, and you put yourself in harm's way.'

'But she died anyway!' Molly swallowed at the futility of it all, and then a thought dawned. 'How . . . how do you know I called out – how did you know I went back?'

'My husband . . .' Marjorie looked at the floor and swallowed. 'His instrument was the accordion.'

The two women locked eyes and Molly smelled once again the potent scent of that moment: a mixture of cigarette smoke, sweat and the stale tang of liquor, all with a base note of fear that she was sure came from her own skin.

'He . . . he told me to run!'

'And you did.' Marjorie nodded.

'And I did.' Molly remembered the way her heart had felt as though it might burst in her chest.

'It was all a long time ago,' Marjorie said, stiffening, as if to indicate there was little point in digging at old wounds.

'Yes, a long time ago.'

'Darren!' A young woman called after a toddler who was now racing down the aisle towards them. 'Can you grab him?'

Marjorie bent down and placed her hand on the chest of the toddler to stop his mad dash; the other she placed on his back. 'Hello there, little one! Are you running away from your mum?' The boy squealed in laughter and showed her the little red and white *Starsky and Hutch* car in his palm.

'Oh, thank you!' Darren's mum caught up. 'He's a rascal – runs away from me at every opportunity, don't you, you little devil?' She bent down and scooped the boy into her arms before smothering his face with kisses. Molly averted her eyes, finding it hard to watch the ease with which the lady cradled her boy, free to do so. 'Sorry, ladies, it comes to something when you can't stand in the supermarket and have a good old natter without being bowled into by a little monster. Come on, you! Say goodbye!'

Darren waved over his mum's shoulder as she carted him off.

'She probably thinks we were talking about the weather,' Molly observed.

'People only see what they want to see, Molly. To her, we are just two middle-aged women buying teabags. She cannot imagine being us, because when you're young or even just younger than we happen to be, it seems unthinkable that you will ever become the older people around you. I think the older you get, the more invisible you become.'

'I suppose that's true.'

'I do think about it sometimes, Molly, the things we did, the things we saw, the way we lived. It shapes you, doesn't it?'

'It certainly does.'

'And then I remind myself that it was all so that our kids, grandkids and that little boy over there' – she pointed after Darren – 'won't ever have to do the same,' Marjorie said thoughtfully.

Molly nodded, knowing this was the truth. 'I don't talk about it much. But I don't . . . I don't ever forget,' she admitted. 'I have always wanted to know,' she added, looking up, 'what her real name was? Violet's name? I've often wondered.'

Marjorie looked a little uncomfortable suddenly, as if making a judgement call. 'Her name was Elizabeth.'

'Elizabeth,' Molly repeated, picturing the beautiful feisty girl with the same name as her own mother. She looked along the aisle at the shelves stacked with foods from all over the globe and suspected that Elizabeth would still, despite the vast array and choice, think that a well-baked spud with butter might be the very best thing to eat in the whole wide world.

'I'd better go,' Marjorie said, looking towards the window. 'It's been good to see you, it really has.'

'It . . . it's been good to see you too.'

Marjorie leaned in and gave her the sweetest kiss on the cheek, then slowly set off down the aisle.

'Marjorie?' Molly called after her, watching as the other woman turned on her heel to look back at her.

'Yes?'

'Did . . . did Elizabeth have family?'

Marjorie swallowed, her eyes misting as if overwhelmed by memories, and then walked away down the aisle past the coffee and hot chocolate.

Molly made her way along Marshalls Drive and turned into the driveway of the spacious home where Joe and Estelle lived. She knocked on the door and Joyce answered.

'Where have you been? We've eaten nearly all the cake! Well, when I say we, I mean Frances.' She whispered the last bit and gave a false grin. 'You should see all the presents Adam's got – quite unbelievable! They have so much these days – too much, if you ask me. Do you remember when we were little and at Christmas we got one doll! One doll! That was it, and we knew we were lucky.'

'We did,' Molly agreed, thinking back to those far-off days.

'Well, you're here now!' Joyce nodded, her gaze a little off.

'Yes, sorry, I got held up; bumped into an old friend I knew donkey's years ago.'

'Oh, from where?'

'From . . . from work.' Molly put her bags down on the floor and shook her hair from her collar.

'And what did he have to say?' Joyce asked curiously as she sipped her Cinzano and lemonade to the sound of kids squealing in the back garden.

'She, and nothing,' Molly replied, as she walked into the party. 'Nothing, really.'

'I see.' Joyce tilted her head and stared at her.

'What?'

'Secrets, Molly. All these bloody secrets.' Joyce rolled her eyes to the heavens and sniffed a little. 'We have this wonderful life and yet it's all underpinned by an enormous secret and I sometimes worry that, when we least expect it, it will fly out of someone's mouth and cut us all, like some wild, loose scythe that will do nothing but irreparable damage.'

'How many of those have you had?' Molly eyed the Cinzano in her sister's hand.

'A few!' Joyce raised her glass. 'I couldn't face not seeing David, couldn't stand the thought of him not being here, and Clara crying into her hankie, and Frances being so very bolshie, so I decided to have a little drink.'

'It's probably best, dear.' Molly tutted, trying to make light of the situation and knowing that she, too, keenly felt the absence of her brother.

'I mean it, Molly.' Joyce gripped her arm now, standing close. 'I've been thinking about this for a long, long time and I want you to promise me something. I don't ever want our situation to be like some known but unspoken thing, like Mr Mason—'

'Why are you talking about Mr Mason?' Molly was perplexed.

'Mr Mason! Our old neighbour!'

'Yes, I know *who* he is!' Molly tutted her irritation. 'But what do you mean, an unspoken thing?'

'Well, surely you must know that he and Mum . . .' Joyce made a clicking noise at the side of her mouth.

'He and Mum what?' Molly needed clarification because she suddenly *thought* she knew what her sister was talking about, but surely to goodness not!

'They were . . . *friends*,' Joyce said with a wink.

'Are you trying to tell me they had an affair?' The prospect was monstrous, not only because the very idea of her mother having sex with anyone was unwelcome, but she could also still picture the sour-faced judgement her mother had poured on her: '*Illegitimacy and infidelity are stains that do not wash off, not ever! As a woman of low moral conduct, what job do you think you might secure, exactly?*'

'Yes, I think it started when Papa got really ill and Mr Mason would drop by the house with bank stuff. They worked together at the—'

'Yes, I know they worked together!' Impatient now, Molly wanted Joyce to get to the point.

'Well, after Papa died, he carried on "popping over" and David and I heard a few . . . noises, shall we say.'

'*David* knew?'

'Well, yes.'

'And you didn't tell me?'

'You were our Little Moll – why would we tell you?'

'Because I have not been "Little Moll" for the last fifty fucking years! I'm a grown woman!' She laughed.

'Molly!' Joyce put a hand to her face, her expression shocked. 'I have *never* heard you use that word.'

'I have rarely felt the need to use the word! But my God! Mr Mason?' She shuddered. 'No wonder he was always turning up. I am so stupid!'

'You're not stupid and I think it's rather lovely that Mum found comfort when Papa was very ill and after he died.'

'I suppose it is lovely. I'm just a bit shocked, partly at my own naivety. But, yes, I'm really pleased she had someone I hope made her happy.' Molly thought of her Victorian mother, who, it seemed, had also been a woman bound by the constrictions of her time. 'I just hope Mrs Mason felt the same way!' She tutted.

'Are you going to swear again?' Joyce stared at her.

'Fuckity fuck, Joyce. Fucking fuckity fuck!'

Joyce laughed loudly and Molly joined in, but in truth she felt on the edge of tears. Her sister pulled her into a one-armed hug.

'Poor old Mum, Joycey. She was miserable and guilt-ridden and judgemental, but she was still our mother.'

'I thought, if she could, she might have sent us a sign after she died,' Joyce said, taking another sip of her Cinzano.

'Like what?' Molly laughed.

'Oh, I don't know – you hear of things, don't you, like doorbells ringing and lights going on and off?'

'Stop it, Joyce, you're scaring me!' Molly shivered, thinking that if Johan could have sent her a sign, he would have by now. 'And if you want to send me a sign, Joyce, do it subtly so I don't jump out of my skin, and I promise I'll do the same for you.'

'That's a deal, my little sunflower.'

'A deal, my darling dandelion.' Molly smiled at her sister, whom she so loved.

Joyce nodded, her tone suddenly serious. 'I want you to promise me something, Molly—'

'What?' Molly asked, pulling away.

'If I die first . . .'

'Oh, Joyce, please don't talk like that!'

'No! I mean it, Molly. It's important.' She took her time now and Molly listened. 'If I die first, I want you to tell Joe. Tell him everything, but I don't think I want to be around when you do. And I know I have no right to ask that, Moll, but you are the dearest thing to me. There's only one thing dearer and that's our boy.'

Molly nodded at her big sister, who was also one of her dearest things. It was a family secret that was kept because the repercussions of letting it out of the bag felt too huge, but maybe her sister was right – with everyone gone, would that be the right time to give Joe his history? It would, she knew, be her greatest moment to be called Mum by the boy she had given birth to.

'All right, Joycey, I promise.'

'Promise me!'

'I just did!' Molly held her gaze. 'I did.'

'We don't need to mention this again, do we?' Joyce asked, leaning in close to her.

'No, dear, we don't.'

And they never did.

'Look at you two conspiring in the hallway!' Joe boomed, as he appeared from the kitchen. 'What are you talking about?'

'Nothing,' Joyce laughed.

'Nothing,' Molly confirmed.

TWENTY

Molly swapped her grocery bag to the other hand and flexed her fingers, newly released from their plastic-handled stranglehold. She had only nipped into the store on her way home for some tomatoes and fresh milk but been swayed by the offers on freshly ground coffee and tinned soup, which now weighed down her bag. She'd also bought a newspaper, which today carried only one story: the end of the year-long miners' strike. Molly hoped that the miners, their families and the communities who had supported them could finally find some kind of peace, but with many of the pits closed for good and many a hard-working man on his knees, she doubted it.

Turning into her road, she spotted a police car parked someway along on the left and her first thought was that she hoped no one had been hurt or anything ghastly like that. Cars and motorbikes tended to roar around these streets and she often thought it only a matter of time before something dreadful happened. The lack of ambulance was, she figured, either a very good sign or a very bad one. Reaching into her jacket pocket, Molly ran her fingers over her house keys. It was a fact that, as she entered her early sixties, her memory had started to sprout leaks. Not for the important or ancient things, oh no, those were locked in with as much detail as if they had occurred yesterday. It was more the everyday stuff, like remembering to take her keys out with her when she left the house, wondering whether or not she had switched off the iron, and trying to recall if she had put the bins out already on bin day – these were the kind of chores and tasks that she found fell through the gaps between intention and action. It drove her crackers and she suspected this was the exact kind of event that would have far less of an impact and be far less of a concern, had she been in a relationship. It wasn't that she was lonely per se, or maybe it would be more accurate to say that her loneliness did not overly trouble her, but there were certainly times when she thought of how much easier life might be for an ageing woman if there was someone by her side to age with. How she envied those with the ability to look over the breakfast table at the person they loved and ask, 'Did I remember to . . .?' It must be nice. She often wondered what kind of couple she and Johan would have become: happy, harmonious friends or bickering, petty rivals, or worse: indifferent to each other? The former, she suspected, and even the thought of it made her smile.

She made her way along the street, her leather-soled loafers barely making a sound on the pavement, and now noticed two policemen who were out of their car and standing in the street – right outside her house. Her heart gave a little skip of nerves.

Mrs Ogilvy – Jean – who lived in a house opposite, came running down the pavement towards her. 'Oh, Molly! Oh my God!' The woman, of whom Molly was not a fan, held her coat clasped at the neck, speaking in haste and apparently keen to deliver the full situation report to her neighbour. Molly found the woman's excitement for whatever unfortunate event had occurred most unbecoming.

'I didn't know what to do! It's all been such a shock. I told the police I might have a brandy with my cocoa tonight.'

'What *has* happened?' Molly asked, her voice steady.

'I saw two men, well' – Mrs Ogilvy breathed quickly – 'the back of two men, but they were tall and big. I've already told the policemen. I watched them go through the gate, and I don't like to be nosy, but there was something about them. So I watched from the window and they walked up the path, bold as brass, and so I thought, "Ooh, must be selling something or doing a survey", you know the type of thing—'

'They walked up your path?' Molly was still trying to ascertain precisely what had happened.

'No, thank goodness!' Jean laughed with evident relief. 'They walked up your path.'

Molly began to walk towards her cottage, quickening her pace, the woman still trotting along beside her. 'They broke in, Molly! You've been burgled!' There was something almost gleeful in Mrs Ogilvy's tone – what was the word she was searching for: *schadenfreude*? Was that it? Ignoring her, Molly looked from the two burly policemen planted at her gate to the front door of her home, which was standing open. It was a strange and sobering moment, especially for someone who lived alone, in a house for which no one else had a set of keys.

My front door is open . . .

Someone has been inside my house . . .

Shock finally bit as one of the officers approached her.

'This is her! This is the lady,' Mrs Ogilvy called out, pointing at Molly. 'It's her house!'

'Mrs Collway?' the policeman asked, doing his best to ignore the overly keen neighbour.

'Yes.' *Close enough . . .*

'I'm very sorry, but it appears your house was burgled this afternoon.'

She shook her head. 'Oh dear, what a rotten thing to do to someone.'

'Yes, it is. But don't worry, we'll come inside with you, and we've called a glazier to come and make the front door secure where they broke the glass to get in.'

'They broke the glass?'

The man had spoken clearly enough, but her thoughts had been elsewhere, wondering what she might find inside.

'Yes. They broke the little window and reached in to open the door. It's very common. They can do that in seconds.'

'Gosh.' Her mouth felt a little dry.

'Thankfully, there's not too much damage; I've seen a lot worse.'

'Do you want me to come in with you, Molly?' Mrs Ogilvy asked.

'That's very kind, madam, but we'll take it from here. Thank you for all your assistance,' the policeman intervened, and Molly was grateful.

'Right then . . .' There was no disguising the woman's displeasure at being summarily dismissed. 'Well, you have my number and you know which house is mine, don't you?' She pointed across the street.

'We do indeed.'

'Because if you want any more detail or need me to go over again what I saw and the times, et cetera, then just knock on my door. I always have the kettle on.'

'Thank you.' He nodded, taking Molly by the elbow and guiding her along the path. It made her feel old.

Now, at close range, she could see the broken glass at the top of the front door. The hallway, however, looked relatively untouched.

'What time did you leave the house this morning?' the other policeman asked.

'Erm, I always leave about seven fifteen, to travel into London. I work at Barts Hospital.'

'And you live alone?'

It was clear Mrs Ogilvy had spared no detail.

'Yes.'

'We need you to walk around the place, Mrs Collway, and give us a rough idea of what, if anything, has been taken. It doesn't need to be a definitive list, so don't worry. You can always call us at the station if you discover anything else gone. We'll leave our number for you.'

Molly nodded and walked into the kitchen. A couple of drawers had been pulled out and upended onto the floor. She looked up at the dresser, and the jam jar with forty pounds' worth of cash in it was missing.

'They've taken some money. I keep a jar on the dresser and put a few notes in it as and when. Forty pounds.' She always knew exactly how much money was in there. 'And some silver cutlery.' She looked at the gap in one of the drawers left hanging open. 'A set of twelve fish knives and forks that I have never used. They were my mother's,' she elaborated, thinking it odd how little she cared about these objects once handled by her mother, but now in the hands of God only knew.

'Are you okay, Mrs Collway?' Both of the policemen were staring at her, as if they expected more. These were boys who she knew had not lived through the war, or they would know that a few upturned drawers was nothing compared to the sight of a flattened house with all its belongings lying splintered for all the world to see.

'I am, thank you,' she offered calmly.

Next she walked through to the dining room, where a silver coffee pot was missing from the sideboard, along with two small carved figurines, in soapstone she believed, although she had no idea how they had come into her mother's possession. Things David and Joyce had set aside for her when they divided up the items after the sale of the house. Things she had kept purely because they had always been around.

'Would you like a cup of tea, Mrs Collway?' one of the officers asked kindly.

'No, thank you, but it's very kind of you to offer.' She felt uncomfortable at the thought of these strangers pottering in her little kitchen, boiling the kettle, touching her things.

She walked now into the sitting room, with the two policemen following on behind.

'The TV is missing.' She pointed to the obvious space on the unit next to the fireplace where the television had sat. Wires still dangled from the points on the wall. 'And my radio – only a small transistor that I like to listen to in the afternoon at the weekend.'

She looked around the room and was somewhat relieved to see that the place was largely as she had left it, bar the seat cushions thrown on the floor and a picture that for some reason had been propped up against the wall. 'Maybe they thought it wasn't worth taking?' she quipped, and the men laughed.

'More likely they found it too big to cart away.'

'Ah yes, probably.' This made more sense. Molly's gaze roved over the surfaces and suddenly her heart rate increased. She walked forward and stopped abruptly at the side table by her favourite chair in front of the fireplace. Plopping down onto the chair, she ran her hand over the surface of the table, despite seeing quite plainly that it was empty.

'Oh! Oh no! Oh!' Sliding from the chair, she got on all fours and with some urgency moved the seat cushion, searching beneath it on the rug, before feeling around on the floor, pushing the chair towards the middle of the room so she could get a good reach around underneath it. 'I . . . I . . .' She was finding it hard to get the words out, and equally hard to get a breath.

One of the policemen rushed forward and dropped to his knees. 'What is it, Mrs Collway? Are you feeling unwell? You don't look too good.'

Molly sat back against the fireplace and emitted a low, soft moan of despair. She closed her eyes and tried to swallow the desperate realisation that her little walnut box was not there.

'I had . . . I had a box, a smallish box made of walnut. Hinged at the back in brass and quite sturdy. I need to find it. I need to get it back,' was all she could manage.

'We'll do all we can, Mrs Collway.'

She caught the subtle exchange of looks between the two officers, which told her it was less than likely her box would ever be returned. The very thought was almost more than she could take. 'Please, I don't . . . I don't care about anything else! They can have it all, but I must get that box back!' She was too distraught to care about the level of emotion on display in front of these strangers.

'Was there anything in the box?'

She nodded sharply. 'There were a couple of small black-and-white photographs in it, an old French franc and a centime' – she paused – 'and . . . and a little brass button with a naval crest and a knot of rope on it.' She looked up at the two police officers, who looked a little bewildered, and said urgently, 'It's the button I really need to get back. I will pay any reward. Please!'

'We'll do all we can, Mrs Collway. There are several things we *can* do that sometimes get results, including putting a piece in the paper with a photo – if people can relate to the person it sometimes urges them to look harder, get involved.'

His words barely registered. All she could do was concentrate on the deep throb of pain in her chest and heart – an old friend, and one she had hoped she might never know again.

Molly decided on an early night. It wasn't the invasion of her home that had caused depression to paw at her senses, but the taking of Johan's button. She felt the loss like a kick in the stomach, just as winding and violent. Curled, she lay for a while, wondering how it might be possible to retrieve this thing that would have no value to anyone but her. The phone rang twice and, each time, she raced to answer it, leaping from the bed with her hair flying and her dressing gown flapping about her shins, hoping and praying it was the police with an update. But it wasn't. The first call came from Joyce, for whom she had left a message. Her sister wanted to hear all the details and offered words of encouragement.

'I mean, don't fret, Molly – the chances of them coming back are extremely slim.'

Molly wrinkled her brow. 'I hadn't even considered the possibility they might come back until you said that.' Molly, in even this most dreadful of circumstances, could see humour in her sister's dire attempt at comforting her.

'I know you're joking, but it must have upset you.'

'Well, of course it has' – Molly thought of Johan's precious button, her irreplaceable talisman – 'but I'm not going to dwell.'

'Well, you know where we are if you need anything,' Joyce offered warmly.

'I do. We'll speak soon, dear.'

The second call was from a very well-spoken Mr Ian Morgan, who was apparently chair of the local Neighbourhood Watch. Molly rolled her eyes and assured him there really was no need for him to drop off a pack, which, according to Mr Morgan, contained a window sticker and a handy leaflet with hints on how best to secure her home.

'It really is no trouble, Miss Collway. I shall be passing anyway, with Hugo. See you in a bit.'

Molly stood in the hallway of her cottage and wondered firstly who Hugo was – his partner? Quite possibly – and then, secondly, how quickly she might be able to get Mr Ian Morgan off her front path. The last thing she wanted was to have to pander to the ramblings of some old dear who had all the time in the world to stand in the cold and give her statistics on how very likely she was to fall victim to a heinous crime on her own doorstep. She had Joyce for that.

Shrugging off her dressing gown, lest she give Mr Morgan the impression that she was a slattern, she put the kitchen drawers back into their grooves, fishing around on the floor for the odd spoon, a ball of string and a nifty pair of mini-secateurs she hadn't seen in an age but had clearly been lurking somewhere and found by her burglars.

The phone rang in the hallway. Again.

'Chelmsford 57286.'

'Auntie M, it's Joe.'

'Hello, darling.' She smiled, as she always did at the sound of his voice, a visceral reaction whenever he made contact.

'Mum called Estelle and she's just told me what happened. Are you okay? Do you want me to come over?'

'No, darling, not at all. I'm fine, I really am. It's not a disaster zone or anything like that; the policeman said it could have been a lot worse—'

'Well, of course it could – they could have murdered you in your bed!'

'Yes, thank you, dear. Joyce was similarly reassuring.'

'Do you need anything?'

'No. That's very sweet, but as I say, I'm fine, and so grateful you called.' And she was.

'Is there much damage?'

'No, a small window broken and a few upturned drawers, and they took the TV,' *and your father's button – all I had, Joe, his little button . . .* 'So not too bad in all. How's Adam?'

She heard her son sigh. 'He's a bloody nightmare!'

'Well, I think if they are going to be, sixteen is the age to do it,' she said consolingly, knowing this only by observation and not experience.

'I suppose so. Not to mention his girlfriend, *Tamara*, who hasn't spoken more than two words to us in the seven months she's been seeing Adam, and who also happens to be a vegetarian, if you will. Have you ever heard the like? She only eats *vegetables*! No meat, not a scrap, and Estelle said the girl gave her a hard stare the other day when she pulled on her leather boots.'

Molly couldn't imagine what the girl ate if not meat for her main meal. 'What does Tamara wear on her feet?'

'Oh, these kind of black canvas plimsolls, hardly sturdy and sure to sog up in a puddle. Anyway, they're planning on both dyeing their hair some lurid colour! What can I say?'

'What colour are they thinking of?'

'Well, that is hardly the point!' Joe laughed.

'Really? I think it's entirely the point! I mean, if you're going to alienate him, fall out with him and comment on his choices for the sake of some temporary wash in his hair, then it would be foolish, but if they're favouring, say, a permanent shade of bright purple, then yes, I would speak out.'

'Hmmm, that's probably good advice. I shall investigate. And if you need anything?'

'Yes, yes, Joe.' She cut him short, touched by his offer. 'I know where you are, and thank you, dear boy.'

The front doorbell rang. 'Must dash, I have a visitor. Love to Estelle and Adam!' She ended the call.

Molly was, despite the shock of her intruder and the loss of her things, feeling quite all right with the world. Talking to Joyce and then Joe was a timely reminder that while bad things might happen, with a loving family only ever a phone call away, things were never going to be truly terrible.

She opened the door to a handsome man with short grey hair and a large nose. He wore a wine-coloured cravat at the neck of his open shirt, inside his tweed jacket.

'Oh!' He stared at her. 'Forgive me. I thought you'd be very old!'

Molly laughed in spite of herself. 'Oh, you did? Well, sorry to disappoint. Who are you?'

'Ian Morgan.' He stepped forward with a slight bow. 'And this is Hugo.'

She followed his eyes downward until they locked with possibly the ugliest dog she had ever seen. 'Oh, Hugo, you poor love.' She bit her bottom lip to stop from saying anything else inappropriate.

'Don't be fooled.' Mr Morgan bent and ran his palm along the white back of the one-eyed bull terrier, whose lower teeth sat proud of his top set. 'He's a massive hit with the ladies.'

'I'll take your word for it. And by the way, I *am* old.'

'No, you're not,' the man laughed.

'How old do you think I am?' She folded her arms across her chest and was surprised that she was, despite the upset earlier, enjoying the rather flirtatious nature of their conversation.

Without any of the usual reticence that might go hand in hand with guessing a lady's age, he tapped his chin. 'Hmm, fifty-four? No, fifty-six!'

She liked his earnest attempt that was in no way overly flattering.

'I've just turned sixty.'

'Ah, close. Well, I'm sixty-two.'

'I wasn't aware I'd asked.' She tried to be curt, but her wide smile belied her tone.

'You're funny!' He chuckled. 'Now, down to business.' His tone and expression changed. 'Rotten luck about your burglary, but it happens.' He shrugged. 'Probably kids, looking for stuff they can sell quickly in the pub, but no less upsetting for that.'

'The policeman said it could have been a whole lot worse.' She kept repeating this cliché, at a loss of what else to say and unwilling to share what she had lost – not only was it too personal, but she knew no one else would understand her attachment to a shiny button.

'I have a pack for you – advice on window locks, front-door protocol for if a stranger knocks, that kind of thing.'

'That's rather ironic, since you're a stranger who knocked.' She took in his height, his neatness and his tan.

'Yes, and you failed to ask me for identification.'

'Because you phoned to tell me you were coming and then arrived. Very promptly, I might add, which is good to know. If ever I need another sticker or advice on window locks, it's a great comfort to know that you can get here so quickly.'

'Now,' Mr Morgan said, taking a deep breath, 'I know you're being sarcastic, but I can't work out if you're being mean or funny.'

'Probably a bit of both,' she responded, to her surprise, and the two held each other's gaze for a beat.

'In that case,' he said, taking a step back on the path and pulling Hugo towards him, 'stay right where you are.'

'Why do I need to stay here?' She was perplexed.

'Because I'm going to get brandy! You're clearly in shock and you're such a very old lady! Back in a jiff!'

Molly closed her front door and leaned against it, wondering what had just happened. She wandered to the kitchen and tidied the work surface, putting the honey pot and loaf of bread out of sight; she then ran the dirty teacups under the tap and set them in the sink for a proper wash later. Next she grabbed her hairbrush from her handbag and pulled it through her straight hair. She caught sight of her reflection in the kitchen window and did not dislike what she saw. Words came to her now, offered in friendship from inside a cramped lavatory during the war:

'*You take a good look and like what you see. It's important. It's hard for people to love you if you don't love yourself.*'

And she smiled at the memory of dear Marjorie.

There was a knock at the door; Molly walked slowly to steady her pulse and opened it. Ian Morgan walked in, holding aloft the promised bottle of brandy.

'Where's Hugo?' She looked towards the path.

'He's asleep, snoring and farting in front of the Aga. And I'd be doing the same, were it not for our chance meeting and your pesky burglary.'

'Did you come back to give me my window sticker?' she asked, feeling a rise of something in her gut that felt a lot like desire.

'I did.' He walked in and she closed the front door.

Molly trod the steep stairs of her cottage and sat on the little stool by the window to phone her sister.

'Morning. Everything all right, Moll?' Joyce was seemingly just as aware as she was of the early hour.

'Yes, everything is fine. Just wanted to call and let you know: I've had sex!'

'Well, yes, dear, I rather gathered as much – hence the whole fiasco back in '44.' It was a wonder they could find any humour in it, and a marker of how far they had come – how far *she* had come.

'No, I mean I had sex *yesterday*!' she whispered, although she was entirely alone. She might have had enough confidence to actually have sex, but talking about it with ease was quite another thing altogether.

'Good Lord, Molly! Who with?'

'A gentleman named Ian Morgan. He's the chair of the Neighbourhood Watch.'

'Well, I have heard that some women find men in positions of power to be an aphrodisiac.'

'Stop it! He's actually very nice, handsome and an architect.'

'Heavens! And he just stopped by and you had sex?' Joyce sounded intrigued and appalled in equal measure.

'Pretty much.' Molly closed her eyes with a flush of embarrassment.

'So are you seeing him again?'

'Yes, yes, I rather think I will.'

'Well, good for you, Molly, good for you!'

'Anyway, cheerio, and I shall keep you informed!'

'Jolly good! Enjoy your Saturday . . .' Her sister laughed.

Molly hung up and immediately felt the lick of disloyalty, as she remembered that she had lost her precious button and then on the same day had sex with Ian Morgan. It was confusing and yet she already knew she wanted to see him and Hugo again, and she definitely wanted more sex. With Ian – Hugo was way too ugly, ladies' man or not.

Molly especially liked Saturdays, not because she ever had any extravagant plans, but simply not having to go to work meant a change in routine. Her hair went without a brush and she didn't bother with lipstick when she was only pottering at home. It felt quite nice, decadent in a way, to spend as long as she liked reading the morning paper or, weather permitting, to dally in the garden with her secateurs primed. And today was especially nice, having enjoyed the company of Mr Ian Morgan until the wee small hours.

Bending down, she hummed as she picked up the post from the doormat and took the little bundle through into the kitchen, where she set it aside while she filled the electric kettle, going back to it when her teabag was in place at the bottom of her grandmother's dainty little bone china cup. The first thing to catch her eye was a circular, reminding every resident in the street that the water was being turned off for three hours next Wednesday to allow for essential maintenance on the pipes. This information raised little more than a shrug; she would be ensconced behind the counter in the patient record office, so no need to worry about the water. She did decide, however, to have her bath the night before and to fill the kettle and a couple of jugs on the morning for the washing up and a cup of tea, just in case. In fact, next Wednesday was going to be special: Janice was meeting her for lunch. Molly couldn't wait to hear about life in Melbourne, Australia, where Janice had been living with her husband and two sons for the last decade. It was only her first visit home and Janice was coming alone, as tickets were too expensive for the whole family to travel. Molly was beyond delighted that the ditsy girl, whom she'd had the pleasure of watching bloom into the most delightful woman, was choosing to spend precious time with her. She was very much looking forward to it.

Crumpling the page into a ball, Molly tossed it in the bin by the side of the fridge. The second item was a handwritten envelope and not the brown variety, so unlikely to be a bill, but instead a plump cream-coloured package that felt comfortingly weighted in her palm.

Molly hummed the tune 'Young at Heart', which she had heard on the radio and persisted as an earworm. Steam was shooting from the spout of the kettle towards the ceiling as she slid her finger under the gummed rim to open the envelope.

The first thing she saw was a folded letter with something nestling inside. Drawing it out, her knees went weak and her breathing grew ragged.

'Oh, good Lord!' Sinking down into the little wooden chair by the stove, Molly studied the black-and-white photograph that she now held up to her face.

'Look at you!' she gasped. 'How handsome . . . And how much you look like Joe! Or rather how much Joe looks like you. I'd almost forgotten – and how young! Oh, Johan, oh my love!' It was some minutes before her gaze was satisfied, her eyes taking in every minute detail from his trimmed moustache to the way the light reflected in his pupils and the wave of his fringe, longer than she had seen it, over his forehead. The flat ears with their fleshy lobes, the almond-shaped nostrils, and his clothes! He was wearing a shirt with the top button open and a jersey over the top. This was the first time she had seen him in anything other than standard Naval-issue uniform. His beautiful mouth wore a slight curve, as if he were trying to stifle a smile, but the slight crinkle at the edge of his kind eyes suggested he was only seconds away from bursting into laughter. It was without doubt the most glorious thing she had ever seen, and since her burglary, when her precious button had been taken, was now a physical link, the only one, to the man she had loved and lost. The irony was not lost on her that this extraordinary thing had plopped into her lap so soon after she had lost her button.

'How on earth?'

She shook her head, beyond curious as to how this had come into her hands, but absolutely delighted that it had. Carefully, she held the photograph in her left hand, while with her right she smoothed out the letter and read slowly, the very first words enough to make her tears bloom. Her first thought was that she did not want tears to land on the precious picture, and so she set it aside on the tabletop and held the letter in her shaking fingers. There was no date and no address.

Molly, my friend, for you are still my friend, aren't you?

'Oh!' She recognised the handwriting instantly. 'Oh, Geertruida! My darling Geer!' She broke away from her reading and said aloud, 'Yes, yes, I am still your friend!' Keen to keep reading, she gathered herself as best she could and wiped her eyes on the tea towel that hung on the grill handle at the top of the stove.

This is a letter I have wanted to write more times than I can remember, but with nowhere to send it I've had to wait until now, when I saw your picture and the details of your burglary in a newspaper! The article made mention of a brass button that you were desperate to have returned – that was Joe's button, wasn't it? I know it! I have kept this photograph of him in an envelope in the distinct hope that I could give it to you one day, and that day is now. How fast the years have flown. Can it really be over forty years since I last saw you? I look in the mirror and don't recognise the ageing face staring back at me – I feel just the same as I did back when we would dance and be damned if Hitler's bombs were going to stop us. No one tells you that, do they? That no matter what happens to our bodies, you feel the same inside?

'No, no, they don't, Geer!' Molly smiled, running her hand over her cheeks and feeling the slackness in skin once taut.

*So much time has passed that it's impossible to talk about
life and what and who and how and where in detail,
and so I won't even try. We moved from Alresford before
the end of the war and my lovely parents didn't make
old bones. I don't think they ever really got over losing
Joe. But I do want to say I am sorry. This is the purpose
of this rather muddled missive: I AM SORRY, MOLLY.
I have always been sorry. My heart was broken when
my beloved brother died and my fury balled and pinged
around inside me. I took it out on you and that was
unforgivable. I said hurtful things that still have the ability to pull me from sleep with shame in the small hours.
The truth is, I know Joe loved you. I know it.*

Molly stopped reading and a wide smile settled on her face. This was
so very wonderful to hear – the *most* wonderful thing! *He loved me,
he did! And I have always felt it and I have always, always known it!*

*And I hope that you and your child have found peace. I
have thought of you both over the years, wondering if I
have a niece or a nephew? But I know that to stoke old
embers might only cause pain. I thought about writing
to the house in Bloomsbury, but then worried that you
might be married and did your husband know the full
story? Did the child? I felt I might be opening the most
enormous can of worms that might only cause you more
harm, the very opposite of my intentions. I have no way
of knowing your circumstances, nor indeed whether you
ever did or are able to forgive me. But time, Molly, is not
on my side and so I take the chance now, having read in
the newspaper that you are still Miss Collway.*

Joe wrote to Mother – I saw the postcard myself. It said simply:

'Ma, I am bringing her home. The one. The girl I shall marry!' And Mother was truly pleased for him and for you, and so was I, my dear friend, so was I! But then in the throes of grief, my jealousy clouded everything. Forgive me, Molly, sweet Molly, forgive me and know that Joe loved you, as did I. Mother took comfort in her final years from the fact that her son, while cruelly taken too soon, had known love . . .

And I send my love to you, old friend.

I think of you often. So often.

Geer xx

Molly read and re-read the words until she knew them by heart. Geer gave no indication that she had received the letter Molly sent to Alresford all those years ago and now, with no return address, she was unable to reply, but this fact did not trouble her. What more was there to say? Digging in the drawer in the dining-room dresser, she retrieved an old silver frame that had been her mother's and placed Johan's photograph in it. It looked splendid on the mantelpiece in a position where she could see it from all angles when in the sitting room. It brought her comfort. Geer's letter had been the most magnificent and unexpected gift. Molly felt as if a weight had been cut from her, one which had inadvertently slowed her recovery and which she had been dragging behind her for so long. And yet here she was, a woman of sixty, with a spring in her step that fired happiness and expectation through her very core; this, she knew in no small part, down to the attentions of Ian Morgan.

Having read confirmation in Geer's note, Johan's words were once again strong and clear in her mind. Her conviction that what they had shared had been true and mutual was restored and that really was the most incredible feeling.

She stared at the picture on the mantelpiece. *How truly wonderful. My glorious, handsome love* . . . She popped Geer's letter inside the pages of the heavy book *A Study of Flora* that lived by her chair.

Molly never saw her little walnut box, her coins nor her precious button again. The Neighbourhood Watch man, however, she saw quite regularly. The glorious Ian Morgan, her lovely friend with whom she had lovely sex, was a ray of sunshine in her predictable life. Their liaison was a surprise to her, this glorious intimacy that had been denied to her for the longest time. It was a joyous connection that she had found with another person, and an even bigger surprise was that she gave herself with abandon, unaware or uncaring of her reputation and all the things that had so hampered her in her youth. It was now the eighties, a new era with new rules, and if Molly, who had only just turned sixty, wanted to have sex with the head of the Neighbourhood Watch on a Wednesday evening after sharing supper in front of the television, with the ugly dog Hugo by their feet, then that was just fine.

Theirs was a casual love affair, hers and Ian's, though no less valued for that. And in truth, on the days when she knew he was going to pop over, she wore a smile on her face as she worked.

'You're positively glowing today, Miss Collway!' the sprightly Mr Kendall would remark, in this, his final year at the hospital before he retired to Spain with his partner Miguel, a dancer, no less.

'Am I, Mr Kendall? It must be the menopause.' How she valued her friendship with this dear man who made every day a little bit better. Dear, dear Mr Kendall. Molly knew he would never fully appreciate what his kindness had meant to her over the years.

'Oh, me too!' he remarked, fanning his face with his newspaper.

Molly had been busy in the kitchen since returning from work, when Ian arrived with Hugo and shrugged off his overcoat and unwound his scarf, laying both on the stool in the hallway.

'Something smells good!' He leaned in and pecked her on the cheek.

'Shepherd's pie.' She smiled. Her repertoire in the culinary arts was small but well rehearsed.

'How was your day?' he asked, taking up a chair at the kitchen table, his manner easy.

'All fairly standard. Mr Kendall was in fine form, as ever. I'm glad I'm retiring too; it wouldn't be the same there without him.'

'Don't be such a creature of habit – change can be exciting! It's amazing what you can get used to when you have to.' He drummed his fingers on the table.

Molly turned sharply, feeling his words as a slight. It wasn't necessarily his fault, but he had no idea what a success it was to live her happy, ordinary life when she had so very nearly snapped for good all those years ago. The life she now led was rich and rewarding.

'You think I don't know that? Gosh, Ian, I have had to get used to lots of things beyond my control.' She couldn't fully explain her flare of anger at his words, but even his drumming fingers were suddenly an irritation.

'Well, yes, we all have. I think it's almost impossible to get to our age and not be scarred by life in some way. I didn't mean to offend you, Molly.'

There was a slight note of apprehension in his tone, and she felt a little mean.

'No, I'm sorry. I was a bit snappy, I don't know why – I think I'm tired.'

'Was that our first tiff?' He chuckled.

'Hardly; more a moment of tension than a tiff,' she said, tipping frozen peas into the boiling water on the stove.

'We're odd bedfellows, quite literally!' He smiled. 'I mean, I get to see you naked, I get to sleep with you, eat with you on occasion, and yet we don't really ever *talk*.'

'We're talking right now.' She put the packet of peas back in the icebox at the top of her humming fridge.

'Ha ha, you know what I mean . . . We talk about the weather, the cricket, our supper, Hugo' – he patted the dog at his feet – 'but we never talk about anything deeper or anything that might take us to the next level in our relationship.'

'I thought we were both happy with how things are?' What Molly meant by this was that *she* was happy with how things were and saw no need to change. What she felt for Ian was enough, but no more. Certainly not what was needed to take things to the 'next level'.

'We are – I *am*,' he clarified, 'but I'd be lying if I said I wasn't curious to see where we end up. I mean, neither of us is getting any younger.'

Molly gave him her full attention now. 'I know I can be a bit of a closed book.' She smiled at the understatement, thinking back to when she had loved completely and her heart had been smashed, and how when she had 'opened up', Rex had run a mile . . . 'I suppose it's a bit of self-preservation.'

'And I understand that, but I talk quite openly about losing Joan and the horror of it, but you . . .' He shook his head. 'Mysterious Molly, you don't give much away.'

'Not much to give away, I suppose. I'm happy you can talk about Joan, but I bet there's something deep in your gut that *you* don't share, and I'm not asking you to!' She raised her palm to make it clearer. 'I certainly have things like that, things that are too personal, too hard to dredge up, and I believe all of us has something inside that we carry around, trapped. Our own secret sorrow or regret . . . I suppose we'll never really know because most of us keep it hidden.'

'And that's my point – we should talk about it, talk about everything!' He flung his arm in a wide arc and Molly knew by the lurch in her stomach at the thought of doing just that that it signified the beginning of the end. She liked Ian Morgan of the Neighbourhood Watch, but to tell him all her secrets? Well, that was another matter entirely.

'You are sweet, Ian, the best – great company and so much fun.' She nodded to emphasise how much he had meant to her. 'But I carry my secret loss like a caged bird that sits in my chest. It's still most of the time and silent, so much so that I don't remember it's there, but then on occasion, it flutters its wings, a gentle reminder of sadness. But that's okay; it doesn't overshadow all the good, all the happy times. I sometimes picture that little bird being set free as I take my last breath, and it will be a relief for us both, I'm sure . . .'

'Well, look at us, sharing our innermost truths.' He drew breath. 'I rather think we're at a crossroads here . . .'

'In what way?' she asked as she sipped her cup of tea.

'In that—'

The phone in the hallway rang, interrupting him.

'Sorry, Ian, just a minute. Can you watch the peas?' She smiled as she ran to the phone.

'Chelmsford 57286?'

'Molly?'

'Estelle, how lovely to hear from you!'

Molly expected the conversation to flow in the way that it did when all was well and it was a chance to catch up on the news with titbits and questions flying back and forth down the line . . . Estelle's pause was therefore enough to tell Molly that all was not well and her heart felt heavy with portent.

'Molly, I'm so sorry to call you like this, but—' The girl paused, clearly crying.

Just say it! Say it! Is it Joe? Is he hurt? Molly could hardly breathe.

'Joe's just had a call from his dad, and it's Joycey.'

Molly stepped back until she was sitting on Ian's coat covering the stool.

'Joycey?' She gripped the phone and pushed it tighter to her face.

'She's passed away suddenly, Molly. I am so sorry, but she's dead.'

Molly expected to feel a crack of grief similar to the one that had threatened to fell her when Mrs Duggan gave her comparable news, but she did not. She waited, but there was nothing. She was numb, entirely numb, with one calm thought that now rose above all others: *What on earth does my life look like without my Joycey in it?*

TWENTY-ONE

Chelmsford, Essex
2002
Aged 77

Molly slowly dragged the black wheelie bin down the narrow path and out onto the pavement. She ground her teeth, exasperated at her weakened physical state, which, while only temporary, was still the biggest irritation to her. She then went back into the cottage, treading carefully in her sheepskin slippers. They were gloriously comfortable and warm, a present last Christmas from Amelie, who was a GP, married to David's grandson, Arthur, also a doctor. They lived in Leith, Scotland. Amelie was a sweet girl who had taken a bit of a shine to Molly; she wrote notes to her on floral paper for no reason at all and sent gifts at Valentine's and Christmas, visiting occasionally too, for all of which Molly was grateful.

She had, since her beloved Joyce died and, sadly, Clara now too, almost by default become matriarch of the family. Without Joyce to phone for the smallest thing, she noticed that Joe and Estelle, Adam and Roz, Frances, Hetty and all of their broods called her with wonderful regularity and spoiled her in the way Amelie did. Molly smiled now to think that when she first gave Joe up, one of her biggest worries had been whether she would have a place in the family, unable to imagine how it might work, living in the shadows, a secret mother, and yet here she was, mothering many and surrounded by love. Not, of course, that she wouldn't have given up her new crown in a heartbeat to have her darling sister back with her for one more day. Geertruida, too, had passed away. Molly bit her bottom lip. It was still a sadness that the two had not reconciled, despite her friend's generous and timely letter, but as the years passed Molly almost understood the toxic combination of grief and anger and the desire to have someone to blame. It was with a level of distress which surprised her that in 1988 Molly came across her obituary in *The Times*:

> Geertruida Hanscombe has passed away peacefully at home in West Sussex after a short illness, aged sixty-three, leaving her husband Benedict, her two children Johan and Anika and her four adored grandchildren.

Molly had wondered at the time whatever had become of Richard, Geer's wartime beau? She wondered if he had made it home from the front and got to write love letters to a woman who might think enough of him not to share them over the table during lunch. How young and giddy they had all been! Molly was sad that Geer had passed at sixty-three, no age at all, but also happy that her beloved friend had found love, with Benedict, whoever he was, and had built a life, had children and known the joy of being called grandma . . .

She smiled now, thinking about them all, as she walked cautiously back along the frost-covered track to fetch the recycling bin, in which, as instructed, she deposited all of her cardboard, tins and glass ready for the weekly collection. It bothered her how much packaging everything seemed to come in these days, remembering a time when she had used one sturdy nylon shopping bag in which she used to lob loose fruit and vegetables, a loaf of bread and meat wrapped in waxed paper, tied with string, and when almost nothing went to waste. Why put bananas and oranges into plastic when they were already perfectly well insulated? It was beyond her. This thought was immediately followed by a memory of the first bag of fresh plums she had tasted after the war, as she prepared Joe's bedroom. She could even now swear they were the sweetest and best she had ever had.

Molly took her time in the kitchen. She braced her arms on the sink and took a deep breath. The scars on her chest were itchy. She rubbed her hand over the two thick rinds of skin that sat in moon shapes, smiling at her mockingly when she dressed and undressed, in the place where her breasts had once lived.

'So that's it, Molly, you have the all-clear. How do you feel?' The nice doctor had been most chirpy about a job well done.

'Relieved, happy.' She thought, a better substitute for what she had been going to say: *Underwhelmed, really.* Molly had been prepared to meet her maker and had made peace with it, but no, it was not her time. Joe and Estelle had fussed over her when she stayed with them after her surgery and she had been glad then that it was not her time, revelling in the opportunity to wake under the same roof as her boy.

'We *can* give you reconstruction surgery. I mean, not immediately, but—' the doctor had offered.

'Oh gosh no, the thought of being pushed and pulled about all over again and having even more surgery—' She shook her head. At seventy-seven, her cancer diagnosis and subsequent treatments had taken their toll. 'I'd rather not bother, if that's okay. But it's a sad day. I can see that my glamour modelling days are finally over.'

'Not necessarily!' he had laughed. 'You're in great shape!'

And she had laughed, too, until the bandages came off and she was standing in front of the mirror in her bathroom, all alone, and her laughter turned to tears. There was something essentially and obviously diminishing in the loss of her breasts, and no matter how much she told herself they were just lumps of fat, entirely redundant, the reality was they were so much more. And if it hadn't sounded so embarrassingly ridiculous to her ears, she would have said that she mourned their loss, but it was the truth no less. This was the kind of thing she would have shared with Joyce. Oh, how she missed her! It was seventeen years since her sister had passed away and yet still Molly was prompted, almost daily, to pick up the phone and call her about something . . . and it was the absence of these small interactions that she missed the most.

Surprising them all, Albert had moved back to Canada, where by all accounts he led a full and active life with his new lady friend, Nella-Rose, a petite country and western singer in her late sixties who wore a waist-length red wig and was, judging by their festive photographs, a little over-generous with the eye shadow palette. Molly could only guess what the very particular Joyce would have had to say about that! The thought of it made her smile. Molly had not, as her sister had requested, told Joe the truth. Not yet. It was complicated. She wanted to honour her sister's wishes but had to factor in that Joyce had been two parts Cinzano when she made the suggestion, and also, what would telling Joe gain? Yes, she had longed her whole life to be called Mum by him, but would he now, a man in his late fifties, feel able to adjust to that huge change, and might it not undermine the wonderful relationship he had shared with Joyce, which had shaped him into the kindest, smartest father, husband and grandfather? She felt that to broach the topic would only be for the most selfish of reasons and so, for the time being, remained quiet. There was still time.

Hubert the cat meowed loudly from the countertop.

'I know, I know: you want your breakfast, but you don't want me to miss the bin men, do you?' She stared at the fat moggy with the lustrous tail, who gave her his usual look of disdain. 'I swear, Hubert, that one day you're going to answer me back.' She laughed and went to the fridge to retrieve the other half of yesterday's cat food, which, frankly, looked good enough to eat. 'There you are, you spoiled pussycat.' Molly watched as he took his time, eating in the same way that he did everything else, daintily and precisely and with a haughtiness that was as funny as it was endearing.

'Right,' Molly said aloud. 'Better get a wiggle on – we're expecting visitors!'

Adam, Joe's boy, his girlfriend, Roz, who was heavily pregnant with their second child, and their little daughter, Maisie Joyce, traipsed into the cottage with so many bags, boxes, bottles and accessories that Molly wondered if they were moving in. She was fascinated by Roz's pregnant form. The girl's large belly rested over the soft waistband of her maternity jeans and emerged beneath her cropped T-shirt, showing off her rounded stomach with its popped-out belly button in all its glory. So very different from her own pregnancy, when she had felt forced to wear a constricting corset to hide her 'shame'. Molly wanted to stare at the girl, who cradled her bump with beringed fingers. How times had changed, *for the better* . . . She heard her sister's voice in her ear: *for the better* . . .

The troupe gathered in the cosy sitting room. Maisie pottered and chattered quite happily, talking to Hubert and fetching him plastic dolls and wooden cars from her endless bag of goodies that he had absolutely no interest in. Maisie, to her credit, persevered regardless.

'So have you heard from Mum and Dad?' Molly asked, keen to hear all about the cruise Joe and Estelle had taken to celebrate their upcoming sixtieth birthdays.

'Yes, he felt terrible about missing Clara's funeral, but obviously he didn't know she'd died until Hetty called, and then Frances organised the funeral very quickly and they were away. Poor old Clara.' Adam looked wistful. 'We went, and it was really sad.'

'They often are.' Molly thought of her own mother's send-off, when her mind had been elsewhere; David's, where everyone was a little shell-shocked; and Joyce's, when each and every one of them had been utterly inconsolable, their grief raw and painful. There was very little that had felt celebratory – people had been angry and felt cheated at her loss, for which they were all unprepared. And then, only last year, Ian Morgan had died, and she had sat at the back of the church, smiling and thinking fondly of the six months of fun they had had at a time in her life when she had felt she had no right to expect such things. They had, much to her joy, remained friends, stopping to chat when they met in the street and sharing at least two bottles of wine and two subsequent nights of passion in the intervening years. She wondered momentarily what might be the nature of her own funeral and inadvertently rubbed the thick rind of a scar on her chest, a reminder of her latest brush with death.

'I was sorry not to go, but I wasn't allowed to travel so soon after my op—'

'You look really well!' Roz offered sweetly.

'Thank you, dear, I feel it. So yes, I missed it too, but sent flowers and cards, of course, to Hetty and Frances.'

Molly thought of Clara, who was only strong and confident with David by her side, recalling how she had sat and cried into a handkerchief in the house in Bloomsbury when Clementine was only a little thing and they were in the midst of a world war, with everyone fearful of leaving their homes and climbing the walls, waiting for life to return to normal. Or as normal as it would get . . . She thought, as she often did, of Johan: just a glimpse, his face, a split-second grin that had not faded.

'Well,' Roz said, shifting forward in her seat, 'there was a bit of a drama at the funeral. Hetty had organised caterers and Clementine had too much to drink and shouted at them! Said they were late and the food was substandard.' Roz pulled an embarrassed face. 'I think she was just a bit stressed. The whole place went quiet and no one knew where to look. Hetty cried and then Lindsey and Frances had a bit of a scrap.'

Molly took a sip of her tea and thought about the warring cousins who had always been rivals. 'Well, Frances and Lindsey should have known better than to act like that. It's disrespectful.' She thought about her sister-in-law, who, towards the end of her life, had been very frail. 'The last time I saw Clara she was really quite far gone. I don't think she knew who I was, the poor love. Dementia is a horrible thing, especially for those who can only watch and do nothing for those they love.'

'Has Frances been over?' Adam enquired about his younger cousin.

'She pops in.' Molly nodded. Her great-niece lived in one of the small Essex villages for which Chelmsford was the main town and, as a result, Frances was her closest relative, physically speaking, and therefore the keeper of a spare key to the cottage, just in case. It wasn't that Molly didn't appreciate having her on hand, or how the girl took time out of her busy life to visit her aunt on occasion, but Frances, who could be a little boisterous, was not always the best company.

Adam sat forward in the chair.

'Dad said the ship's really snazzy and Mum is loving the cocktails, but he would have been happy to stay in Nice, where they boarded, and spend some time in the south of France.'

'I'm with Joe,' Roz said loudly. 'I can't think I'd enjoy being stuck on a boat.'

'Well, they're hardly stuck, babe, and they're being spoiled rotten – it's a huge ship.'

'Maisie, be gentle with Hubert!' Roz called to her little girl, who was stroking him a little too vigorously. 'I know they're being spoiled, but I'd prefer to hire a little car and tootle around France any day.'

'Not that we have the cash for either,' Adam pointed out. 'Not with babies, who cost money!' Adam reached out and ran his fingers over his girlfriend's stomach, an act so intimate, so beautiful, that it caused a lump to rise in Molly's throat.

'And not with my partner being a poor artist!' Roz said, teasing the man she loved.

'I think it's lovely to chase a passion rather than money.' Molly meant it.

'Have you ever been to France, Auntie M?'

'Hmmm?' She tried to think how best to answer.

'Have you ever been to France?' Adam repeated, looking at her, as she felt the colour slip from her face.

'No,' she lied, unsure why exactly, but knowing it felt easier than having to go into painful detail that seemed to have no place in this world in which she now lived. And just like that, words from her training came into her head:

Lie if necessary, rather than get drawn into any lengthy conversation that might give you away, might put you in danger . . . I am Claudette Menard, secretary. I am here to visit my sweet cousin Violet. I'm married to Benoît. We have no children. I'm quiet, myopic, and très réligieuse . . .

'Auntie M?' Adam rose and placed a hand on her forearm, 'Roz was just asking if you might like to go to France? Her grandad was involved in the Normandy landings and we went to have a look around. I think you'd like it there. We went on the ferry, had a mooch and some lunch, ham and French bread – although I suppose they just call it bread, don't they?' He laughed.

'And they probably just call it kissing!' Roz added. 'We had a glass of wine and sat on the beach to toast my grandad. It's funny to think that just a few years earlier and we'd have had Germans firing at us from the sea!' Roz took a mouthful of her tea.

'Now there's a thought!' Molly nodded and kept her eyes on Maisie – a welcome focal point while her thoughts tumbled.

They weren't in the sea, they were on the land. Our soldiers and allies were in the sea with packs on their backs so heavy they drowned the boys who carried them. The Germans were on the land with snipers poised, hidden in the cliffs and behind scrub, in sandbag castles, waiting to pick off the sons of women in houses all over the UK. Women who sat in chairs by the wireless with their hands folded in their laps and a handkerchief threaded through their fingers, waiting to hear news of how their son was faring, while that boy took one last breath, and one last look at the blue, blue sky, and sent one last message of love to fly across the miles to land in her ear as she fell asleep. And my love . . . my man died rehearsing for it . . . What a waste – what a terrible, terrible waste . . .

'But I think you'd love it, Auntie M, France. I mean, it's foreign, but lovely. I like to see all the signs written in French and the menus, and we go to the supermarket and laugh because we haven't a clue what half the stuff is! I think they eat bloody anything over there!'

Molly nodded and smiled at Maisie, who was now trying to show Hubert her alphabet book.

You'll eat anything if you're hungry enough . . . even if your mouth and mind crave a jacket potato with butter and salt, the crispy skin saved until last when you can put a fresh knob of butter into it, fold it over with your fingers like a charred . . . and for pudding, blackberries, so plump you put them on your tongue and push them up to the roof of your mouth, where they burst . . .

'Don't touch that, Maisie!' Adam called to the toddler, who had jumped up and was grabbing a book from the shelf. A leather exercise book from which tumbled yellowing sheets of paper.

'Oh.' Molly walked over, glad of the change in conversation as she gathered the sheets. 'These are poems and musings written by your great-great-grandpa, Maisie! Can you believe that? Mainly about Brussels sprouts and dancing moles!' Maisie stared at her with a look of disinterest and started chewing the bottom of her dress.

It had been a lovely day. Molly was tired, quite unused to the hours of continual conversation. She yawned as she waved Adam and Roz off from behind her garden gate, watching as their little car tootled off. They were such a lovely little family, her grandson, his girlfriend and her great-grand-daughter . . .

'Had visitors, I see?' Mrs Ogilvy called over from her front garden.

'Yes, it's chilly, isn't it? Hope the rain holds off!' Molly looked skyward and made out to have misheard rather than converse with Mrs Ogilvy, who had a knack of bettering any and every story Molly told. If Molly had bought a stamp, then Mrs Ogilvy had met the Queen whose head graced it. It was most wearing and impossibly dull.

Molly closed her front door and pulled Hubert in for a cuddle.

'People, eh, Hubert? Is it any wonder I sometimes prefer the company of you, my lovely cat?' And, of course, he looked at her with utter disdain.

TWENTY-TWO

The hospital
Chelmsford, Essex
December 24th 2019
Aged 94

'Here we go, sweetheart.' The bustling porter in his comic Santa hat checked some paperwork, smiled and placed the sheaf of paper on her legs. 'Right, we're going to move you from this corridor and get you settled in a room away from all this noise. Looks like you've been in the wars! I hope the other fella came off worse – eh, Charlie?' He laughed, and Charlie released the brake from the end of her trolley and smiled at her too. They moved deftly, cheerily snaking her along the corridor and into a cavernous lift. She was wheeled along another corridor and into a small room where blinds hung vertically in strips, linked by little chains that, had there been any doubt, placed her very firmly in a public building.

'Hello, Miss Molly! Now, let's get you comfortable and I will give you a little clean-up and something for the pain. How about that?'

The nurse was short and wide, a young woman in her thirties, but with the furrows on her brow of a much older woman, or at least one who didn't sleep easy. She was quickly joined by a stocky male nurse who, despite his size, was gentle and patient as they carefully transferred her rather crumpled body onto the bed, taking with her the catheter and drip. Molly winced in pain at the movement and again out poured the gravelly mewl that had replaced her voice. And then came more tears, which embarrassed and frustrated her. She couldn't seem to stop crying, but knew she needed to try. *How was she going to get the letter into Joe's hands? How? If she couldn't say a word!*

The irony was not lost on her that she had in her life landed in a field in the dead of night, arriving in a plane with the lights turned off, flirted with the enemy, dodged Hitler's doodlebugs – good Lord, she had even beaten cancer in her seventies! And yet here she was, crying in a safe bed a few miles from her home at a ripe old age. It was hard for her to imagine that this time yesterday she had been standing admiring the view from her kitchen window, a sight that had never grown tiresome: the back wall where the gnarled knots of her lilac nestled in an intricate pattern. With the kettle set to boil and a teabag nestling in her favourite china cup and saucer, Molly had surveyed the rest of the garden where winter now crept, spindles of bloomless branches and woody stems shooting up into the sky where only months ago bright-headed flowers had almost made her weep with their beauty. The breeze was suddenly sharp instead of gentle, as if aware that to have an effect on the reddening stems of the dogwood and the last leaves that clung still to hardy twigs it needed to ramp up its game. Birds were scarcer than they had been in the warmer months. Adam, often with his son, the eighteen-year-old Joe Junior, or JJ, as he was known, were the greatest help when it came to maintaining her precious outdoor space. They pitched up in all weathers, even the grimmest arctic day when everything was damp and soggy, waterlogged. Just this weekend, with quite a lot of leaf cover on the grass, the old chestnut shedding and the sycamore too, JJ had raked up all the leaves. And for the thousandth time he had pulled that stubborn dandelion that insisted on popping up in the middle of the patio, only for it to reappear . . .

The porters left with the empty trolley. The male nurse, too, but not before tucking the top sheet over her legs.

'This must all seem very strange and a bit scary, Miss Molly,' the lady nurse said with a smile, 'but don't worry, I'm right outside the door, and if you need anything you only have to press this button.'

What I need is for someone to get a letter to my son! But I can't tell you and I don't know what to do about it!

The nurse laid the thin red pulley against her arm and over her palm. 'Plus I'll be checking on you every so often. I expect you're tired, so you'll sleep well. The doctor has reviewed your CT scan and he'll be along at some point to discuss it all with you. You took quite a tumble, didn't you, lovey?' She smoothed Molly's hair from her forehead. 'Try and close your eyes now.'

'Paws!' she managed, irritated by the word, but also strangely glad of its clarity. The nurse quietly left the room, her soft-soled shoes squeaking a little on the linoleum.

Molly looked around the room. It was a little depressing, but clean and quiet, and she was thankful for both. It was a moment when she very much missed her small sitting room, thinking how she would have liked to be at home, where, having refused the various invitations to go to their homes, she knew she would receive endless calls from the family over Christmas. She allowed herself to picture the log burner, the two comfy chintz-covered chairs lined with dented soft cushions to support her back and their sturdy arms, on which she liked to rest a steaming cup of tea. Also the soft, honey-coloured glow of her pretty china lamp which seemed to make even the greyest or dampest of days cosy. She fought the temptation to cry again in lament of just how much she wanted to be at home in that moment and not to have fallen down those darned stairs. To be able to say to Joe on the telephone, 'Darling, I've written to you . . .' She had made a promise. *A promise!*

She parked her sadness, knowing she could cry later when her catheter was emptied and her dentures lurked in the bottom of a glass on the nightstand and when she heard the distinct *thunk* of the overhead strip lighting being turned out for the night. Then she would know she was quite alone and free to acknowledge her distress and able only then to vent the rather odd variety of noises that now accompanied her crying. It was thought-provoking that, in her ever-reducing world, she should now find herself in this one sparse room with none of her things around her, nothing at all. Curious, really, the importance she had placed on the collecting and maintaining of pretty objects, precious books, works of art, bits of furniture, trinkets . . . when in this, her final winter, she needed nothing more than the bed on which she had been placed, the soft pillow beneath her head and the bag of liquid that fed into the shallow vein of her arm.

She could now at ninety-four look back at her story, every chapter, every event and all the people who had played a part, and she realised as she lay in that bed that it was in fact *all* she had, all anyone had at the end of the day: their story. And what a story it was! Yes, she might, if pushed, admit to having one regret: the fact she had lived in a time when circumstances beyond her control had shaped her life in the way that they did. But despite everything, Molly never forgot that life was good. Precious! And the moments of joy that had taken her breath away, the moments when she looked up to the starry sky and felt dizzy at all the gifts the universe had sent her way – her first, deep and all-consuming love! Her boy! Would she have traded any of it for a guarantee of no sadness, no pain?

Well, as her grandmother would have said: not on your nelly!

She chuckled to herself at the thought and yawned before falling into a deep and restful sleep.

After her morning of being pulled and shoved, Molly closed her eyes and must have fallen asleep. The door opened slowly and she silently cursed the disturbance under her breath; all she wanted was peace. She felt exhausted, which really was quite funny, considering she'd spent the best part of twenty-four hours lying in bed in a state close to dozing, and yet it was the truth. She was really awfully tired. Her broken bones caused her pain and she was mindful of her overly tender, bruised skin. The painkillers they prescribed were effective and, as long as she remained immobile, she would best describe her physical condition as 'almost comfortable'. The door closed quietly and she could sense a presence. It felt like a chore to open her eyes. Molly feigned sleep, fairly certain that whatever pill needed swallowing, lotion applying or pressure reading taken, nothing, nothing was half as important as letting her sleep, but she was wrong.

She became aware of the soft tread of shoes, the creeping manoeuvre indicative of someone unaware of the lack of formality when it came to entering a room here. She heard the knock of the toe of a shoe against the skirting board beneath the radiator and the slight metallic twang as the radiator made contact with something like a belt buckle or ring. Slowly, she opened her eyes and saw the back of a head, a man with grey hair. He turned around and Molly let out a mewling sound, an almost visceral reaction to the sight of Joe.

Oh my boy! My son!

How very, very happy she was to see his face, possibly for the last time. It filled her heart! In that moment she wished more than anything that she could go and move the hair from the ear of her younger self, as she sat broken-hearted in her bedroom with her baby boy recently whisked away by her sister, and whisper to her in her darkest hour,

It will be all right, Molly. He will come back to you . . .

Joe smiled at the sound she made. Her tears fell across her temple and down her nose.

'Hey, Auntie M, don't cry! I've come all this way to see you and the last thing I wanted to do was make you cry. Frances called to say you'd had a fall on those bloody stairs and I couldn't let you lie here on your own on Christmas Day now, could I?'

His voice carried the same pitch as his father's. And Molly tried to smile. She realised that to let frustration at her lack of voice cloud this moment would be a waste. Instead, she breathed deeply, liking this new sense of calm. There was no one but her alive who knew the truth, the secret – she wondered if he would ever see the letter? And then the thought struck her that she had written to Johan, the letter informing him that he was to have a child . . . a letter he, too, was never to receive, which also lay tucked inside the pages, along with Geer's note . . .

Maybe Joe would find the letter and maybe he wouldn't. What would it matter in the great scheme of things? Would it change the way she had loved and had received love? Of course not. What would be, would be . . .

'Igloo!' She spoke with as much enthusiasm as she was able.

'Ah yes, Frances also told me about the igloo, paws conundrum. That must drive you plain crazy.'

It does! It does! But I could kiss Frances right now, that's for sure.

Joe sat in the chair next to her bed and she wished she could stop crying, as it fogged her view and she wanted to drink in every single detail of him.

'Now, Auntie M, you are obviously on the nice list this year because Father Christmas left this under our tree for you! Fancy that! What are the chances?'

In his hand he had a present wrapped in shiny gold paper with a red ribbon tied in a beautiful bow on the top. She might have been ninety-four, but the prospect of being spoiled still ignited sparks of joy, a feeling she had quite forgotten.

'I'll open it for you.' Sitting in the chair, he placed the box on his lap and, very carefully, in the manner of someone who had every intention of reusing the wrapping, slid his finger under the folds, removed the sticky tape and folded back the sheet to reveal a cardboard box. Molly knew that, had she still access to her words, she would have been shouting in jest, 'Get on with it, man!' The anticipation was excruciating.

Joe raised his shoulders excitedly and opened the box, reaching in to pull out none other than a big fat snow globe. It was so beautiful!

'Look!' He stood with the precious glass ball in his palms. It balanced on an ornate base of gold, green and red. He shook it in his hands and tiny flecks of snow drifted. And there in the middle of the glass ball stood a tiny, stunningly decorated Christmas tree with two people in front of it who appeared to be mid-waltz. The man, handsome in a navy suit, held the woman as she dipped backwards and her full red skirt swept down to the floor.

'I saw it and it reminded me of you. I know you used to like dancing – you told me.'

Oh, I did! I really did! What a wonderful, wonderful thing to say to me. I danced with your dad.

The snow settled in the globe and she had a clear view of the two little people dancing and the sight made her heart sing. The woman in the full red skirt looked so incredibly happy, and why wouldn't she be? Dancing at Christmastime in the arms of her beau? Joe picked it up and shook it again. For the next ten minutes, they both watched transfixed by the couple captured in their own tiny world. Molly felt quite overcome. It was in truth one of the loveliest gifts she had ever received. And this was most fitting, as it was to be her very last.

'I just really wanted to say happy Christmas, Auntie Molly.'

Joe reached out and took her hand in his and she thought her heart might burst out of her chest; it was still her greatest joy to be in his company, to feel his touch.

'Please don't cry. I really can't stand to see you so sad.'

I am not sad! I am moved and so very thankful to see you one last time.

'I hadn't realised quite how much you look like my mum.' Joe paused and swallowed, as if the thought of Joyce was almost too painful. Without understanding the full irony of his words, they were like music to Molly's ears.

Because I am your mum . . . I am your mum, my darling!

'I still miss her.' He smiled ruefully. 'Silly really, but I do. She always spoke about you when I was growing up; she was so very fond of you, Auntie M. You and she were like a double act in my life when I was a kid. She was my mum and you were like a second mum.' He chuckled. 'She used to tell me of all the things you and she got up to when you were children, hiding away in the attic of that grand old house in Bloomsbury and the adventures you had learning to smoke!' He wheezed with laughter. Molly pondered the fact that Joyce had supplanted their brother David in the story, and made it a tale of her own . . . *Oh, Joyce, how I miss you too! My sister – my only sister!* She thought of Joyce's face on the day she had driven away with baby Joe, Molly waving after her with her heart almost dissolving with grief.

'I know you were a very important part of her life, and mine too.' He smiled at her with creases of kindness at the edge of his eyes that were just like his dad's.

'Adam and Roz send you their love, of course, as does Estelle; she wanted to come too, but is on turkey duty, as you can imagine – and did you hear, Maisie has met a chap and is moving to Eindhoven, in the Netherlands.'

Molly thought of the little girl who had tried desperately to make friends with Hubert the cat. It felt like a mere blink ago.

'She's a clever girl.' Joe beamed with grandfatherly pride. 'As you know, she graduated a year ago and has a fascination for all things Dutch. I thought it was the art of Rembrandt, the canals, the windmills, the tulips.' He laughed. 'But no, it turns out to be much simpler than that. Her fascination is for a boy called Daan to whom she's now engaged! We found out last night and, boy, do I feel old – my granddaughter getting married! They met at college, but Holland will be their home. Her Dutch is impressive and he's a very nice boy. Adam approves and, as you know, Roz loves everyone and JJ was wondering if he could move into her bedroom, as it's slightly bigger, so we are all good.'

My great-granddaughter – just wonderful!

'Estelle was fretting about her being abroad, but I said to her that Maisie is loving life and if that isn't the whole darn purpose then I don't know what is. To find love and hold on to it.' Again that smile . . . 'But it'll be strange to think of her so far away from home. I will certainly miss her, and I know Adam will too.'

No, Joe, no! She's not far from home, she's gone home! She is home! The land of her great-great-grandfather! Now isn't that something?

'Oh, Auntie M, come on now, not more tears. Nothing good gets solved by crying. That's what my mum used to say. I think she got it from her mum – your mum too, of course! I think she used to say it.'

She did indeed.

'I've been told by the nurse not to stay too long and I don't want to tire you. So that just leaves me to wish you a merry Christmas,' he said, with an obvious crack to his voice. 'I do love you, Auntie M. I hope you know that. I hope you've *always* known that.'

Oh, Joe! And how I love you and how I have loved you since the moment I saw you . . .

His words were like balm to a restless soul, sincerely offered and the very sweetest gift he could have ever given her to see her on her way. It was as if the hole left in her gut when she handed him to Joyce on that terrible day was finally sealed with his perfect words. And at first she had worried that history might damn her for giving up too easily on her boy, but now she hoped history would mark her as a woman who did the very best for him and who made the ultimate sacrifice for his well-being. Joe stood slowly to leave. He pushed the snow globe forward on the nightstand so she could see it. She did her best to nod at him, gratefully accepting the gentle kiss he placed on her cheek as he left her.

Goodbye, my boy, my son. Thank you for coming into my life, and thank you for shaping it in the most wonderful way. Goodbye, my darling . . .

With the sound of his words in her ear, Molly decided to close her eyes, just for a minute . . .

She wasn't sure how long she had slept, but now opened her eyes slowly and stretched her arms above her head before twisting her neck to the left and right. Joe had clearly left and things felt . . . different and, as she tried to put her finger on what exactly, she spoke.

'I must have nodded off. I wonder what the time is.'

These words were immediately followed by a gasp – her voice! Molly ran her fingers along her throat. She had said the words out loud and they were clear and smooth and rounded – the voice she had not heard at all for the last few days and had not heard with this velvety clarity for years!

'What on earth?' she laughed, delighted by the sound. Even her laughter was light and gay.

She became aware of a fluttering sound and looked towards the window, surprised to see a small bird sitting on the windowsill.

'Well, where have you come from, little chap?'

Only as she swung her legs to the side of the bed and looked down at the full red skirt she was wearing did she realise she was no longer broken.

'Oh! Oh my goodness!'

This was what was different! This was what was missing – the pain. Gone were her aches and grumbles, all of it, gone! She looked at the back of her hands, where the skin was smooth and creamy, unblemished by distended veins and liver spots. Flexing her fingers, she ran her palm up her forearm and over her décolletage towards her sharp jawline.

Leaping now from the bed, Molly ran to the window and opened it wide, watching as the little bird flew out of the room and soared high into the inky blue sky of approaching dusk.

'Be free, little bird!' she called after him, watching until she could see him no more and then gazing down over the dismal car park before smiling at her reflection in the window. Running the tip of her finger beneath her full bottom lip, she checked to make sure her lipstick was pristine. She felt absolutely brand new. Her focus was sharp, her hearing clear and her muscles sat snugly attached to strong bones – feeling like this, she could climb a mountain or chop a log! She loved the sensation of the full red silk skirt beneath her fingertips and very much liked the white shirt tied at her slender waist. Her hair was neatly coiffed and so delighted was she with her appearance that she jumped up and down on the spot.

There was a knock at the door. Molly turned and watched as it slowly opened. She wondered who it might be and couldn't wait to show them the transformation – Frances? The sweet nurse? Joe? But it was none of them.

First she saw the buttons of his uniform, shiny brass with their naval crest and knot of rope.

'Johan!' The word was as sweet in her mouth as honey and her heart swelled to see the man she loved, handsome and . . . and somehow here! Here in this room!

'Marvellous Molly! My darling M.'

The two collided as they met, holding each other fast in a tight embrace with as much of their bodies touching as was possible, hip to hip, cheek to cheek, thigh to thigh, as if nothing less would do. Molly felt the heat from his hands and it warmed a place deep inside her that had been cold since the moment he left her.

'Oh, how I have missed you!' She whispered the understatement with her eyes tight shut for fear of opening them and he not being there. 'I have missed you every single moment of every single day.'

'And I you, my love. Every single day.' Johan tipped her chin with his finger and tilted her face to his before kissing her firmly on the mouth.

'Don't ever leave me again, Johan. Please don't ever leave me again!'

'I shan't. I promise.'

He stepped back and held out her hand, safe and warm within his. 'You look beautiful.'

Molly beamed. She felt beautiful.

'Listen!' Johan put his finger to his ear and cocked his head slightly, and there it was, quiet at first, but unmistakably the strains of their song . . . 'I'll Be Seeing You' – the deep melodic tones of Billie Holiday masking the crackles and scratches of the record.

'You know, Marvellous Molly, I should tell you now that if you don't immediately say no to a dance, I will always assume it's a yes.'

'It is a yes – it will always be a yes!' She twirled inside his arms, as he suddenly dipped her backwards, one strong arm beneath to hold her, and there she stayed, staring up into the face of her handsome love. A love that had endured beyond life. Her very ordinary life . . .

EPILOGUE

Joe put the key in the lock and pushed open the front door. The cottage still smelled like Aunt Molly and it made him miss her. It was her scent and her fondness for all things lavender that lingered. Standing in the hallway, he shook his head; it seemed unbelievable that she had left him her house, and he was more than happy to pass it on to Adam and Roz, who could not quite believe it. He wished more than anything that he had been able to thank her for this most extraordinary gift. It wasn't only the bricks and mortar and their value, or the fact that Adam and Roz would finally have space and a garden of their own! It was also a piece of their family history. Joe had loved coming here since he was small.

He touched his finger to the newel post and looked up at the steep wooden stairs where his aunt had taken her last tumble. He trod the stairs and came to a halt on the landing, where the door was open to the guest bedroom. An unremarkable room, really, with a small fireplace and walls that had been painted a rich blue for as long as he could remember, but what was remarkable were the six hand-painted balsa-wood planes that had been strung from the ceiling at different heights.

'Well, aren't they something!' Joe looked up at the planes, marvelling at their detail.

'Hel–lo?' Adam called from the open front door.

'Up here, son!'

Adam walked in with excitement in his limbs and a smile on his face. He joined his dad, staring up at the ceiling. 'Hey! They look old.'

'I think they are.' Joe nodded.

'Have you checked out the other bedrooms yet, Dad?'

'Not since Auntie passed away. I'll go and take a look. Why don't you go and put the kettle on in your new home.'

Adam danced on the spot with childlike excitement. 'I will. Roz and JJ are just unpacking the car.'

Joe walked along the narrow corridor and made his way into Molly's old bedroom. He liked her collections of things, the paintings, ornate chairs and ornaments. It reminded him of his childhood. He sat on her bed, where her stack of pillows still carried the dent of her form, and swallowed the emotion that threatened. He had loved her, that was for sure. His eyes were drawn to a heavy book on top of the bedspread, which he gathered into his hands.

'*A Study of Flora.*' He read out the title, before putting it on the floor, where he would pile all the bits and bobs destined for storage or for charity. He'd let Adam and Roz decide, but had been given firm instructions from Estelle not to bring any more clutter into their own house.

'Tea!' Roz called up from the kitchen.

Joe made his way downstairs and walked into the cosy sitting room with the two chintz-covered chairs in front of the fireplace. He gazed out over the beautiful garden. Staring out of the French doors, he spied a large dandelion in the very middle of the patio. He bent down and gripped it by the root, before pulling it from the crevice between the slabs. As it came loose, something caught his eye where he had disturbed the moss, something shining in the sunlight. He stuck his finger into the space where mud had gathered and wiggled out a small gold object which he wiped on his jacket sleeve and held up to the sunlight.

'Ha! A button.' And there it sat in his palm, a shiny brass button with a naval crest on it and a knot of rope. Joe stared at it, holding it up to the light. There was something about it that was strangely familiar. He couldn't place it, but as ridiculous as it sounded, it seemed somehow that the button was just where it belonged: right there in the palm of his hand.

'What's that, Grandad?' JJ called over his shoulder.

'I just found it. I'd say it's pretty old and possibly naval. Treasure, JJ!'

'What are you going to do with it?' his grandson asked, munching on shortbread Roz had brought over in her mother-in-law's old tin.

'I'm going to keep it, son.' Joe smiled at the boy. 'It's a good-luck charm, I think. I'll keep it in my wallet.'

It felt like the right thing to do because in that perfect moment with good fortune shining down on them, surrounded by love, and all because of Molly, Joe certainly felt like one of the lucky ones . . .

ABOUT THE AUTHOR

Photo © 2012 Paul Smith
www.paulsmithphotography.info

Amanda Prowse likens her own life story to those she writes about in her books. After self-publishing her debut novel *Poppy Day* in 2011, she has gone on to author twenty-six novels, seven novellas and a memoir about depression co-authored with her son, Josiah Hartley. Her books have been translated into a dozen languages and she regularly tops bestseller charts all over the world. Remaining true to her ethos, Amanda writes stories of ordinary women and their families who find their strength, courage and love tested in ways they never imagined. The most prolific female contemporary fiction writer in the UK, with a legion of loyal readers, she goes from strength to strength. Being crowned 'queen of domestic drama' by the *Daily Mail* was one of her finest moments. Amanda is a regular contributor on TV and radio but her first love is, and always will be, writing. You can find her online at www.amandaprowse.com, on Twitter and Instagram at @MrsAmandaProwse, and on Facebook at AmandaProwseAuthor.

Printed in Great Britain
by Amazon